D0446901

The Iowa
Baseball
Confederacy

BOOKS BY W. P. KINSELLA

Dance Me Outside

Scars

Shoeless Joe Jackson Comes to Iowa

Born Indian

The Ballad of the Public Trustee

Shoeless Joe

The Moccasin Telegraph

The Thrill of the Grass

The Alligator Report

The Iowa Baseball Confederacy

The Iowa
Baseball
Confederacy

W·P·KINSELLA

A TOTEM BOOK
Toronto

First Published 1986
by Collins Publishers

This edition published 1987
by TOTEM BOOKS
a division of Collins Publishers
100 Lesmill Road, Don Mills, Ontario

© 1986 by W.P. Kinsella

All rights reserved. No part of this publication may be reproduced,
stored in a retrieval system, or transmitted in any form or by any
means, electronic, mechanical, photocopying, recording, or otherwise, without the prior written permission of the publisher.

All inquiries regarding the motion picture, television or related
rights in or to this book should be addressed to the author's representative, The Colbert Agency Inc., 303 Davenport Road, Toronto,
Ontario M5R 1K5. Representations as to the disposition of these
rights without the express written consent of the author's representative are strictly prohibited and will be vigorously pursued to the
full extent of the law.

Canadian Cataloguing in Publication Data

Kinsella, W.P.
    The Iowa Baseball Confederacy

ISBN 0-00-223129-8

I. Title.

PS8571.I57I57   1987   C813'.54   C87-093429-5
PR9199.3.K59I57   1987

Portions of this novel appeared in slightly different form in *Descant,
Saturday Night, New Quarterly, Arete,* and *Buzzard's Luck* and
in the story collection *The Thrill of the Grass* (Penguin Books,
1984). Several excerpts were broadcast on CBS Radio and the
MacNeil/Lehrer News Hour.

Printed and bound in Canada.

For Ann . . . always

PART ONE

The
Warm-up

Nothing bleeds quite like devotion.
—Gary Kissick

1

MY NAME IS Gideon Clarke, and, like my father before me, I
have on more than one occasion been physically ejected from
the corporate offices of the Chicago Cubs Baseball Club,
which are located at Wrigley Field, 1060 West Addison, in
Chicago.

My father's unfortunate dealings with the Chicago Cubs
began with his making polite requests for information concerning the 1908 baseball season: player records, box scores,
nothing out of the ordinary. At first, the Cubs' public relations people were most cooperative. I have their letters.
However, the information they provided was not what my
father wanted to hear. His letters became more pointed, critical, accusatory, downright insulting to the point of incoherence. The final letter from the Chicago Cubs Baseball Club —
their stationery has a small picture of Wrigley Field at the top
— is dated October 7, 1945, and states clearly: "We consider
the matter closed and would appreciate it if you did not contact us again."

After that letter my father began to make personal visits to
the Cub corporate offices.

My father's quest began in 1943. I was born in 1945 and
grew up in a home where the atmosphere was one of vague

3

unease. I sensed my father was a troubled man. The general anxiety and discomfort that permeated the air also affected my mother and my sister, Enola Gay.

My father's problem was this: he was in possession of information concerning the Chicago Cubs, our home town of Onamata, Iowa, and a baseball league known as the Iowa Baseball Confederacy, information that he *knew* to be true and accurate but that no one else in the world would acknowledge. He *knew* history books were untrue, that baseball records were falsified, that people of otherwise unblemished character told him bold-faced lies when he inquired about their knowledge of, and involvement with, the Iowa Baseball Confederacy.

As a child, though I sympathized with my father, I never fully understood the significance of his obsession. As the Indians say, one cannot walk in another man's moccasins. I was never able to conceive what he suffered, until, upon his death, when I was sixteen, I received his legacy, which was not money, or property, or jewels (though I was not financially bereft), but what I can only liken to a brain transplant. For upon my father's passing, I inherited not only *all* the information he alone had been a party to, but also his obsession to prove to the world that what he knew was right and true.

His example taught me well, for no matter how futile his efforts seemed, he would not be moved from his goals, just as I shall not be moved from mine. I will pursue the elusive dream of the Iowa Baseball Confederacy until it is admitted that the Chicago Cubs traveled to Iowa in the summer of 1908 and engaged in a baseball game against the Iowa Baseball Confederacy All-Stars.

As there are stages in grieving, in aging, in acceptance of illness, so there seem to be stages in the development of the inherited obsession of which I speak. I began my investigation by making the same polite written inquiries to the Chicago

4

Cubs and other sources who should have known of the Confederacy, and ended with the same personal confrontations and shouted accusations, which resulted in my being firmly escorted from the Cub offices.

Two years ago, I learned, by eavesdropping on a conversation in the box next to mine at Wrigley Field, that the Cubs were in the process of hiring a junior public relations person. I applied for the job; in fact I submitted a twelve-page letter of application, outlining some of the facts I knew about the Chicago Cubs, past and present. The personnel department didn't even have the courtesy to acknowledge my application. However, by phoning the Cub offices on various pretexts, I was able to learn that the person hired was to begin work the following Wednesday. I also learned that the executives held business meetings on Monday mornings.

I showed up on Monday, dressed in a rented three-piece suit, looking as eager, expectant, thrilled, and breathless as I anticipated the new employee would feel.

"Hi! I'm supposed to start work this morning," I said, smiling brightly. For the occasion I had had my hair cut and dyed a neutral brown. My hair is usually shoulder length, white as vanilla ice cream, which makes it difficult for me to appear inconspicuous. I am not an albino, for though my skin lacks pigmentation, my eyes have color: a pale, translucent blue.

My job — or, rather, the job of the new public relations person — was to write copy for the Chicago Cub yearbook. A young woman whom I remembered having a confrontation with a few years before kept checking the dates on her calendar and staring at me, trying, I'm sure, to place me. She assigned me back issues of the yearbook to read, promising to give me more substantial employment after lunch when the public relations director returned.

As I glanced at the yearbooks, I eyed the rows of foot-locker-green filing cabinets, my mouth watering for the opportunity to leap into history. Shortly before lunch I made my

5

way to the supply room and secreted myself behind several thousand Chicago Cub yearbooks. I lay on the floor and covered myself with the glossy little magazines, their slick surfaces smelling like new-car interiors. I slept for a while, dreaming I was in the hold of a fishing vessel, covered with slippery tropical fish.

When the fluorescent hands on my wrist watch showed 6:00 P.M., I ventured out. The offices were deserted, silent, smelling of paper and coffee grounds.

I spent the entire night skimming through the filing cabinets, reading everything I could find concerning the years 1902–1908, which were the years the Iowa Baseball Confederacy was in existence.

It was sad to find out that, to the Cubs, baseball was not the least magical; it was strictly business. The files contained little but contracts, tax forms, medical expense forms. There were no elaborate personnel files, no newspaper clippings, no fan testimonials.

Here was the Cubs' greatest pitcher, Mordecai Peter Centennial "Three Finger" or "Miner" Brown, in a manila folder labeled M. BROWN and smudged with fingerprints. Not even a first name. No mention of his 239 victories or of his induction into the Hall of Fame. No mention of his injury, the cropped finger that allowed him to put a special spin on the ball. Just a file with the barest of records.

I did find some of my own correspondence in a file labeled CRANK LETTERS, filed away alongside a letter claiming the Chicago Cubs would win the last pennant before Armageddon and another containing what purported to be conclusive evidence that Ernie Banks and Billy Williams were extraterrestrials. Seeing them side by side, I had to admit that those letters made as much sense as mine.

There were penciled notes on one of my more inflammatory letters: *Dangerous? F.B.I.? Relative of E. G. Clarke?* My sister, Enola Gay, is a fugitive from justice.

6

I emerged at 6:00 A.M., disheveled, dry-mouthed, red-eyed, and without one shred of evidence that the 1908 Chicago Cubs ever visited Big Inning, Iowa, or, for that matter, that there ever was a Big Inning, Iowa.

"It is a fact that there are cracks in time," my father repeated endlessly. "Weaknesses — fissures, if you like — in the gauzy dreamland that separates the past from the present." Hearing those words like a musical refrain all through my childhood, I came to believe them, or, rather, accept them; it was never a matter as simple as belief. To me they weren't remarkable; after all, some children were taught to accept the enormities, the absurdities, the implausibilities of scripture as fact.

"Time is out of kilter here in Johnson County; that's my conclusion," my father said to me often. "But if something is out of kilter, there's no reason it can't be fixed. And when it's fixed I'll be proven right."

Briefly stated, here is what my father believed: through those cracks in time, little snippets of the past, like small, historical mice, gnaw holes in the lath and plaster and wallpaper of what used to be, then scamper madly across the present, causing eyes to shift and ears to perk to their tiny footfalls. To most people they are only a gray blur and a miniature tattoo of sound quickly gone and forgotten. There are, however, some of us who see and hear more than they were ever meant to. My father was one of those, as am I.

My father, Matthew Clarke, dreamed his wife. He lay in his bedroom in the square frame house with green shutters in the Iowa town called Onamata, which, long ago, before the flood, when everything but the church was washed away in the direction of Missouri, was called Big Inning. Wide awake, eyes pressed shut, Matthew Clarke dreamed his ideal

7

woman, conjured her up from the scarlet blackness beneath his lids, until she rose before him like a genie, wavery, pulsating.

"There's always been a strangeness hovering over all this land," he used to tell me. "Even before I dreamed Maudie, before I learned of the Confederacy, I knew there were layers and layers of history on this land, like a chair with ten coats of enamel. And I sensed some of those layers were peeling off, floating in the air, waiting to be breathed in, soaked up like sunshine. I tell you, Gideon" — and he would scratch the tip of his long, sun-bronzed nose and run a hand through his black curls, which were as unruly as twitch grass — "there are all kinds of mysteries dancing around us like sunbeams, just beyond our finger tips." When I'd look at him as if I didn't quite believe him, he'd go on, "They're there, like birds in a thicket that you can hear but can't see."

And I would listen to him and marvel at his energy and dedication, and I'd believe him or at least accept what he told me, but with a total lack of awe. If my father insisted that he alone was in step, the rest of the world a ragtag of shabby marchers, who was I to disagree? Nothing, including the resurrection of the dead, would have surprised me.

My first experience of the floating magic he talked of was when the hollyhocks sang to me. I suppose I was eight the first time I heard those hollyhocks, tall, sturdy flowers the color of sun-faded raspberries. They grew high and physical outside my father's bedroom window, their stocks like broom handles, saucer-sized heads bowed silently, gathered together like a freshly scrubbed barbershop quartet. "Ooooooh, ooooooh, ooooooh," they sang at first, softly as a choir.

As I listened I knew they were performing for me alone, that if a playmate appeared he would hear nothing. I remember thinking, Why shouldn't the hollyhocks sing? And I pictured a nebulous rock wall, desert-rust in color, cracking open

8

like an egg, the tall flowers ducking their heads as they emerged, eerie as aliens. As I sat cross-legged on the lawn in front of them, their song grew louder, the tempo increased: "DA da DA da DA DA, DA da DA da da, DA da DA da da, DA da DA DA DA." It would be years before I discovered the source of their music.

One thing I don't understand is that I did not tell my father of the experience. How he would have loved to have had me as an ally. In that credulous way children have of accepting what life offers them, it didn't occur to me then how lonely my father's quest must have been. By the time I realized, my mother had long since left us and taken my sister and my cat with her to Chicago. Father was devoting his whole life to proving the existence of the Iowa Baseball Confederacy and having precious little success.

I didn't understand his obsession well enough to be the kind of son I should have been. Now, years after his death, after he has been dead for more years of my life than he was alive, after I have come to have an obsession of my own, I understand all too well what he went through, and I sympathize, too late though it may be.

But back to my father's dream. I won't tell what I know about the Iowa Baseball Confederacy just yet. It is more important to explain about my father and my mother, the woman he dreamed to life.

"She was so real sometimes, I could smell her and taste her and do everything but touch her," he used to say to me. "When you get older you'll understand what it was like, Gid." I wonder if all parents tell their children things the children don't understand but will when they get older. I wanted to understand *then*.

Matthew Clarke knew he wasn't likely to find his dream among the residents of Onamata, or even in nearby Iowa City. It was the summer of 1943, the war was raging, and

Matthew Clarke was just graduated from the University of Iowa with a degree in American history.

"I had a choice to make and make quickly," he used to say to me. Some of my earliest memories are of hearing this story. We — when we were still a family — used to sit on the wide verandah on humid summer evenings, Mother and Father on slatted wooden chairs, hers enameled white, his vermilion, while my sister and I sat on the floor, our legs in front of us in V shapes, rolling a ball back and forth.

"It was either the army or graduate school," my father would continue. "In fact, I had the graduate school application, all filled out, in the back pocket of my pants the night I dreamed your mother to life." He'd laugh a low, soft chuckle, and look across at my mother, who would be sitting forward in the white chair, dusky as an Indian, her eyes unfathomable and molasses-black.

I have often imagined Matthew Clarke as he lay on top of the old black-and-red patchwork quilt, which still graces the bed and still looks as if it might at one time have served a Gypsy as a cape, the graduate school application folded and stuffed in his rear pocket, crinkling to remind him of its presence each time he moved slightly.

"That evening, I was just like a bear gettin' a whiff of honey, Gideon. I stood up, my arms out in front of me like a sleepwalker, and I headed for the truck, drove off to Iowa City, went to the carnival, and the rest is history."

That was the short version of the story. The tale became longer and longer, I think in direct proportion to the time my mother was absent from us. As the years passed, my father recalled more and more about that fateful summer night. And as I grew older he supplied more details, and told more and more about what he felt on that magical evening.

After telling the short version, my father would look over at my mother and down at us children and smile. He would wipe imaginary sweat from his high forehead, raise his hands palm up in a gesture of wonder. I would stare at my dark-haired father, at my dusky mother and sister, who would blend into the summery shadows of the porch until I sometimes wondered if they were there at all, and silently question why or how I came to have lank blond hair and eyebrows the color of corn silk.

⊖

Matthew Clarke had lived all his life near Iowa City, where sun-blond girls with browning skin and endearing overbites flocked around the campus of the University of Iowa. A few even lived in some of the two dozen houses that made up his home town of Onamata. In the summer of 1943, those sweet, sincere, interchangeable young women wore saddle shoes and pleated skirts. The skirts were made of red, yellow, or green plaid, often with a six-inch safety pin worn just above the knee to keep them modest. Many of these young women were beautiful; most were scrupulously laundered, smelling clean as fresh ironing. They were cheerful, dutiful, God-fearing, and ravenous for husbands. Matthew Clarke wanted none of them.

He knew what he wanted. He had even gone to Chicago in search of her.

"I ever tell you about the fat woman in Chicago?" I remember him saying to me. We were on our way to St. Louis to see a Cardinal double-header. It was a Sunday and we'd left Onamata at five A.M. to be sure to get there in time to buy good seats.

"Fifty times," I was tempted to say, but didn't. I was about fourteen and thought anyone as old as my father must be partially fossilized and fully retarded. But I was cautious. He didn't wait for an answer from me.

"Seemed like every street I walked on in downtown

11

Chicago there were women every forty feet or so, posed like statues, in suggestive stances. And there were loud women in the bars I went to, women with quarrelsome voices and stringy hands. But they weren't the kind I was lookin' for. Stay away from those kind of women, Gid. They're nothin' but trouble."

"Your experience with women hasn't exactly been trouble free," I thought of saying, but again, didn't.

"Then I met this woman, Gid. And I think she was the start of this whole thing with the Confederacy."

"She'd slipped through one of the cracks in time, " I said, staring out the window, resisting the temptation to say something about its being a *wide* crack.

"I was just off State Street, I think. A dark street with sidewalks covered in grit and glass fragments. There were boarded-up buildings, and bars with blue neon beer bottles bleeding down their windows. She ambled out of a doorway, wide as she was tall, so ash-blond I swear she gave off light, an aura. She was as blond as you. She had bangs to the middle of her forehead. The rest of her hair was straight and chopped, as if a bowl had been set on top of her head. She might have been twenty-five or she might have been fifty. Her face was wide and mottled, her nose flat as a baby's. She was wearing a tentlike dress that stopped above her pale knees; the dress was a swirl of color, like scarves blowing in the wind.

"Her eyes were a pale, pale blue, and she was barefoot. She walked splay-legged right into my path, her stubby feet with their gray, sluglike toes grinding sand. She'd come out of a run-down building where dirty velvet curtains were strung across a storefront. A few stars and triangles were painted on the glass in front of the curtains. The words FORTUNE TELLING had been hand-lettered on the windowpane by an amateur.

"That woman looked a little bit like Missy, you know, except she was a lot fatter than Missy, and she wasn't a . . . a mongoloid, although before she spoke I thought she might be. As I stood staring at her, the only thing I could think of was a white Gypsy, an albino Gypsy.

" 'Excuse me,' I said, and tried to step around her. But she didn't move; in fact, she leaned into my path until I had to stop.

" 'No, no,' she crooned, like she was talking to a child. And she put her pudgy hand on my arm. Her fingers were white as fresh fish, the nails chewed down to the quick.

" 'I came to meet you,' she said in that same purring voice. 'I could feel you getting nearer.' Her bottom lip was turned down like that of a child about to cry. Her teeth were short, crooked, and stained.

" 'Go home to Iowa,' she said. 'You're not supposed to be *here*. Go home.' I glanced down at her huge knees; they were dimpled and scarred.

" 'What are you talking about?' I said. But she was gone. I swear it, Gid. Gone, vanished. There I was, standing on that sleazy sidewalk, lookin' like a fool, talking to a parking meter, a big, prehistoric, beast-headed thing, all pitted and ugly and metal-smelling.

"I got out of there, let me tell you. But I never forgot that woman or her voice. And she was right. Because I no sooner got back to Onamata than I dreamed your mother. And then went out and found her."

☺

Ah, yes, my mother. I think it better if *I* tell the story of how Matthew Clarke met his wife. I was raised on that story. My father told it to me for the final time on the way to Milwaukee the day he was killed. It is the first story I remember hearing from my father, and the last.

The events that disrupted my father's life, and in turn

mine, happened in the summer of 1943. Part of the story involves my father being hit by lightning.

On that sultry Iowa evening, storm clouds swept in from the west like a fleet of tall ships. Silver zippers of lightning decorated the evening sky, and a lightning bolt struck my father as he and Maudie, the strange girl he had just met, sought shelter from the storm. He wasn't killed; he wasn't even injured seriously; he wasn't fried by the heat of the bolt, disfigured, or melted down like a record left in the back window of a car. He was, however, forever changed. For as a piece of stationery is squeezed between the jaws of an official seal or as liquid metal is struck into a shiny new coin, my father's life was altered.

As well as gifting him with a wealth of information about a baseball league known as the Iowa Baseball Confederacy, the lightning tampered with my father's blood, rearranged his chromosomes gently as a baby's breath turns a mobile, rattled his bone marrow, disrupted his immune system. That is how he passed the Iowa Baseball Confederacy along to me. When I was born, two years after the lightning struck him, my little flower of a brain was crammed with the same statistics, the same league standings, the same batting averages, the same information that plagued my father. Yet my knowledge was veiled, covered by one of those layers of history my father was so anxious to expound on, hidden from my view like a dove cuddled beneath a magician's handkerchief. Eventually the Confederacy came to me full-blown, one fateful day at County Stadium in Milwaukee, the day my father died. But that comes later.

After Matthew Clarke was struck by lightning, the nut of information that was the Iowa Baseball Confederacy began to grow like a summer pumpkin. The Confederacy crowded in on his life until it became like a fat man in an elevator with two huge suitcases.

To say that my father was regarded as an eccentric in those years after he became obsessed with the Confederacy would be mild understatement. Luckily, eccentrics are tolerated, even encouraged, in small Iowa towns. "Like father, like son," the people of Onamata say about me. "That Gideon Clarke is a right odd fellow," they say, "but he comes by it honestly." I think they whisper about me more than they did about my father because I don't work steadily, a cardinal sin in America's industrious heartland. Thanks to my mother and my sister, I have more money than I will ever need.

But to the story. As I've explained, my father was carrying his graduate school application in his back pocket the dreamy August evening he felt compelled to travel to Iowa City and take in the Gollmar Bros. Carnival and American Way Shows. As he approached through the parking lot he could see that the carnival was a small, sorry operation: rusty, square-fendered trucks were mired in a confusion of mud and cables. Behind the trucks was a string of blunt-nosed buses with bulging tires, some with frayed curtains at their windows. Portable generators, which powered the frail carousel and the paint-freckled Ferris wheel, roared deafeningly.

As Matthew set out for Iowa City that day he'd had the feeling that there were presences all about him, that there was hidden life in the poplar leaves that fluttered alluringly in the yard; he'd turned back toward the house once, as if beckoned by the group of slim hollyhocks that stood under the bedroom window at the side of the building. For a few seconds Matthew had thought he could hear them humming to a mysterious military music. The hollyhocks were surrounded by cosmos, themselves tall. The pale pink, wine, and mauve cosmos, peering from the frilly green lace that was their leaves, looked like delicate children appealing to a parent.

Matthew stood absolutely still for several moments, staring at the tableau, waiting expectantly. There was something eerie about the flowers; he had the feeling they wanted to speak to him.

During the drive to Iowa City, Matthew had thought he'd seen an Indian walking in the ditch, loping along with enormous strides, an Indian wearing only a breechcloth. But as he came abreast of the spot he'd seen that it was just a trick played by the sun as it slanted through the emerald cornstalks.

Matthew slouched down the midway, his hands deep in his pockets, his dark eyes, though downcast, taking in everything. He stared and stared at the rides and the booths. He spent no money. The trampled and muddy grasses of the fairgrounds were frosted with cedar shavings, and their perfume filled the air. Matthew craned his neck, brushed stubborn curls from his forehead, stopped and scrutinized a brightly lit booth where a pyramid of milk bottles repelled puffy baseballs, until he was certain the booth held nothing of significance.

As he continued along the midway he eyed the banner advertising the obligatory girlie show. DARLIN' MAUDIE was painted in garish red letters across a canvas banner; at each end of the banner was the same drawing of a girl with rosebud lips, sporting a 1920s hairdo. The drawing ended at the girl's navel. She was clad in a silky red blouse, vaguely Chinese in nature. The fingers of each hand gripped the scream-red material as if she were about to tear the blouse wide open. EXOTIC! DARING! REVEALING! NAUGHTY! was printed in smaller capitals under the main headline.

Matthew noticed that the barker for the Darlin' Maudie show was not attracting many patrons, partly because his voice could not be heard above the thundering generators, and partly because it was wartime and the sparse crowd was made up mainly of women and children. What few men were present were middle-aged or older and had women and children in tow.

After watching the barker for a moment, Matthew cut between the girlie-show tent and a barrel-like wooden structure where motorcycle daredevils rode only inches away from multiple fractures. As he rounded the corner of the tent he could hear arguing voices. He continued to the back of the tent, and there he saw Darlin' Maudie standing at the top of some makeshift stairs, just outside the door to a tiny, aluminum-colored trailer that appeared to be held together by rust. The first thing he noticed was her mouth. It was wide and sensuous, nothing like a rosebud. She was dressed in celery-colored satin pantaloons, the kind worn by harem girls in movies. She had on the same blouse as the girl on the banner, only all the buttons were tightly closed, each snap surrounded by what dressmakers call a frog.

Darlin' Maudie was pointing accusingly and cursing as if a cow had just stepped on her. The man at whom she was cursing had a red, moon-shaped face. His wiry hair was brushcut; he wore construction boots, jeans, and a soiled white T-shirt, which humped out over a sizable beer belly.

"No matter what you say, you can't make me do it," Darlin' Maudie was shrieking. "You . . ." She reeled off every curse Matthew had ever heard, plus a few totally new to him.

"If you don't do it today, you'll do it tomorrow," drawled the crew-cut. While Maudie whirred curses at his back like poisonous darts from a blowgun, the man ambled away, his boots making sucking sounds in the mud.

Darlin' Maudie eventually turned back toward the trailer, and as she did she saw Matthew standing there wide-eyed as an orphan in front of a magician, one hand gingerly touching the rusting metal.

"What do you want?" she said, making her dark eyes large in an imitation of Matthew's surprised stare as she produced a pack of cigarettes from somewhere on her body. Matthew stood rooted to the spot, gaping up at her as she lit a Phillip Morris and inhaled deeply. Matthew knew he must look like a farm boy staring at his first skyscraper. But the odors that floated slowly in the sultry air had enchanted him — the tangy shavings, the burning-oil smell of the generators, Maudie's perfume, the acrid odor of her cigarette.

"Can I do anything to help you?" Matthew finally stuttered. He pictured himself astride a shining steed, his lance turned orange by the setting sun.

"What are you, a cop?" said Darlin' Maudie.

"You sounded as if you were in some kind of trouble," said Matthew.

"Nothin' I can't handle," she said, still eyeing him suspiciously. The sun sparked off her blue-black hair. She wore one large ringlet at the front of each ear. After a few seconds she smiled, showing small, even teeth with delicate spaces between. "Yeah, you can do something for me," she said, still smiling. "You can carry me someplace where I can set my feet down on solid land. I can't get these goddamned shoes dirty." She pointed with her cigarette at the high-heeled red pumps, the same color as her blouse.

Matthew, his breath constricted with love, knowing the color was rising up his neck like mercury in a thermometer, stepped forward, his own shoes sinking uncomfortably deep in the mire.

"I won't have to carry you far," he said. "Your trailer's parked in a low spot."

"We'll see who does what," Maudie said defiantly as she stepped carefully down the rickety steps and deposited herself in Matthew's arms. He carried her across the lot and fifty yards up an embankment to the edge of a cornfield.

18

"Thanks," said Darlin' Maudie, looking carefully at her benefactor for the first time. "What's your name?"

"Matthew."

"Your friends call you Matt?"

"No. They call me Matthew."

"I might have figured," she said, making her eyes large again. Then she spotted a wide, squat tree about a hundred yards into the cornfield. "Let's go in there," she said. "It looks so peaceful."

The corn was armpit high and the field smelled fresh as dawn. Darlin' Maudie tested the earth with one crimson shoe.

"I told you it would be dry up here," Matthew said, and taking her hand he led her toward the tree.

The tree sat like a party umbrella, trunk sturdy, branches gently arcing. Wild grasses grew around the base of the tree, where roots ridged above the soil like exposed veins.

They sat down on the grass, Matthew picking away twigs and pieces of fallen bark so Darlin' Maudie wouldn't dirty her exotic costume.

The corn swaddled the noise of the carnival. They could feel the rhythm of the generators, thumping away like distant music.

"This is so quiet," Maudie said, looking tiny and frightened, a ragamuffin of a girl lifted out of her noisy and reverberating environment and deposited amid the silent corn. "I ain't been anywhere quiet for months and months, since we left Florida in the spring."

Matthew could see her shoulder blades chopping at the material of her blouse. As his gaze flashed across her black eyes, he saw that she had a beauty spot on her cheek, about an inch to the right of her mouth. He couldn't tell if it was real or painted on, but he felt himself salivating. He was mad to caress the mysterious spot with his tongue. Maudie smiled again and he counted the spaces between her lower teeth. He held out his arms to her, tentatively, afraid she would laugh rudely or ridicule him. She moved close, there under the canopy of leaves, but with her head down so there wouldn't be any kiss. She rested her head on his chest as he put one hand on her upper arm, which was so thin he felt as if he were holding a paper girl and not a real one.

But he could smell her. Her hair held the dusky, musky odors of soap, perfume, and smoke. If Matthew bent his neck at an odd angle he could just manage to kiss the top of her head. Her hair was a tangle of black velvet; and the sun rays, about the same height as the corn, made every tenth hair or so look as if it were on fire.

While they embraced, the sun vanished as if it had been switched off. Thunder grumbled and a sudden breeze set the leaves trembling and rustled the corn.

Maudie remained absolutely still, light as a kitten against Matthew's chest.

"If you're lucky, in a lifetime you get one moment in which you'd like to live forever," my father said each time he recounted the story to me. "One moment when you'd like to be frozen in time, in a landscape, a painting, a sculpture, or a vase. That was my moment. If I had it all to do over again, Gideon, I'd do it the same way. Even if I knew then what I know now."

Back then in the cornfield, Matthew said, "We'd better leave, find someplace to get out of the storm."

"No," the bird-light girl replied emphatically, pushing herself closer to him. "I want to stay out here. I want to see what the storm is like."

"But your clothes . . ." said Matthew.

"To hell with my clothes. I ain't goin' back. He can't make me do it."

To his dying day Matthew Clarke never knew what it was that Maudie didn't want to do. It turned out that Maudie *was* her name. The one extravagance Gollmar Bros. Carnival and American Way Shows allowed itself each spring before the troupe hit the road was to print a new banner for the girlie show, using the name of the lead performer.

In the cornfield, the first penny-sized raindrops plopped down.

"We'll have to move closer to the tree," Matthew said as a drop splattered on the toe of one of Maudie's scarlet shoes. They moved closer to the trunk.

The wind gusted and the tree above them shuddered. But beneath the leaves it was eerily silent, the air heavy. Matthew thought it was strange to see the wind bending and flattening the corn just yards away, while beneath their canopy they could scarcely feel a breeze.

Lightning buzz-sawed across the sky, leaving ragged silver incisions. The rumble of thunder was followed by a bulletlike whine and a sizzling crash as lightning struck somewhere nearby. As the thunder rolled wildly, Maudie pressed against Matthew. When she turned her face up to him he saw fear in her almond-pointed eyes.

"I didn't know it would be like this," she whispered. "I'm not from around here."

Matthew kissed her then, awkwardly, his lips touching her nose before covering her mouth. The rain hurtled down around them; a few drops leaked through the leaves, dripping onto the frilly grass at their feet. Maudie wrapped her arms tightly about Matthew and returned his kiss. Her tongue felt small and hot against his own.

I'm so happy I could die, Matthew thought. At that moment there was a violent, ripping, crunching sound, as if kindling was being broken right next to their ears. The tree screamed. Afterward, Maudie claimed it was her, or possibly

Matthew. But Matthew knew it had been the tree, a long, shrill sound like a rabbit's death cry.

The tree was struck behind and above them. The lightning ripped off a huge limb. Matthew found himself on the grass, staring up at a fresh white scar where the limb had been. The fallen branch lay beside him, some leaves brushing against one arm.

He was nauseated; his left arm and leg felt full of pins and crawling ants. When he tried to blink he realized his left eyelid was paralyzed. In another second or so he discovered that the only part of him he could move was his right eye, and it was full of Maudie.

Darlin' Maudie stood in the drenching rain at the edge of the corn, her arms raised above her head, her legs braced as if she were supporting a monstrous weight on her upturned hands. From where he lay, it looked to Matthew as if she held lightning in each hand, bolts the color of molten silver, crackling like cellophane, long as the sky. They stretched from her hands clear to the clouds, which were wild and black and rolling like locomotives.

Matthew felt heavy drops of rain hit his face. The drops sizzled as they spattered on his lightning-seared skin. He watched from his one good eye as Maudie's eyes blazed in some kind of mystical triumph, her fingers dazzled with lightning.

"I won't!" Matthew heard her say. "I won't! I won't!"

He never knew whether she was drawing the lightning in or warding it off.

The next thing Matthew remembered, Darlin' Maudie was kneeling beside him on the wet grass, her cheek against his, whimpering like a puppy, alternately kissing him and imploring him to show some sign of life.

As he came around, Matthew realized he could see from both eyes, that he could blink his left eyelid. The pins were retreating from his left arm and leg, leaving an ache in his hip and knee. His fingers and toes on the left side felt like candles that had been lit and then extinguished.

"I'm all right," Matthew said as Maudie planted more kisses down his cheek.

Matthew could feel her hot little breasts against his chest, burning right through her blouse and his shirt. He managed to get his right arm around her shoulders and pull her even closer to him. Her breath was warm against his cheek and holding her was like clutching an armful of flowers. The odors about her were somewhere between sweet clover and heaven. But painted on the inside of Matthew's eyelids was the frightening image of Maudie, arms raised to the sky, joined to the lightning.

When the rain stopped, Maudie helped Matthew to his feet. He was limp as laundry and had black dots the size of tapioca floating in front of his eyes. As they moved down the rows of corn toward the carnival Matthew said, "I can't carry you this time," and tried to muster an apologetic smile.

"No need to," said Maudie.

"But your shoes . . ."

"To hell with my shoes. I ain't goin' back," she said, looking down past her mud-splattered costume to where her shoes were all but covered in muck. "That is, if I can come with you?"

Matthew took her hand. "It's a long, messy walk to my truck, especially if we avoid crossing the carnival grounds."

"I'm with you," said Maudie.

An hour later, wet, bedraggled, mud-scoured, Matthew Clarke and Darlin' Maudie arrived at Matthew's home in Onamata. As he helped Maudie out of the truck he glanced at the sky, which appeared troubled: dark fleeces of cloud glided across the night, covering and uncovering a tangerine-colored moon. Matthew tucked Maudie into the huge, black-walnut four-poster, which still dominates the downstairs bedroom, and covered her with the Gypsy quilt.

"How do you feel?" he kept asking.

"It was you got struck by lightning, not me," Darlin' Maudie replied.

⊖

I still live in the town of Onamata, two miles south and west of Iowa City, a hundred miles east of Des Moines. I am the only person who knows the origin of the name Onamata; yet explain as I might, no one will pay the slightest attention to me. In *Place Names of Iowa*, Onamata is described thus: "Origin unknown. Possibly a corruption of the Black Hawk Indian word for magic. Town established 1909."

Onamata now consists of thirty houses, a general store, a café, a Conoco service station, a John Deere subagent, and the Clarke & Son Insurance Agency, of which I was until recently the proprietor. My grandfather was the original Clarke, and my father the son. Then Matthew Clarke was the father and I was the son. Now I am the Clarke and there is no son. The agency fronts on the main street of Onamata, a hundred yards from the banks of the Iowa River, where the water runs placid, the color of green quartz. The false front of the insurance agency building is painted a vibrant peach. The building once housed a bank, and before that an undertaker. Underneath the peach paint can still be seen BANK OF ONAMATA, the dark letters looking as though they want to push themselves to the surface.

Only I know that long ago Onamata was called Big Inning. That was before the flood of 1908, before the Iowa Baseball Confederacy was erased from human memory for thirty-five years. When the Confederacy did resurface, its origins, history, and secrets were known only to my father. His knowledge of the Confederacy destroyed his life, and some say my knowledge of the Confederacy is destroying mine. Personally, I feel somewhat like a prophet, and prophets are meant to be derided and maligned.

I have spent the past seventeen years of my life trying to prove the existence of my inherited obsession. Whatever was done to erase the Confederacy wasn't enough. Bits and pieces have survived, like rumors, like buried evil unearthed and activated.

⊖

My grandparents, Justin and Flora Clarke, retired to Florida in 1942, leaving my father the insurance business and the two-story white frame house with a wrought-iron widow's walk centered by a tall silver lightning rod. From a distance the top of the house resembles the helmet of a medieval soldier.

Grant Wood, the world-famous Iowa artist, could have known my grandparents. They could have posed for *American Gothic*. They were dry, meticulous people. My grandfather retired precisely on his sixty-fifth birthday, which was a Wednesday. He had been forty-one and my grandmother thirty-nine when my father was born. There had been an older child named Nancy-Rae, born to them in their late twenties, who, shortly after her fourteenth birthday, when my father was a toddler, stole off in the dark of night, walked out to the highway, where someone they knew saw her hitchhiking toward Chicago, and disappeared from the face of the earth.

"Our greatest sadness," was how my grandmother described the loss of my aunt Nancy-Rae.

I saw my grandparents only once. When I was about eight my father and I drove to spring training in Florida. I saw Curt Simmons, Robin Roberts, Allie Reynolds, Vinegar Bend Mizell, Yogi Berra, and my grandparents.

They lived in a very small house on a side street in Miami. There was an orange tree in the back yard. The house and my grandparents smelled of Listerine, peppermint, and Absorbine, Jr.

They left Iowa irrevocably behind them when they retired. They never returned for a visit, never invited anyone from Onamata to visit them, including us, I suspect, although my father never said so.

What he did say, on the drive back, as if he was trying to explain something to me but was not exactly sure what, was, "We are haunted by our past, which clings to us like strange, mystical lint. Of the past, the mystery of family is the most beautiful, the saddest, and the most inescapable of all. Those to whom we are joined by the ethereal ties of blood are often those about whom we know the least." I think he was talking about much more than just my grandparents.

I listened to my father's tales with half an ear. I knew he was obsessed with something no one else cared about. He wrote letters, articles, talked of a book, which he eventually wrote. Complained. I didn't pay half the attention I should have. Children, thinking themselves immortal, assume everyone else is too. He died when I was a few months short of seventeen.

☉

The morning after being struck by lightning, Matthew Clarke woke in the cavernous double bed in the front bedroom, one of his long arms draped over the frail shoulders of Darlin' Maudie. He stirred slightly, his finger tips touching her ribs. At his touch she moved closer to him. He had to restrain himself from counting her ribs with his fingers, one, two, three. Her body felt cool as it curved against his.

He could see her back, the skin the soft brown of tanned leather; her ear, protruding through tangles of coal-colored hair, seemed anxious to be kissed.

26

Matthew remembered the carnival, the rain, the lightning, the drive home with Maudie, scruffy as a drowned muskrat, at his side. He recalled adding whiskey to the coffee he made in the spacious kitchen at the rear of the house. And later, Maudie wild with passion in the big bed, her nails sharp against his shoulders, their bodies slick under the quilts as their sweat blended.

As I listened to various versions of this story, time and again, told to me as other children were regaled with fairy tales, I was always embarrassed. I realized as I grew older that it was because, as with most children, I wanted to deny my parents' sexuality. I reluctantly have to admit that even now as I recall my father's voice I am embarrassed. It is only when I distance the story by using my own words that I am comfortable with the telling.

There is one part of the story that wasn't embarrassing, only puzzling. On that morning when Matthew awoke with Maudie beside him, he awoke with an awareness of something he knew was going to become the most important element in his life, more important than his business, than his home, than even the strange, fragile girl, who, next to him, trembled as she dreamed.

In Matthew Clarke's brain, which that morning felt bright as chrome, full of white light and blinding metal, the complete history of the Iowa Baseball Confederacy was burned in, deep as a brand, vivid, resplendent, dazzling in its every detail.

⊖

Two weeks later, on a humid August afternoon in 1943, Darlin' Maudie and Matthew Clarke were married at the stone courthouse in Iowa City.

"I tell you, Gid, during those two weeks there was a terrible volume of mail from Onamata to Miami. Everybody within a ten-mile radius of Onamata felt it their duty to let the old folks know what I'd done. I'd not only moved a girl into the holy confines of my father's house, but I'd moved in what was known as a 'carnival girl.' A few of the more morally indignant canceled their insurance policies with my agency, but only a few.

"After the wedding, the same straight-backed, blue-nosed women who had written scurrilous things about me to my parents came pussyfooting around the house bearing casseroles, pies, good wishes, and wedding presents.

"After I wrote to them about the wedding, my mother added a little postscript to her next letter. 'We hope you'll be very happy,' it said. They never sent a present, never met Maudie."

The same week he was married Matthew was accepted as a graduate student in the History Department at the University of Iowa. He was accepted reluctantly, by a vote of three to two, strictly on his undergraduate record. At his interview he was bright-eyed and only moderately coherent as he babbled about writing a thesis on some kind of baseball league that had existed near Iowa City in the early 1900s. The majority of the committee blamed his exuberance and incoherence on the fact that he was to be married in a day or two.

"By October he'll be back to normal and we'll convince him to write a thesis on the Civil War," said E. H. Hindsmith, the man who cast the deciding vote in Matthew's favor.

In the months that followed, Matthew Clarke continued to operate his insurance business from the dusty-windowed storefront in Onamata, not soliciting business but gently reminding local people when their fire, auto, farm, or crop insurance was up for renewal. He accepted new business when it came to him.

"My Joseph's gettin' married next month," a sturdy farmer might say, standing awkwardly in the office, which smelled of varnish and paper and held a large, rectangular, wax-yellow desk, a wooden filing cabinet, and two severe wooden chairs. "He'll be around to see you about life insurance. That is, if you'll be in Tuesday evening."

"If Matthew Clarke sends you a bill, you know it's an honest one," people said. They also said, "Matthew Clarke could have made something of his life if he wasn't so interested in those baseball teams of his." They also whispered, in the gentle, misty heat of Iowa summer, "Matthew Clarke had a wife but couldn't keep her."

Matthew was hard at work on a proposal to write his thesis on the history of the Iowa Baseball Confederacy, though occasionally, when he tried to confirm some detail by consulting various books on baseball history and was unable to do so, he had doubts. But he quickly put them aside. He didn't *need* any confirmation from outside sources. The history of the Iowa Baseball Confederacy was carved on stone tablets in his memory. He couldn't know such things if they were not true.

During that time he also made Darlin' Maudie pregnant.

Try as he might, Matthew learned little of Maudie's past.

"Why do you keep asking?" was the way she would answer his questions. Or else she would say, "Do you love me?"

"Of course I love you," Matthew would reply.

"Then what else matters?" And she would stare across the oversized oak table in the dining room, her chin resting in the palm of her left hand, her fingers hooked on her lower lip, a smile, full of love, gently crinkling the skin around her eyes.

It was Matthew's nature to ask questions. He felt as if Maudie's past was a rock that needed to be battered into gravel.

It was years later, long after Maudie was gone for the last time, that Matthew realized how lonely she must have been. He had the business, his studies, his obsession with the mysterious baseball league. But he had few friends, and much of his life was lived in solitude. Maudie maintained the old

29

home, which still smelled of his retired parents. But she had no friends. There were simply no friends for her to have. The young people lived on the farms; the houses in Onamata were occupied mainly by retired farmers and businessmen. There were fewer than ten children in Onamata. And the mothers of those children were tight-lipped Baptists with protruding teeth and hair pulled back until their eyes bulged. The women were the same color and texture as the dusty streets of the town. Maudie walked barefoot to the general store, wearing her celery-colored pantaloons. And she smoked in public.

About the only change Maudie made to the house was to open the heavy, lined drapes with which Matthew's mother had covered the enormous bedroom window that looked out onto a lilac-and-honeysuckle-choked yard. Maudie insisted the curtains remain open day and night. She opened the window, too. She brought a garden hose indoors and sprayed years of dust off the screens. In doing so she let the trapped odors of camphor, floor wax, and moth balls escape.

In the rich mornings they lazed in bed, the room shimmering with sunlight; they made love slowly, Matthew taking a long time to get used to the light, to the trill of birds outside the window, the flash of a cardinal across the pane, a wren or finger-sized hummingbird staring in at them over the saucer-like edge of a hollyhock.

Maudie's skin, the color of creamed tea, both aroused and fascinated Matthew. He teased her about being Indian, remarked on her high cheekbones, her flattish nose, her sensual lips, hoping for some response that would reveal her past. In the huge bed, fragrant with their lovemaking, Matthew would lick his way slowly across her belly, thrilling to the salty sweetness of her, sure he could feel the life growing inside her, though she was barely pregnant.

"My name is Maude Huggins Clarke. I'm nineteen, and I used to travel with a carnival. That was all you knew when you asked me to marry you; that's all you ever need to know," Maudie would say in reply to whatever questions or implied question Matthew posed.

"Hereditary diseases," Matthew cried one morning. "We have to think about the baby. Did anyone in your family suffer from hereditary diseases? Your mother? Father? Brothers? Sisters?"

"Is clap hereditary?" Maudie laughed.

"You know what I mean."

"I don't have any idea who my father was. I don't think anybody has any idea who my father was."

"And your mother?"

"I didn't have a mother."

"Everybody has a mother."

"I was one of those babies janitors find wrapped in newspaper in a garbage can."

"In what city?"

"Jesus, Matthew, don't you ever quit? My father was an Indian rodeo rider, my mother was a camp follower, a rodeo whore. Oklahoma City. How's that?"

"Is it true?"

"Only if you want it to be."

Matthew would laugh, wrap his arms around her, and roll her across the big bed. He believed she told him the truth when she said she didn't know who her father was. One crack in the rock.

⊖

My father ignored the suggestions, and later the recommendations, of his advisers at the University of Iowa History Department. He finally decided his thesis would be called *A Short History of the Iowa Baseball Confederacy*. His advisers were at first tactful, forgiving, tolerant; later they became businesslike, orderly, methodical, and demanding of proof.

"It is highly unlikely that we will recognize your efforts unless you can provide us with some documentation as to the existence of the so-called league about which you propose to write," is a sentence from one of the many letters my father exchanged with members of the History Department.

My father, at that point totally unperturbed, replied that since a number of prominent Iowans, many associated with the University of Iowa, were among the founders of the Iowa Baseball Confederacy, he would have no trouble providing the required documentation. He kept every piece of correspondence connected with his project. I also have his finished thesis, his book, all 288 pages of it, from which I will quote occasionally, though sparingly. When I do quote, it is first to show the mystifying problems my father was up against, and second to demonstrate the seeming genuineness of the information my father quoted as truth.

In fact, right now I am going to transcribe a letter my father wrote and the reply he received, as well as an excerpt from *A Short History of the Iowa Baseball Confederacy*.

My father, when he woke the first morning after being struck by lightning, with Darlin' Maudie snuggled against him, knew unquestionably that the Iowa Baseball Confederacy was founded in the early months of 1902. The idea for the league came about during a casual conversation, in a bar in Iowa City, between Clarke Fisher Ansley, one of the founders of what eventually became the Iowa Writers' Workshop, and Frank Luther Mott, an eminent Iowan who was a teacher, scholar, and baseball aficionado.

My father's history of the Confederacy is divided into three sections — Origins, Emergence, and Growth and Consolidation — with each section having many subsections and even the subsections having subsections. The Origins section takes a full seventy pages of text. Very little of it requires repeating here. I can assure you the information is accurate in every detail.

Here is my father's letter to Mr. Mott, who in 1943 was retired but very much alive.

Dear Mr. Mott:

My name is Matthew Clarke and I am doing graduate work in American history at the University of Iowa in Iowa City. My interest is in the Iowa Baseball Confederacy, of which you were co-founder.

I will not presume to ask the many questions I wish to ask in this introductory letter. However, I would be most grateful if you would consider granting me an interview, at which time I would be pleased to learn whatever you can tell me about the formation, duration, and history of the Iowa Baseball Confederacy.

Yours very truly,
Matthew Clarke

Mr. Mott's reply follows.

Dear Mr. Clarke:

I have your letter before me and, I must confess, am rather mystified by it. I am totally unfamiliar with the Iowa Baseball Confederacy and certainly had nothing to do with the organization of such a league. I am, however, a baseball fan of long duration, and had any such organization existed in Iowa, I am certain I would have known about it.

I was associated with amateur and professional baseball in a number of capacities during my years in Iowa City. You must certainly have the name of the league wrong. If you could be somewhat more specific I would be happy to answer your inquiries.

Best wishes,
Frank Luther Mott

So you see the problems my father faced. He possessed a brainful of information, bright and beautiful as diamonds swaddled in midnight-blue velvet, yet it was information no one else would validate. The letters I have reproduced are merely the tip of the iceberg. There were tens, dozens, and finally hundreds of letters to anyone and everyone who might have come in contact with anyone who organized, played in, or was even a spectator at a game during the seven seasons that the Confederacy operated.

I feel as if I might have written *A Short History of the Iowa Baseball Confederacy* myself, for my father has catalogued in it the exact information that is burned into my brain. The only difference is that I am one generation further removed from it. The number of people who might remember the Confederacy decreases almost daily. My own task becomes more and more difficult.

I am going to reproduce another letter — the final one my father wrote to Frank Luther Mott. There was an exchange of eleven letters between them, with my father's letters becoming more detailed, more demanding, more desperate, while Mr. Mott's letters became shorter, more curt, and finally almost condescending.

Dear Mr. Mott:

After all our correspondence I am still unable to understand why you do not remember the Iowa Baseball Confederacy. I realize it has been a long time since 1902; perhaps if I refresh your memory. It was the evening of January 16, 1902, when you and Mr. Ansley met at Donnelly's Bar in Iowa City.

"Some of these young fellows who play in the Sunday Leagues are awfully good," you said to Mr. Ansley.

"We should get them all together and form a semiprofessional league," Mr. Ansley replied.

"I'd be willing to do some of the work if you would," you said.

"It sounds like a good idea," said Clarke Ansley. "There's that team from out around Blue Cut, call themselves the

34

Useless Nine; they haven't lost a game for two seasons. I was up to Chicago in September and some of those boys could play for either the Cubs or the White Sox."

"I know a couple of other people who would be interested," you said. "Why don't we arrange an organizational meeting for next Wednesday?"

There you are, Mr. Mott — that was the way the Iowa Baseball Confederacy was born. Surely that must jog your memory.

Waiting anxiously to hear from you,

Yours truly,
Matthew Clarke

What follows is Mr. Mott's final letter to my father.

Dear Mr. Clarke:

Although as you say it has been a number of years since 1902 and I have indeed spent considerably more years than you on this planet, I assure you I am not senile, demented, forgetful, or a liar. I resent the implications of your last correspondence. Once and for all, I know nothing of an organization called the Iowa Baseball Confederacy. I had nothing to do with the conception of such a league. To my knowledge, and my knowledge is considerable, such a league never existed. And on the off chance that it did exist in some remote part of the state, I certainly had nothing whatever to do with it, and neither did my friend Clarke Fisher Ansley.

I will thank you not to write to me again.

Sincerely,
Frank Luther Mott

I quote from *A Short History of the Iowa Baseball Confederacy:*

The Iowa Baseball Confederacy consisted of six teams, representing, with the exception of Iowa City and Big Inning, rural districts rather than actual towns, although Frank Pierce did have a post office in a farmhouse, as did Husk. Blue Cut and Shoo Fly were loose geographic areas defined by the districts from which their baseball teams drew players. Shoo Fly was in the general region now known as Lone Tree, while Blue Cut was in and around the town of Anamosa.

The league standings, as of July 4, 1908 — the time at which, for reasons as yet undetermined, the Iowa Baseball Confederacy ceased to exist forever — were as follows:

Team	Won	Lost	Pct.	G.B.
Big Inning	32	16	.667	–
Blue Cut	27	21	.562	5
Shoo Fly	26	22	.541	6
Husk	22	26	.458	10
Frank Pierce	21	27	.436	11
Iowa City	16	32	.333	16

"Something happened," my father would say, always making the same palms-up gesture of incomprehension. "Something happened on July 4, 1908, that brought history crashing down on the Iowa Baseball Confederacy. Something happened that erased the league from human memory, changed the history of Iowa, of the U.S.A., maybe even the world. I'd give anything to know what it was. I don't know if there was something in the air, or if a mysterious hand reached down out of the clouds, and patted tens of thousands of heads, wiping minds and memories until they were clear and shiny and blank as a wall newly covered in white enamel. Or maybe some phantom surgeon went into all those brains with long-handled magic scissors and snipped out all the memories of the Iowa Baseball Confederacy."

My own knowledge also ends as of July 3, 1908. The day before a scheduled game between the Chicago Cubs and the Iowa Baseball Confederacy All-Stars.

I have spent years of my life studying the *Iowa City Daily Citizen* and the *Chicago Tribune*, searching for some mention of the game or some mention that something unusual happened in the baseball world that summer. I know a great deal about the Chicago Cubs of 1908 and have written to their heirs and survivors — but I have drawn a blank.

2

My SISTER WAS BORN in 1944, and was, in some prophetic manner, named Enola Gay, a full year before the bomber droned over Hiroshima, its womb bursting with destruction. I was born a year after my sister and named Gideon John — Gideon, because my father, like the biblical Gideon, played the trumpet. He had a fascination for what he described as "soulful music." When he played, the instrument often seemed only a shadow of itself. The muted notes reflected his moods, burbling like water when he was happy, ticking like a clock when he felt reflective, wailing like an animal in pain when he was sad or frustrated, as he often was. Deep in the night I'd hear him in his study, or in the living room, the music soft and sad as angels. I'd shiver and cover my head with my pillow, for I'd know that his playing usually, in my early years, predicted my mother's leaving, and later it meant his frustrations were building to unbearable proportions. On the occasions when my mother did leave us, he would climb to the second floor, pull down the old spring ladder that spent its life nestled against the hall ceiling, and climb to the widow's walk on top of the house. There he would release all his anger and hurt and disappointment, and I would cry softly, as much for him as for myself, while he hurled the notes toward the blue-and-silver night sky.

I found out early on I had the same easy ability with the trumpet as my father. Neither of us ever took a lesson. When I was barely school age, after we had returned from a weekend of watching baseball in St. Louis, I picked up the horn and tooted "Take Me Out to the Ball Game." My version was as muted and sad as anything my father had ever played.

Instead of blood grandparents, I had John and Marylyle Baron. Only for the first five years of my life did I have a blood sister, but for all my life I've had Missy Baron. Missy, the eternal child. Like Raggedy Ann she has a candy heart with I LOVE YOU written on it. One of my first memories, perhaps my very first, is of Missy staring down into my crib, cooing to me in a voice of universal love. Missy, her straight red hair dangling like shoelaces across her bland, freckled face, her pudgy hands touching me as if I were made of gossamer. Missy is well over fifty now, an advanced age for one who suffers from Down's syndrome, as it has come to be called.

The Barons, both over eighty, still live on their farm a mile out of town in the direction of the Onamata Catholic Church, which was built in anticipation of a new railroad and never relocated after the fickle iron highway chose another route.

"We always tried to be a friend to that mama of yours," Mrs. Baron said to me just recently. "She was a strange lady, Gideon."

In small towns, events that would be forgotten by all but intimate family members become community property, remain ripe for rehashing. My mother deserted us, taking my sister with her, when I was going on six.

"Your papa was a fine man, a bright young man too, until he started carrying on about that baseball league of his. You know, Gideon, I trained as a nurse for three years, in the hospital in Iowa City, back when I was a girl. We were taught to look for symptoms, and I used to watch you with a professional eye when you were growing up, looking for signs of the same disease in you."

39

She stops. She has talked herself into a corner. It is all right to mention my father's obsession, but mine is never discussed seriously; certainly no criticism is ever offered. It is also all right to mention the strangeness of my mother, but Sunny is never mentioned, though she is my wife and, like my mother, a woman who comes and goes at will.

"I caught the disease all at once. There were no symptoms."

"Maybe I shouldn't say this, but I always thought it was kind of like that polio that used to go around in the summers; it just snuck up and paralyzed your body. But what you got kind of affected your mind." She pauses. "Well, now I have put my foot in it, haven't I? But you really didn't have personal knowledge of this baseball league until after your papa died?"

"I knew only what he told me. I was just a kid, purposely uninterested in what my father was doing, kind of contemptuous too, the way teenage boys are."

"And you were suddenly filled with it, just like religious fervor? But why keep at it? A smart young fellow like you should know when he's beating a dead horse."

"I don't think anyone knows when he's beating a dead horse. But the reason I keep on trying to prove the existence of the Confederacy is that *I'm right and everybody else is wrong!*" I laugh wistfully, trying to show that I do have some understanding of the futility of my quest.

"Well, Gideon, I wish you luck. You still planning on having the town's name changed?"

"I don't want to change the town name. I just want it acknowledged that Onamata is named for the wife of Drifting Away, the great Black Hawk warrior."

"I don't suppose you have any proof that there ever was an Indian named Drifting Away?"

"Not an iota. Except I *know* it's the truth, and so did my father, and neither of us has ever been known to be a liar."

It will take some monumental action on my part to have the Iowa Baseball Confederacy recognized and legitimized. I read of a man who climbed up a pole, vowing to sit on a platform twenty feet above the earth until the Cleveland Indians won the pennant. That was sometime in the mid-fifties. I assume *he* came down.

"Well, I wish you luck, Gideon." And Marylyle Baron tightened up the strings of her speckled apron and hobbled up the steps of her farmhouse. I do odd jobs for the Barons. Out of love, not because I need the money. Today, I mow the big front yard; the sweetness of cut grass fills the air. I am bare to the waist and streaming sweat.

☺

In the past year or so I have tried a new tack: I have begun to approach the subject of the Iowa Baseball Confederacy from an oblique angle. I liken it to driving a wedge in a rock.

Part of the information my father passed on to me concerned an Indian named Drifting Away, a Black Hawk warrior and chief. I know the facts I have about Drifting Away are true, but, as with the data about the Confederacy, there is not a shred of proof. But if I can get one person to acknowledge the existence of Drifting Away, if I can convince one person that the town was named for Onamata, Drifting Away's wife, who was murdered by white settlers in the 1830s, I'll have a real wedge in the rock.

From *A Short History of the Iowa Baseball Confederacy:*

Drifting Away remembers. He remembers the gentle, rolling Iowa landscape in days when buffalo still grazed idly, the only sounds the grumble of their own bones. The creak of the wheel was only a prophecy, the oxcart a vision, the crack of the whip and the crack of the rifle known only to those who made their eyes white as moonlight in order to stare down the

41

tunnel of the future. Drifting Away remembers the haze of campfires hanging, smooth as a cloud, in the tops of dappled poplars . . .

⊖

Why baseball? Was it because of our obsession with the game that my father and I were gifted, if it can be called a gift, with encyclopedic knowledge of a baseball league?

I inherited my knowledge of the Confederacy and my interest in baseball, but what of my father? My grandfather never attended a baseball game in his life.

"How did you come to love baseball?" I asked my father repeatedly. And he told me the story of how his passion was roused by a visiting uncle, a vagabond of a man who parachuted into their lives every year or so. He would appear clutching a deck of cards and a complicated baseball game played on a board with dice and markers. He also arrived with an outfielder's black glove and a baseball worn thin by time. He claimed the baseball was once autographed by Walter Johnson.

The uncle — I'm not clear about which side of the family he was from — first charmed my father into playing catch, then into investigating the intricacies of the board game.

"My uncle was named James John James," my father reported. "He owned nothing but a blue serge suit, a crumpled felt hat, and the articles to do with baseball.

"My imagination had never been exercised," he went on. "My folks weren't that kind of people. Uncle Jim pulled my imagination out of me like a magician pulling a string of light bulbs from my mouth. We played his board game, moving little nubbins of yellow and blue around the cardboard baseball field. Strange as it seems, it was through that board game that I learned to love baseball, for my uncle could bring

42

that small green board to life. Every roll of the dice was like a swing of the bat. My uncle arrived with a tattered copy of the *St. Louis Sporting News,* and as we played we invented leagues, furnishing them with teams plucked from the *Sporting News* standings — teams from dreamy-sounding places like Cheyenne, Quincy, Tuscaloosa, Bozeman, Burlington, York, Far Rockaway. We created players, gave them names and numbers and histories. They pitched, batted, ran the bases, were benched if they didn't hit or made too many errors, or were moved up to clean-up if they hit like crazy. We drew up a schedule, had double-headers on July Fourth and Labor Day, played out a whole season during the few weeks that my uncle visited.

"And then he took me to a real game. We went into Iowa City and watched a commercial league in action, and it was just like I'd discovered the meaning of the universe.

"After my uncle left I kept on exercising my imagination. If you look around on the side of the garage, Gid, you'll see a piece of board nailed to it in the shape of a strike zone, and if it hasn't rotted away, you'll find a piece of plank imbedded in the earth right in front of that strike zone. Me and my friend from down the street, we made our own baseballs, according to my uncle's recipe. We soaked *Life* magazines in a mixture of milk and kerosene. Uncle Jim said that combination made the balls tough but spongy. They certainly smelled bad enough. Dried them in the sun, we did. We used a little piece of one-by-two for a bat. There were no bases or running or anything like that. It was pitcher against batter. I sneaked some lime out of the garage and we made white lines down the middle of the garden, like lines on a football field. If the batter hit the ball a certain distance it was a single. A little farther, a double, then a triple, and finally over the garden fence was a home run. We spent most of the time searching for the ball in among your grandmother's cucumbers. In the

43

fall, when we raked up the leaves and vines from the garden, we'd find a dozen or two of our baseballs. But, oh, the imagination we had."

I played the same game; my father taught it to me. There was nothing surreptitious about our laying white lines across the garden until it looked like a golf driving range. Eventually I found a playmate with an imagination; his name was Stan Rogalski, and though he played real baseball, too (in fact, Stan is still playing semipro ball), he and I passed hours on summer afternoons and evenings, batting and pitching, searching for the ball among the cucumbers, keeping accurate box scores for our imaginary teams. Then, after the game, we would sit in either my or Stan's kitchen and bring all our statistics up to date.

Neither my father nor I ever played anything but sandlot baseball. I was on the Onamata High School team, but only because there were just ten boys in our high school and one of them was in a wheelchair, making his handicap only slightly worse than mine, which was lack of ability.

"Why not baseball?" my father would say. "Name me a more perfect game! Name me a game with more possibilities for magic, wizardry, voodoo, hoodoo, enchantment, obsession, possession. There's always time for daydreaming, time to create your own illusions at the ballpark. I bet there isn't a magician anywhere who doesn't love baseball. Take the layout. No mere mortal could have dreamed up the dimensions of a baseball field. No man could be that perfect. Abner Doubleday, if he did indeed invent the game, must have received divine guidance.

"And the field runs to infinity," he would shout, gesturing wildly. "You ever think of that, Gid? There's no limit to how far a man might possibly hit a ball, and there's no limit to how far a fleet outfielder might run to retrieve it. The foul lines run on forever, forever diverging. There's no place in

America that's not part of a major-league ballfield: the meanest ghetto, the highest point of land, the Great Lakes, the Colorado River. Hell, there's no place in the *world* that's not part of a baseball field.

"Every other sport is held in by boundaries, some of absolute set size, some not: football, hockey, tennis, basketball, golf. But there's no limit to the size of a baseball field. What other sport can claim that? And there's no more enigmatic game; I don't have to tell you that. I'm glad what happened to me happened to me, Gid. I created imaginary baseball leagues when I was a kid. Now I have a *real* imaginary league to worry about, if there can be such a thing. But I'm glad it happened to me. I consider myself one of the chosen. I'm an evangelist in a funny sort of way. It ain't easy, but you should be so lucky."

I am.

⊖

A few statistics on batting from *A Short History of the Iowa Baseball Confederacy:*

Batting Averages

1.	Bob Grady, Husk	.368
2.	Simon Shubert, Blue Cut	.360
3.	Jack Luck, Iowa City	.358
4.	Horatio N. Scharff, Big Inning	.357
5.	Henry Pulvermacher, Shoo Fly	.351

Home Runs

1.	Ezra Dean, Blue Cut	27	(1906)
2.	Orville Swan, Big Inning	26	(1903)
3.	Jack Luck, Iowa City	22	(1906)
4.	Bob Grady, Husk	20	(1905)
5.	William Stiff, Frank Pierce	20	(1907)

In the summer of 1907, the Detroit Tigers, who were burning up the American League, were invited to Big Inning, Iowa, to play the Iowa Baseball Confederacy All-Stars on July 4. In May, the Tigers sent a former player of theirs named Norman Elberfeld, known as the Tabasco Kid, to Big Inning to scout the IBC. The Tabasco Kid sent back a report saying that though the players were for the most part unknown, the caliber of play in the Iowa Baseball Confederacy was so high that it could prove embarrassing to a major-league team experiencing an off day. The Tigers politely declined the invitation.

◍

My father submitted his thesis, his 288-page manuscript, to the University of Iowa, Department of History, in the spring of 1946. It was about the same time that my sister, Enola Gay, poured a large tin of Golden Corn Syrup into my crib, very nearly causing my demise.

A few days later, my father was called to the office of Dr. E. H. Hindsmith, his supervisor.

"He looked at me over the top of his bone-rimmed glasses, his eyebrows like crusted snow, his face grizzled, snuff stains in the creases at the corners of his mouth.

"'There is no evidence to indicate that the Iowa Baseball Confederacy ever existed,' he said, coming right to the point. 'In fact, Mr. Clarke, it seems that I and my colleagues have repeatedly warned you against writing on such a topic.'"

My father could reproduce the exact inflections of Hindsmith's voice. I interviewed Hindsmith after I became obsessed with the Confederacy, and it was like speaking with an old friend. Hindsmith's voice inflections betrayed his roots, he having been born in a place called Breastbone Hill, Kentucky, the son of a miner. My father reenacted that conversation at least once a month for all the years I knew him.

"His eyes met mine, sending out a frank, blue stare, solid as steel rods. 'This is a masterfully written thesis,' he said, pausing dramatically. He did not pronounce the *r* in masterfully. 'We have voted five to zero to reject it completely as historical fact. However, we are much impressed with your writing ability; in fact, we took the liberty of showing a copy to Paul Engle at the Iowa Writers' Workshop. Mr. Engle, also, is very enthusiastic about your writing style. He suggests that with, say, one semester of study in fiction writing, you could use the same material as a novel and probably find a publisher, at the same time earning yourself an MFA degree in English.' He kept staring at me to see how I was reacting.

"'But it's the truth,' I wailed. 'Every word of this thesis is true. I don't care who denies it. I don't care how many people are in league against me, for whatever reasons.' Oh, I made a proper fool of myself.

"'We urge you to consider our recommendation, Matthew,' Dr. Hindsmith said. 'It is the unanimous opinion of the History Department that your field of endeavor should be fiction.'"

⊖

Drifting Away remembers, stares around at a world cut into squares. The white man's world is full of squares. The cities are measured out in squares and rectangles — houses, factories, tables, automobiles — the white man always obsessed with bending the lines of nature, attacking the natural circles of nature, straightening the curving lines into grids, breaking circles, covering the land with prison bars.

Squares have no power, thinks Drifting Away. Power lies in the circle. Everything in nature tries to be round — the world is round, the sun, the moon, the stars; life is circular; the birds build round nests, lay circular eggs; flowers are round.

Indians knew. Tepees, round, set in circles, a nest amid many nests. Drifting Away remembers the undulating trails, smooth and easy, long as rivers, bent as snakes. At first the white man followed the Indian trails, but, always in a hurry, he could not take the time to follow nature; he had to defeat nature. The white man's trails were straight, no matter that the going was sometimes impossible. Then came the straight iron rivers, always intersecting at right angles.

Drifting Away, in one of his lives, built a round lodge, draped it with hides, was a proud hunter, rich, provided well for his squaw and children. Owned many horses. Built that round lodge on the edge of a grove filled with every kind of bird, near the gentle Iowa River, miles from the nearest white settlement.

But the whites carved the land into squares, claimed to own it, claimed it as their own, though everyone knows you cannot sell the land upon which the people walk. The land, like the sky, is not for sale.

The white men came, riding across the hills, loudly, no fear in their hearts, for their guns and engines make nature cringe. They take measure of the land, stake out the earth as if they could tie it down.

They look at Drifting Away's lodge, make solemn faces.

"You can no longer live here," they tell him.

"The earth is for all men," Drifting Away replies.

"Not for you, Indian," they say. "For you, there is a reservation. By law you have to live on your reservation."

Drifting Away pretends not to understand, prays they will go away. They do, but leave behind a warning, like a cloud bank groaning with thunder.

"One moon," they say. "There will be trouble if you are not gone."

⊖

How has my father affected my life? He has been like a giant smothering me with his shadow. For every inch my memory

48

of him recedes, his shadow grows a foot taller. His memory holds me aloft; he is a Cyclops, a colossus, angry, tossing me in the air, dangling me by one arm while I struggle, tiny as a toy.

Still, it is very hard to take someone seriously who was killed by a line drive. No matter how macabre it is, there is something humorous about being killed by a line drive. It is much the same as being fatally struck by lightning. A couple of years ago, in Iowa City, a man really was fatally struck by lightning. He was walking up the sidewalk to his fiancée's home when, *splat*, he was fried like an egg on her sidewalk, cooked like a hamburger, spread out like quicksilver to shimmer in the sun. Turned out he was a churchgoer, too — a deacon or an elder or something. I've often wondered what a preacher could possibly say, with a straight face, about someone fatally struck by lightning. It is so biblical. So prophetic. So funny.

I am the only one who knows *this*: that my father committed suicide. I have never told Sunny, or the Barons, my sister, my mother, or my best friend, Stan. I'm sure, on the bright blue September afternoon at County Stadium in Milwaukee, where the air was crisp with the memory of frost and tangy with the odor of burning leaves, that my father saw the line drive coming. Bill Bruton, the Milwaukee center fielder, swung late at a Harvey Haddix fast ball and sent it screaming over the top of the visitors' dugout, at a speed of more than a hundred miles per hour. My father was writing on his scorecard and supposedly never saw the ball, which struck him full on the left temple, bursting a blood vessel and killing him instantly. But I was there, too. He had indeed been writing on his scorecard. I still have the scorecard, the final pen line wavering downward like the graph of a failing stock. I, for some reason, while pouring the last of my popcorn from the box into my right hand, was watching my father out of the

49

corner of my eye. He sighted the line drive — I swear I saw the ball reflected in his pupil — and instead of ducking or pulling his head back, he almost imperceptibly moved his head forward, a weary gesture of resignation, and allowed the ball to strike him, thus ending his long and unsuccessful struggle against his tormentors, those craven bureaucracies which, for whatever reasons, refused to acknowledge the existence of the Iowa Baseball Confederacy.

As he lay crumpled there in his shirtsleeves in the brilliant afternoon sunlight, I knew he was dead, because at the same instant I was filling up with the information he alone had been party to for so many years; it was like water transferred from one lock to another. There in County Stadium, with the smell of fresh-cut grass and frying onions in my nostrils, I was suddenly illuminated like an old Wurlitzer, garish neons bubbling. I was overflowing with knowledge, and boiling with righteous indignation because not a soul in the world cared about what I knew.

Whatever had been visited upon my father was now visited upon me. The history of the Iowa Baseball Confederacy was transplanted into my brain like a pacemaker installed next to a fluttering heart.

If I had to choose a way to die, I suppose I would do the same as my father. What better way to go? The lulling quality of the sun, the crack of the bat, the hum of the crowd. Surrounded by everything he cherished. I don't begrudge him his one instant of resignation, if that's what it was. He had been chasing the elusive Iowa Baseball Confederacy for eighteen years and for all that time it had remained just out of his reach, the uncatchable mechanical rabbit of his dreams.

On the way back to Iowa City, I drove our green Fargo pickup truck while my father's shell rode in a satin-lined casket on a railroad baggage car at double regular fare. I made the arrangements myself. I didn't phone anyone. Who was there to phone? I would let the Barons know after I got back to Onamata. If I had let them know sooner, they would have insisted on coming to Milwaukee. After all, I wasn't helpless.

It never occurred to me not to pursue legitimizing the Confederacy. At least I didn't have to worry about money. My father certainly was not wealthy, but the big old house in Onamata and the small building that housed the insurance agency were both paid for. My father had employed a charming woman, Mrs. Lever, to manage the business. She was tall, flat as an ironing board, with gray hair combed back at the sides and mother-of-pearl-rimmed glasses. She was the wife of a corn farmer who retired to the city and let his eldest take over the farm. She must have been a lot younger than she looked, or perhaps at going-on-seventeen I thought everyone looked old, for she still runs the agency.

About four years ago I said to her, "Give yourself a raise of a hundred dollars a month. Keep running the business as you always have. At the end of the year we'll split the profits."

She fussed a little but she didn't turn me down.

The next year I gave her another raise and sixty percent of the profits. Last fall I said, "It's all yours. Just promise me you won't change the name."

My mother remarried and apparently settled down. At what age? On her marriage license when she married my father, she listed herself as nineteen, but did she have to show proof or did they take her word for it? If nineteen was correct, then she was about twenty-two when I was born, twenty-seven when she deserted us for the last time, thirty-four when she married a man named Beecher, who, it was rumored, had some connection with the Wrigleys and the Chicago Cubs.

I know virtually nothing about my mother that my father didn't tell me. I remember the warmth of her, her dark, hazy eyes. It seemed to me, when I got older, that she really didn't know how to kiss. I remember her brushing her lips across my cheeks or forehead, but brushing was what she did, not kissing. I always felt as if her and Enola Gay's leaving might

51

somehow have been my fault. Perhaps I was so strange a child neither of them could stand me. Perhaps she hated my blondness, my potato-white skin, my hair the color of new stationery. What if she had good reason to leave? What if my father mistreated her? He was never violent, but mistreatment can take much subtler forms. What if she couldn't stand being ignored? What if she couldn't tolerate my father having a mistress, one far more demanding than anyone alive and sexual and sensuous, one she couldn't fight either physically or mentally? The IBC is like that. I know.

Mother settled down at thirty-four, to life in a Chicago mansion.

Sunny isn't thirty-four yet. Perhaps there is hope. Perhaps Sunny will settle down with me.

⊖

To my surprise, Darlin' Maudie and Enola Gay returned for the funeral. I had thought of notifying them but didn't. Certainly my father's death didn't make the *Trib*. Unless, of course, it was in one of those columns of oddities in the news: RABID FAN KILLED BY BASEBALL, or FAN KILLED BY RABID BASEBALL. There were six dark-suited, nervous men from the Milwaukee organization at the funeral. The Braves were so afraid I was going to sue them for some astronomical amount and win that they paid for my father's transportation back to Iowa City, the hearse and the undertaker, and the silver-handled oak casket — that was a small settlement in itself. There were floral tributes from the owners, manager, and players which looked as if they belonged in the winner's circle at the Kentucky Derby.

I was sent a sack of twenty-five baseballs, each personally inscribed by a member of the team, and a lifetime pass to a box seat, which, of course, expired with the team in 1965.

My mother and sister arrived in a black limousine, driven by a large-eared youth with a white, cadaverous face partially hidden by a chauffeur's cap. They were both dressed fashionably in black and both looked much smaller than they had been in my memory. Mother was no more than five foot one, and Enola Gay was of identical height.

In the chapel of the Beckman-Jones Funeral Home in Iowa City, there was a curtained-off area for family members, but neither Mother nor Enola Gay sat there with me. In fact, they didn't come near me at all. It was as if they were attending the funeral of a distant acquaintance, one whose family they had never met.

The Barons drove me to the funeral home. I sat in the back seat of their comfortable old Dodge, which smelled of dust and machine oil, as Missy hummed and smiled, twisting the skirt of her dark brown dress.

"You don't want to be all alone in that little room, Gideon," Marylyle Baron said to me. "Come and sit out in the chapel with us."

"You come inside with me," I said. "I don't feel like having everyone stare at me. I suppose there are rumors." I smiled weakly. "It's not every day the community's number-one baseball fanatic gets killed at a baseball game."

"You don't want to hear them," Mrs. Baron said. "People have small minds and mean mouths."

So the four of us sat on pastel chairs in the curtained-off room, separated from the chapel by a peach-colored curtain translucent enough for me to recognize many of the mourners by their silhouettes.

I peeked around the edge of the curtain once: Darlin' Maudie and Enola Gay sat about halfway back, demure and expensively dressed. They left as the pallbearers were preparing to carry the coffin outside to the hearse for the ride to Fairfield Cemetery in Iowa City. Their leaving was a good idea. The pallbearers might have mistaken their limousine for the hearse.

It was only a year or two later that Enola Gay became one of

53

America's first urban guerrillas. I have to admit Enola was a pioneer; perhaps she inherited her spirit from my father. She was years ahead of the Chicago Seven, the Weather Underground, and the Symbionese Liberation Army. She has also, as urban guerrillas go, been quite successful. Her first venture was to bomb a Dow Chemical subsidiary in Chicago — $250,000 damage and no injuries. She and her cohorts left a note, signed with their real names, with a P.S.: *Catch us if you can!*

They have not been able to catch Enola Gay, though one of the original bombers came forward in the early seventies and spilled his guts in return for three years' probation and a reunion with his wealthy family. He is now vice president of a bank. Another member of the group blew himself up in 1969, near an Omaha packing plant where a labor dispute was taking place. Every post office in America has posters showing Enola Gay as she looked some fifteen years ago and as they imagine she might look today. Her list of offenses takes up two sheets of Wanted paper. There is a women's collective named for her in Iowa City, and the abortion clinic in Winston-Salem, North Carolina, bears her name. Occasionally a car full of bedraggled-looking women in sloganed T-shirts stops in front of my home and a few pale faces peer at Enola Gay's birthplace.

⊖

After the graveside service, Marylyle Baron grabbed my arm as I tried to edge away — from the Barons, from the polite condolences of neighbors and acquaintances who, having nothing to say, tried to say it anyway. It's too bad there are no Hallmark cards saying, "Sorry your loved one was killed by a foul ball."

"You're coming home with us," Mrs. Baron said. "You're not going back to that big, lonely house. In fact, I think you should come and live with us. You can finish your schooling. Only thing is, you'll have to walk a mile instead of a block to school." John Baron stood behind her, nodding his big, gray-thatched head.

"I'll bake you cookies," said Missy. "Gideon won't be so sad if I bake him cookies, will he?" she said to her mother, smiling her innocence, hopping a little in her excitement.

Missy bakes wonderful gingerbread cookies; always has. Marylyle was able to teach her how to mix the ingredients, divide the dough into small balls, flatten the balls with a rolling pin, make tracks in each cookie with the tines of a fork, and place the tire-tracked cookies on a greased cookie sheet ready for the oven. I've watched her countless times; she sings under her breath as she performs the ritual, concentrating, brows furrowed like those of someone puzzling over a mathematical problem.

"You always make me feel good, Missy," I said to her and patted her arm.

I lived with the Barons for two years, until I finished high school in Onamata. I insisted on paying my own way. It was the least I could do.

It was during that time that Marylyle Baron told me what I call the oral history of Big Inning, Iowa. From her I learned that I wasn't quite as different as I at first thought. I shared my stories of the Confederacy with her, and though she had no memory of the events I knew as fact, she was able to add some rather astonishing folk tales to my repertoire.

⊖

Drifting Away remembers the shining desert, the Dakota hills roiling with green and silver grasses. Drifting Away fought beside Crazy Horse, rode with him into the wilds, shared his deepest dreams, was there when Crazy Horse's only daugh-

ter, They Are Afraid of Her, lay dying, strangling on her own phlegm, not yet five years old.

Drifting Away was there when Crazy Horse died, murdered by a soldier named Gentles, held from behind by his traitorous brother, Little Big Man. With a knife blue as moonlight Drifting Away cut out the noble heart, carried it to Crazy Horse's elderly parents, who buried it in the clear, sweet water of Wounded Knee Creek.

3

"I THINK I'LL TURN IN," I said to the Barons, early on the evening after the funeral. I was just not able to face any more conversation, no matter how loving or concerned.

But in my room, between the crisp linen sheets, I could not sleep. I got up and dressed, then tiptoed down the hall and stairs like a burglar, carrying my shoes in front of me.

The sky was clear, the stars like tinsel, the soil still warm from the sun of the afternoon. I walked down the silent midnight roads, past the small Onamata Catholic Church, its spire the middle of a trinity of shadows; evergreens on either side of the church had grown to almost equal height. Along the roads, the corn stood crisp and blond, chittering like small rodents in a whisper of a breeze.

Onamata was quiet; the streetlights hummed. Above a hedge an occasional firefly twinkled; something scuttled in an overgrown yard. I let myself into the empty house. I went to my room and retrieved my horn from where it lay encased in fuchsia-colored velvet in its old black case.

The moon trickled over the horn, sparking until I might have been carrying golden water in my hand. I headed for the gentle elevation on the edge of town, where the land rises steadily up from the sleepy Iowa River. The river that night

57

was so silent it might have been painted on the landscape. I climbed the easy slope I now knew had been the Big Inning baseball grounds. I knew that something terrible, something of history-changing magnitude, had taken place there. I walked on past the furthest reaches of center field, stopping on a precipice that must, long ago, have been a buffalo jump. I stood staring out at the rolling acres of corn, the pinprick of yard lights in a farmstead or two. Behind me was the eerie glow of Onamata, like a campfire just over a ridge.

I pointed my horn toward the sky and let it cry for me, let it translate my sorrow into notes. I played such a version of "Take Me Out to the Ball Game," the music plaintive as a loon's call, the melody melancholy as taps. When I finished I rested for a few seconds, then went at it again, moving the tempo up to nearly normal but still soulful. Finally, knowing my father would not want me to grieve for long, I blasted it out with a Dixieland wail, as if I were playing during the seventh-inning stretch in front of a hundred thousand frenzied fans in a pennant-deciding game.

☻

Once in the days after I moved back into my own home, before I met Sunny, I brought Missy Baron home with me to the cool, high-ceilinged kitchen with its tall cupboards and the rectangular, flat-bottomed sink. The sink boasted high steel faucets capped with porcelain. I made soup and grilled cheese sandwiches, a bachelor's specialty. Mainly I wanted to see if Missy would be a party to any of the unusual goings-on in my kitchen. I think, too, I simply wanted some confirmation of what I had seen, something to let me know my obsession with the Confederacy was not tampering with my sanity.

We finished our meal, Missy being elaborately careful to spoon up the last few drops of her soup and to blot up the last crumbs of her sandwich with her middle finger.

58

"You do a very good job of cleaning up your plate," I said. Missy smiled like sunshine.

"Can't let good food go to waste," she said, and I could hear Marylyle Baron's tones echoing in Missy's slightly nasal sing-song.

"No, we can't," I said. Then, "Let's go sit in the sun porch."

As we stood to leave the room, the water began gushing into the sink, the dish detergent gulped out of the bottle, and a froth of suds rose to the edge of the sink. The dishes, as if carried by invisible servants, floated to the sink and immersed themselves gently like children sliding into a bubble bath.

When the washing and rinsing were done, the plates, cups, and cutlery glided off like butterflies, each to its proper place on the shelves, and the cupboard doors and cutlery drawer closed softly.

Missy stood entranced the whole time. I was vindicated. What I saw was actually happening. When our eyes met, I was smiling from ear to ear, nearly bursting with excitement. I had never shared the mystery of it before. My father was always talking of the magic in the air, but I never knew how much of it he experienced. Until now, the dishes had performed their sleight of hand only when I was alone with them.

"They rinsed themselves only once," Missy said, with deadly seriousness. "Mama says you rinse once to get the soap off and once to kill germs."

If the eeries in my kitchen heard, they were not about to let on, though I imagined I heard a cupboard door tugged tightly shut, from the inside.

⊖

After the funeral, Missy did bake cookies, and I helped her. Sometimes I teased her gently by taking a fork and making a cross pattern on one of the cookies, or marking one well off center. Missy would pull her lips tight in exasperation; she became the mother, I the child.

59

"Oh, Gideon, that's not the way to do it," she would say, scowling. Then she would deliberately take the improperly marked gingerbread back, roll the fork marks out of it, and with extreme care redo it properly.

It was a good distraction for me, taking my mind off the death of my father and the multitudinous fund of information concerning the Iowa Baseball Confederacy that whirled and flopped in my head like clothing tumbling in a dryer.

Later, from the hallway, I listened to Missy splashing her bath water, giggling like a five-year-old. "Gideon, come see me sail my boat," she called between splashes.

And then from behind the door came Marylyle's firm voice saying, "You're too grown up for Gideon to see you in the bathtub."

But I did hear her prayers. We all did. John Baron would stand just inside the white-trimmed doorway, in the room where ballerinas forever danced on the wallpaper and where a bed with a ruffled canopy sat against a far wall. He wore bib overalls and a black-and-red-checkered shirt, his white hair combed in a high pompadour, his face wide and windburned. He appeared slightly uneasy, as if he feared he might drip oil on something. Missy knelt by the bed, her nightgown a riot of black-eyed Susans, her hair still damp from her bath.

"Now I lay me down to sleep," Missy said.

⊖

My tribulations. Wealth is a tribulation. I was happy enough before I had it; the insurance agency always earned enough to pay the taxes on the house and keep us in food and a new pickup truck every few years. The only thing I've done with my new wealth is a little advertising. You've probably seen the ads I've run in everything from the *Christian Science Monitor* to the *National Inquirer*. The small ads ask that anyone having memories or any kind of information concerning the Iowa Baseball Confederacy contact me at a P.O. box in

Onamata. I receive a lot of religious tracts, offers to sell me Rhine Valley cuckoo clocks, pamphlets on numerology, brochures advertising trips to Hawaii, and instruction on how to become a Rosicrucian. I've also discovered that the peace movement is heavily into junk mail. So far, I've received polite letters from a number of baseball experts, real and imagined, who tell me the IBC never existed.

The way I became wealthy was this. My mother, Maude Huggins Clarke, married a man named Beecher, who, it turned out, was indeed related to the Wrigleys, the Chicago Cubs, and several million dollars. He died when I was nineteen and, inexplicably, left no will. My mother was about to inherit everything — he had no relatives close enough to raise legal objections — when the executors of his estate discovered that Mother had children from a previous marriage. Because of some quirk in Illinois law, Enola Gay and I became heirs to his estate — fifty percent went to Mother, twenty-five percent to each of us.

They have never been able to pay Enola Gay her share, for by the time the legal entanglements took their course, Enola Gay had embarked on her career as an urban guerrilla. I don't know if Enola Gay is aware that I have barely touched my inheritance; I would guess she is, however. Late at night the phone will ring, and though I suspect it is Enola, I always answer just in case it is Sunny. Enola wants me to give her some of my money, or to claim her share, which I am apparently legally entitled to do, and then pass the money on to her. I am interested in doing neither. I doubt that she was very kind to my cat, Shoeless Joe, in his old age.

"Live in fear, you bastard," Enola Gay said to me the last time she phoned. It must be frustrating for her to be so near that much money, to have a cause she wants to give it to, and yet not be able to get her hands on it.

"I think the FBI has a tap on the phone," I said to Enola, and she hung up.

My share of the money was deposited in trust with a law firm in Iowa City. I signed a power-of-attorney form; they invest the money, pay my taxes, and keep me informed as to how wealthy I am. I can't think of a single thing I want that all my wealth can buy me. I want:

(a) Sunny to love me enough to stay with me.

(b) To vindicate my father and myself by proving the existence of the Iowa Baseball Confederacy.

(c) To do something for Missy Baron.

It doesn't surprise me that none of the items on my list requires great wealth.

☉

The cat. I would hug him and he would hang down the front of me like a big orange bath towel. When he was hungry, he would rub around my ankles, nearly knocking me down. I think I learned some of my indifference from the cat. He demanded to be fed, or petted, let in, or let out. When he got what he wanted, he was disdain incarnate. When he didn't, he could be as obsequious as a dog.

When he was content he would lie on his back and let me squeeze his front paws gently, feeling the moccasin-like pads, flexing his claws in and out. He was warm, and almost adoring, soft as the velvet pillows on the back of the sofa in the living room.

Enola didn't like Joe. I have never understood why she took him with her when I was going on six years of age. If she hadn't taken my cat, I would have claimed her money, put it in a suitcase in small bills, and left it for her in a garbage can in some suburban Chicago park on a rainy night. When I told her that, she spit curses in my ear and hung up.

☉

The men who cleared and leveled the land to create a baseball diamond on the outskirts of Big Inning often saw, or thought they saw, flashing like a deer through the fluttering poplars beyond the outfield, the figure of a giant Indian.

He loped beyond the poplar grove, knees raised high, back bent forward as if he were performing some ritual dance or high ceremony. Sometimes, in the clean morning air, as they bent picking roots, they would hear his voice, yipping like a coyote or trilling a plaintive birdcall. Other times, they only felt his presence. Occasionally on a humid afternoon the men would stop what they were doing, notice the all-encompassing silence of the land, the trees, the nearby river. One of them would shiver, though sweat tracked in rivulets down his face and chest.

"Someone just stepped on my grave," he would announce, and laugh self-consciously.

Someone else would say, "That damn Indian is somewhere close. I can smell his ornery hide, but I can't see him."

Everyone would stand still in the stifling afternoon and stare around them. Then a bird would squawk or a horsefly would bite or a frog would sing from the riverbank, and everything would be back in order just as if the moment of silence had never happened.

Drifting Away, who had been near enough to smell the white men's sweat, near enough to reach out and touch their glistening wet backs, disappeared into the poplars, chuckling softly as a breeze.

⊖

"Walt 'No Neck' Williams, do you remember him?" my friend Stan asks suddenly, in the way he has of jumping from subject to subject.

We are with our wives, driving back from a night game in Cedar Rapids.

"Mm-hmm," I say noncommittally. "I know the name, but the details are fuzzy. He ended up playing in Japan, didn't he?"

"He played for the Sox. The White Sox. They called him No Neck because he didn't have one." Stan laughs his long, stuttering laugh, sounding as if he has peanut shells lodged in his throat. There is a car following us closely and the headlights bury themselves in the rearview mirror, which then paints a moonlight-like bar across Stan's face. As I glance across the front seat at him he looks as though he is wearing a golden mask.

"Last summer I met No Neck Williams on the street in Chicago," Stan goes on. "I just about went crazy. 'Hey, No Neck,' I called to him, and I set down my suitcases and went running after him.

"You remember that, Gloria?" He directs the last words at his wife, turning toward the back seat to acknowledge her, the mask of light slipping around his ear as he does.

Gloria is a big, blowzy Polish girl, cheerful and resilient. She has so far fouled off all the curves life has thrown at her, though I notice that her brows have squeezed together in a mini-scowl, as if she has been staring too long at the horizon.

"He actually edged away from me. You remember that, Gloria? I guess you must meet a lot of nuts when you're in the Bigs. I mean, I kept sayin' to him, 'Man, I used to watch you when you played for the Sox. You were great, man. You were great.' And I hauled out my wallet and looked for something he could sign, and I didn't have any paper, not even a Master Charge slip or anything, so I got him to sign the back of Gloria's picture. It's one I've carried around for ten years, with Gloria in jeans and her hair up in a beehive, standing beside her old man's '69 Buick. No Neck looked at me like I was crazy, leaving my wife with our suitcases and chasing after him for a block like that. Don't you remember him, Gid?"

"I don't get involved with modern-day players the way you do, Stan."

My wife, Sunny, is squashed into the corner of the back

64

seat behind me. She hasn't said a word since we left the ballpark in Cedar Rapids. I catch a glimpse of the red glow of her cigarette. She is tiny as a child, sitting back there. I wonder how someone so small and insignificant-looking can tear me apart the way she does.

"No Neck's only a couple of years older than us, Gid," Stan says. "Played his last game in the Bigs in '75. You know how that makes me feel? A guy just two years older than me, retired. And me still strugglin' to make the Bigs?"

"You'll make it, Stan," I say automatically, just as I have been saying every year for over half my life.

Stan and Gloria have come to visit Gloria's mother in Onamata; she's the only family either of them has here anymore. Stan's father is dead and his mother has gone to Florida to live with a married sister.

Since spring, Stan has been playing Triple A ball in Salt Lake City, but he sprained his right hand pretty badly a couple of weeks ago and the club put him on the disabled list and brought up a kid from a team in Burlington, Iowa, to replace him.

"I wanted to ask No Neck how much he practiced. I bet he practiced like crazy or he never would have got to the Bigs. God, but I used to practice. Remember how I used to practice, Gideon? Gloria? Hey, Sunny, you're bein' awful quiet. I ever tell you how I used to practice?"

Sunny draws deeply on her cigarette but does not answer.

Stan is tall and muscular, his head square, his hair cut short, but his face is wide and innocent as a husky child's. His eyes are pale blue and wide-set; his hair, though it's darker now, was a lemony color when we were kids, and Stan was forever watering it, as if it were grass that would grow stronger when wet.

"My old man never liked baseball, but I used to make him come outside and he'd stand in front of the barn, and I'd make him hit fly balls to me. I spent all my pay on baseballs — all

65

the money I earned working for Old Piska, the cement contractor. Saturdays I used to carry a bucket of cement in each hand, from the mortar box to the sidewalk we were laying, or the garage floor. I took the money I earned and bought a box of baseballs, a whole dozen.

"I laid them out on my bed like a bagful of white oranges, and I smelled them and touched them and handled them like a miser handling his money. Too bad I couldn't have made real ones the way we made balls to play in your back yard, eh Gideon? God, they used to stink, but it was fun.

"Speakin' of stinking, the old man wasn't a very good batter, and every once in a while he'd foul one into the goddamned pigpen. I'd have to wash the pigshit off it, and sometimes when I went into the pen, one of those big red buggers would have the ball in his teeth, and I'd have to whack his snout to make him let go, and then the ball would have tooth marks on it forever."

Stan stops for a second or two. The highway is dark. There is an orange flash behind me as Sunny lights a new cigarette. I see that her left eye is closed, squinted up against the smoke. There is an inch-long scar, pink as a worm, on her dusky skin, running vertically from the corner of her eye onto her cheekbone. There are fine age lines spreading out from the corners of her eyes. Sunny aged a good deal the last time she was away.

"I love the game, I've always loved the game, right, Gid? I used to dream about a career in baseball. It wasn't just vague hopes like a lot of kids have. I knew what I was doing. I've made a living from the game for almost fifteen years. And I'm gonna make the Bigs yet, you wait and see."

"You'll make it, Stan. We know that," I say.

"I mean, I've seen guys with twice as much talent as me throw it all away. They party all night and stagger in ten minutes before a game, wearing their hangovers like badges. It's not fair that my reflexes are one one-hundredth of a second slower than theirs. I mean, I work out three hours every afternoon. I've always hustled, haven't I, Gid?"

"You've always hustled," says Gloria from the darkness. Her voice is lifeless. She answers by rote. She, like me, has learned to agree with Stan without even listening to him.

"And I put a washtub on its side, used it for home plate. I'd make the catch and rear back, and I got so I could hit that tub on the first or second bounce about nine times out of ten. You know what the difference is between the Bigs and the minors?" Stan waits only one beat, not expecting a reply. "Consistency. The whole thing is consistency. There are players in the minors who make spectacular plays and hit the ball just as hard as in the majors, but the guys in the Bigs are more consistent. They make the plays not just nine out of ten times but ninety-nine out of a hundred." He pauses thoughtfully for a moment. "You know, I'd hit that tub nine out of ten times, but the tenth one might end up thirty feet down the line, or hit the barn door fifteen feet in the air, making a sound like a gun going off. Hey, Gideon, how about you come out and hit me some flies in the morning?"

When we got home after the game, I kissed Sunny gently and pulled her against me. Her lips were dry and she made them thin and did not return my kiss. I did everything I could think of to please her. I touched her with my finger tips, gently undressed her, massaged her, fondled her, loved her with my hands, my tongue, held back my own passion, waited for a response from her, received none.

I remember once, at a time like this, when Sunny was in one of her moods, she said something bitter, something designed to make me hate her.

"Can't you tell by the way I touch you that I love you?" I said.

"No," said Sunny, precipitating a long silence.

Eventually I made love with her. Her body was unpliant, mannequin-like. I wanted so desperately to rouse her, I controlled myself carefully, rocked her gently for a long time, until our bodies were slick and delicious.

"Can't you finish up?" Sunny said, not even in a whisper. "I'm tired."

If she had known how close I came to killing her then, it would have made her happy.

I threw myself off her without a word and lay like a rock in the darkness, my body taut, nerve ends twitching. Late in the night I heard her leave. I woke to the tinkling of hangers in our closet, knew she was packing a few blouses, a couple of pairs of jeans, in the same battered suitcase she arrived with twelve years ago. I lay, tense as piano wire, afraid to speak, afraid not to. She closed the front door quietly; I listened to her tiny footsteps descend the stairs, fade away as she moved down the sidewalk.

Where does she go? How does she get there? There are no buses, no traffic. I suppose she walks to the interstate, stands like a waif at the side of the road. I can hear the sinister hiss of air brakes as a truck pulls over . . .

I recall a night, many years ago, when I ran out of a restaurant after her, frantic that I might never see her again. I recall the face of a man in a Tennessee pickup truck who was losing her. I don't suppose he was over thirty-five, although he looked old to me. I have never forgotten the uncomprehending look of loss and pain on his face. I have seen that look many times since. My reflection wears it like a tragic mask.

Within the recent past Marylyle Baron has begun telling me more of her memories.

"I can't believe you're serious about your baseball league," she says to me. "There've always been a lot of odd goings-on here in Johnson County. I suppose you're too young to remember what we called the Backwards Plague?"

"I suppose I am," I say, looking questioningly at her.

The Barons have a big, old-fashioned kitchen; there are marks on the green linoleum where the cream separator used to sit. There is a flowered couch in the kitchen, too. On it Missy sits sideways, carefully dressing her doll, Susan, in some of the clothes Mrs. Baron has made. Missy hums and talks soothingly to the doll.

"It was in the early nineteen hundreds; I was just a girl. People were a lot more superstitious than they are now. For all our pioneer spirit, we were pretty ignorant people. Medicine was still primitive, too. Not that it isn't now. But neither medicine nor the church, or even folklore, could explain the Backwards Plague.

"What happened was that a bunch of young people, all in the seventeen-to-twenty age range, started to lose weight, a pound a week exactly. It took a while for anyone to notice because there were no two in a family afflicted, and only one or two in each community. There were two here in our community, two more out toward Blue Cut, four in Iowa City, and some as far south as Frank Pierce and Boscurvis.

"When the families of the young people themselves started to notice the weight loss, many of them went to doctors. The only hospital in those days was in Iowa City. Well, the doctors were completely stumped. They gave them young people every test that was known at the time, but couldn't find anything wrong; the young people were healthy but they were losing a pound a week, no matter what they ate or how little they exercised.

"What the doctors quickly discovered was that not only were these young folks losing weight, but they were shrinking; their bones were getting smaller, everything was getting smaller.

"And then the doctors discovered that the victims were regressing mentally as well as physically." She stops and stares at me from her faded blue eyes.

"So what happened?"

"If you believe *that*, you'd believe anything, Gideon Clarke."

"I'll believe anything," I say, laughing. "That's not half as strange as my story about the Confederacy. Besides, the hollyhocks talk to me. Always have. I've always wanted to tell you that."

"Is that all?" says Mrs. Baron. "Flowers have always talked to Missy." She looks at me again, only her eyes smiling, her old mouth looking as if it has been sewn shut.

"The Backwards Plague," she goes on. "Those kids just kept regressing and losing a pound a week until they hit their birth weight. A couple of the ones from around Iowa City were big, strapping farm boys, must have weighed close to two hundred pounds. Took a couple of them nearly four years to shrink down to tiny babies again. But as soon as they hit birth weight, why they started to grow again, as if they'd just been born. But, of course, they didn't remember that they'd lived before; they grew up just as they did the first time, same diseases, same broken bones and all that." She stares at me, daring me to call her a liar.

"I believe you," I say. "Why shouldn't I? The world's a weird place."

"The preachers had a field day. Fire and brimstone rained down from the pulpits of Johnson County. It must be every minister's dream to have a genuine Old Testament plague to preach about. Divine retribution, the wrath of God being heaped on the heads of these young sinners. But what they had to say never rang true, for the young people who were afflicted were no better or worse than anyone else.

"There was one really touching story came out of the Back-

70

wards Plague. One of the Hannichek girls, Alberta May — she was my age, I guess, about seventeen when the plague struck her. She was a pretty little thing, only weighed about ninety pounds, and was engaged to Walcomb Andrews, a fine young man five or six years older than her.

"He was heartbroken. He'd fallen in love with her at her fourteenth birthday party and her papa said she couldn't marry until she turned eighteen; young people listened to their elders back in those days. When Alberta May regressed back to about twelve years old, she didn't know Walcomb Andrews any more, but he didn't stop coming around. She was one of the first to get the disease, so they didn't know if she was gonna die or what. I remember seeing Walcomb Andrews in his Sunday suit, driving his buggy out to the Hannicheks', his suit too big for him as if he was wasting away too, his huge hands holding on to the reins.

"When she got down to baby weight and then commenced growing again, Walcomb Andrews didn't know what to do. The family decided to christen her all over again, and Walcomb Andrews walked down the aisle beside the father, who was carrying this girl baby in a long christening dress, a girl who used to be engaged to Walcomb Andrews.

"When he seen she was healthy and growing and all, Walcomb he went away. He was a smart man; he went to Omaha, dealt in cattle and hogs and got himself an interest in a packing house there. He built himself one of the grandest houses in Omaha, so they say; I never seen it myself.

"The summer Alberta May turned fourteen, Walcomb Andrews showed up here in Onamata. By this time he had to be close to forty. Must have taken a lot of nerve for him to turn up like that. I mean, you know what most fourteen-year-old girls think of forty-year-old men. But she took to him like they were long-lost friends, and her papa, who was getting on in years himself, wasn't so particular now about her being eighteen to get married. They got married when she was fifteen, and they had over thirty years together; I hear they raised a nice family over in Omaha and was happy as could be."

⊖

The Iowa Baseball Confederacy came about by accident. On a quiet February evening in 1902, Clarke Fisher Ansley and Frank Luther Mott met, some say in Donnelly's Bar, some say in one of the private clubs in Iowa City, probably for a friendly drink, although the more pious suggest the beverage was coffee. It is unlikely that they had preconceived ideas of discussing baseball in a serious way.

Mott admits, in later correspondence, that it was he who first suggested the idea of a league. Most of the small towns in eastern Iowa had baseball teams, while in Iowa City many of the trades and even a few employers had loosely organized baseball teams. But the schedules, if any, were haphazard, and play was confined mostly to weekends, where various communities sponsored tournaments in conjunction with their sports days or church picnics.

As a result of their conversation, Ansley and Mott called together interested parties from twelve "towns, hamlets, and various rural districts," as Mott described them, each of which had fielded a team at some time the previous season.

The idea of an organized league was well received, and several more meetings followed. It was eventually agreed that there should be six teams. Many alliances were quickly formed and just as quickly broken before the final six entries were decided upon.

Representatives from Husk, Boscurvis, and Phlange River are said to have cut cards to determine what name the team from their area should carry. Husk turned up a king, compared to a seven for Phlange River and a four for Boscurvis. The entry in the Iowa Baseball Confederacy was known as

Husk; they played their home games at the Deep Valley school grounds, which was roughly at the center of a triangle made by lines connecting the three post offices.

The name Iowa Baseball Confederacy was adopted without an argument, and on March 14, 1902, Frank Luther Mott of Iowa City was named the league's first and only commissioner. It was decided that the six teams would play a ninety-six-game schedule in two sections, the first to end on July 3, the second to start on July 6, with winners of each division to meet in mid-September in the Iowa Championship Series.

4

I MET SUNNY twelve years ago, at a restaurant in Iowa City, where I filled in occasionally for a friend when he wanted a weekend off. She came in accompanied by a large, rumpled-looking man who was dressed in a blue pinstriped suit. He was tall and cadaverous, and it was impossible to guess their relationship. He might have been father, husband, lover, brother. As they crossed the dining room she trailed after him, covered in a feathery, calf-length dress of some material that attached itself to her as if both she and it were charged with static electricity.

Her chest was flat, her dark hair hacked in a boyish cut; her lips were thin, and when she did open her mouth there were spaces between her teeth. She took a crumpled pack of Winstons from a very used-looking handbag, which had once been black leather. The man ignored her as she searched the tiny purse until she found a book of matches. She squinted her left eye to keep the smoke at bay, drew deeply on the cigarette, and licked her lower lip with a cat-pink tongue.

By the time I approached their table to ask if I could get them anything from the bar, I was in love. Sunny was hunched over the table, smoking as if she expected to be arrested for it. Her eyes were brilliant, the irises fawn-brown,

74

floating in untarnished whites. I tried to imagine my tongue
bringing her tiny nipples erect. I wanted to taste her mouth,
feel her tongue exploring my teeth. There was no way to
judge her age; she might have been fifteen, she might have
been thirty. It didn't matter.

All through the meal, I circled their table like a hawk,
replenishing their water, coffee, lighting Sunny's cigarettes,
asking again and again if the meal was satisfactory.

The man had a deep voice with a strong southern accent;
Sunny's voice was breathy in a peculiar sort of way, as if she
were acting, speaking in a voice not entirely her own. They
talked very little. I eavesdropped on every word, ignoring my
other tables. In spite of my attentiveness I was unable to learn
her name, their business, or their relationship.

In desperation I followed them to the parking lot as they
left the restaurant, first tearing off my apron and grabbing my
jacket, which hung on a many-pronged chrome hook next to
the bar. They got in a faded red pickup truck with Tennessee
license plates. I memorized the license number — in fact I
still remember it: PNT-791 — and I stood helplessly as they
pulled away, envisioning myself writing to Motor Vehicle
Registration in Nashville to obtain a name and an address.

To my immense relief, the truck simply pulled across the
street and stopped in the parking lot of the Evangelical Christian Church. The man got out, lumbered toward the door of
the church, and disappeared inside.

As I walked up to the passenger side of the truck, Sunny
glanced at me. I motioned for her to roll down the window,
which she did.

"You're very beautiful," I said.

She looked at me, really looked at me for the first time. I
prayed she'd like what she saw. She smiled then and I could
tell it was involuntary. I bet I'm the first person who's ever
told her she's beautiful, I thought. And she was, to me, in

that magic way no one can explain. Her nose was too flat, and her hair looked like she cut it herself to spite someone. She was covered in freckles — even her fingers were freckled. And I smiled at her as if I was witnessing a miracle, and recalled how, when she brushed past me as she entered the restaurant, I got the first whiff of her, a tangy sweetness, not of perfume but of *her*. And I could feel my tongue rearranging the freckles on her neck, her breasts, her belly.

And the feeling has never left me, will never leave me — the breathlessness, the tightness in my chest, when Sunny enters a room. The desire that makes my knees weak. The love that makes me able to endure the way she tortures me. Sunny is one of those women who comes and goes. Whatever demons she wrestles with require that she be on the move a goodly part of her life. She vanishes for days, weeks, months, then returns as mysteriously as she left. She is alternately plucked from my life and parachuted back into it.

Sunny eventually climbed down out of the truck. Reaching over the tailgate she heaved out a small, scarred suitcase. We stood talking for a while. I babbled nervously about the restaurant, about my big old house a few miles away in Onamata, about my interest in baseball history. I told her about my ongoing quest to prove the existence of the Iowa Baseball Confederacy, although I didn't let her know how all-encompassing my obsession was. I didn't realize at the time that she told me nothing.

"Can I buy you a drink?" I finally said, waving vaguely toward the restaurant, toward the rest of the town. "That is, if you're old enough to —"

"I'm old enough to do anything," said Sunny, and I think that under her breath she added, "and I have."

Just as we were leaving the truck, the side door of the church opened and the truck owner stepped outside. I didn't know what was expected of me. Sunny seemed willing to continue right on. But I stopped, feeling that we owed some sort of explanation. I turned my head in the direction of the man, who held up suddenly, his feet making a skidding sound on the gravel.

Sunny turned and waved, a cheery, impersonal gesture.

"Thanks for the ride," she said. "Maybe I'll see you around."

The man raised a hand, not waving, but making a gesture as if he were reaching out for her. Then he joined his two large, helpless hands together at belt level. He didn't speak but his gesture and his stricken face said more than he intended.

We continued across the street and toward downtown. Sunny never looked back. I glanced over my shoulder once and saw the man standing in the same position.

"So," said Sunny, eyeing my head, "what do you do to your hair?"

"I don't do anything. I was born this way."

"Marilyn Monroe's hair wasn't as white as yours."

My hair is the color of sewing thread; it has no pigment in it.

"You're not one of those — what do they call them?"

"I'm not an albino," I explained patiently. "Look, my eyes have pigment; they're a pale blue."

I was about to go on with a prepared speech I had memorized about albinos and combinations of pigments, but Sunny interrupted me to say, "I'm not *that* curious, I just wondered if you dyed it, was all."

In grade school a couple of boys took to calling me White Rat, but my friend Stan, who was the largest boy in class, banged a couple of heads together, and I was never called White Rat again.

"There's an old-fashioned bar downtown," I said. "Dark wood and dark mirrors. You'll like it."

"First thing I want is to hit the john and get rid of *this*,"

77

Sunny said, running her hands down the slippery, clinging material of her dress. "*This* was his idea."

⊖

Why do I stand what Sunny does to me? Why do I put up with it? It all defies logic. I suspect — I *know* — that there are hundreds of women out there who wouldn't mind having a clean, sober, wealthy husband. They would tolerate my eccentricities, keep the house clean, feed me when I forget to eat, joyfully give me the armful of daughters I have often fantasized, allow me to pursue my elusive dream, and recognize what percentage of my life was theirs and what percentage was not. In other words, the horizon is illuminated by the pearly glow of bridal gowns, each occupied by an attractive, faithful woman.

The truth, sad or otherwise, is that I am uninterested in anyone but Sunny. I am thrilled by her indifference, aroused by her deceit. I sometimes think I would like to be ensconced in amber, like an insect, encased in the sweetness of Sunny's odors, the bittersweet taste of her forever on my lips. For even when she doesn't try to please me, I melt against her body. The others may be there, but to me they are as asexual as money, and, like money, unless they can engender passion, they are useless to me.

A car stops on the gravel deep in the night. There is a long silence. I picture her standing, small as a child in the darkness, psyching herself up for what she is about to do. Then comes the crunch of her small steps on the gravel. The door opens. Silence while her eyes get used to the dark.

At the bedroom door: "Gid?" She is smoking a cigarette.

"Over here."

She bumps a table, finds the ashtray on it. I always keep one there, although I have never smoked. There is a tiny crackling as she puts out the cigarette.

She takes off her jacket and tosses it on the floor. Her arms go up in a supple motion and her T-shirt skids over her head. She kicks one boot off with the help of the other, bends and dispatches the second one. My desire for her is so wild I feel as if I'm all liquid. I can smell her, the tart, sweet scent of her sweat. The odor of a car interior. I grab the waist of her jeans, pull her toward me until she stands at the edge of the bed. Her nipples are like hard candy. The musky, smoky taste of her fills my senses. Her mouth finds mine. Her tongue is like a bird set free. She tastes faintly of whiskey.

"Fantasyland," I say, tossing back the covers, pulling her down on top of me.

⊖

There was never any question about her coming home with me that first night. As we sat in the bar sipping drinks, I talked while Sunny studied me, eyeing me as if she were figuring some kind of odds, trying to guess how I would react to her secrets. She pursed her lips each time she laughed, making laughter seem a gesture of self-control.

When we first entered the bar, Sunny opened her small suitcase, fished out some clothes, disappeared to the washroom; she emerged, empty-handed, in jeans, a white blouse, a tattered denim jacket faded to the color of skim milk. The dress was nowhere to be seen.

"I have more lives than a cat," she said in reply to my questioning look. "I just used one of them up. What's past is past."

"You'll need a dress to get married in," I said.

"You mean that, don't you?" she said, crinkling her nose, her polished-oak eyes measuring me again.

"I mean it," I said.

"Then you'll have to buy me another one."

Later, when I stopped the truck in front of my home, I

turned toward Sunny, toward where she sat with her thigh touching mine.

"You wear your clothes as if you want to be helped out of them," I whispered, my fingers undoing a button on her blouse. Suddenly Sunny grabbed onto me fiercely, her mouth melting into mine. She held me as if her life depended on getting closer to me than anyone had ever been.

She loved the house, my tall, square, white-painted house. I know it was built in 1909, though neighbors claim it is older than that. It has green shutters the color of spring leaves and is solid, permanent, an anchor, a rock, a root. Sunny explored it the next morning, tentatively, poking her head into each room before allowing her body to follow. The floors of the bedrooms and living room were a sunshine yellow; the rooms smelled subtly of wax, of dust, of old upholstery.

"Do you like it?" I asked.

"It's a fairy tale. You're sure it's yours?"

"It can be yours, too. I need to share this with someone." I placed my arm tightly around her waist.

"This is really yours? I've dreamed of a big, solid home like this. If I drew a picture of the house that I've dreamed about, this would be it. And it's really yours? You're so young. You're sure your parents aren't coming home from their holidays next week?"

"My father's dead. I have a mother in Chicago and a sister who blows up buildings."

"Sounds like a normal family," Sunny said, laughing.

"Everyone should have an outlaw for a sister," I said.

⊖

I've always felt that Sunny's biggest quarrel with me is that I don't treat her as badly as she thinks I should.

"I'm trouble," she said, in the sweet darkness of my bedroom. "Don't say I didn't warn you."

"I'm warned," I said.

"I'm a little like smoke," Sunny said. "There isn't a door I can't get under, or over, or through, or around."

"I'll take my chances," I said.

Two years ago, while Sunny was gone, I even tried dating. I hung around the University of Iowa Bookstore, a bar called the Airliner, which was frequented by students, and a restaurant known as Bushnell's Turtle. But just as they were ten years before, the girls I met were too young, too silly, or too serious. I hate dewy-eyed girls who talk about meaningful relationships; I hate perfumes, deodorants, hair sprays, sweaters and bras and knitted dresses, manicured nails, cosmetics, loud music, football pennants, stuffed animals, and vegetarian dishes. Each girl I met was so eager and so inexperienced. I talked a lot about Sunny.

"I've done things that would curl your hair," Sunny said to me once in the warmth of our bed. She had just returned from a two-month absence.

"Don't tantalize me," I said fiercely. "If you want to tell me, tell me. If you don't, shut up. There's nothing you can tell me that will change the way I feel about you."

"Maybe I should try."

"Sunny, whatever it is you want, I won't do it. I won't punish you. I won't abandon you. I won't send you away. I refuse to cage you. If you stay with me, it has to be out of love."

☺

I had my revelation as I stood staring into the half-empty closet the morning after Sunny left me for the first time. As if I were stepping out of a fog bank, I realized that I was married to a woman as like my mother as it was possible to be.

I want a girl, just like the girl that married dear old Dad.

Why had I never seen it before? I had never considered myself unintelligent. Shades of Oedipus, his father struck down by a staff on the road to Thebes. Until that moment it had never occurred to me that Sunny, like my mother, was one of those women who come and go.

I suddenly remembered my father rambling through the empty rooms of this same house, stopping to stare into the same half-empty closet, shaking his head in disbelief, then going into his study and staying there for days. It is the same study where I have spent half my life pursuing the same elusive dream my father was never able to capture. My father was not an easy man to live with. I always felt that my mother had some justification for her extended absences. This was almost more than I wanted to think about.

Chasing a dream, a dream no one else can see or understand, like running after a butterfly across an endless meadow, is extremely difficult. Now I could see that my father and I shared not only the dream of the Iowa Baseball Confederacy but something else as well, something he must have passed to me through his genes: a fatal fascination for transient women.

⊖

I remember a conversation I had with Gloria last week in Iowa City. I bumped into her on Dubuque Street and we walked over to Pearson's Drug Store for malts. Tall chocolate malts, thick as cement, served in perspiring glasses.

"Gideon, you understand Stan better than anybody, maybe even me," Gloria said. "He looks up to you. If you could hear him talk about you all the time. He wishes he had your intellectual ability. He'd like to be able to read and understand things the way you do, you know.

"I bet Stan's never told you, but two springs ago, the year he turned thirty-one, I talked him into retiring."

"No, he didn't tell me," I said.

"We'd wintered in South Carolina. He got a job in a warehouse; we had a nice apartment; I started thinking about

82

getting pregnant. It was really nice: Stan home every night, me being able to cook supper for him — *you* know.

"Stan was adjusting. He really was. He was nervous as a coyote in a pen, but he was getting by. Then him and a couple of guys from work hooked up with a softball team. The league started in late April and at first I figured it wasn't such a bad idea. He could still play, you know; that way I figured he wouldn't miss the game so much. The team was sponsored by Red Ryder's Pizza Parlor. The uniform jerseys were cardinal-red, made of slippery material, with the silhouette of a square-jawed cowboy on the back where the numbers should have been.

"Oh, God, Gideon, it was sad to watch him. I mean, he was the star of the team; he hit about .500 and the team hardly ever lost. But it wasn't baseball. It didn't mean anything to him. The guys would all go back to Red Ryder's after a game and the owner would give them all the pizza they could eat and all the beer they could drink. After six weeks, Stan was starting to develop a paunch on him.

"About the first of June, he came home from work one evening and he was sitting on the edge of the bed putting on his jersey. I couldn't stand watching him no more; I reached over and stopped him from pulling that slippery cloth down over his head. I grabbed hold of it, peeled it off him, tossed it into a corner, and leaned down and kissed him. I never seen Stan smile so hard, except when I said I'd marry him. I thought his face was gonna bust.

" 'Glory,' he says, 'I hear there's a team down around Tidewater is in a bad way for players. I think they might be glad to see a veteran outfielder.'

"And I says, 'I'm with you,' and next morning we were packed and headin' south."

"He'll always get by, Gloria, as long as he's got you." I reached along the counter and squeezed her hand.

"But now, I think maybe I done the wrong thing. I don't know what to do, Gideon. He was batting .220 and playing hurt, and his legs are gone. He was never fast, but now he's like a big bear in the outfield. The fans boo him when he can't get to a long ball or a Texas leaguer."

"I'll do what I can," I told her. "But take care of him. He needs you."

"How are you and Sunny doing?" Gloria asked.

"Not very well, I'm afraid."

"She's been awful quiet. She seems down."

"She'll be gone again soon."

"I'm sorry, Gid."

"There's nothing anybody can do. She'll go and she'll come back. She'll be changed ever so subtly, like a piece of furniture that's been shipped across the country one more time. And I'll get a little more eccentric while she's gone. I'll haunt the university, do some more research on the Confederacy; the more my ideas are ridiculed the more stubborn I get, Gloria."

Gloria takes her lips away from the straw in her malt. She lifts her eyebrows; there is genuine concern in her eyes.

"When you have the name, you might as well have the game," I go on. "The university people, the baseball people, they all think I'm crazy to keep on pursuing the Confederacy. They say, 'Gideon Clarke's spent most of his life on some crazy research project. Something to do with baseball. Gideon Clarke lives most of his life all alone in that big old house, plays the trumpet at night, and takes odd jobs when he's got more money in the bank than he could spend in two lifetimes.' That's what they say, Gloria. That, and 'Gideon Clarke had a wife and couldn't keep her.' "

☯

I get up early the morning after Sunny leaves me again. I spend all day in the University of Iowa Library, doing little research, sitting silent, dreaming of Sunny.

As I open the door to my house, smells of abandonment rush past me. Though it is nearly July, the air that meets my face is as cold as a meat locker. Without Sunny, I don't think I will ever be able to live in these drafty rooms again. I close the door. The screen door makes a sharp snap. I need at least two doors between me and Sunny's memories and odors. In the fresh, moist warmth of the Iowa night I bed down on the cushions of the wide, white-painted porch swing.

Footfalls on the sidewalk and front steps awaken me. A dark silhouette stands before the front door, hand poised to knock.

"I'm over here, Stan," I whisper. Stan starts as if someone has walked over his grave, throws his head back in a gesture of surprise.

"My God, you scared me, Gid. I was trying to decide how hard to knock."

I ease myself to a sitting position. The swing slices back and forth, cutting the air.

"Is it late?" I ask.

"Very," says Stan. "I can't sleep. Why are you out —"

"Sunny's gone again," I say.

"I'm sorry, Gid. I know how much you care."

I nod my head. The porch and yard are silvered by moonlight.

"Makes my problems seem pretty small, I guess," Stan goes on. "A telegram arrived at the house last night. I told the club there was no phone there — I couldn't stand the thought of some secretary phoning to tell me I'd been cut."

"Is that what the teleg—"

"I haven't opened it. Gloria went to bed mad. I wouldn't let her open it either. Gloria's old lady looks at me with her lips all sewn shut . . . like I was something in a zoo."

"Do you want me to be there when you open it?"

"I don't know what I want. It was just lying there like a death sentence on that dark table in the front hall. Geez, but that's a depressing place, that hall. That table, covered with a linen runner; those tall baseboards, enameled black; the newel post, black and shiny as a skull. Like a funeral home. I wanted to turn and run. I don't run from many things; you know that. The yellow telegram just lay there on the linen runner like a stain. Gloria's old lady was standing there, her hands clasped in front of her, her hair pulled back tight. 'For goodness sakes, open it,' Gloria said. But I wouldn't touch it or let her touch it. I mean, I know what's in it. I'm not dumb. There was something rotten in the air when they put me on the disabled list. The manager had a crafty look about him. I'm thirty-three years old and I been playing hurt. I've been released. I know it."

"Maybe it's not —"

"I *know*," Stan says emphatically. "You understand better than anybody. I need to go for a walk or a drive. I want you to come with me."

"Okay," I say.

"Man, you should have come to our place when you found Sunny was gone. You shouldn't be alone."

"Let's go," I say, standing up. The arc of the swing lessens until it is barely trembling.

"It's not fair," Stan says, as we make our way down the silent, leafy streets, the air slightly sweet from the last lilacs of the season.

"What isn't?" I reply.

"I want to go into Iowa City," Stan says. "My car's just around the corner. I parked there a while ago and tried to walk it off, the way I do when I take a foul tip on the shin. But it didn't work."

We try to close the car doors quietly. We are probably the only people awake in the whole town of Onamata.

"This cast is supposed to stay on for ten more days," he says, banging the white plaster against the steering wheel as he turns the car out onto the dark, silent highway. "But I bet I could get it off in seven if I concentrated. You heal faster if you concentrate all your energy on the sore part of your body, did you know that?"

"No." I think vaguely of concentrating all my energy on my heart.

"Well, you can. A week and I'll be good as new. It was unfair as hell for them to let me go, instead of letting me work my way back from the disabled list. I've still got a few good years left in me. I might still make it to the majors. I know I'll never be a starter, but I could still be a utility man, fill in a game here and a game there, pinch-hit once in a while, play defense in the late innings. I've still got a few years left in me, haven't I? Thirty-three ain't too old, is it?"

"It's not too old," I say. I look in the rearview mirror, expecting to see Gloria's form in the back seat, the glow of Sunny's cigarette.

"You know, yesterday, when I went into Iowa City, I went to see Gloria's brother, Dmetro. I went down to the railroad yard and he showed me around. I did it only to please Gloria and her old lady. Dmetro's a checker there in the yards. I'm not sure what he really does — they don't let him touch the switches or nothing like that. He has a chart and a clipboard and I think he makes sure the right cars are on the right trains. He started that job the day after he turned fifteen. His old man made him quit school and got him that job. Made Gloria quit on her fifteenth birthday, too, but she went back after she got out on her own. Her old man worked for forty-nine years for the flour mill; he died within six months after they retired him. Dmetro's my age; he's got a job for life. He'll never get laid off or bumped or anything. I guess he's happy. 'I can do my job in my sleep,' he says. 'I don't have to think or nothing.'

"Dmetro offered to get me a job there. Did I tell you that? Gloria wants me to take it. I mean the three of them set it up. They think I'm so dumb I don't know. I'd be kind of a gofer to start with, working the midnight shift, not very steady at all." Stan pauses, looks over at me.

I want to say something to comfort him, but the right words are elusive. Instead, I gesture helplessly with my hands, my palms turned up.

"You know, Gid," he goes on, "last week I drove up to the stadium in Iowa City; I was running in the outfield, doing stretching exercises on the grass, stuff like that, when I happened to look up at the sky. There were little white puffs of cloud all across it, like a cat stepped in milk and then walked across the blue. I thought it was so beautiful I told Dmetro about it. He just stared at me. 'I ain't looked at the sky in ten years,' he said." Stan guides the car with the tips of the fingers that peek from the white cast, and slaps his other meaty hand on the dashboard.

"There was something else, too, something that really bothered me, Gideon. Dmetro was telling me the names of the spur lines, the dead-end tracks where they store boxcars or move them in and out of the yards. There was the Exxon Spur, the Texaco Spur, and the Miller Spur that runs right down to the brewery. There was the Icehouse Spur from when they used to cut ice from the Iowa River and store it in sawdust in big old slab sheds. Then there was a spur out at the edge of the yards that had ties piled across it. 'They use that one to store broken boxcars,' Dmetro said. He didn't name it at all, but later he spotted a boxcar with a cracked wheel and said it would have to be moved to the Baseball Spur.

" 'Where's that?' I asked him, pricking up my ears.

" 'Back in the old days,' Dmetro said, 'why, the Baseball Spur used to run out of town for a mile or so. There was a ballpark out around Onamata. I heard that on Saturday and Sunday afternoons whole families used to get dressed up and pack picnic lunches and catch the train out to the baseball game. My old man said there used to be two trips both ways. He remembered it, though he never went himself. But they tore down the grandstand, maybe as far back as the twenties, and the railroad figured it was cheaper to let the roadbed rot than to tear up the tracks. Some junk dealer eventually made off with most of the steel, but the track still runs for a few hundred yards, and you could still follow the roadbed if you really tried. All that's used of the Baseball Spur now is the hundred yards or so inside the railroad yard.' "

"You don't have to tell me about that line," I said. "I *know* all about that. That's where *the game* was played, back when Onamata was still called Big Inning. That spur ran right out to the ballfield. There were concessions, and they rented bathing suits and boats."

"Oh, yeah," says Stan. "I guess you have told me all that . . . A few thousand times," he adds, his voice full of irony.

"The ballfield was abandoned in 1908," I say. "There was a flood, and someday I'm gonna find out— But I never heard that line called the Baseball Spur before. Something new and it could lead to something else. That's how discoveries are made. People remember the twenties and thirties and before, but no one remembers when Onamata was Big Inning. They think Onamata just appeared there in 1909, that it was dropped from heaven, that there was never a flood, never another town —"

"Someday you'll find out everything you want to know, Gid. You don't have to convince me. Have I ever said I didn't believe you?"

"No, you haven't, Stan. I'm sorry. I'm getting a little

touchy, a little more eccentric all the time. Maybe someday you'll have to have me put away."

Stan takes the wheel in his left hand and taps my shoulder twice with his cast-covered fingers as if my T-shirt were a piano.

☉

Speaking of eccentric, I'm not sure if I dreamed this while I was sleeping or dreamed it while I was awake. The other morning I truly thought of building a geodesic dome, adding it on to the front of the house as a place for me to live, something more substantial than the sun porch. But the dome would be in the shape of a baseball. I can see it sitting like an igloo on our quiet green street, shiny, white, with red-stitched seams. It doesn't matter what condition I was in when I fantasized it; what matters is that the more I think about it the more it seems a good idea.

But what about Sunny? Would it be too much for her? Would it frighten her off? Would she come tiptoeing down the street and see the addition all silvered with moonlight and be spooked by it? Or would it be a message to her: "Stay away. I've had enough of your coming and going"?

☉

Stan eases the car to a stop on a dark side street not far from the railroad yard. Again, we are both careful as we close the doors.

"Hey, Gid," Stan says, in a voice too loud for the night. "Remember how in high school I spotted that the West Branch pitcher stood a certain way on the rubber when he was gonna throw a curve?"

"I remember," I say.

"And I wouldn't tell anybody else what I knew, just you and me?"

"I remember."

"If I stand with a bat on my right shoulder, it's gonna be a curve, I told you. You whacked a triple to deep center."

"The only triple I ever hit."

"Yeah, you were never much with the bat, were you? When I came up he got two quick strikes on me before I saw him set his foot in that certain position. I took a deep breath and waited. The ball was still rising when it cleared the fence, and those two runs put the game right out of reach."

The railroad yard looms in front of us as we top a rise: acres of boxcars, and blue ribbons of track crisscrossing like tangles of wool.

"Is this where we're going?" I ask.

"Yeah, I want you to see this place, Gid."

In the yard, outdoor lights sway slightly, casting long, ghostly shadows. The roundhouse hulks in front of us, high as a grain elevator. There are men in coveralls scurrying about; the air is steely-smelling, full of grease and hot metal. Bright blue stars from welding torches bloom in the yellowish light. The door of the roundhouse gapes wide. Inside there are figures in white T-shirts climbing like ants over a tall black engine. No one pays any attention to us.

"We fit right in," says Stan.

He's right. We are both wearing white cotton T-shirts and jeans.

"That's the Exxon Spur," Stan whispers, pointing.

Picks and sledgehammers lean haphazardly against the corrugated metal wall of a shed. Stan stops; he picks up a sledgehammer, hoists it on his shoulder like a bat. I bend and pick one up too. It is heavier than I imagined.

"The Baseball Spur is way back here," Stan says, pointing between two dark rows of boxcars.

There are two cars on the spur, each with a wheel partially broken away, the fractured surface bright as a new coin. We amble past the damaged boxcars, walk between the rails; ankle-high grass heavy with dew wets our shoes and cuffs.

"This feels good," Stan says, hefting the sledge and moving into a batting crouch. "Rogalski in the on-deck circle," he announces. "Rogalski beat out Reggie Jackson for the right-field spot on the Yankees. 'It's a shame to have a player of Jackson's caliber sitting on the bench,' the Yankee manager said, 'but Rogalski's just too good.'"

We come to the edge of the railroad yard and the end of the Baseball Spur. Across the tracks there is a barricade, consisting of a sturdy six-by-eight driven spikelike into the roadbed on either side of the track, then five ties stacked across the tracks and bolted at the ends to the six-by-eights.

I walk behind the barricade, where the spur passes into a tangle of raspberry canes, willows, and saplings. In the distance I see a tiny scratch of silver where the wind and snow have scrubbed the rust away from the rail. A moonbeam touches down on it like a wand and it shimmers bright as a needle in the creamy warmth of the night.

"See, what did I tell you? It's here, just as I said it was. Think about all the history here, Gid. Doesn't it just make you tingle? Like the first time I knew a girl was gonna let me put my hand down her blouse."

Stan grins wildly, his face turned up toward the moonlight. I am tempted to remind him that I am the historian, but I don't.

"Hey, Gid, do you remember how when we were kids there used to be ads on the backs of comic books and sports magazines? I don't remember who sponsored them, but they were aimed at groups — you know, churches and boy scouts and things like that. They wanted to see who could sell the most salve or Christmas cards or wrapping paper. And the grand prize for the group that sold the most was a baseball field. They claimed they'd come out to your town and build you a baseball field — you know, level it, sod it, put up a backstop. I don't know if they built an outfield fence or not. But they always showed a picture on the back of the magazine with new bases sitting out there, white as Leghorn hens, and the grass an unreal green, a heavenly green, and the whole field covered in kids wearing red-and-white uniforms. You know what I always dreamed, Gid? That I was a charity or a church group, and I sold the most salve or whatever, and they came and built me a baseball field."

I'd like to step around the barricade and hug Stan and tell him I understand his fears and how trapped he feels, that I appreciate his dreams and have had a few of my own.

The barricade across the Baseball Spur has been put there to stop any boxcar that might manage to coast that far. Stan and I grin at each other as if we've just completed a double steal. The moon is so bright that the yard looks almost beautiful in the distance. The tracks are blue and silver and gold, while only feet away, behind the barricade, they are coated in rust and disappear into weeds and wild grass. There is just a hint of ground mist in the ditches and there are mosquitoes purring about my face.

Stan squares his shoulders, takes the sledge and swings it back sideways as if he were going to ring a gong, and brings it forward, landing a mighty blow to one of the ties. The barricade barely budges. But Stan swings again and again, chipping the ties, splintering them, breaking them away from the blue-headed bolts. He sets down the hammer and lifts the broken ties one by one and tosses them into the ditch. Each time, a little puff of coolness, sweet with the odors of grass, rises and envelops us.

☉

"Sometimes I feel badly about Missy," Mrs. Baron said to me recently.

I was about to inquire why, but she pressed on, not looking at me. She was working at the sink, rinsing and stacking dishes, polishing the faded blue Arborite countertop that was covered with white, wormlike squiggles.

"We didn't have to take her, you know. The doctors said we could wait for another baby. They found this young woman for us, one who planned to put her baby out for adoption. Poor young thing. I can still see the fear in her eyes. She was scrawny and covered in so many freckles it was like she was paved with them, and even though she was barely seventeen, her shoulders were stooped and she looked like she never had a good meal in her whole life. Her name was Melissa Ann Jeffcoat, came from a hillbilly family that lived fifteen people to a shack, somewhere down near the Missouri border. Well, the upshot was, even way back then, they could tell right off that our Missy wasn't right. 'You don't have to take her,' the doctors told us. 'We'll find you another girl who wants to give up her baby.'

" 'The hell you will,' John said to them. He felt real strong about it. 'We agreed to take this baby and raise it like it was our own. If Marylyle here had been able to have a child, and it turned out sickly or downright deformed, we'd take it as our own. So why not this one? We made an agreement not only with you, but with the Lord. This little girl's ours, for whatever time the Lord allows us with her. I won't have it no other way.' "

"Doesn't sound as if you have anything to feel bad about," I said between swallows of coffee and tart rhubarb pie.

"Oh, not that we're sorry we took her. She's been the joy of our life. What I feel bad about is that we didn't know way back then all the things they know now about Down's syndrome. I still don't understand what causes it, something about these x and y chromosomes not being in balance; I've had it explained to me, but it doesn't sink in. Back in those days they just said, 'You got yourself a mongoloid child, won't ever be able to do for herself.'

94

"We believed them; wasn't no reason not to. We never sent Missy to school or tried to teach her much of anything. Nowadays, these little Down's syndrome kids go to special schools and they learn what they call life skills. Most of them can read and write at a passable level; they can read signs and ads, and they can learn to bank and pay their own rent and survive in group situations. Now here's poor Missy, lived way longer than anyone ever expected her to. John's on his last legs and I'm not far behind. What's gonna become of her when we're gone?

"Missy don't even understand the church services, though we had her confirmed. That was mostly John's idea; he's much more of a believer than I am. At her confirmation, Missy had the prettiest white lace dress you ever seen, Gideon. Old Father Rafferty, he looked at Missy and he said, "If ever I saw God's child, Marylyle, Missy is it. Innocence and love and goodness, what more could God or man ask for?' He confirmed her in the church, though the poor thing didn't understand a word of what was going on.

"And I feel bad about the way Missy speaks. I was reading just recently how they can do an operation on these Down's children, sort of fix their nose to look more normal and repair the cleft palate or whatever it is makes them talk the way they do. I just wish I'd known those things early on."

"You did the best you could."

"I suppose parents always feel guilty, and I think children always feel resentful, except Missy, of course, She's just so full of love."

I remember Missy, when I was a child, looking down at me, speaking in her slow, squeezed voice. "Do you like to be hugged?" she asked me.

I said yes, and Missy held out her arms to me. I suppose I was about three, standing at the fringes of my memory. Missy took my hands in her blunt, freckled ones and drew me to her. She wore a speckled dress and cloth running shoes, and even then had a gentle little belly, soft as a friendly cushion.

Now, when we meet, I often greet Missy, her plump hands veined with age, her orange hair streaked with gray, with the words, "Do you like to be hugged?"

⊖

In the first months of our marriage I tried to explain to Sunny how I knew what I knew, and why I somehow had to prove to the world that the Iowa Baseball Confederacy had really existed. But it was like trying to write a description of how to tie shoelaces in a bow for a person who has never seen shoes. Everything I said suddenly seemed silly and unimportant. I felt like a television pitchman, one of those with a bulging gut and alcoholic face, extolling the virtues of a sleazy used-car lot, full of vehicles with bald tires and sawdust-stuffed transmissions.

"Your're more of an evangelist than Memphis Ray ever was," said Sunny, and I gathered she was talking about the man in the Tennessee pickup truck. "But you're funny, too," she said, and hugged my neck, and we were enough for each other, then. One of us lonely and tired of fighting a losing battle against shadowy and unwilling enemies, the other tired of being a lonesome traveler, each of us willing to overlook the peculiarities of the other.

And then Sunny asked the question that I have asked myself so many times. "Why do you care? You got a nice house in about the prettiest place on earth. You claim to have money in the bank, and you got me and I got you and we got better lovin' than I ever supposed. So why can't you treat that baseball stuff like it was somethin' useless you was taught in school? Just push it off to the back of your head."

"Everyone's got to have interests," I said. "The world's a big place. Life lasts a long time. What about you?" I went on,

96

thinking I was cleverly changing the subject. "What are you interested in?"

"Oh, well . . ." said Sunny.

"You must be interested in something," I pressed.

"I'm interested in you," she said.

"That's not enough," I replied, without thinking. I could feel the pain heavy in my chest before the words were cold; it was as if I had swallowed a rock. "You know what I mean," I said lamely.

I'm sure she did.

⊖

"You mean we can really do anything we want to do, go anywhere we want to go?" Sunny asked repeatedly.

"What would you like?" I asked. "Name it. Do you want a big car? A limousine half a block long? Or a Rolls-Royce? Any color you want. Or one of those low, flat things that look like ugly bugs, Corvettes or XKLs or whatever?"

"No. I don't want none of them."

"How about clothes? It could be just like on TV; we could go to a fashion show in New York, or I suppose Paris, if you wanted to. You could have anything you wanted."

"Where would I wear stuff like that? I'm not comfortable in anything but jeans. And I'd look funny by you in that damn baseball cap you was born in." She tried to grab the red-and-white cap with ORKIN on the crown that I had indeed worn ever since she had known me.

"Maybe I'd like to travel, though," she said seriously. "In a year or two, when I get rested up. After you been on the road a while, you grow feathers on your feet."

"You choose the place."

"I don't want to go nowhere where they don't speak English. But I do want to travel. I get real nervous sometimes, Gid. My arms feel like they might grow wings, and I just

97

crave to strike out for somewhere. I crave it real bad, the way
a drunk must yearn for liquor. It scares me sometimes. When
I get to feelin' that way I turn on the record player and listen
to some Hank Williams or the Jimmy Rodgers train songs,
with the volume way up, and I wait for the feelin' to pass."

"I've never heard you do that," I said.

"You're never here," she replied.

We went to Hawaii, flew first class, stayed in a room at the
Illiki Hotel that was almost as big as our whole house in
Onamata. We rode the glass elevator up the front of the building, where Sunny, momentarily disoriented, grabbed the arm
of a stranger she thought was me and squeezed for dear life.
The man was good-humored and had a block-long Texas accent.

"I'm honored, little lady," he said. "I got bit on the bicep
by an angry possum once, didn't grab on near so tight as you."

I brought a bulging file folder with me and haunted the
libraries in Honolulu and at the University of Hawaii, hoping
I might find a clue to the Confederacy that had somehow
flown across the ocean like a strange and wonderful seed.

*It was due to the persistent efforts of Frank Luther Mott, the
first and only commissioner of the Iowa Baseball Confederacy, that an exhibition game was finally arranged with a major-league club. Mott made the necessary contacts with the
Chicago Cubs and a verbal agreement was reached that the
Cubs would visit Big Inning, Iowa, on Saturday, July 4, 1908.*

Mott sent Paul Eicher, the publisher of the Iowa City Citizen, *to Chicago to finalize the arrangements. Mott and at
least one representative from each team were at the Iowa City
railroad station when Eicher, smiling like a cat drinking out
of a cream pitcher, stepped down onto the cinders, amid the
smells of steam and creosote.*

98

Word spread around Iowa City faster than pinkeye. People were lined up in front of the Citizen *office the next morning to see the details posted.* CUBS COMING TO BIG INNING, *the headline read.*

A raging controversy soon ensued as to whether the Cubs should face an all-star team from the Confederacy or the Big Inning Corn Kings, who were champions of the Confederacy in 1907 and were leading the league by six games on the day of the announcement.

After a stormy eight-hour meeting, the best the team representatives could do was a deadlock. Big Inning, Iowa City, and Husk voted in favor of Big Inning, while Blue Cut, Frank Pierce, and Shoo Fly voted in favor of an all-star team.

That left the final decision to Commissioner Mott, who, although he lived in Iowa City, was an eminently fair man and bound to do what he considered best for the Confederacy. His decision was never in doubt. The Iowa Baseball Confederacy All-Stars would host the Chicago Cubs in a doubleheader at the Big Inning ball diamond on Saturday, July 4, 1908.

5

THE FIRST TIME Sunny deserted me, it was in a bleak January with a foot of snow on the ground, an ice storm lurking like a coyote in the hills. Desperate with grief, yet angry at the betrayal, I carried Sunny's plants — each spindly geranium, each African violet, each phallic cactus, and her favorite, a delicate lipstick plant — out of the house, across the wide porch, and I set them in the snow in the middle of the front lawn. Then I watched them from the living room window, wondering if I would be able to see them shrivel in front of my eyes, grow dark, bend down, limp as old celery, as the frost destroyed them.

But the plants sat where I put them, like multicolored splotches of paint on the unspoiled snow. They did not turn black; they did not wilt. In the night the ice storm slammed Iowa, coating power lines, trees, and fences with a half inch of ice, clear as springwater. By dawn, trees groaned and exploded, staples shrilled in wire fences, eavestroughing sagged.

In the yard the snow was paved with clear ice, yet each plant stood as it had in the house, erect, protected by its coating of transparent ice. When, a few days later, a warm breeze melted most of the ice, Sunny's plants remained encased. When the winter winds howled and new snow fell, the plants were still brilliant beneath their coating.

Spring finally arrived, and in a few sun-mellowed spots, crocuses popped from the earth. Only then did the coating disappear. The plants remained on the greening lawn, like tall, cool, fruit-flavored drinks in long-stemmed goblets.

⊖

Drifting Away remembers Onamata, remembers riding into a Blue Cloud village and seeing her, dressed in white, in front of her father's tepee. It was a feast day for the Arapahos, and Onamata's face was decorated with lines of yellow paint, the color of dandelions. She looked him in the face and smiled, not shy or sullen, but daring, unafraid.

Her skin was tobacco colored, seeded with darker spots, her eyes a warm brown. He felt the sickness of love radiate outward as if the sun was at his center. He leapt from his horse, landing on his toes, soundless as a dancer. He saw each yellow line was like the petal of a sunflower. Still she did not look away.

"I am Drifting Away," he said. "I come from a far-off place."

"And you are on your way to . . . ?"

"Another far-off place."

"I am Onamata. It is the word for traveling woman."

Drifting Away had an Arapaho friend, Afraid of His Own Horses, whom he enlisted to speak on his behalf to Onamata's father. The father loved his daughter very much and wished for her to stay within the camp, to marry someone from their village. But Afraid of His Own Horses bragged of Drifting Away's prowess as a hunter and warrior, told of how rich he was. When the father suggested five horses as dowry, Afraid of His Own Horses said a warrior of Drifting Away's caliber would not hear of paying less than ten horses, and that rather than make a long return journey to his own camp, he would steal them from the Crow, whose camp they had passed only recently.

☺

"The more of these unlikely stories I tell you," Mrs. Baron says, "the more I remember. Of course no one recalls these tales but me. Thing is, I don't feel badly about being the only one. I feel kind of special, in fact. Your life would be a lot simpler if you could do the same, Gideon."

"Wouldn't it, though," I say, smiling my most rueful smile.

"Why do you suppose you remember those baseball things that no one else does? Doesn't it bother you? Don't you want to know why?"

"I suppose there are cracks in time, like those invisible gaps in hedges that only children know about. Plus, whatever is *up there*, or *out there*, has an evil sense of humor. Life is full of evil jokes."

"You know it, Gideon, and you fight back. You fight back."

"Don't you?"

"I suppose I might. If the jokes were cruel enough. Sometimes I want to fight back for Missy. I think about how she's been cheated. How unfair it is. Then I look at Missy. She doesn't know what she's missed. In her own sweet way she's happy. So then I calm down. But I could fight, for myself, or John. John would never do for himself. He trusts in —" She points toward the sky. "Oh, I gave up on that a long time ago."

"I think the reason I fight is that my father's death *was* a cruel enough joke. How many people do you know have been killed by line drives?"

"It was indeed," says Mrs. Baron. "Now for that story . . ." She stares at me, a crease like a wound between her brows. "His name was Sigmund Foth. Odd duck if there ever was one. I think he came here direct from Germany, though I

102

couldn't swear to it. He had an accent, but a lot of second-generation Germans still had accents.

"He didn't look like the Germans around here; he wasn't apple-faced and stolid as a Clydesdale, the way the rest of them were. He was downright scrawny. Had a pointed face like a fox and was dark skinned; looked Spanish or Italian. His eyes were blue, but set deep in his face. They gave off light sometimes, like jewels way down in a bag.

"He farmed a quarter-section south and east of here, had a ratty cabin, a few cattle, some sheds, a few acres of corn. Anything went missing in the neighborhood, Foth got blamed. Got caught red-handed with a stolen water pump one time. One of the Snell boys owned the pump. He took it back and told Foth not to do it again. Said Foth behaved like a dog that had just been whipped.

"One day, after he'd been living around here for five years or more, a wife and a couple of kids turned up. Girl and a boy, eleven or twelve, and a tall, pale woman with reddish-blond hair and a hangdog look about her. The girl was a pretty little thing, dark like her father, but with a charming smile and her mother's freckles.

"The rumor was that Foth abused his family pretty bad. Though they weren't Catholic, the boy went to see Father Rafferty one time, sort of as a last resort. He said Foth beat the mother and the girl with a belt and with hame-straps off the harness. Said he used to do awful things to the girl; you know the kind I mean.

"The boy ran away not long after that. Couldn't have been over fourteen. They say he threw a pitchfork at old Sigmund, pinned one arm to the log wall of the barn with the middle prong. There was a doctor in town in those days. Foth eventually showed up because he thought he had blood poisoning.

"A year or so later, the wife — I think her name was Irma — ran off, too, with a drummer from Chicago who traveled from farm to farm selling fancy kitchen ranges from a picture catalog.

"Folks said they saw her sitting up on the seat of the drummer's buggy, a carpetbag in the back, her wearing a bright-colored sunbonnet.

"Well, no one was surprised that Sigmund Foth's wife had left him. But what happened next certainly did surprise us all. Foth wandered around town like a lost soul for a few days, eyes downcast. 'You know my wife left me,' he told everyone he met. People didn't offer him much sympathy and I guess one or two told him his pigeons were coming home to roost and he was getting what he deserved.

"But Foth just looked at them kind of wild-eyed and mumbled about his Irma and how he missed her. 'My wife left me, you know,' he'd say just as if he hadn't told them that but two minutes before.

"Foth had worked part-time on the railroad, and about a week after his wife went riding off on the drummer's buggy, he went into one of the railroad's storage sheds and stole enough dynamite to blow up the whole district. Tied the sticks together and draped them over himself like armor, walked through the town scaring everybody out of their wits, down to the baseball field near the river. He sat out behind second base for an hour or two, and then he set off the dynamite. Blew a crater ten feet across and four or five feet deep, broke half the windows in the town, and deafened most of the dogs that were within a mile of the blast.

"They didn't find enough of Sigmund Foth to bury. The draymen had to haul in I don't know how many scrapersful of earth just to fill up the crater so's the teams could play baseball that weekend. Some say they found a few scraps of him out on the field and a few pieces caught up in the chicken-wire backstop behind home plate. Someone put the pieces in a gunnysack and took them to the Lutheran minister, who took them to the farm to see if the girl, who must have been about fourteen, had any wishes for them. 'Feed them to the hogs' is what she told the minister. She spit at the sack and slammed the door.

"Community had some kind of meeting, tried to decide what to do about the girl. They say the minister said a few words over the gunnysack and buried it in the Lutheran graveyard. They had the meeting in my papa's undertaking parlor; John's father was there and probably some of your kin. They decided to employ a hired man to run the farm and add his cost to Foth's taxes, all the time hoping the wife would come back or some other relative would turn up.

"You know, Gideon, I just thought of something. When I was a girl, when I was still Marylyle McKitteridge, my family lived *above* the undertaking parlor, the same building where your agency is now. But now there's no upstairs to the building . . ."

"The building *you* were raised in was destroyed by the flood."

"I don't remember any flood."

"Haven't I been telling you about the flood for years, ever since my daddy died? And he must have told you about it, too."

"I think I'd better get back to my story. I don't know as I want to think about that building. I was brave as anything a while ago listening to you talking about 'cracks in time' when they didn't have any direct effect on me. When you get old, Gideon, you only have to think about what you want to. Now, I was telling you about Foth.

"That woman came back. Irma Foth. Only there was something changed about her. She arrived by train in Iowa City one day. All alone. Those who saw her said she carried herself differently. She seemed to know what had happened to her husband. Newspapers picked up grotesque stories like that, just like they do today. Even the *Citizen* did that, and they used long subheadlines, like in the story about Foth:

FARMER DYNAMITES SELF ON BASEBALL
DIAMOND

CRATER SEVEN FEET DEEP BLOWN IN THE
OUTFIELD

"Sigmund Foth Not Known to Be
a Baseball Fan," Says the Manager

"First thing she asked was 'Where is he buried?' and then she started carryin' on as if she was really bereaved. I would have thought she'd have breathed a sigh to be rid of that weasely Foth, sold off the farm, and taken her daughter to Chicago or wherever she lived now.

"Instead, the first thing she did was marry that girl off — her name was something awful, Gunhilda, or Sigfrieda, something that sounded like a piece of hardware — to the Amish boy the town had hired to run the farm. The Amish were always lookin' for new blood in their colony. They got married in town and then he took the girl home with him, and her probably young enough to still be playin' with dolls. Someone said they saw them drivin' toward the colony. The girl took off her sunbonnet and dropped it over the back of the buggy, where it lay in the fine, reddish-brown dust, all twisted-like and broken.

"Then Irma Foth went to the mayor of the town and asked to see the place where Foth had blown himself up, and she also asked to claim the few pieces the Lutherans had buried."

"I notice you've taken to saying *the town*, not Onamata, and that you always pause slightly, as if you'd like to say something else. Could it be you have *Big Inning* on the tip of your tongue?" I say eagerly.

"You've just told me your stories too many times, Gideon."

"Even so, you're making me feel hopeful again. Now, what happened next? To Irma Foth, I mean."

"She brought him back to life."

"Who?"

"Foth, of course. She brought him back to life."

"How?"

"She went around like a diviner, only instead of a forked stick she used her fingers. I seen her once; lots of people used to go down to the baseball grounds to look at her. She was tall and pale, wearing a long, flowered housedress that fit her poorly, as if she'd lost a lot of weight while she was away. She was keening like a sick cat all the time, she was. She'd walk a few steps, her right-hand fingers splayed and stiff, pointin' at the ground. Then she'd stop, sort of frozen like a bird dog, and that Amish boy would start digging with his long-handled shovel. And when he got something dug up, why she'd sift the soil until she found what she was lookin' for, and she'd stuff it into a canvas sack, the kind the mail used to travel in.

"She'd walk a step or two more, circle around almost as if she was dancing, or playing a child's game, howlin' like a banshee all the time, until she'd freeze and point again, and the boy would dig again.

"By the time she finished, the baseball field looked as though it had been shelled — lucky it was fall and the season was over — and she had a half-dozen bags full of sod and soil and, I guess, pieces of Sigmund Foth.

"On the day she was done, her son-in-law drove into town in one of those black-painted Amish coaches; they still use them today, look like little stagecoaches all painted up for a funeral. He loaded all those bags into the back and Irma Foth climbed up on the seat of the buggy beside him, and they drove off toward her farm.

"There was a lot of people standin' around rubbernecking

that day, and they all said there was chittering sounds coming from those sacks. 'Sounded like they was full of squirrels,' one woman said. And them sacks bumped and tumbled as if they was trying to arrange themselves into some form or pattern.

"The next Sunday Irma and Sigmund Foth came to the Lutheran church. He was dressed in a suit and a shirt with a wing collar, and she was wearin' a dress that brushed on the grass and a wide-brimmed straw hat with bluebells growing all around the crown. He held on to her arm and helped her in and out of their buggy, acted the perfect gentleman. And she was as cool as you please, sort of starin' at a spot on people's foreheads."

"Maybe he had a brother," I say.

"You wait until you hear the rest of the story and judge for yourself. Foth nodded and smiled at people he knew. He became a model citizen; he worked his farm, joined the church, paid his bills, and, as far as everybody knew, gave up stealing. And when somebody had nerve enough to bring up the subject of him being dead, he just laughed and said he'd been called away on business, and he thanked the town for caring for his farm and paid them back the wages they'd paid the Amish boy.

"Now this left the Lutheran church in a peculiar position. They had erected a small cross over what they thought were Foth's remains:

SIGMUND FOTH
1864–1906

Somebody eventually carried the cross inside and stored it away.

"For the next few months you never saw such a devoted couple. Then, in the spring, on this lush Sunday morning, just as everyone was coming out of church, that little black

Amish buggy come driving down the street, Foth's son-in-law guiding the horses. It pulls to a stop in front of the church and Foth's daughter climbs out of the coach part. She's all dressed in black and she's holdin' on to a big, old-fashioned six-shooter about half as big as she is. Foth is halfway down the steps, and when he sees her he doesn't break and run but continues right toward her, a half-smile on his face. That girl pulls the trigger and hits him dead center of the chest. The recoil very nearly knocks her down. Foth falls face down at the bottom of the church steps; the girl recovers herself and stands over him and fires two more bullets into his back.

"Right before that whole Lutheran congregation and the Reverend Clyde Pulvermacher, who was by that time kneeling down over the remains, the body of Sigmund Foth then changes form, turns from a body into a stack of canvas mail sacks, each one of them bumping and chittering like something wants out real bad. The girl is still standin' there and she fires two more shots into the mail sacks, and they quiet down, all but one that whimpers and wiggles. 'Too bad,' the girl says to her mother, who's been standing like a post through it all. 'I'd saved this one for you.' And she fires the last bullet into the mail sacks and they all become quiet. Then the girl turns and walks off toward the edge of town.

"Well, the Lutherans buried him again. Only this time, the cross over the grave said:

SIGMUND FOTH
1864-1906-1907

And they say the grave marker's still down there, if you was to go and look."

"The grave markers were washed away in the flood," I say.

"And no one ever saw the daughter again. She just vanished like smoke."

"I'm all too familiar with the phenomenon," I say.

Suddenly Marylyle covers her faded lips with her fingers. "Oh, Gideon, I don't think I should remember this. That girl, she was called Sunny, just like your . . ."

"Can the story possibly be true, Marylyle?"

"It's the story that counts, Gid. Once it's been told it's as good as true."

⊖

Tonight in my empty home, I hear my father's voice again. "Don't you think the world was meant to know about the Confederacy?" he used to shout rhetorically. "Otherwise why do I know about it? Why do you know about it? You do know about it, don't you?"

"Only what you've told me. Maybe it's like the business about 'If God had meant man to fly he would have given him wings.'"

"How does that fit in?"

"How do you think the first man to envision flight must have felt? He must have had a hell of a selling job to do."

"Maybe I'm going against the ways of the world. Maybe that's it. Maybe whatever powers there are out there, floating suspended in the silk and satin of the darkness, erased the Confederacy from the minds of the millions of Americans who must have known about it. I have to think of it as if they were just doing their job. But nothing is perfect. If it was, *I* wouldn't *know*. Their eraser missed some recessive gene in my father or mother, or the lightning blew the fog out of my brain. Anything is possible. I read about a man breathed a pear seed into his lung, and darned if it didn't sprout right there in his chest cavity; it tickled and wiggled and jiggled, curlicuing around, groping for light the way potato shoots used to grow in your grandma's cellar, long, pale, pearl-like tendrils reaching up toward the cellar door.

"This whole business has got to have something to do with survival. Somewhere out there there's energy, or memory, or *something*, that wants the Confederacy to survive. And I'm gonna do everything I can to see that it does."

But though the essence of dreams is gossamer-light, the reality of dreams can be heavy as hundred-pound bags of cement.

Drifting Away continued to defy the white men. In the fall, when the leaves turned orange as marigolds, he moved his white-skinned tepee deep into the poplar grove, two hundred yards from the Iowa River, where Onamata drew water and fished with a white-birch spear.

Earlier, in the heat of the summer, he cut long branches from the nearby cottonwoods, watched as the sticky leaves dried on the branches, a green-black color, banked the tepee with the cottonwood branches and with moss.

There had been other encounters with the sullen, buckskin-clad men, other threats.

"There is land enough for all," Drifting Away said to them, moving his arm in a wide circle. "See how small my own circle is, my charmed circle. The land births us, feeds us, reclaims us."

"It's gonna reclaim you right soon, Indian, if you don't get on your way."

Drifting Away carried arrows, chipped out rock arrowheads, made a rock blade for his tomahawk. Sometimes he followed the white men so closely their horses shied at the smell of him. Sometimes he entered their camps at night, felt them breathe on his hands, studied their faces in the glowing embers from their fire.

Early this morning Mrs. Baron phoned and asked if I could drop by. When I arrive, she and Missy are standing in the lane near their front gate. There are brown-and-black tiger-striped butterflies dancing over the grasses, and Missy, bent forward from the hips, her left arm akimbo, is carrying on a conversation with them. The sounds she makes are sweet, breathy, unearthly. Missy scratches her straight red hair, setting her yellow sunbonnet askew, but her voice never misses a beat. She reminds me of a musician, improvising.

"How's your research coming, Gideon?" Mrs. Baron says to me.

"Not very well, I'm afraid. I'm still the only one who believes. I'm a regular one-man religion." I smile in what I hope is a sardonic manner. "But I'll keep at it."

"I'm sorry to hear you're not making any progress," she says, and pauses. The only sounds are a bumblebee droning over the ditch full of sweet clover and Missy's singsong. "I don't need any work done, Gideon," she goes on. "I asked you out for another reason. You know I'd help you with your research in any way I could."

I nod. "You have helped," I say. "Your stories help me. Reminds me that there are others aware of the magic all around us. Those cracks in time are going to widen until time splits wide open."

As I am speaking, Mrs. Baron is listening, a hand cupped on her chin, her eyes fastened on me, her brows closed in a scowl.

"I have a confession to make, Gideon. I tell you those stories because I feel guilty."

"About what?"

"Well, I *know* those events in the stories I tell you — I know they're true . . . just like you *know* your baseball league existed."

"That's nothing to feel guilty about."

"Well, it is and it isn't. The reason I asked you out here is, I think I can be of some help to you."

"Go on."

"But there's some real bad news, too." She pauses for a heartbeat. "John's as sick as I've suspected he was. You know how I've been nagging him to go to the doctor. Well, he finally did. Was in to Iowa City for some tests. He's had a good long life, but I reckon there ain't all that much of it left for him."

John Baron has been looking peaked for the last month or two; he's lost weight and his shoulders, always so square, have sagged noticeably. His white hair looks matted and dry, like that of a sick animal.

"I'm sorry to hear that, Marylyle," I say.

"Thank you, Gid. But I didn't drag you out here to tell you my troubles. Missy, honey, push your bonnet back off your forehead."

Missy is bent almost double, cooing to the butterflies where they dance over the grass and clover like snippets of brown cloth.

"You know, Gideon, I'm only four years younger than John, but I have no memory of your baseball league. I would have been old enough to remember. By 1908, I was almost fourteen."

"You say that as if John remembers the Confederacy."

"Do I?" Her face has an odd expression, one I've never seen before. "I can't find anyone who remembers these odd stories I've been telling you, but still I don't remember your baseball league."

"But John does?"

It is Marylyle Baron's turn to nod.

"But why has he never told me? And why didn't he tell my father?"

"Well, now, he says he feels right bad about that. Thinks

your father might be alive if he'd . . . But let me tell you another story, Gideon, a short one this time.

"When we were young, just a year or two after we were married, John woke up one night with a jump and a whoop. Woke me up fast, as if I'd been poked by a cattle prod. John was sweating and trembling and he grabbed on to my arm so hard I had black prints on it for weeks.

" 'Somethin' happened to me, Marylyle,' he said to me. 'Oh, I don't know if it happened or not. Or if I dreamed it. No, it happened. Do you remember the Chicago Cubs coming down here and playing a Fourth of July game at the ballgrounds on the edge of town, only . . .' — and he paused a long time — 'the town was called Big Inning then?'

" 'Of course I don't,' I told him. 'I'd remember something as important as that. You just had yourself a doozy of a bad dream.'

"Well, then, Gideon, he told me a story as crazy as I've been tellin' you. All about a baseball game going on for a month or more. And in a rainstorm, too. And there was something about lightning. Oh, and a big Indian, and a dead midget, and an albino. The river flooded and carried away the town while the game continued right on, as nice as you please, and the sun sucked ballplayers right up into the sky. John ended up by claiming he played in the game. Said the team he played for was the Iowa Baseball Confederacy All-Stars."

She stops and looks over at me, waiting for my reaction. But I'm too stunned to react. *Someone else knows*, I'm shouting inside my head, over and over. *Someone else knows! Someone else knows!*

" 'If something like that happened, don't you suppose I'd know about it?' I said to John.

" 'But I played on that team, Marylyle,' he said several times. 'You know I'm no liar.'

114

" 'You've just had a dream about one of your dreams,' I told him.

"For a few weeks John he asked around, kind of casual, about if anybody ever heard of the Chicago Cubs visiting Iowa City or Onamata. And I know he went to the library and looked through some old newspapers. But he didn't find anything and nobody he asked could recall such a thing as he described."

"But why didn't he tell my father, or me? He knows what we've gone through."

"He sure was surprised when your papa came askin' around about the Confederacy baseball league. 'I'd be giving him false encouragement, Marylyle. What could I do but tell him what I remember and then there'd be two of us bangin' our heads against History? I figure what I know is some kind of freak of nature and best forgotten.' "

"Then why bring it up now?"

"Yesterday, when we got back from Iowa City, after the doctors told John the truth of his condition — or after John forced them to, you know how John is. 'No blarney,' he told the doctors. 'If I'm goin' to cash in, I want a chance to close all my accounts and pay all my debts.' Well, after we got home, he just turned to me and said, 'I think I should tell Gideon what I know.'

" 'I'll ask him out in the morning,' I said to him."

When John appears in the yard he looks as though he has aged in the week or so since I last saw him. He looks brittle. His overalls seem baggy. The veins on the backs of his big, rough hands are distended, a troubled blue.

"Let's go for a walk," he says to me. He touches Marylyle's hand briefly, glances over at where Missy croons softly.

We walk along the edge of a cornfield, behind the boxcarred barn and machine shed. The air smells of moist earth and the sweet greenness of corn.

"Even now I have no idea if I'm doing the right thing, Gideon. I thought old men were supposed to be wise. You know how sometimes there is one cloud high in the sky and its shadow makes a dark spot, like a stain, on the ground near you, or over you? That's the way this odd business has been to my life. I always thought I knew something nobody else did, until your father came around asking questions. Ever since then, that cloud has been like an odd-shaped personal shadow. Often I think it's as if I glanced over and saw I had the shadow of a horse or a truck instead of my own. I suppose Marylyle's told you her story about shadows?"

"No, she hasn't."

"Oh, well, I suppose it's just as well for you not to know." He pauses, stares around as if he has momentarily lost his train of thought. I make a mental note to ask Marylyle to tell me the shadow story at the first opportunity.

"I don't know how I come to know all this information, Gideon, but I guess you're familiar with the feeling." He claps a hand on my shoulder. Even on this humid summer afternoon the hand feels cold. "A long time ago, I even went down to the church and told Father Rafferty about what I knew. He's been retired for years. They came down and carried him away to wherever they take old priests. It was just like ripping an old tree out of the ground.

"I told Father Rafferty everything I knew, and he said, 'John, there are some things that cannot be explained, and it's better not to occupy our minds with such problems, but instead to think uplifting thoughts.' I don't know if priests have a manual with quotes for all occasions, but that certainly sounded like one to me. So I told him a part that I'd held back. I told him about the night that Little Walter, the mascot of the Confederacy, died, and how Father Rafferty himself came out to Big Inning in the dark of the night, in the height of the rain, holding a lantern in front of him like he was this fellow searching for an honest man. I told him how I led him to one of the tarp-covered wagons where the players from the Chicago Cubs were sleeping. Water was sloshing around his ankles, wetting the the hem of his cassock. I told him how he administered the last rites to that little fellow."

John sighs and massages the back of his neck.

"I think we should go down to the baseball field, Gideon."

"Let's go right now. We can take my truck."

"No, not in the daytime. There's a softness about it at night, almost a holiness. And more, but you have to be there. Maybe that's not the best way to describe it, but you'll see when we get there."

I want to tell him that I *have* been there. That I've danced like a witch doctor and played my horn, trying to devise some ritual that would raise the dead.

Instead, I say, "So there *was* a game with the Cubs."

"Of course there was a Cubs game," he snaps. "Went on for forty days and forty nights."

"Really. I didn't know."

"At least that long — more, I think."

"Why didn't you say something before? Why have you let me . . . ? Why did you let my dad . . . ?"

"Well, you see, until your papa started talking up the Confederacy, I thought I was the only one in the world who remembered it. Even Marylyle didn't remember the Confederacy. I thought I was best to keep quiet. And when I seen how folks treated your papa — well, I knew I was best to keep quiet."

"But you were his friend!"

"Sometimes friends have to do unkind things. There would have been only the two of us. What could we do? I thought if he was alone he'd give up."

"There are only the two of us now."

"That's different."

"How so?"

"I'm gonna die soon. Marylyle must have told you."

"Why does that make a difference?"

"What can they do to an old man like me?"

"Who's *they*?"

"Don't you know?"

"No."

"Neither do I," he says, and he chuckles softly, wiping the back of his hand across the white stubble on his chin.

☒

Later in the evening, full of Marylyle's blackberry pie, and after hearing Missy's prayers, we drive into Onamata, past the town center and to the bluff overlooking the Iowa River where the ballfield used to be.

"I came out here with your pa once," says John Baron. "Just on some pretext or other. Never let on that I knew anything. Just wanted to see what it was he was raving about. And I suspect I was considerin' telling him what I knew. But things just didn't smell right."

When he stops talking the night is soft and silent, warm as cashmere. The moon hangs like a neon scythe over the countryside. The stars are tinsel-bright and seem to move down closer to us, as if they are curious.

"The ball diamond was right over there," John says, pointing to a tangly area full of scrub poplars and tall grasses. "They built two new bleachers, one on the first-base side, one in right field, built them specially for that double-header with the Cubs. Could smell the spruce gum in the air. The boards of them new bleachers was white as sliced chicken, not like the others. The ones behind home was painted dark green and had little seat numbers written on with white paint. The ones behind third base and down in left field weren't painted and were weathered to the color of mist."

118

"What do you think caused all this, John? Why do you remember the Confederacy? Why was my father struck by lightning? Why did I inherit the obsession?"

"Slow up, Gideon. I don't have any answers. As for me, I just think I was missed."

"Missed?"

"Maybe I was in a root cellar, though I don't know when that could have been. Maybe I was sleeping too sound for that witch dust they splattered to penetrate my senses. Maybe I had my pillow wrapped so tight around my head the vapors couldn't get to me. I used to sleep like that, pillow over my head, wake up with my arms aching like I'd been pitching bundles into a threshing machine."

"Who do you think *they* is?"

"I can't rightly say. Whatever power there is that lurks around and evens things out. I'd say God, but I don't suppose you believe in things like that. God has a different meaning to every man anyway. I've been a churchgoing man all my life, but it doesn't mean I believe everything put in front of me. I liken it to the big meal my mother used to put out for the threshers: outdoor tables groaning under a dozen varieties of every kind of food. Normal man couldn't sample but a third of what was put in front of him. Religion's like that. Sample here and there, pick and choose what to believe. If you claim to believe it all, you're a liar. If you claim to believe none, you're likely one too.

"But I was talking about evening things up. Nature always balances things out in the end. There may be a drought" — John Baron pronounces it *drouth* — "or too much rain, but eventually one balances the other. Same principle applies to the Iowa Baseball Confederacy." John stops and stares straight at me as if he has explained something to me.

"The Confederacy? I don't understand."

"Well now, there was this game, and things got a little out

119

of hand. The powers that be straightened things out. They erased the Confederacy."

"But how?"

"Somehow they reached in and, like plucking eggs from under a hen, slipped away with that part of everyone's memory that had to do with the Iowa Baseball Confederacy."

"Then it really existed as I know it. Six and a half seasons, six teams. The town *was* called Big Inning. The Chicago Cubs came to Big Inning to play a double-header on July 4, 1908. I'm not crazy."

"Or, just you and your father and me are crazy."

John laughs, but pain strikes as he does and his face becomes sober as the laugh turns into a cough.

"Sorry, Gid," he says, straightening his shoulders. He smiles again but the pain has left his eyes watering. "I should have come forward when your papa was having his trials over the Confederacy. I should have . . . but I was in the prime of my life, and your papa was a young man. I figured he'd find someone else who remembered, or else he'd convince people by himself. Do you figure he was gettin' too close? Do you think he was given an impossible task and was about to accomplish it, so they killed him?"

"I don't know if it was an accident or not. Marylyle says you played in the Confederacy. Is that true?"

"Oh, I played, all right. I was good, too. Tall for a shortstop. But I could range away back in the outfield grass and throw to first like I had a clothesline strung between my hand and the first baseman's glove."

"What happened to the Confederacy? What went on at the game?"

"I'm no wiser on that point than you, Gideon. My memory's pretty spotty. Most people's memories were blanked out from about 1902. The whole business of the Confederacy, erased like wiping off a slate. The Cubs were there, though —

I can see it like it was yesterday. They were getting ready to come to bat. We'd been introduced and I shook hands with Frank Chance, Three Finger Brown, the whole crew. They were polite, older than I would have expected them to look, and serious. 'I wish you good luck,' Frank Chance said to me. We had a big, mean left-hander, name of Arsenic O'Reilly, on the mound warming up. He was six foot four at least and was known to be bad tempered. The commissioner of the Iowa Baseball Confederacy was the umpire. He was wearing a frock coat and a silk top hat. He was standing behind the pitcher, going to call the whole game from there. O'Reilly finished his warm-ups. Frank Luther Mott called, 'Play ball.' The crowd roared. And that's where my memory stops. Gid, I didn't bring you out here for fun. I think there might be a way to find out."

I look across at him as if he is about to give me the combination to a safe with a billion dollars in it.

"Things smell right to me, Gideon. I think some of the magic that was here in 1908 is still here. There are cracks in time, Gideon, and I think one of them may well be here. Tomorrow is July third. Seventy years from the date the Confederacy disappeared, for everyone but me."

"Was there an Indian? Do you remember that much? Marylyle says there was."

"Yes, there was an Indian."

"You act as if it's just me that's going."

"That's right."

"But you have to. You know your way around. You've lived there. And . . . and if there is another side, your illness might be gone, and —"

"No, Gideon, I've had a full life. I'll learn the answers to *all* the mysteries soon enough."

"Then I'm gonna ask someone to come with me."

"Not Sunny," says John. "Not that I don't like Sunny . . ."

"Stan."

"He's a baseball player, all right. But what does he know of the Confederacy?"

"Only what I've told him."

"Does he believe you?"

"He doesn't really listen. He's too busy with his own dream. He still thinks he can make the big leagues."

"Bring him along."

"Tomorrow night?"

"About eleven. I'll be here."

"What should I bring?"

"What you think you'll need."

"There really was an Indian?"

"There really was."

☻

All these years I have felt like a private eye in a 1940s movie. In those ancient black-and-white movies full of snap-brimmed hats, square jaws, snub-nosed revolvers, and voluptuous heroines, the private eye always knew what was going on. He knew who the villain was and what dastardly deeds were planned. He knew who had done what and with what and to whom. He was full of dangerous information; he knew who the killer was, where the McGuffin was stashed, at what time the prison break or bank heist was to take place. The trouble was, nobody believed him when he told them the truth. The tough police captain or chief of detectives always scoffed at the private eye, told him to get lost, get off the case. The private eye would find himself on the cold sidewalk in front of the police station, brushing himself off in a bitter wind.

That is how I have felt for years. Stuffed with dangerous information and ignored. Treated like an eccentric. I have spent over half my lifetime picking myself up off gritty sidewalks, brushing the sand from my clothes, hunching my shoulders against the bitter wind of rejection.

Suddenly, for the moment, I have an ally. What do I do?

I start by spending a sleepless night. I can't tell Stan yet. I don't want to give him time to think about my request and turn me down. I stalk through the rooms of my house like someone mad. I take up my horn and blast out "Cherry Pink and Apple Blossom White" so loud I picture the notes driving their way through the roof of the house and heavenward in a molten stream of sound. I play "High Hopes" and "It's a Small World" over and over again, imagining I can hear the hollyhocks bumping softly against the dark windowglass of my bedroom, their sound gentle and rhythmic, like a baby wielding a stuffed toy.

I pack a bag. I stuff two shirts, some shorts, two pairs of socks, my electric razor, and a toothbrush and toothpaste into an orange-and-black flight bag. Then I fill the bag with my notes and writings on the Confederacy. I set the bag by the front door. I stop.

How, I wonder, does one pack for a possible trip to another dimension? I feel like a fool.

I think of Sunny, feel as if I am bleeding deep inside, because I love her so much and she loves me so little. I play my horn again, madly. I throw the horn on the bed, rush to the closet, bury my face in a piece of Sunny's clothing, searching for some trace of her odors, something to feed my heart.

Outside, I walk rapidly toward Stan's, not on the sidewalk but on the boulevard, kicking dandelion heads as I go, like a boy on his way to ball practice or a music lesson, watching dandelion heads arc and fall, exploding like puffballs. My orange-and-black bag is back at the house, sitting morosely beneath the newel post. The only thing I have brought with me is my horn.

As I walk, I remember something else Marylyle Baron told me.

"Did a man named Lonely Stern ever play in your baseball league?" she asked.

"No."

She looked puzzled. She cupped her chin in her hand and scowled. "You're sure?"

"Yes. I know the name of every player who ever appeared in the Confederacy. Most of them are names that are still common around here, grandfathers of people still farming around Onamata or Lone Tree. I can't understand why no one remembers . . . By the way, as far as I know, John Baron never played for the Confederacy."

"Well, Lonely Stern must have been before your Confederacy. He was a ballplayer, though. Herman Stern was his name. And a heck of a pitcher — at least that's what my father said. You know almost the only thing I know about baseball, Gideon? I know the distance from where the pitcher stands to home plate is sixty feet six inches. Do you want to know how I know that?"

"Does it have anything to do with Lonely Stern?"

Mrs. Baron chuckled softly. "He never had a nickname until *after* he quit playing baseball. The fall he decided to retire from baseball, he also decided he would never allow anyone to come closer to him than sixty feet six inches. He farmed up toward Blue Cut. Built a fence around his house and around his barn, sixty feet six inches in all directions. He'd leave notes on his mailbox down by the road, and one of the local boys would do his grocery buying and that sort of thing.

"Folks would come by, stand outside the fence, and have hollered conversations with him while he stood in the doorway of his house. They pointed out that his infielders was closer to him than sixty feet six inches, but it didn't do any good. 'No one is ever gonna be closer to me than my catcher was' was all he'd say. He was still called Herman then, but it didn't take long for 'Lonely' to catch on as his nickname."

"What became of him?"

"He died lonely," she said, and she laughed heartily. "He never let anyone inside his fences. Once, when he was sick, he let a doctor come to his fence. Lonely yelled his symptoms from the doorway, and the doctor made the diagnosis from sixty feet six inches away.

"The big graveyard up on the hill in Iowa City, where the Black Angel sits, was the largest graveyard in Johnson County, even back then. Lonely Stern arranged to be buried sixty feet six inches from the nearest grave, paid extra for a stipulation that no one would be buried closer until he'd been at rest for ten years. I've always wondered why he chose ten years. But they honored his request."

Θ

The day is dying as I reach Stan's. The western sky is the color of orange mousse. I knock but receive no answer, so I push open the door to Gloria's mother's house. It is as depressing as Stan has described it. The interior is so dark it brings back my father's words about potato tendrils struggling toward light. I envision Stan and Gloria, white and spindly, reaching like babies toward the light of the world.

The TV is going in the living room and I pop my head in there first. But only Mrs. Orosko is there, sitting deep in a flowered couch, a remote control clutched in her bony hand. The blue flashes of the TV make her appear alien-like. Her tiny eyes stare at me, boring in. Her hair has been snatched cruelly off her face.

"Excuse me, I need to see Stan."

She doesn't speak, just makes a motion with her thumb toward the kitchen at the back of the house.

I duck down the hall and push open the swinging door to the kitchen, bathing the closed hall in yellow light. Stan and Gloria are sitting across the gray Arborite table from each other; their hands are joined, their elbows rest on the table. I am struck by the absurd thought that perhaps they have been arm wrestling.

"Stan, you've got to come with me," I almost shout into their startled faces.

"Hey, Gid. I thought I heard something in the hall."

"Stan, you're the only one who understands this. Sorry, Gloria, what I mean is, this guy's a dreamer just like me. I'm gonna meet John Baron out at the end of the Baseball Spur in a little over an hour. You gotta come with me, Stan. Something's gonna happen. I know. John Baron's discovered one of those cracks in time I've been babbling about for years."

I feel like a messenger who has just run a hundred miles to deliver a message.

"Take it easy, Gid. John Baron's got to be close to ninety years old. What's he doin' out on the Baseball Spur in the middle of the night? And why are you waving your trumpet around like it was a weapon?"

"Trust me, Stan. I want you with me, man. You know how much the Confederacy means to me."

"What is it that's gonna happen?" says Stan.

He has a half-amused grin on his face. Perhaps he thinks I've been drinking.

"Where is it you're going and how late are you gonna be?" says Gloria. "You want coffee, Gid?"

"No, I don't want coffee. And we're gonna be gone for a while."

I grab Stan by the arm and try to pull him up from his chair. He stands reluctantly.

"Don't worry," I say to Gloria, "if we're gone for a few days." I've already got Stan to the kitchen door. "If Sunny comes back, tell her I love her and I'll be back as soon as I can."

"Do I need anything?" says Stan as I wheel him down the hall toward the front door.

126

"Come on, come on," I say, propelling him past the blue-shadowed living room and onto the front porch. Darkness has fallen. "You don't need anything. John will be waiting for us. It's only a ten-minute walk." I can see Gloria's outline behind the screen door.

Fireflies glow like planets in the moist, silent darkness that envelops us.

"Something's going to happen," I keep repeating as we tramp along. I am swinging my horn, which glints like broken glass under the stars.

We hike past the edge of town. The air along the riverbank has a nighttime chill to it. But the temperature rises as we scramble up the briar-choked hill to the plateau where the baseball field used to be.

John Baron is already there when we arrive. He is standing quietly amid the brambles and scrub growth.

"I see you brought a friend," he says. His shoulders are hunched and he is wearing a black-and-red-checkered mackinaw.

"I told you I would."

"You game?" he asks Stan.

"I'm with Gideon, in whatever he's up to."

In the distance are the lights of the town; on the horizon, the pinprick windows of farmhouses.

"Oh, you should have seen this field back when I was a boy. A fellow named Frank Hall was groundskeeper. He lived in a shack down on the riverbank. This field was like carpet. Frank rigged up a pump, and he piped water up from the river in wooden pipes —"

He stops and stares up at the moon, which has one corner sliced off like a bite trimmed off an apple with a knife.

"Feel the softness," says John Baron. "It all feels right to me."

"What do you think will happen?" I ask.

127

"What are you talking about?" says Stan.

"There are cracks in time," says John. "Just stand and absorb the silence, the softness, the history. If it works, it will be smooth as butter."

He takes a step back, then another. The brambles snatch at his cuffs for the first step, then grow silent. He takes another step, then another. He becomes only a shadow, then only an outline in the delicate darkness, then only a voice.

"Absorb, absorb . . ."

Stan and I remain still as scenery. Stan sighs. I feel the tiniest of tingling sensations, as if an insect brushed against my arm.

As we wait, the scents in the air seem to change subtly. The air is pungent with water. The delight of fresh-cut grass reaches my nostrils.

The lighting is different, too. The sky is exactly the same. But the town is different. The buildings are closer than I remember, and there is less light. The farmhouse lights are gone. I look all around, but there is only one faint orange speck in the distance.

"What's happened?" says Stan.

I breathe deeply.

"We've slipped through one of those cracks in time," I say, my voice louder than I intended. I can hear water sprinkling softly in the darkness.

"Who's that out there?" a male voice hollers. "Get off my outfield before I get my gun."

PART TWO

The
Game

. . . to fuel magic. It takes risks. It takes EXTREMES.
—Tom Robbins

6

FOR SOME REASON the first thing I want to do is to look at my wrist watch. I move my right hand across my left wrist with the intention of pushing the tiny button that will illuminate deep red numbers on the face of the watch and tell me the time, which I estimate to be twelve-thirty A.M. What I find is my naked wrist, though I can still feel the patterns of the watchband on my skin.

"Who's that out there?" the voice shouts again. "I'll give you one more chance."

"Don't shoot us," yells Stan. "We're just lost."

Off to our right, perhaps half a block outside the left-field foul line, there is activity. Lamplight belches from the open door and single window of a long, whitewashed log building with a crude spire. There are horse-drawn wagons tied to trees around the building; the nervous jingling of harnesses sounds loud as tambourines in the night. Suddenly a pump organ cries out and a dozen or two voices rise like fire into the blue-black night:

> "It was midnight in the valley
> And the camp was dark and still
> When a blinding flash of torches

> And a trumpet loud and shrill
> Rang up and down the valley
> And echoed o'er the hill."

I realize for the first time I am clutching my trumpet, holding it in the strangest of positions, on my left shoulder, as if it were a musket.

"What are you, drunk?" says the voice, which has a strong Irish brogue to it.

"No, sir, but we're new to town, walked all the way from Iowa City on the Baseball Spur, but we stepped off at the wrong place."

"God damn, I knew the town would be overrun with fools tomorrow, even suspected they might ooze out from under their rocks tonight, is why I'm out here — only me and the fanatics up at this hour."

"What time is it?"

The man moves toward us and we toward him. He is tall and is carrying a rake and a large watering can with a swan neck and a nozzle at least five inches wide.

"We're sorry we walked on your field," says Stan. "This is where the big game will be, right?" He continues before the man can say anything: "Even in the dark I can tell the field's perfect. I can smell a field that's loved. I can tell right through my shoes that the outfield is perfect, that you've shaved the hummocks and filled in the depressions, planted new grass a seed at a time,"

"Well, now," says the man, "it is nice to be appreciated. Are you a ballplayer yourself?"

"I am," says Stan, and I can see him grinning wildly — he has not spoken out of flattery.

> "Blow ye the trumpet,
> For the Lord hath made us free.

Your blazing lamps raise bright and high
On every signal tree.
The sword of the Lord and of Gideon
Shall be our battle cry."

"I'm Frank Hall," says the spindly man, placing the rake in the crook of his arm and extending a hand. It is dry and scratchy, like shaking a root.

"Now, about the time," he says and digs in his watch pocket, extracting a fried-egg-sized silver watch. I suspect somewhere on it it says RAILROAD TIME. He takes a wooden match from another pocket. Bursting the head of the match with his thumbnail, he bends close to the watch face. Blue-gray tendrils of smoke rise from the match like wool. The bitterness of sulfur permeates the air.

"One o'clock," he says.

"Thank you," I say. "I'm Gideon Clarke and this is Stan Rogalski."

"Gideon, eh? They're singing about you over yonder."

"Coincidence," I say, tucking the horn under my arm. Then I go on. "If it's one A.M., why is the church full, and why are they singing hymns?"

"Well, now, it's a little embarrassed I am by them." Frank hooks a thumb in their direction as if he were an umpire calling them out. "That's the Twelve-Hour Church of Time Immemorial, it is. They operate either twelve hours ahead or twelve hours behind the world, I can never remember which. It's either yesterday afternoon or tomorrow afternoon." He stops for a moment, resting a heavily calloused hand on his chin. His face and neck, even in the bad light, are whiskey-red, the color of turkey wattles. "It must be tomorrow: *they* hold services on Saturday."

"King Jesus is my Captain,
I shall not be moved.

133

King Jesus is my Captain,
I shall not be moved.
Like a tree
That's planted by the water
I shall not be moved."

People in white choir robes, each person carrying a candle, file from the church and walk a few yards toward the massive shape of the biggest tree I have ever seen. Its bulk is illuminated by the moonlight.

"What is *that?*" I say.

"It's called the Indian tree," says Frank Hall.

"Is it a weeping willow?"

"Nothing I've ever seen before. They say the Indians used to camp under it. See how its branches sweep out and down like a woman's hair."

"But what are they doing?"

"They part the branches and go inside, walk around the tree three times, blow out the candles, and everybody goes home. Odd lot," Frank Hall goes on, waving his arm to where the lamplight lies in a pale swath outside the church door. "Sleep all day and plant their corn at night, have miners' lamps strapped to the heads of their workhorses. It's bizarre, the things that are done in the name of religion."

"It is."

"Can we help you?" asks Stan.

"Thanks, but I was about to call it a night myself. Want to get an hour or two of sleep before all hell breaks loose."

"We'd like to get a little sleep, too."

"Not in Big Inning, you won't. Not a room in the whole town. No hotel here. Mrs. Berry has a boardinghouse, but it's been full ever since the announcement about the game. The Lutheran church rented out pallets and there's people sleeping on pews and on the floor."

"It's warm," I say. The night is like flower petals, the air moist as a damp cloth. "Guess we'll just walk around and look at your town."

"I'd offer you a place to stay, but I've only one bunk in my shack." He gestures into the darkness. "I rent a few boats, sell treats to the Sunday people."

"There'll be lots of time to sleep after the game," says Stan.

Though neither of us has mentioned it, the cast is gone from Stan's hand. He is carrying a glove, but not the huge orange scoop shovel of a glove he usually wears. His right hand is encased in a black glove, thin and limp, not much larger than a quality ski mitt.

"The metropolis of Big Inning, such as it is, is right over there. We're a one-streetlight town." Frank chuckles softly. "Town council met for over ten hours before they voted to do it. Only five buildings in Big Inning have the electricity."

Frank Hall goes on his way. In the blue light of predawn, Stan and I walk the main street of Big Inning, Iowa. The Twelve-Hour Church of Time Immemorial has let out. There is the sound of harness bells, the nervous fumbling of horses, a creak of wagon wheels in the dark. The only other sounds are a few voices mixed with the cheeping of early morning birds. No motors. No horns.

The wooden sidewalk is resonant under our feet. This is land I have lived on all my life. The contours are there, the sky is there, the river is there, but everything else is different. I've dropped into the well of the past, seventy years deep. I shiver.

Stan bounds beside me like a large, overanxious dog.

A false-fronted building bears the hand-lettered sign BIG INNING GENERAL STORE. It has a bay window, poking pillow-like toward the street. Our reflections in the glass are mildly distorted. Stan, hatless, looks a little foolish: an overgrown boy in dark trousers and an ivory-tinged shirt with a circular

135

celluloid collar. Stan's arms bulge from rolled-up sleeves. He's wearing heavy, obviously handmade shoes.

"Geez," Stan whistles softly through his teeth. He runs a hand through his blond hair, which appears freshly watered. "This is the place, isn't it? You've been telling the truth." His face is wide and innocent, open to miracles.

"I thought you believed me."

"Never a doubt, man." Stan laughs his long, stuttering laugh and claps a meaty hand on my shoulder. "Never a doubt." Then Stan's eyes widen as he really sees me. "Geez, Gid, where'd you get those duds?"

I nod toward his chest and he stares down at himself, touching the silky shirt, the rough cloth of his trousers.

"July 4, 1908. Big Inning, Iowa," I say.

"Onamata?" whispers Stan.

"In location only. The houses out there are different. There *was* a flood."

"Are we gonna be here for it?"

"I don't know. We'll just have to play it by ear."

For the first time I look closely at myself, inspecting the fabrics, examining the ghostly vision in the bay window. I am wearing a summer suit, pale tan in color, too tight in some places, too loose in others, as if I picked it off a rack in a Goodwill store. I, too, have sturdy leather shoes, a white shirt. My worn black belt with the Indian-head buckle is gone, replaced by suspenders, though my baseball cap still sits on my head. My white-blond hair is still shoulder length, straight as wet binder twine.

"Dressed for the times," I say, and smile.

I tingle. My breath is short. I worry I may have a heart attack and not survive to see the rest of what lies before me.

Next to the general store, after a thirty-foot gap like a missing tooth, is a small frame building with lettering on the only window: BIG INNING PRINTING COMPANY. In the window, yesterday's newspaper, the *Iowa City Citizen*, has been hung with its front page facing the street.

BIG GAME

TOMORROW

reads the headline.

But what I find next is even better. Beside the printing company is the Big Inning Barber Shop, identified by a wooden pole painted with the traditional red, white, and blue stripes. In front of the barber shop on the sidewalk is a bench; on the bench, abandoned newspapers. I leaf through them rapidly, holding them close to my face in the mauve light. The single streetlight Frank Hall spoke of glimmers weakly.

July 1, 1908. Here it is.

IOWA CITY PREPARES FOR EXODUS
AS BIG GAME APPROACHES

A subheadline: *Cubs to Arrive Evening of July 3.* And the story:

> Iowa City will be deserted on July 4, as
> thousands plan the two-mile excursion to Big
> Inning for the exhibition games between the
> Chicago Cubs and the Iowa Baseball Confeder-
> acy All-Stars . . .

"I knew it," I exult. "Look at this, Stan!" I'm almost shouting.

I feel like running down the street waving the newspaper, or perhaps running right back into 1978 clutching it in my hands. I'd like to slam it down on the desk of old E. H. Hindsmith, the man who engineered the rejection of my father's thesis. For this paper is different.

My father spent several years of his life in a windowless

room at the University of Iowa Library, reading and rereading the 1908 issues of the *Iowa City Citizen*. I followed in my father's footsteps, or thumbprints — the only difference is that I read the material on microfilm, in another windowless room, hoping to spot some detail my father might have missed, feeling close to him as I struggled to adjust the focus, read ends of sentences obliterated by the sweat of his hands.

I've read the July 1, 1908, issue of the *Iowa City Citizen* so many times I even know what's missing from the first page of the copy I'm holding: a headline reading BOY SERIOUSLY BURNED and under it a story of twelve-year-old Raymond Pilcher, whose pocket caught on fire after he picked up some phosphorus on what must have been Ralston Creek, though in the paper it is identified as only "the creek."

Inside is a familiar ad: "Eat at the Bon Ton. Meals 15¢."

Below the ad, an article states: "George M. Chappel of the Iowa Weather and Crop Service finds conditions just about ideal."

But the game is here. The information about the game is here. Oh, to show Sunny. To show my mother. To show everyone who ever laughed behind his hands at Matthew Clarke or his strange son, Gideon.

I read. As the sky wears the first blush of morning, I dissect the newspapers.

Stan walks the length of the main street, paces back and forth in front of me and the bench, walks around the block.

"I think I found the spot where Gloria's old lady's house is," he says.

Later in the day, after the game is in progress, two newsboys will come through the crowd offering a still-damp copy of the *Iowa City Citizen* for two cents. The front-page story will read in part:

> After a comfortable night at the Jefferson Hotel
> in Iowa City, the Chicago Cubs, eighteen strong,

gathered in the lobby at 9 A.M. and headed for
the Bon Ton Café, where they packed away
steaks, chops, plate-sized slices of ham, and dozens upon dozens of eggs, sausages, and bacon slices.

⊖

The town eases to life. The moist air of morning smells of
honeysuckle and horses. A large woman waddles around the
corner, inserts a long-handled key into the lock of the Corn
State Lunch Room. She props the door open behind her,
using a flatiron that has been enameled white.

Stan and I are her first customers.

"Coffee," we say together. She stuffs what look like split
shingles into the fire drawer of a huge, black stove with a
silver-trimmed warming oven. The brand name of the stove,
FORGET, is written in fancy letters on a foot-long piece of
porcelain set into the door of the warming oven.

"Up early," she says, as we all wait for the tall, blue-
enameled coffee pot to boil.

"Up all night," I say. "Came last night to beat the crowd."

"Takes all kinds," she says, wheezing asthmatically.

"Do you know Justin Clarke?" I ask on a whim.

"Of course. Everyone knows Justin Clarke. A bit of a
stuffed shirt, but —" She stops. "Relative of yours?"

"We have the same last name," I say, vaguely.

"Honest young man. Pretty wife. Baptists, though. Known
to talk religion to strangers. You know the type . . ."

"I do."

"Dear little daughter. Two years old or so. Mrs. Clarke
walks downtown every day, dresses the girl in beautiful pink
dresses and patent leather shoes. Sweetest thing. I can't think
of her name, though . . ."

"Nancy-Rae."

"Right." She looks at me, squeezing her brows together. I
blush.

139

As we're wolfing down thick slabs of bacon, fried eggs, and hash browns, along with toast made by holding thick slices of bread over an open flame, it suddenly occurs to me that money may be a problem. What did currency look like in 1908? I have perhaps three hundred dollars, mostly in twenties, plus Visa, Master Charge, and various oil credit cards. What could I use for I.D. if I were asked? Certainly not my social security card, my picture I.D. from when I was a student at the University of Iowa, my library card, or my driver's license. Nothing. People knew each other in 1908. And if they didn't know you, your word as to who you were was good enough. The whole meal costs us fifteen cents each.

I pull out my money, held in a clip with a yellow-and-black hawk's head, the emblem of the University of Iowa — I wonder, did they have a hawk as an emblem in 1908? My bills and change are in the currency of the day. I riff the change and see no coin dated after 1907. I touch my other back pocket and discover my I.D. folder is gone. I am adrift in the past, roughly thirty-five years before I will be born. And I can be anybody I want to be.

The café is full by the time we leave. The morning burns in a golden haze. July 4, 1908, will be clear and warm; the dew is almost gone, promising a scorching afternoon. The humidity is low, the air full of summer fragrances: ripening corn, mellow earth, dandelions, red and white clover. I breathe deeply, squinting my eyes against the sun. We loaf along the street past the McKitteridge Funeral Home with its sign, M. J. MCKITTERIDGE, REGISTERED UNDERTAKER. As near as I can guess, the building sits about where the Clarke & Son Insurance Agency will stand — but then, I'm not good with directions. Marylyle would be — what? — about fourteen now, the schoolgirl she's so often told me about who received a book as a prize at a community event — just awakening, longing to fall in love. I'm not sure I want to see her, knowing as I do how her life turns out. All I want is to clear up the mystery of the Iowa Baseball Confederacy.

"I can't believe we've just walked across time," Stan says quietly as we return to the street.

I notice that people are staring at me with more than casual interest, their necks spinning around on their shoulders. I check my fly, try to catch a glimpse of myself in a window. Is there something about me that identifies me with the future?

"Why are people looking at me?" I ask Stan.

"Beats me. You look okay to me. We both look as if we just stepped out of an old sepia-tinted photograph. But as far as I can tell we look just like everybody else."

"Maybe it's my hair. Maybe nobody wore long hair in 1908."

"Don't know," says Stan. "I'm having enough trouble believing where I am. I mean, signs don't lie. I guess this really is your Big Inning, Iowa."

"You guess!" says a boy's voice. "You'd have to be awful dumb not to know that."

When I look, I see an urchin of about ten accompanied by what must be an older brother. Both are leaning against the hitching post, which is a peeled hickory log.

"Davey," says the older boy, putting a hand on the urchin's sleeve. The child wears a tweed cap, held in place by his teacup ears.

"We're from out of town," I say, as if that will explain our ignorance.

"From where?" says the child. "I was to Des Moines twice. Once to get my appendix out."

"Welcome to Big Inning," says the older boy. "We're proud to have you here. Came for the big game, did you?"

"I'm a sportswriter," I hear myself saying. "*Kansas City Star*. Gid Clarke's the name."

"I'm Johnny Baron," says the boy, "and this is my kid brother, Davey."

"Johnny's gonna play this afternoon," shrills the youngster. "He's gonna play for the Cubs someday, too. He's the best player I ever seen."

"He's a little prejudiced," says Johnny Baron, grinning disarmingly. He is tanned, freckled, wearing a faded baseball uniform with black lettering, CORN KINGS, on the chest.

I introduce Stan. "Stan's a ballplayer," I say, "come to see how the big leaguers play. He's hoping to catch on."

Johnny Baron. He must be about eighteen. And Davey at sixteen will run away, lie about his age, join the army, die in a muddy trench at Ypres. Now I really know more than I want to, but there is no turning back.

But something is wrong here — John Baron playing for the Confederacy. Nothing in my memory or my father's memory deals with that. Simon Shubert, the power-hitting shortstop from Blue Cut, is supposed to be the starter. Two or three other players could replace him if he is unable to play. John Baron does not play in the Confederacy.

"I was sent a preliminary line-up for the All-Stars," I lie. "I didn't see your name on it."

"Oh, well," says Johnny Baron with a smile, "it took kind of a minor miracle to get me here. Simon Shubert was supposed to start, but he's caretaker of the Fairfield Cemetery in Iowa City and was mowing the grass when something spooked his horses, dragged the mower in among the tombstones and Simon with it. Broke his arm in four places; he may never play again."

"That's too bad. Heard he was quite a home-run hitter."

"He claims the Black Angel, a huge old statue up there in the cemetery, flapped her stone wings. Says that's what set the horses off."

"I know of the Black Angel," I say. "In fact, I've seen her."

Stan gives me a look that says, Enough is enough.

"I wasn't even on the list," Johnny goes on. "Dick Wheelwright from Iowa City was second choice, but he got called to his father's funeral in California. Will be gone for weeks. And Horace Flowers, from Frank Pierce, came down with pneumonia about the time they decided he was to be an all-star."

"And the others weren't near as good as Johnny," Davey Baron pipes up. "So they raided the Business League in Iowa City and asked him to play. What the Cubs don't know won't hurt them at all."

We all laugh good-naturedly.

"Well, congratulations," I say. "I'll look forward to seeing you play. By the way, we need someplace to stay. Do you know of any place that isn't filled up?"

"We live a mile out of town, might be able to arrange something — "

But the child interrupts. "Game will be over by evening. Everybody will go home. Anybody'll be able to get a room at the Jefferson in Iowa City."

"I suppose you're right," I say. "Didn't think of that." I wonder what he'd say if I told him the game is not going to end today, or tomorrow. But I don't know how to say that, so I say nothing.

I notice that the boy, Davey, is staring at me, but so does Johnny, and he gives the boy's arm a shake and whispers, "Don't stare."

"What chance do you reckon you have against the Cubs?" I ask, trying to sound like a reporter or as I imagine a reporter should.

"O'Reilly's the key," says John Baron. "Best pitcher I've ever seen. And I've been to Chicago four times. Seen both Chicago clubs, and most of the teams in both leagues. Only Mathewson and Three Finger Brown are as good."

"If he's so good, why isn't he in the bigs?" says Stan.

143

"You'd have to talk to Mr. O'Reilly about that," says Johnny coolly.

I hear a steam whistle, two long blasts, and I see the gray whoosh rise in the air from the valley near the spur.

"First train in," shouts Davey, dancing a few steps down the wooden sidewalk. "That means Frank Hall will be all set up." And he looks expectantly at Johnny.

"Go ahead," says the older brother, and the boy dashes away, one hand in the air above his cap to catch it if his momentum should tear it from his head.

7

THE BASEBALL FIELD in daylight is even more remarkable
than we had imagined. Frank Hall is truly a magician. The
infield looks as if it has been tended with a flour sifter. There
isn't a pebble, a clod of dirt, a weed, a mound, or a depression
of any kind. The earthen surface is fine, soft dust, warming in
the midmorning heat. The grass is smooth, fresh-cut, one
perfect green blanket.

"Better than any big-league park I've ever been in," I say to
Stan.

"I could sense it last night, remember?" he says. "Still,
there's something too perfect about it. It's as if after you once
played on this field, you'd never feel quite the same way
about playing anywhere else. I mean, what if you found the
perfect woman, everything you ever dreamed of, and she
liked you, loved you back, anticipated your every wish . . ."

"I'd consider myself the luckiest —"

"But if something happened to her, you'd never be able to
look at —"

"It's not the same," I say loudly, my voice much more
fierce than I intended.

"What are you doing with the horn?" says Johnny Baron.
"Going to play the anthem or something to start the game?"

Maybe that's why people continue to stare at me. Perhaps they're not used to seeing a grown man walking around with a golden trumpet tucked under his arm.

"Can you play?"

"Don't get him started," Stan says, laughing. "He goes up on the hill there and plays in the middle of the night, keeps the whole town awake. Some of the —"

"I thought you'd never been here before," says John Baron quickly.

"Haven't," I reply. "He's a kidder. Talking about Kansas. I play the horn in Kansas."

"Right," says Stan, "a slip of the tongue."

Admission is twenty-five cents. The bleachers behind home plate are already jammed. The seats on the first- and third-base sides are almost full. In the distance we can see people in the outfield, creating a human fence where they stand or spread blankets to claim space.

We pay our admission. John Baron has joined a couple of other players nearby; they seem reluctant to go to the field. Johnny said earlier, "I don't think we should take the field until the Cubs have had a chance to warm up."

"Here they come," cries someone.

A mass of people surges up the hill from the direction of the Baseball Spur. There is the sound of a wagon, and a horse-drawn vehicle appears, garlanded in red, white, and blue, followed by children running and yelling.

The Chicago Cubs, in full uniform, are standing in the wagonbox, smiling, tipping their caps to the crowd.

"Looks like they're being hauled off to market," says Stan.

The Iowa Baseball Confederacy All-Stars gravitate toward the Cubs. Soon the wagon is stopped behind the main bleacher. I recognize most of the Cubs, though I wish the players wore numbers on their uniforms.

But the men in the line-up for the Confederacy are like old

146

friends, so thoroughly has my father described them in his book.

O'Reilly is there, Joseph Francis "Arsenic" O'Reilly, his windburned face centered by a lopsided nose that has been broken more than once.

Bob Grady, the right fielder, smiles affably, shaking hands all around. He is pink complexioned with lemon-colored hair and blue eyes that catch the sunlight and seem to spark with energy.

Scorecards, printed by Sentinel Printing Company of Big Inning, are being sold by a man in a straw boater. The starting line-ups and space to keep a box score are surrounded by small advertisements for local businesses, among them Justin Clarke Insurance Agency, Est. 1903, "A Reputation for Honesty and Integrity."

The starting line-ups:

CHICAGO CUBS		IBC ALL-STARS	
Jimmy Slagle	CF	William Stiff	LF
Jimmy Sheckard	LF	Ezra Dean	CF
Johnny Evers	2B	Oilcan Flynn	3B
Wildfire Schulte	RF	Orville Swan	1B
Noisy Kling	C	Henry Pulvermacher	C
Battleaxe Steinfeldt	3B	Bob Grady	RF
Frank Chance	1B	Bad News Galloway	2B
Joe Tinker	SS	John Baron	SS
Three Finger Brown	P	Arsenic O'Reilly	P

The Confederacy match the Cubs in size, may even be larger man for man.

"A pretty mean-looking crew," says Stan, referring to the Confederacy's players. "I wonder if they play as tough as they look."

The Cubs push through the crowd and take the bench on the first-base side. The last one out of the wagon is their mascot, Little Walter, a hunchbacked midget a little over three feet tall, his head not much bigger than a doll's. His eyes are bird-small and bright; he is trying to drag a canvas bag full of bats out of the wagon, laboring like a horse. The Cub players ignore him.

Bob Grady, grinning good-naturedly, grabs the bag with one hand and eases it to the ground.

The midget snaps a profanity at him. Grady takes his big paw off the bag as though it were hot.

"I can do my job," the midget cries, his voice high and whining like a cricket. He adds an unkind reference to Grady's size, intellect, and ancestry.

"I was just trying to be kind," says Grady, removing his cap and running a hand through his thick hair.

The midget, huffing and wheezing, drags the canvas sack by standing in front of it, digging his heels in the earth, and pulling it along a few inches at a time.

We move with the Confederacy players to the area behind third base, where we respectfully watch as the Cubs take infield practice. The players smile involuntarily as they observe Joe Tinker sucking up ground balls and scooping to Johnny Evers at second, who pivots and fires to Frank Chance at first. We all know we are watching the greatest double-play combination in the game.

The Confederacy players begin to toss balls back and forth. We wish Johnny Baron luck and have started to fade toward the stands when a voice booms out, "Not so fast. Come here, boy."

Arsenic O'Reilly, the Big Inning pitcher, bears down on me.

"Me?" I ask. I don't like the tone of his voice. O'Reilly spits tobacco juice at my feet.

"What's that word on your cap say?"

"Orkin," I reply, then realize the word has no meaning to these men. "It's a team I play for in Kansas."

"Look at the color, and what's it made of? I never seen stuff like that before."

I want to say, "It's just nylon mesh and foam rubber, with an adjustable plastic strap," but realize that would be like speaking in tongues. I see the other Confederacy players closing in on me. I take the cap off, begin to extend it toward them.

"My mother made it for me. Material came from my grandfather's army uniform. He was a general in Serbia." Was Serbia around in 1908? I wonder briefly if plastics are impervious to time travel, just as they are impervious to everything else.

But then I see it isn't the cap they're closing in on, it's me. I am surrounded. I feel like a hamster in a cage, a whole kindergarten class about to pet me.

"Will you look at this," says O'Reilly, putting a large, calloused hand on my head, an almost rapturous look on his face. "We are gonna beat those Cubs today. We been sent a genuine albino for a mascot. Don't you go nowhere, boy," he says to me. Not that I could. There are five or six hands touching my head, others resting on various parts of my clothing.

"What are you doing?" I ask wildly.

"You ought to be used to getting handled."

"Why?"

"You're one of them albinos, ain't you?"

"I'm *not* an albino," I hear myself yelling. "Stan!" But Stan has taken a few steps backward.

My hair is being tousled back and forth as if I'm in a crosswind.

"Hey!" yells O'Reilly in a commanding voice. "Don't go rubbin' him bald-headed before the game starts. Detroit had

149

an albino when they won the series. You sit down on the bench there, boy. If you don't, we'll have to tie you down. Luck like you don't come along too often."

"Ouch!" I yell as someone pulls a hair from my head. "I'm not an albino. Look! Look at my eyes. My eyes are blue. Albinos have no pigment in their bodies. Albinos have pink eyes. I have some dark pigment in my body; it's called melanin."

"What are you talkin' about, boy?" says Henry Pulvermacher, the catcher. He is built like a barrel, scarred, and mean-looking. He smells of snuff.

"I'm just blond. Look, you're blond," I say to Bob Grady, who is beside me but not mauling me.

"Don't try none of that on us. You're an albino and that's all there is to that," says O'Reilly. "You're gonna sit on the bench with us and we're gonna rub your head for luck. Albinos are luckier than hunchbacks; everyone knows that."

I notice the Cubs are vacating the field, to the cheers of the huge crowd.

"And a lot rarer, too," says big Henry Pulvermacher.

At least I know now why people have been staring at me with such interest. I slap a hand away from my hair. The hand belongs to Oilcan Flynn, the third baseman.

"I'll make you a deal," I squeak.

"What?"

"Who's manager here?"

"I'm manager," says O'Reilly. Then he glowers around at the other players to see if anyone objects. No one does.

"The reason I came was to bring you a player." And I point at Stan. They all look at him.

"Is he any good?"

"His bat's like a lightning rod. Slams blue darters to every part of the field."

"What's he call himself?"

Instead of naming Stan, I recall the story of the Blue Cut team billing itself as the Useless Nine. And stories of Shoeless Joe Jackson and the White Sox who were barred for life, playing in many places under a variety of aliases and assumed names.

"I can't tell you his real name," I say. "You'd all know it if I did. He was barred in the South — not supposed to play pro anymore. He's known as the Left-handed Farmhand."

"Can you hit like he says?" O'Reilly says to Stan.

"Give him a bat and he'll show you."

O'Reilly tosses Stan a splintered bat blackened by creosote and stalks out to the mound with six baseballs in the crook of his right arm.

Henry Pulvermacher, the catcher, starts toward the backstop.

"Don't need a catcher," says O'Reilly. "If he's any good, the ball will never get to the catcher."

I smile weakly at Stan. He gives me a look. I don't know exactly how good these guys are and neither does he. We can only hope he doesn't disgrace himself.

O'Reilly sets five balls beside the mound, taking the sixth in his huge left hand; he winds up, rearing back until his body appears parallel to the earth, and fires a blur of horsehide toward the plate.

Stan slashes at the ball, pulls it foul, deep behind third.

O'Reilly winds again. This time the ball is a curve, looking as if it is going to hit Stan in the ribs but at the last second hooking over the plate. I would have been flat on my belly in the dust. Stan does not flinch and, waiting on the ball, slaps it smartly to right field.

The next pitch is very high; Stan reaches up and fouls it off. The fourth is a fast ball and he laces it up the middle.

Stan hits a fly to straightaway center on the fifth pitch. The sixth, another curve, he belts into the gap in right center.

151

"He got wood on all six," I shout. "Two foul, three hits, and one out."

"We can see that," O'Reilly shouts back. "All right, you can sit on the bench with us. We may need an extra hitter."

"This here's an all-star team," says Henry Pulvermacher.

"And him there is an all-star," says O'Reilly, grinning. "What those Cubs don't know won't hurt them a bit."

"Then I can go?" I say.

"Go where?" says O'Reilly.

"Don't you want to bring your friend luck?" says Henry Pulvermacher, standing in front of me like a closed door.

Stan strides to the bench, still swinging the bat. "See, what have I been telling you? I've got a few hits left in me, haven't I, Gid?"

"You sure have, Stan."

"You boys have the funniest accents," says Henry Pulvermacher. "Sound like some Englishman who came through here once. Everybody down Kansas City way talk like you two?"

"A lot do," I say.

"Can't hardly understand him," says Ezra Dean. "Sounds like he's makin' up his own language. I was at a ree-vival show once in Memphis where there must've been three thousand people all goin' 'Umm, umm, umm' like they was singin' their own songs, and some was gobblin' like turkeys and others makin' what sure sounded like birdcalls, and some just babblin' a mile a minute."

"You could be the bat boy," Grady says.

"Just don't let him get away," says Oilcan Flynn, the third baseman.

"Dee-troit had to keep theirs hog-tied for the first month or so," says Grady. "At least that's what I heard. Albinos are downright good luck. I heard tell they can point to the proper spot to dig for gold."

"Wouldn't I be rich if I could do that?" I say.

"Got to be prodded to do, so my daddy said," Grady goes on, glowing with self-satisfaction at his display of knowledge, "and they only do it for other people, never for themselves."

Stan and I are now surrounded by the whole contingent of IBC all-stars.

"Well now, we don't want to appear too unfriendly," says O'Reilly. "We don't want to hold you prisoner or tie you down or anything, but we need all the help we can get to beat the Chicago Cubs, and if you was to sit on the bench and allow the boys to touch your head for luck, we'd be indebted to you."

O'Reilly smiles, displays long, white teeth like a beaver's. The statistics for the Confederacy list O'Reilly as six foot four, but I think he is taller. He is muscular even in his baggy uniform. His head is long and equine; his hair, the shiny black of axle grease, curls over his forehead and collar. His eyes are a deep blue.

"I'd be honored," I say, staring not at O'Reilly but at Stan, noting the look of bewilderment on his face. "I'll do whatever I can for the Iowa Baseball Confederacy."

☙

By game time, the train, with two extra cars attached, has made an unprecedented ten trips from Iowa City. The ballpark is jammed, and people are lined up along both foul lines. After the outfielders establish their positions, fans wander across the outfield behind the players as whole families choose spots to set down their picnic baskets on the fragrant grass.

Frank Luther Mott, the commissioner of the Iowa Baseball Confederacy, walks to the mound with the mayor of Iowa City, who is appropriately named W. G. Ball; Arsenic O'Reilly, captain of the All-Stars and manager of the league-leading Big Inning Corn Kings; and Frank Chance, the player-manager of the Chicago Cubs.

The crowd finally hushes. There is some minor confusion;

153

Mott beckons to someone behind the backstop, and a full-figured woman holding a tambourine large as a pail top takes a few steps out, then retreats. She is joined by a skinny man with a fiddle under his chin, then a quartet of white-shirted men who sport boaters and red bow ties. They all come about halfway to the mound and then retreat a few steps.

"God damn, Luther Phillips is gone again," says Ezra Dean. "Guess it's the middle of the night for these people anyway. Those folks are from the Twelve-Hour Church over yonder. Luther was the town bum until they saved his pickled old soul, but I guess he's backslid a little today." He pauses. "Say, do you play that thing?" He looks at my horn.

"I do."

"Maybe you'd care to join those folks. They'll be playing 'I Shall Not Be Moved.' It's sort of become the theme song for Big Inning — we tried to make the railroad come here, instead of our having to go to them, over to Iowa City. We lost. As you can see, all we got is that miserable spur line. But we're still here. Stubborn as tangle grass."

"Why not?" I say, rising. I swing my horn, which flashes like a sword in the sun, and head toward the mound.

Mott introduces the managers, who doff their caps to the crowd. Both teams receive rousing applause. He then welcomes everyone on behalf of the Iowa Baseball Confederacy and announces that the league teams will begin play on the second half of their schedule on July 6, with games at Blue Cut and Husk. He then announces that a group of singers and musicians from the Twelve-Hour Church of Time Immemorial have risen in the middle of their night to perform the special song of Big Inning, Iowa.

Everyone stands and removes their headgear. I confer briefly with the large lady with the tambourine. The fiddle man taps his toe, the tambourine lady shakes her silver bells, and I raise my horn.

Surprisingly, we start together and in the proper key. The quartet members drape arms around one another's shoulders and harmonize:

> "Don't let the world deceive you
> I shall not be moved
> I shall not be moved.
>
> I shall not be moved
> Like a tree
> Planted by the water
> I shall not be moved."

Five verses later we grind to a halt, amid wild cheers from the crowd. Sweat trickles into my eyes as I make my way to the bench. Arsenic O'Reilly throws his final warm-up pitches.

Frank Luther Mott, dressed in a black suit and a high silk hat, takes his place behind the pitcher; from there he will call the whole game.

"Play ball!" shouts Mott.

The leadoff man for the Cubs is the Human Mosquito, Jimmy Slagle, the center fielder.

Henry Pulvermacher holds up a beefy finger as a signal; O'Reilly winds and fires.

"Strike one," intones Mott. The crowd roars its approval.

A sweeping curve ball breaks in for strike two. The fans roar louder. O'Reilly must appear ten feet tall as he winds up, leaning back so far it looks as though he might topple backward. He fires a fast ball straight down the middle of the plate. Slagle strikes out. I imagine the crowd can be heard all the way to Iowa City.

Jimmy Sheckard, the Chicago left fielder, taps the first pitch, an easy roller to Oilcan Flynn. Two out.

O'Reilly strikes out Johnny Evers on four pitches. The fans

both roar and sigh as the inning ends, an eerie, animal-like sound, hollow, wild.

"We're as good as they are," a fan says. "Haven't I been tellin' you that all along?"

William Stiff, the lithe young left fielder, is the leadoff batter. He walks back from where he was swinging two bats and stands awkwardly in front of me. Almost apologetically he reaches toward me. I take off my cap and he touches my damp hair, then proceeds to the batter's box.

"He's almost as blond as I am," I say to O'Reilly, who is sitting beside me. "Why not use him as your mascot?"

"Because you're an albino," he says crossly, sweat running into his eyes. He wipes his sleeve across his forehead. "You be careful, Gideon. You be careful them church folks don't get ahold of you. They got some strange ideas about Gideon leading them to the promised land. I wouldn't tell them my name if I was you."

"I won't if you won't," I say.

On the fifth pitch, William Stiff strikes out, a mile in front of a "slow ball," what I would call a change-up. Dean pops up. Oilcan Flynn taps back to the pitcher.

CHICAGO CUBS	0
IBC ALL-STARS	0

⊖

There is still no score when, with two out in the fourth inning, Oilcan Flynn gets the first hit for the Confederacy. He slams a single up the middle under the glove of a diving Johnny Evers. Orville Swan, the long-legged first baseman, hits a weak looper to right field that drops in for a single, Flynn going to third.

Henry Pulvermacher wipes his big, dirty hand through my hair, rattling the vertebrae in my neck.

"Henry runs the feed store in Blue Cut," whispers O'Reilly. "You ought to see him toss hundred-pound sacks of corn around."

"I can imagine."

Three Finger Brown gets two strikes on Big Henry, then delivers his slow ball, which Pulvermacher waits on and slaps cleanly into left field for a single. The Iowa Baseball Confederacy has its first run. The fans pound their feet on the wooden bleachers, making a rumbling, earthquake-like sound.

The crowd buzzes as the Cubs come to bat in the fifth. The Iowa Baseball Confederacy has held what may well be the best team in the world scoreless and hitless for four innings.

But that ends quickly. Wildfire Schulte pounds the ball to deep right center. Bob Grady can only wave at it as it lands twenty feet deep in the spectators' territory. The pro-Iowa crowd parts like water; someone knocks the ball down. Grady skips over blankets, picnic baskets, and babies to retrieve it. Bad News Galloway has run most of the way to center field to take Grady's throw. Schulte is no speed merchant, but it takes a long time to get the ball to Johnny Baron near second base, who fires to Pulvermacher. Schulte is across home a full stride ahead of the throw. The game is tied.

The Cubs do not get another hit until Schulte returns to the plate with two out in the seventh and singles up the middle. But Noisy Kling forces him at second to end the inning.

Pulvermacher gets his second hit in the bottom of the seventh, but Grady immediately grounds into a double play.

CHICAGO CUBS	000	010	0
IBC ALL-STARS	000	100	0

Four teams are still in contention for the National League pennant at this time. The standings in the July 3, 1908, *Iowa City Citizen*:

PITTSBURGH	41 25	.621
CHICAGO	39 24	.618

The New York Giants and the Cincinnati Reds are still within striking distance. Three Finger Brown must have an iron arm, for only a day ago he pitched an eight-hit shutout over the Pirates to move Chicago into a virtual tie for first place.

The seventh inning over, there is a conference near home plate. Mott is there, and Frank Chance stalks over from his bench; the IBC players have not taken the field for the top of the eighth. Little Walter, the Cubs' midget mascot, scissors along beside Chance, holding on to a fold of Chance's uniform with one of his baby hands.

They beckon toward our bench.

"If he can drag his mascot with him, so can I," snarls O'Reilly, wiping sweat from his high forehead. He grabs me by the arm and pulls me with him. I feel like the scarecrow from *The Wizard of Oz* as I spin rather helplessly off the bench.

"What's the problem, Francis?" says Frank Luther Mott in a congenial manner. I notice he is quite sunburned in spite of his top hat.

"First game of the double-header was to be seven innings," says O'Reilly. "Game's a tie. We'll take a half-hour intermission before the second game."

"Like hell," growls Frank Chance. "Game ain't decided. We play extra innings."

Both managers look to Frank Luther Mott for a decision.

"Gentlemen, since this is a friendly game, an exhibition game, I think perhaps Mr. O'Reilly has a valid point." He pauses. "And since a double-header is scheduled, and since I'm sure your team, Mr. Chance, wants to get a propitiously early start on your return journey —"

"The hell he does," says Chance, with an amazing amount of venom in his voice.

The Peerless Leader is not a man to fool around with.

"No game I manage goes undecided," he goes on. "We play extra innings or we don't play at all."

The midget jumps up and down like a monkey. I catch his eye; he makes a rude face and spits in the dust at my feet. He mouths a number of profanities at me in his high, tuning-fork voice, which has some kind of European accent to it.

Mott is genuinely taken aback by the hostility of Frank Chance.

"I had no idea you felt so strongly, sir," says Mott, taking off his hat to show a sweaty white forehead with a red crease just above the eyebrows. "Since you are our guests, I suppose we should accede to your wishes. Mr. O'Reilly, do you have any objections?"

The crowd is getting nervous; some catcalls, a few boos, rise in the muggy air.

"I think it's a damn fool thing to do. We've got a second game to play."

"We'll play one game at a time, worry about the second one when we start it. That's why you're bush leaguers and we're big leaguers."

"We haven't fallen apart like bushers and that's what you're sore about," says O'Reilly.

"I really don't think this sort of hostility —" Frank Luther Mott begins, but Chance abruptly turns his back, nearly upsetting the prancing midget, and stalks back to his bench.

"To keep the peace," Arsenic O'Reilly says with a shrug, and trudges toward the mound, waving a big hand to signal the other players to take their places. I am left standing alone near home plate. Henry Pulvermacher shoves me rather rudely out of the way as he takes his place in the catcher's box.

"You won't have to be a mascot much longer," says Stan, grinning, as he slides down the bench toward me.

"Why?"

"These dudes have muddied your hair so you look almost normal," he says, then emits his long, coughing laugh.

"You have brought us luck," says a lanky boy named Don Poston who has sat at my right in silence the whole afternoon.

"I do the best I can," I say, trying to load my voice with sarcasm. "This is not my regular job."

"What *do* you do?" asks the boy.

"An excellent question," I reply, struggling for an answer. What do I tell him? Do I say, "I'm a baseball historian of sorts. My particular interest is in this league, this game, this day. You see, for some reason, everyone except me has forgotten that the Iowa Baseball Confederacy ever existed, that this game ever took place . . ."? Or perhaps I could say, "I am the beneficiary of inherited wealth. I live in the 1978 version of this town — quietly, without ostentation."

But the Cubs are out in the eighth, and Bad News Galloway rubs his sweaty hand in my hair before singling up the middle. The fans applaud wildly. But Three Finger Brown strikes out the next two batters and the inning ends on a pop-up to second.

As the ninth begins, a single pillow of a cloud floats across the sky; it covers the sun, darkening the afternoon. Sun specks, like black sand grains, prickle in front of my eyes. I stare up at the cloud, which shows a black center like a deep smudge of dirt and a fierce, electric fringe where the sun prepares to reemerge. But what I notice, which no one else seems to in this sultry moment of relief from the brazen sun, is that the shadow, coasting slowly across the ballfield and seeming to stop for a few seconds just back of second base, is in the form of a profile with an Indian headdress, like the image smelted into an ancient coin. It seems, too, that in amid the murmur and buzz of the crowd are a few yips and fragments of chant. I look across at Stan, but he is concentrating on O'Reilly's warm-up pitches. Perhaps the sun has been soaking into my scalp for too many hours.

It looks as if the Cubs will wrap it up in the ninth. Three Finger Brown doubles down the right-field line. Slagle singles him home. Sheckard walks. Evers triples to deep left and scores on a soft grounder to the right side by Schulte. Four runs across in under four minutes. O'Reilly gets the next three outs, but going into the last of the ninth, the line score reads:

				R	H	E
CHICAGO CUBS	000	010	004	5	5	0
IBC ALL-STARS	000	100	00	1	5	0

The parched fans head for the refreshment stand behind the main grandstand, where orange- and lemonade are dipped from washtubs, a block of ice like an iceberg in the middle of each. Frank Hall must be ecstatic as the concession, in spite of a dozen women working full out, is unable to cope with the demand.

Frank Chance kicks dirt around first base and shouts encouragement to Three Finger Brown. After fouling off six pitches, Dean draws a walk to start the inning. Chance growls at the umpire. Oilcan Flynn pops out. Orville Swan doubles. Henry Pulvermacher singles, scoring Dean. It's 5–2. Grady, the amiable right fielder, is hitless today; in fact, he has not had his bat on the ball. He rubs my head with both hands, both before and after spitting on them.

"Just watch my fire," he says. He has taken a few steps toward the plate when O'Reilly calls him back.

"Get in there and hit," he says to Stan. "He really doesn't have a name?" he says to me.

"Not one you can use."

O'Reilly strides out to Frank Luther Mott. They confer. Mott addresses the crowd.

"Batting for the Confederacy, the Left-handed Farmhand," he intones.

Stan swings two bats, does some bending and stretching exercises, heads for the plate.

"You forgot to touch your friend for luck," yells Grady.

"I don't believe in that stuff," Stan shoots over his shoulder.

"Around here, that's like saying you don't believe in God," says Grady as he flops down beside me.

O'Reilly calls time, marches out to the plate. He speaks rapidly and forcefully to Stan but is not shouting. Stan shrugs, walks back toward us with a disgusted half-smile on his face.

"Not my idea," he says, and touches the top of my head with stiff fingers, walks back to the plate, takes a ball high and inside, wallops the next pitch about twelve picnickers deep in right center field. There is no play at home plate.

We are all gathered at the plate as Stan scores. He gives me the high five, which draws a few stares from both players and fans.

"I've still got it, Gid. By golly, I've still got a few hits left in me, haven't I?"

"You sure have, Stan. But you know it's because you touched my head."

"That's a crock and you know it, man."

"Hey, how many other times have you touched my head before you went to bat?"

"Never."

"Then I'm one for one." And I remember the words, "Things are out of kilter in Johnson County."

There is no reason why I shouldn't have some power as a good-luck symbol. Things are, indeed, out of kilter in Johnson County. Somewhere in this crowd is Marylyle McKitteridge, at fourteen, watching her future husband play shortstop for the Confederacy.

After nine innings the game is tied 5–5.

⊖

Each team scores a run in the thirteenth. As the top of the sixteenth inning is about to begin, Frank Chance, Arsenic O'Reilly, and Frank Luther Mott hold a conference at the plate. Mott once again addresses the crowd:

"By mutual agreement, the baseball day will end when this game is decided. The second game of the double-header is hereby canceled."

A few fans boo good-naturedly. The game resumes.

The players are hot and sweaty, red-faced and red-eyed as the sun fries down. The line-ups for iced drinks and food are long. Fans are irritated and snap at each other. Sunburned children whine and cling to parental legs. The line-ups for the two slant-roofed privies are at least a block long; many people head over the hill behind center field to relieve themselves in the brush-covered slope that winds down to the river.

The scorecard in the program was good for only one nine-inning game. Now, in the sixteenth, I have lost track of who is up. But the players know. Frank Chance has not yet used a substitute; O'Reilly's only change has been to put Stan into right field.

After eighteen innings, the game is over four hours old and the crowd is thinning because of the heat. The air has become thick; we all sweat profusely. We pass the bucket of water with the white-enameled dipper up and down the bench. A number of players have taken to pouring dippers of water on their heads.

Frank Luther Mott calls everyone together again and suggests the game be called.

"This is just an exhibition game," he says. "You've fulfilled

163

your obligation, you've given the fans eighteen innings of good baseball. Let's call it a day. There's a dinner at the Big Inning Community Hall, a dance, fireworks. What do you say?"

"Play ball," bellows Frank Chance, his eyes ferocious.

Mott, taken aback, looks to O'Reilly for support.

"This game must be decided," says O'Reilly, not so loudly, but with no less conviction. The players behind him give a cheer, all except Stan and me. The Cubs sit sullen and baked on their bench. Not one indicates any disagreement with Frank Chance.

"Gentlemen, I have the power to call the game."

"Like hell you will," shouts Chance, kicking the dirt.

"I'll allow it to continue until six P.M., at which time we'll retire to the Community Hall for a chicken dinner —"

"Let's end it," says Chance, lofting a bat. He is to lead off the nineteenth. He rubs the head and hump of Little Walter, who has been clinging to his legs, and strides toward the plate.

But Chance fouls out to Orville Swan at first. Tinker and Brown go down without a whimper.

☺

The twenty-fourth inning ends with the score still tied at 6–6. It is five forty-five.

Frank Luther Mott raises both hands above his head, as a football referee might to signal a touchdown.

"The game is a tie after twenty-four innings. We will retire for supper to the Big Inning Community Hall. The game is over."

The fans cheer and applaud.

O'Reilly lumbers toward the mound, pulling me along with him. Chance is already there.

"Gentlemen," says Mott. "The game is over. Thank you for a fine exhibition." His voice is becoming hoarse.

"The game is not over," says Frank Chance. "We'll be back after supper."

"Fine with me," says O'Reilly.

"What time does the sun set?" asks Chance.

"At eight fifty-two," I hear myself saying.

"How do you know?" he says sharply. I suppose there are some questions one is not supposed to answer, even when one knows the answer.

"It's in the top right-hand corner of the newspaper every morning," I squeak. "I make a point of remembering."

"Only person in the world who does," says Chance.

"Gentlemen," says Frank Luther Mott with great patience. "There will be no more baseball today. This is July Fourth, a celebration of our independence, and we shall celebrate. We shall retire to the community hall and eat a meal the women of Big Inning have prepared for us. We shall then watch the fireworks display, which will be followed by a dance and musicale. There will be no more baseball today. Do I make myself clear?"

"What time does the sun rise?" O'Reilly asks me.

"At five forty-seven," I say.

"We'll be here at dawn to continue the game," growls Chance.

"As will we," says O'Reilly. "And you, sir?" he says to Mott.

Mott pauses for a few seconds, studying the depth of emotion in the eyes of both managers. "I'll be here," he says quietly. "I'll pass the word tonight, so any fans who care to may also be here at sunrise."

"Don't you go disappearing," O'Reilly says, clapping a firm hand on my shoulder.

"I wouldn't dream of it," I say. "Me and the Left-handed Farmhand here will be out at dawn." Then I pull Stan away quickly before O'Reilly decides he wants to keep an eye on his mascot to make certain I don't run off.

8

WE WALK THE MAIN STREET of Big Inning, which is teem-
ing with people. A sign, red on white, catches my eye — ICE
CREAM PARLOR.

"I need something cold," I say, and Stan agrees.

We buy heaping dishes of vanilla ice cream for five cents
each. Sunlight filters through a tall cottonwood and dazzles off
the glass of the window, dappling the interior.

I look up from spooning my ice cream, and for an instant, in
the flickering light of the ice cream parlor, I think I have seen
Sunny. I half rise from my chair. Stan looks up expectantly.
Three girls have entered from the street. The middle one
tosses a shawl off her shoulders, quickly, recklessly — Sunny's mannerisms. She has Sunny's features, the flattish nose,
the dark complexion seeded with freckles, the black hair.
Why does that particular combination of features excite me
so? One of the girls with her is much more attractive, long-
limbed, with pale yellow hair, white skin, lashes half an inch
long. But if that girl came and sat in my lap and began kissing
along my cheek, I'd ease her gently away from me and walk
toward the small, dark girl, just as I am doing now, trying not
to show that my heart is clattering, loud as dishes in an earth-
quake.

"I'm Gideon Clarke," I say, speaking only to the dark girl. "Could I buy you . . . and your friends dishes of ice cream?"

She looks at me. Her eyes are hazel and gold, the lashes short, like Sunny's.

"That would be very nice of you," she says, her voice full, throaty, with a plains twang to it. "But we're only looking for someone. We can't stop."

"Then later? Will you be —?"

"At the dance," she says, and is gone in a second, lost in the crowd on the street.

We eventually repair to the long wooden tables inside the Big Inning Community Hall, where we are served steaming plates of roast chicken, sage dressing, potatoes, gravy, peas, corn, and carrots. There are apple, cherry, and rhubarb pies, coffee or lemonade. The coffee is accompanied by china pitchers full of thick, sweet cream. The teams sit at opposite ends of the hall, shoveling in food.

"I'm two for five since I came in," Stan says between mouthfuls. "That's not bad, is it, Gid? I've still got a few hits left in me."

"Of course it's not bad," I snap. "That's .400. Any damn fool knows that's a good average."

Stan's face clouds like that of a child reprimanded for being too noisy, but I don't pay any attention. I am tired of consoling him. I have other things on my mind.

Strangely, I haven't minded being the mascot–bat boy all that much. It puts me at the center of the action. There is a certain charm to being regarded as a magical object.

Johnny Baron leans across the table, his face still stained by sweat and dirt.

"I spoke to my pa a few minutes ago," he says. "You're welcome to stay with us. That is, assuming you're staying around for the game tomorrow."

"That would be very nice," I say. "We'll pay, of course, whatever your father thinks is fair."

"It's a mile walk. After the dance we'll head out."

I realize that Stan and I have missed a whole night's sleep.

"We'll meet you after the dance," I say, grinning. "That's if none of us get lucky." Johnny stares at me, puzzled. The phrase apparently has no sexual connotation in this time and place. "You taking Marylyle to the dance?" I ask Johnny.

"Who?" He narrows his eyes.

"Marylyle McKitteridge."

"The undertaker's girl? No. Why would I? She's just a kid. And what do you know about her? I thought you were strangers here."

"I don't know anything," I say innocently. "I swear I heard one of the other players say she was your girl. I must have been wrong."

"I guess you were."

"Wait a few years," I say, but under my breath.

As soon as the meal is over, Frank Chance and the Cubs depart; their wagon has been summoned and a space saved for them on the train to Iowa City.

"We'll be at the baseball field at five forty-five in the morning, all ready to play," he reiterates to O'Reilly.

O'Reilly, his mouth stuffed with pie, acknowledges the statement with a deprecating wave of his hand.

The fireworks, "imported at great expense from the mystical Orient," are, even by present-day standards, magnificent. They have a roughness about them, like uncut jewels, that is both refreshing and spectacular. The starbursts are wild extravaganzas of color; the reds, blues, and greens are purer and brighter than I remember. The fireworks I have seen in recent years have a refined quality about them — like fast-food restaurants, they produce a bland and repetitive product.

A red flower has a silver center. A long arc of green stars

rains down from the bluff overlooking the Iowa River. There must be three thousand people standing beneath the silver-blue sky centered by a peach of a moon three-quarters full, hanging like part of a permanent backdrop. On the ground a fiery manifestation spells out BIG INNING as the crowd cheers. Colored stars burst and fall, leaving smoke-shaped stars in the night which are quickly blown away by a small, sweet breeze.

As a finale, the star-spangled banner explodes across the night sky, hangs for several seconds in awe-inspiring splendor.

Stan and I and Johnny Baron watch from a spot near the Twelve-Hour Church of Time Immemorial; waist-high corn glistens just yards away. As people are slowly preparing to leave, accepting that the day is at an end, there is the long whine of one more article of fireworks being shot skyward, and a burst of brilliant red stars fills the sky. It is in the shape of an Indian head, a war-bonnet-clad profile, with a single green eye bright as a jewel. The head fades, leaving behind its smoky ghost. There is a noise from deep within the cornfield. It sounds to me like a long, low chuckle.

The Big Inning Community Hall has been cleared and a three-piece band, consisting of a fiddler, a pianist, and a tall man with an accordion, is playing polkas and waltzes. The lamps have been dressed in pale blue coverings, and streamers of pale blue, some decorated with a glittering substance, crisscross the hall only a few feet above the heads of the dancers.

I sit and watch the crowd. I am an object of minor curiosity since I am easily recognizable as the All-Stars' mascot and because of the horn I carry. People introduce themselves, wish me, meaning the team, luck in the morning, most saying they will not be present for the continuation of the game.

Small boys stop by and ask to rub my head. I consider giving them a lecture on superstition, but it is easier to comply. I must look a sight — no sleep, my chin stubbly. I've managed only to wash my face and hands in an enamel washbasin full of cold, gray water.

At the first break in the music, the fiddler approaches and asks if I play the horn I'm clutching.

"A little," I say modestly, though I'm sure I saw him in the crowd at the ballfield.

"Would you care to join us for a few numbers?" he asks. "Our horn man, Luther Phillips, hoisted a jug of bad whiskey this afternoon. He's sleeping on the grass out back."

I wonder about changing history. Should I participate any more than I already have? I've resisted predicting history, so far. But it's tempting. The Democratic nominating convention is upcoming, has been mentioned several times over dinner and even here. I have volunteered that William Howard Taft will win but have refrained from insisting on it as fact.

"I'd be happy to join you, but only for a couple of numbers. There are some beautiful young women here." I smile as ingratiatingly as I know how.

"What would you like to play?" the fiddler asks.

"Do you know 'Cherry Pink and Apple Blossom White'?" I inquire.

"No, but start off. There's nothing we can't follow."

I'm sure "Cherry Pink and Apple Blossom White" won't be written for another forty years. Will it matter if I play it? Will it change history? If I change history, will it be for better or for worse?

The dusky-skinned young woman I met at the ice cream parlor is across the hall, almost hidden in a gaggle of schoolgirls. Her coloring, her bone structure, set me atingle. She wears an emerald-green, long-sleeved blouse closed at the neck by a cameo brooch.

I play it safe and launch into "Greensleeves." I know *that* has been around for a few years. I let my eyes wander across the hall. Does she know the song is for her? Are the other girls teasing her? Halfway through I stop and begin playing "Cherry Pink." The band is slow to pick up on what I am doing. The fiddler eventually joins in, though the pianist takes longer. The audience doesn't seem to mind and the floor is soon full of dancing couples.

I let the band lead me in a polka. I join in quickly and the hall shakes with the pounding feet of the dancers.

Another waltz. I tilt my horn and the music fills the bluey, romantically lit hall. I remember Sunny and the good times, our bed damp with our lovemaking.

"It's like blue light when you touch me," she'd say. "Electric blue light sparking between us." She'd cry softly into my shoulder, tears of passion, because she couldn't get close enough to me.

"Gideon Clarke, from Kansas City," the fiddler announces, and leads the applause for me as I retreat to my table.

At the next waltz, I seek out the girl who looks like Sunny. She smiles the same secret, knowing smile I've lived with for twelve years. My heart is flopping like a fresh-caught fish as I lead her to the dance floor.

I hold her close, closer than I imagine this society deems acceptable.

"Sunny," I say, half question, half statement.

"Yes, it was," she replies, and as I look down at her I see she is smiling, probably in embarrassment at my feeble attempt at conversation.

"Sunny is a name," I say. "You look like someone I know named Sunny."

"I'm Sarah. Should I be sorry? Was Sunny someone you liked very much?"

"Very much."

"Where is she now?"

"Lost."

"It must be very sad to lose someone you love."

"But not something we should be talking about on the Fourth of July. I'm Gideon Clarke."

"I know; I just heard. I'm Sarah Swan. My brother plays on the ball team."

"You were at the game, then?"

"I seldom miss one." She pulls herself back from me.

"I've never been a mascot before. I'm not an albino, you know."

"If you bring them good luck, it doesn't matter what you are."

"Thank you. I . . . I played the song for you. The . . . 'Greensleeves.' "

"I know."

"How did you know?"

But the music ends. I escort her back to her giggling friends. I try to decide if one of them is Marylyle McKitteridge.

Touching Sarah's hand, I feel desire for another woman for the first time since the night Sunny walked into the restaurant in Iowa City. I let myself visualize her in my arms, our bodies twined together.

It is a shock to realize I can feel this way about a woman other than Sunny. Perhaps crossing the barriers of time has freed me. There is certainly a reasonable chance that both Stan and I are here in the past forever.

Later in the evening, I dance with Sarah twice more. She is eighteen, helps her mother on the farm, wants to be a nurse.

I suggest we go for a walk.

"I can't; my brother is watching me. He keeps his eye on me."

I look across the hall to where the tall, gaunt Orville Swan is standing. He is indeed watching me. The baseball players have changed their shoes and taken off their caps, but they still wear their uniform blouses and pants. Orville Swan's straight black hair sticks up in a huge cowlick. His eyes are narrow, his face and neck windburned.

"Perhaps I could see you home after the dance?"

"Well . . . What kind of rig do you have?"

"Rig?"

"I live six miles south, near the Frank Pierce post office. It's much too far to walk."

"I'm afraid I hadn't thought of that. I'm a city boy."

She wrinkles her nose and squeezes my hand to let me know she is not offended by my stupidity.

I play another set with the band. But when it is time for "Good Night, Ladies," I stash my horn with the band's personal goods, slice across the dance floor, cut off a red-faced farm boy, and lead Sarah to the dance floor.

"Look, I'm not from around here, so how do I get to see you again? I don't want to offend you or your family or anybody."

"Tomorrow is Sunday," says Sarah. "You could come by the farm in the afternoon . . ."

"I'll be at the ball game."

"Oh, it will be over by then. The Cubs have to be back in Chicago."

"But if it isn't — "

"I'll know why you didn't show up."

The music ends. I picture walking with Sarah in the firefly-speckled darkness, kissing her . . . But my dream lasts only a few seconds because we are met at the door by Orville Swan, who, without a word, blocks my path and guides Sarah out into the night.

"See if I let him touch my head tomorrow," I say to Stan. I don't think Stan has danced once all evening.

"I was concentrating on my hitting," he says as we wait on

the wooden sidewalk for Johnny Baron. "I figure if I spend all my time concentrating I can squeeze a couple of extra hits out of myself. What if I beat the Cubs with a homer? They'd have to notice me."

"They'd notice, Stan."

Johnny appears and we walk the mile down a dirt road that has soft dust in the wheel ruts.

"We're gonna be tired in the morning," I say.

"I'll set the alarm for five A.M.," says Johnny.

The Barons' house is the same one I will occasionally make repairs on. It will be insulated, re-sided, painted, will have a basement slipped beneath it, but it is the very same house I will share, after my father's death, with John, Marylyle, and Missy. In fact, Stan and I are housed in *my* bedroom. There are twin bedsteads with blue-and-gray-striped mattresses. Mrs. Baron, Johnny's mother, gives us each two sheets from the linen closet at the end of the hall.

I am inclined to talk of the miracles that have befallen us this day, but Stan, like a tired child, is asleep the moment his head touches the pillow. I, on the other hand, am wide awake. I have that vaguely nauseated, overtired feeling lack of sleep brings on. My ankles are swollen from my being upright for so many hours. I keep blinking and shaking my head as if that act will clear my vision; all day I've seen forms, like shadows on a TV screen. I have seen the shadowy figure of a giant Indian, loping along the top of the hill behind center field. I have seen the face of a young woman, not exactly Sarah, not exactly Sunny . . .

I try to make my mind blank to let sleep come. But my nerve ends are raw. I soon have the top sheet twisted around me, the bottom one loose from the mattress. Half-dollar-sized mattress buttons pick at me as I squirm.

Finally, I get up, dress, and creep out of the house. The July night is soft and moist, almost tropical. Only the sky is unchanged. It is the same deep blue, sequined with silver, that I looked upon a day ago in 1978. The countryside has undergone many changes, some subtle, some more devastating, but the sky is changeless.

I breathe in the honeysuckle, pick a few plump, translucent berries, toss them like pebbles as I walk across a moonlit cornfield in the direction of the Catholic church, which must practically smell of new lumber.

As I near the church and the grove of trees that surrounds it, my eyes pick up a movement, no more than the wind pulsing a few silvery leaves, but something is not right. I approach the grove of trees; rough grasses, stiff-stemmed asters, caraway, pick at my pantlegs, their fragrances spicing the air. I skirt the edge until I'm sure I'm at the spot where I saw the movement. Recalling my one or two abortive attempts to make my high school football team in Onamata, I leap without warning into the tall undergrowth, arms foremost as if I'm tackling a fleeing runner.

A sapling stings my face, and no one is more surprised or frightened than I as I make solid contact with a crouching figure. I have grabbed bare flesh. My right hand holds solidly to a muscular upper arm as we both roll into the grasses.

"Eeeyuh!" says the party I have tackled. He rolls on me, crushing my face into his chest. He smells of campfires, leather, sweetgrass. What could have possessed me to behave so foolishly? The man is half again my size, and I am no fighter at the best of times. I expect to see a knife blade glint in the moonlight, feel searing pain, and watch my life bleed out of me.

He flips me over and pins my hands behind my back.

"Don't kill me. Don't kill me. I have a family, little children . . . I come in peace."

Oh, how could I have said that? All the lies the white man has told the Indian have begun with that phrase.

"Don't kill me," I say again. I have read accounts, from both Indian and white viewpoints, of how the soldiers were rubbed out at Little Big Horn. Not pleasant deaths. Not the kind I want to die.

"Be quiet. If I wished you dead, you would already be with your grandfathers."

"Are you Drifting Away?" I ask. Now it is his turn to register surprise. I cannot see his face, but I can feel his hand relax. He does not answer but he eases his grip, and when I force myself not to thrash and struggle he releases my hands and turns me on my side so he can get a look at what he has captured. He raises himself on one knee, allowing me to be turned onto my back.

"How do you come to know my name?" His voice is flat, emotionless.

"I saw you all day long, skulking around the edges of the crowd, peering around the corner of the church, peeking through the branches of the tree by the river."

He purses his lips, stares at me, the moon reflecting in his eyes.

"You believe in me?" he says.

"I know all about you." And I begin reciting from memory pages from my father's book about the Confederacy.

He listens attentively.

"My magic may be stronger than even I have thought possible," he says. "Perhaps we need to talk." With that, he jumps to his feet soundlessly. He takes my hand and pulls me to my feet. I feel lightheaded.

"Something is going to happen, isn't it?" I say. "You have some stake in the baseball game?"

"I have an interest in it," he says, his voice still toneless, his mouth almost curving but not quite.

"Is Johnson County your own private puppet theater?" I ask.

"*Puppet theater?* I believe I detect your meaning. To answer in terms with which you are familiar, yes, I tamper with the reality of Johnson County, Iowa."

"Why?"

"That I do not have to answer," he says and draws himself up until what I thought was nine feet in height appears to be twelve, maybe even fifteen. "I *am* the reality of Johnson County. I can take life or I can give it; I can make you gobble like a turkey —"

"Capricious as a bad-tempered child. Why?" How much of the Trickster is there in Drifting Away? The Trickster, mischievous primitive from assorted folklores, a being given to deceptive acts, sly deceits, terrible violence, often sexually outrageous acts.

When he does not answer but only stares coldly at me with his arms folded across his chest, I go on. "I knew you as a hero, a warrior defeated by treachery, overrun by time. Is this what you've come to? Threatening to make someone gobble like a turkey?"

"I am only telling you what I am capable of doing." It seems to me there is a trace of regret in his voice.

"Let me in on some of the secrets," I say. "Why me? Why my father? Why baseball?"

Drifting Away stares at the sky for a few seconds before replying.

"Baseball is the one single thing the white man has done right." He chuckles deep in his chest, a soft, soothing sound like a mother plumping a pillow.

"But baseball has solid lines, like so much of what the white man makes," I say to him, "and diamonds are close to squares."

"Think of the circles instead of the lines — the ball, the circumference of the bat, the outfield running to the circle of the horizon, the batter running around the bases. Baseball is as close to the circle of perfection as white men are allowed to approach."

"Are you taking revenge against baseball? That seems so narrow. If I had your powers, I'd devastate, I'd destroy, I'd bring down plagues and pestilence. I'd make the doom-sayers of the Old Testament smile with righteousness as all their prophecies were fulfilled."

"But think of how a cat teases and tortures a mouse," he replies. "If the cat snaps the little animal's neck with one flick of his paw, the revenge is very short-lived, but when it allows the wounded mouse the illusion of freedom, then snatches it away again and again . . . Swift retribution is not very satisfying."

"But why me?"

"My magic is small as a firefly."

"You're too modest. But baseball, I don't understand the connection."

"My power vision was of your game," says Drifting Away.

"Of baseball?"

He nods, his eyes bolted to mine.

"But what year? Only young men have power visions, so yours would have been long before there was baseball here. Long before the white man."

"True," he says.

"How could you know what to make of it?"

"It was a vision, a prophecy. Sometimes it is many moons, cycles, lifetimes, before a vision becomes a reality. A medicine man named Takes Many Hides saw the coming of the white man, saw the iron rivers with as many white men as fish in fresh water. In the time of Crazy Horse, another medicine man, named Drinks Water, saw the death of the Indian nation, saw Indians living in square buildings, staked out to one spot like hides drying in the sun, defying all the laws of nature, going against the hoop of the world, the roundness that is life. And those visions have all come to pass."

"How did your . . . power vision come about?"

"I was fifteen, already a man, a hunter, a warrior. Already I had chosen Onamata as my woman. Paid her father, Greasy Grass Man, dearly that she would be my bride. I decided to dream, to search for my power vision, for I felt I was someone special, that I was meant for important deeds. I fasted for eight days. Our medicine man told me eight was my number. I came far into the wilds, walking without food or weapons. I chose as my dreaming place the bluff overlooking the river, the high place where the baseball field now ends. I dipped my hands in the earth and powdered my face to show I come from earth and will return to it. There I sat cross-legged in the swaying grass for eight more days. And I dreamed. I carried only a bag of water, sipping only when I felt I would die without it.

"On the fourth or fifth day I had my vision. I remember a hawk circling so high in the sky he looked the size of a sparrow. And then there were more than one, the sky was speckled with a dozen brown hawks, scything the air, cutting a hole in the center of the sky so that they might take me there. As I dreamed in the summer sun, the hawks dove at me, one after another, straight for me, as if I were a mouse that would be their food. When they came close to me they didn't slow; their bodies were knives, long, sharply pointed, and they pierced me from the neck to the ankle with their sharpened beaks. And I lay back in the warm grass, feeling no pain, only a sweet desire for sleep.

"Then I was raised in the air by the hawks, impaled on their beaks; the flapping of their wings was close and furious. They carried me as if I was light as a cloud, up into the blue of the sky and through the hole they had cut. There they laid me down and pulled their beaks from me, and I sat up.

"The grandfathers were there, sitting in a circle looking down at the earth.

" 'Much will be expected of you,' a black-faced grandfather said to me. 'Your people have seen you drifting away to the top of the sky. They will want to share your wisdom when you return.'

"It was then that I knew my name would forever be Drifting Away. Until that time I had another name. But I can no longer speak it.

" 'Look down and see the earth as it will be,' a yellow-faced grandfather said to me. I looked and saw the land intact, but changed, covered with square gray boxes like stacks of bones."

The yellow-faced grandfather Drifting Away is speaking of must have been the grandfather of the south. I know enough of Indian legend to know the earth was quartered and a color associated with each quarter — black for west, yellow for south, white for north, red for east.

"But the land above the river, above the holy tree, was staked out with sacred markings, and men were stationed about like ants," Drifting Away continues. "Imagine watching your game from above, from the center of the sky.

" 'It *is* a very holy business,' I said to the grandfathers. 'But there are white men doing the ceremony. Will they learn our ways? Have we become one people with them?' I asked the stony-faced grandfathers.

" 'The vision is yours, my son,' said the grandfather of the north. 'What you do with it is for you to decide. We can only place the images in front of you. If you are wise you will understand what is required of you. We would not have chosen you if we did not think you wise.' And the old man spoke no more to me.

"I looked down at the land I loved, the sacred tree, the markings on the land. The ritual of the white men. I watched until I became dizzy because of the height. I felt weak and lay back on the top of the world and saw the hawks coming for me again. I was very tired and welcomed their sharp beaks into me. The hawks carried me down gently as a leaf falling on a windless day."

"I know a lot about you. Your history . . . your— "

"We were not to meet yet. *I* was to find *you*, not the other way. It is a bad omen."

"I have more questions — "

"Not now," says Drifting Away. He almost makes a farewell gesture, but instead he turns, moves sideways into the woods, and is gone.

9

I MUST HAVE HAD only about two hours' sleep when Johnny
Baron bangs at the door. Stan is up instantly, sitting on the
side of the bed, stretching his arms, flexing his muscles. Mine
has been *hard* sleep; I have slept with my body pushed into
the mattress, as if a huge weight held me in place. My eyes
have sand in them, my arms and legs are weighted, my throat
is dry.

"I bet I'm gonna get a hit today," says Stan, "maybe two.
What do you think, Gideon? If they start Brown again, he'll
be tired; I'm gonna go for him the first time up, swing for the
fences."

"You do that, Stan," I say, dashing cold water on my face
from the crockery bowl and pitcher by the side of my bed.

Johnny Baron has cooked slabs of bacon and has fried
potatoes in the grease. I force myself to eat a few bites, drink a
cup of strong coffee. Then we strike out on foot through the
dew-soaked grass, Johnny and Stan talking baseball, Stan
pounding his glove.

When we arrive, the eastern horizon looks as though it has
been insulated with pink cotton batting. The other players
from the Confederacy are arriving by foot and on horseback.
The sky becomes an expectant, robin's-egg blue.

The sound of a steam engine chugging ever closer fills the predawn air. The engine stops, then chugs off again. I wonder what strings Frank Chance pulled to have the train and the Baseball Spur made available to him this morning.

There is apparently no wagon waiting for the Cubs as there was yesterday. Eventually we hear the voices of men, short, staccato bursts like crows scrapping, and the Cubs appear, a ragged squad, carrying their equipment themselves.

There is no joy this early in the morning. I am reminded of my own college days, when on a morning a term paper was due I'd rise long before dawn and stand, stunned by sleep, in the bathroom, running hot water over my hands so my fingers would behave like fingers on the typewriter keys rather than like the large, paralyzed blobs that hung from my wrists.

It appears that the game is about to end in the first inning of the day, the top of the twenty-fifth. The Cubs immediately load the bases against a creaky O'Reilly, who does not appear to be rearing back and firing the ball the way he did yesterday.

A double down the right-field line — by Frank Chance, no less — scores three runs. Taking a walking lead off second, Chance taunts O'Reilly with vicious insults both personal and professional.

O'Reilly steps off the mound and walks toward second; he and Chance stand nose to nose and curse into each other's faces. An unshaven and less formally dressed Frank Luther Mott lets them go at it for a moment or two, then steps between them.

The game goes on. O'Reilly strands Chance at third. The Iowa Baseball Confederacy comes to bat for what appears to be the last time.

⊖

In present-day Iowa City, among the undulating hills and umbrella-like shade trees of Fairfield Cemetery, stands the Black Angel. Surpassed in height by only two or three extremely phallic granite obelisks thrusting skyward, the Angel, sweet-faced, with all-encompassing wings spread in benevolent protection, stands like a silent shadow over the lush green of the graveyard.

The citizens of Iowa City think they know the history of the Black Angel. Students in sociology, history, and women's studies regularly write papers, even master's theses, on the awesome monument. The Angel has her own folk history. She is alternately praised and blamed for changes in society. She has been blamed for changes in the weather; forecasters claim they can tell what the winter will be like by the shade of green corrosion on the Angel's extended wings. Some nearby residents claim to receive electrical impulses from the Angel, and everyone would like to connect a mysterious death or disappearance to the Angel, but even the rumors are vague.

The Angel has been blasted from a variety of bigoted pulpits for somehow influencing the morals of the young, for contributing to disrespect for elders, for increasing consumption of liquor, cigarettes, and marijuana, and for the supposed increase in sexual promiscuity, illegitimate births, and abortions. All claims are unsubstantiated.

The most prevalent folk tale is that if, one summer midnight, a young man kisses a virgin beneath the Black Angel's gaze, the statue will turn white. The statue has, however, remained black for over a half a century, which says something about either the veracity of the folk tale or the number of virgin women in and around Iowa City.

Other than the golden-domed Old Capitol building, there are few points of interest worth touting to tourists or new arrivals to Iowa City. I took Sunny to see the Black Angel, I suppose on only the second or third day we were together.

The day was warm, the air fragrant, and I was so much in love I could walk without touching the ground.

I told Sunny the legend; she laughed and threw herself into my arms, her mouth melting into mine.

"She hasn't changed a lick," I said, coming up for air, peering over Sunny's shoulder.

"What did you expect?" Sunny laughed. "I think your old Angel knows what she's about."

It was a Saturday afternoon and we were interrupted by a wedding party, complete with flashbulb-popping photographers. It is common practice in Iowa City for newlyweds to be photographed kissing beneath the Angel's dark wing.

We watched from a distance.

The recorded history of the Black Angel is that a woman, an immigrant from Czechoslovakia, grief-stricken at the death of her son, decided to build an unforgettable monument to him. The Angel was commissioned, and was created in Italy, out of black bronze, and shipped to Chicago, then somehow transported to Iowa City and erected so the benevolent wing of the Angel would shade the grave of the son, which has a small granite marker above it. The Czech woman was eventually laid to rest beneath the Angel. There are many stories about the Angel not being what the Czech woman expected, about the account being disputed; it is even suggested that the Angel was not always black but turned black because she was not paid for.

Of course, I know the true story of the Black Angel. My father knew the true story of the Black Angel and catalogued it in *A Short History of the Iowa Baseball Confederacy.*

After the murder of Onamata, Drifting Away went into a raging grief. He burned the tent made from albino buffalo hides. Destroyed all his possessions. The few that could not be eaten by fire he cast deep into the Iowa River. He carried the body of his beloved across the river, where in the placid summer mosquitoes and daddy longlegs balleted on the smooth, ice-green surface. A mile or two northwest of the fatal campsite, on the side of a gentle knoll, beneath the green canopy of a flutter-leaf cottonwood, Drifting Away buried his wife. Then, as the peach-and-silver moon brightened the night, Drifting Away chanted his sorrows to the sky. Sculpted by moonlight, glowing like a coin, his chant rose to the cloudless expanse of night. On a distant hilltop the dark shadow of a coyote was silhouetted, nose pointed skyward like a church steeple, as it answered Drifting Away's sorrow with its own howling chant.

On the spot where Onamata was buried, the Black Angel grew out of the earth, rising like a mushroom, pushing up, shedding the rich Iowa loam.

The Angel took the fall and winter to materialize, learning the feel of the bitter cold and hearing the tick of snowflakes against its own surface.

It was there when the scouts for the railroad rode through the next spring. They were not sure whether to scorn or worship it; in the end they chose to ignore it. It grew in the silence of the plains, was there when the first settlers gathered on the banks of the Iowa River, south of what is now Iowa City, created a settlement, then a town, called it Napoleon. The Angel was there when Iowa City was built along the river, became the state capital. When a cemetery was necessary, it seemed only logical to locate it next to the Black Angel, on the gently undulating land, fifteen minutes by wagon from downtown Iowa City. People were not as skeptical then, were more willing to accept unusual and unexplainable acts. The present history of the Black Angel is all post-1908, and therefore highly suspect.

After Onamata's burial, Drifting Away continued to grieve with a ferocity even his grandfathers had not anticipated. His

186

extravagant mourning poured out in such fury that the gentle Iowa River, which until then had stretched like a ribbon of jade across the plains, now changed its course, slithering snakelike through the buffalo grass to escape Drifting Away's wrath.

Eventually the grandfathers, tired of his furor, sent Coyote, the Echo of the animal kingdom, the touchstone of the prairie, to deliver him a message.

"The spirit of your beloved Onamata has fled to the four quarters of the earth," Coyote told him, speaking from deep within a grove of spruce, only an occasional glint of amber, telltale as a moonbeam, scratching an eye, betraying his location.

"One part of her spirit will remain close by. If you are patient, the other parts will eventually be reborn, return here, be reclaimed . . . and you will be united."

"When?" Drifting Away demanded.

"When all the parts of Onamata's spirit have been reclaimed by the grandfathers, she will be returned to you."

"That could take a lifetime," wailed Drifting Away.

"It could take several lifetimes. Amuse yourself in the meantime," said Coyote. "It is not often the grandfathers are so generous."

Drifting Away continued his keening, but with diminished fervor, for scarcely were Coyote's words uttered than deep in his chest Drifting Away felt the first warm embers of hope begin to smolder.

My father's belief was that the Angel was anchored to its spot by bronze roots that ran deep into the heart of the earth. He petitioned the Iowa City town council to let him do some exploratory digging around the base of the statue. Each time his request was presented, the council voted unanimously to reject it.

⊖

187

The game does not end in the twenty-fifth inning. Though the Cubs are only three outs away from victory, they manage to kick it away. The first Confederacy batter grounds out. But Orville Swan walks, and Harry Steinfeldt makes an error. Stan swings for the fences and very nearly reaches them, but Jimmy Slagle, the Cubs' center fielder, runs up the embankment, which this morning has no picnickers on it, and snares the ball, well over four hundred feet from home plate. The runners are able to advance a base. Bad News Galloway then lofts a fly to right center which should be caught, but neither Wildfire Schulte nor Jimmy Slagle can decide who should take it. The ball falls and, as if it has eyes, rolls fifty feet toward the horizon. Galloway and the other runners score. The game is tied.

They have played nine innings by eight A.M.

"What time are the Cubs supposed to catch their train for Chicago?" I ask Johnny between innings.

"Noon," he replies. "Surely the game will be over by then." But it isn't.

By noon the game is still tied. The Cubs have scored single runs in the thirty-sixth and fortieth innings, only to have the Confederacy come back each time and score.

As the fifty-first inning ends, Frank Luther Mott lifts his hands in the air. "Gentlemen, I suggest we adjourn for lunch."

Frank Chance scuffs dirt all the way from first base to the mound. "Keep the game going," he shouts.

"What about your train, Mr. Chance? I have been informed it is waiting for you at the station in Iowa City."

"Let it wait," says Chance, red-eyed and stubble-cheeked.

"What do you have to say, Mr. O'Reilly?"

"We can't stop now," says O'Reilly. "Let the game go on."

A crowd is beginning to gather in the stands.

A small boy in short pants arrives on the run, decides I look like someone he can talk to. I take his message to the captains and Mott, who are still bickering on the mound.

"The lunch problem is solved," I say. "The ladies of the Twelve-Hour Church of Time Immemorial have prepared sandwiches, coffee, and pie. It is ours for the asking."

"One hour only," says Chance.

"Fine with me," says O'Reilly.

It is at this point that Frank Chance makes an important decision. He sends all his reserve players back to Chicago.

"We have a league game to play tomorrow," he says. "If for any reason we don't get back in time, you and the fellows who didn't make the trip will give them a good game, I'm sure," and he pats the unused players on the back and sends them to the waiting wagon.

I have just seated myself at a picnic bench outside the church and begun chewing a roast beef sandwich and sipping coffee when a stout woman in a housedress approaches me.

"I heard you play your trumpet last night, and I was hoping you might join us in a hymn of praise — after you finish eating, of course."

"I'd be happy to. You seem to dwell on a couple of favorites of mine."

And I do join them. The stout woman waggles a tambourine and someone inside the church plays an unseen pump organ while I toot my horn. The women sing; some of them have very good voices. Some of the players mouth the words, but most remain silent and slightly suspicious of the music:

> "The Church of God is marching,
> I shall not be moved
> I shall not be moved
> I shall not be moved.

189

Like a tree
Planted by the water
I shall not be moved.

When my burden's heavy
I shall not be moved."

We move right on to "The Sword of the Lord and of Gideon."

"The only reason I've ever heard of that hymn is that my name is Gideon," I say to the stout lady, who, it turns out, is a Pulvermacher, a second or third cousin of Henry, the catcher. "How does your church come to be so fond of it?"

"Well, it is a biblical story," she says, as if that answers my question. "Gideon went into battle with a sword, a lamp, and a trumpet."

"I know *that*. But it's an obscure story, Gideon is an obscure character. Why all the interest?"

"Oh well . . . I'd have to get Elder Womple to explain it to you. 'I Shall Not Be Moved' is very significant, because this land wasn't ours originally. Elder Womple was out walking one afternoon, reading his Bible, when the book was plucked from his hands by an unseen source. Slammed the book on the ground, it did, and the book was petrified and rooted to the earth when Elder Womple tried to pick it up. 'We'll build our church on this spot,' he said, and we did, though the town of Big Inning, Johnson County, the state of Iowa, and I think even Washington, D.C., tried to keep us from doing it because this was 'river right of way' or some such foolish thing, and before that it was reservation land, but the government took it away after some ungrateful Indian massacred a bunch of white settlers on this spot."

In the distance, behind center field, a dark shadow skulks in the undergrowth, bent forward, arms and legs pumping.

"Of course, the Good Book was frozen open to the story of

Gideon," Mrs. Pulvermacher says, closing her lips tightly in a self-satisfied lock.

☺

Drifting Away cut like a knife through the silk-smooth water of the Iowa River. He made no sound as he emerged and slithered up the bank beneath the sacred tree.

The white men were camped beneath its branches, their campfire banked and smoldering. Ten men lay in their bedrolls about the camp. A sentry, rifle across his knee, his back to the river, stared into the firefly-peppered darkness.

This was the third night Drifting Away had visited their camp. He stood behind the trunk of the sacred tree and prayed to his grandfathers for success in his mission. He plunged his knife into the tree. When a few drops of sap appeared like tears in the wound, he caught them on the broad blade of his knife, then cut his thumb and mixed the blood and sap. He licked the mixture off the knife blade, crossed the clearing, and soundlessly cut the sentry's throat with one deft movement.

"Why didn't they hear them coming?" the search party repeated endlessly when they found their massacred friends. "All killed in their sleep. They all had guns handy, but not one reached for his weapon."

The air was rank with death. Drifting Away, not ten feet from the searchers, slipped into the placid water, smiling.

☺

They play thirty-four more innings between lunch and darkness, for a total of eighty-five. The scoring for July 5 looks like this:

Inning 25					40			
CHICAGO	300	000	000	001	000	100	000	000
IBC	300	000	000	001	000	100	000	000

	52			55				
CHICAGO	000	0	*Lunch*	00	000	000	000	000
IBC	000	0	*break*	00	000	000	000	000

	70						85	R	H	E
CHICAGO	000	100	000	000	000	000	0	11	?	?
IBC	000	100	000	000	000	000	0	11	?	?

We long ago ceased to keep a record of hits and errors. It is like a pickup game on a summer afternoon; everyone knows who bats after whom.

All afternoon I fidget on the bench, remembering Sarah's invitation to visit her at her home. I wonder if it will be like scenes I have encountered in books and movies. Will there be a wide verandah with a porch swing, perhaps a grandmother dozing in a wicker chair, and Sarah, beautiful and golden-eyed in an ankle-length dress, entertaining an assortment of beaus, farm boys with their heels hooked on the rungs of wooden chairs? How will I fit in? Or will I? But I am anxious to find out. I consider bolting and running. I could probably get away. But what if the Confederacy lost? They would blame me, and perhaps with good reason. Stan seems to believe in my effect as a good-luck talisman. He rubs my head before each turn at bat. Stan is keeping a scrupulous record of his average. He is hitting .333 as play ends.

Finally, I compromise. I stay, but I stretch out on the grass behind the bench, put my head on a spare glove, and sleep. The players grumble about my shirking my duty as bat boy; nevertheless, they let me doze. I scarcely stir as each batter rubs his fingers in my white, white hair.

The game should have ended in the eighty-fourth inning. With one out and Frank Chance on second, Three Finger Brown slapped a single through the box and over second. Dean, the Confederacy center fielder, charged the ball and made a remarkable throw to the plate. Chance slid and his foot crossed the plate just as the ball was hitting Henry Pulvermacher's glove. Pulvermacher put the tag on Chance's thigh and Frank Luther Mott, who was halfway between the pitcher's mound and home plate, gave the out signal.

Chance moved like lightning. He was face to face with Mott before the umpire moved a step. The Cubs all rushed from their bench and surrounded Mott and Chance. We had all leapt to our feet after the call, first in surprise, then in jubilation. Chance backed Mott toward second base, a step at a time, nose in his face, mouth rasping out obscenities like coal pouring from a scuttle.

But Mott remained silent, refused to be drawn into the confrontation, refused to become a part of it, and eventually Chance wound down. With his years of experience as a major leaguer, he knew exactly how far he could go with an umpire without being thrown out of the game. Mott, in spite of his lack of experience as an umpire, knew the limits, too. No obscenity was taboo as long as it was directed against fate and not the umpire.

The decision stood; the Cubs eventually retreated to the bench. O'Reilly struck out the next batter. The Confederacy went out in order at the bottom of the inning. The Cubs would, but for the bad call, have won. Chance knew it. We knew it. And I suspect Frank Luther Mott knew it.

When play ended, Chance and the Cubs returned to Iowa City, where Frank Chance got on the telephone, not to the executives of the Chicago Cubs, as might have been expected; he ignored a half-inch-high batch of telegrams from them. He called an old friend-enemy of his, stayed on the phone for over an hour, begged, pleaded, threatened, called in old debts, used the ransom of friendship, hung up with a half-smile on his sunburned face.

A small, brisk man caught the night train from Chicago to Iowa City. He was white-haired, might have been a banker, a cattle buyer, or a preacher. But he was none of those. Chance would pay for a cab to be waiting at the station the next morning, and the uncorruptible Bill Klem, the most honest umpire in the history of baseball, would arrive to take charge of the game.

⊖

On the night of Mott's bad call, as soon as we'd eaten I excused myself from Stan and Johnny.

"I have somewhere to go," I say.

"You be careful," says Johnny. "Calling on a girl on Sunday afternoon is one thing, but going courting in the evening is something else again."

"Gid, are you sure you know what you're doing?" asks Stan.

"As much as you do," I reply, smiling sardonically.

As I walk through the cooling evening, I think how amazing it is that one can adapt so quickly to what seems to be a wholly untenable situation.

I think I understand how people rally themselves to start over after a fire or tornado or flood. I suspect that even if I weren't dying with curiosity about the Confederacy, I would still allow myself to become their mascot, just to be close to the action, to be an insider, if an insignificant one.

It is after ten-thirty when I reach the Swan farm. An ample, unpainted farmhouse with a wide verandah across the front sits near the road. When I first see it, there is a light in an upstairs window; it goes out when I am about a quarter of a mile away. There seem to be lights, bouncing slowly as tumbleweeds, in the distant cornfield, but they must be reflections or foxfire.

I walk in the soft dust up the lane to the house. Fireflies rise and glow, twinkle and vanish in the humid warmth.

I try to guess which room is Sarah's. As I circle the house, somewhere in the distance a coyote yahoos in the darkness. I

194

try to visualize the floor plan of the house. It can't be too different from my own home back in Onamata. The room where the light went out would be the large upstairs bedroom, the parents'. I don't know how many other children there are. My guess is that Orville has the downstairs bedroom. I'll try the upstairs one at the rear.

I creep toward the back steps but am frozen where I stand by a deep growl. An old dog, his eyes glowing amber in the moonlight, lies head on paws on the back step.

I retreat around the corner. I pick up a few pebbles from the yard. I have never tossed a pebble at a window. Have never known anyone who has.

P-took goes the pebble against the glass; then it makes a small scuffling sound as it falls in the grasses below.

What if I've picked the wrong window? What if Orville Swan's sunburned face and shoelace-like black hair suddenly protrude from the window? It is not easy for me to be inconspicuous, even in the dark, for my white hair glows like radium in the moonlight.

P-took, p-took. I keep tossing pebbles, hitting the glass. Finally a face appears at the pane. I can't make out the features, but the person is wearing white. The window shuffles upward and the head emerges. It is Sarah.

I call her name.

"Gideon?" she says. "What are you doing here?"

"The game lasted until dark. I couldn't get here this afternoon, and I wanted to see you," I say in a stage whisper.

"You don't have to whisper — everyone's out working. Orville's sleeping. I'm making beds."

"Working?" I hold my arms open, beckoning for her to join me. She laughs lightly, covers her mouth with her hand. She withdraws, closing the window as she does.

I hear the back door creak, and Sarah appears around the corner of the house, her white dress billowing as if she is making an entrance. Behind her the old dog moves arthritically, a mangy chaperon.

"Let's walk," I whisper. And then I remember the time difference. How stupid of me. It is midmorning for Sarah and her family. What I saw in the field were horses at work, miner's lamps attached to their foreheads.

"I'm sorry," I say. "I just forgot about the time. I thought it was evening."

"Better this way," says Sarah. "Everyone else is in the fields. We have the place to ourselves. Ordinarily, I'm told, a girl's family are always under foot when beaus come courting."

As Sarah takes my hand, an image flashes before me, is snapped in marble in my brain, will be carried with me as long as I live. Sarah's wrist protruding from the long-sleeved gown. I feel so tender toward her, want more than anything to please her. I think of Drifting Away riding into the Arapaho village and seeing his love in front of the tepee made from albino hides.

Sarah is barefoot. We walk in the moonlight down the soft, dusty road until the house is only a shadow. The corn rustles sweetly. The night smells of earth and water. I hold tightly to her hand, try to let my feeling flow into her. I am struck dumb by the night, Sarah's presence, my confusion.

"Tell me about Kansas City," she whispers.

What have I told her so far? I can't remember. I have only the vaguest of ideas of what Kansas City was like in 1908.

"Have you ever been there?" I ask. To me my voice sounds full of cunning.

"I've never been anywhere but Iowa City. Do they have tall buildings there? And are the streets full of automobiles? And are there theaters that show only moving pictures?"

"Yes, all of those. Skyscrapers, buildings so tall you could stand in them and look down on the roof of the Jefferson Hotel in Iowa City and it would be like being in an airplane."

"A what?"

"A balloon, a hot-air balloon."

"Oh."

The lyrics of all the songs about Kansas City rampage through my thoughts. I'm so tempted to say, "Everything's up to date in Kansas City."

"Is that where your wife died?" asks Sarah, stopping and turning to face me.

I didn't realize she thought Sunny dead. *Lost* and *dead* have quite different connotations for me.

"Yes," I say finally.

"You loved her very much, didn't you?"

"I did."

I put my arm lightly on Sarah's shoulder and pull her toward me.

"You can't live in the past," she says logically, raising her face to be kissed.

⊖

Next morning, when I appear in the kitchen puffy-cheeked, I can see tears of rain on the window glass behind the lamplight.

"Guess we might as well go back to bed," I say. "There'll be no game today."

"Don't count on it," says Johnny.

"Can't play in the rain," I say.

"Best if we check in anyway, may be just a shower."

When we venture onto the front porch, it is apparent that it is raining steadily and seriously — not the downpour of a shower, but a steady drill of chill rain.

Johnny outfits us in slickers the color of flypaper, and we go outside. The walking is slippery, the sky low and toothachy.

"Won't be anyone there," I say. "This is about the only thing I can think of will get the Cubs back to Chicago; they're scheduled to play again this afternoon."

197

"It will take more than a little rain to stop this contest," says Stan, slogging along, head down.

We arrive at the ballfield, our heads soaking wet, water trickling down our necks. The other players for the Confederacy are arriving, some on horseback, some on foot, in the bleak predawn. At five-forty the train whistle blasts from the Baseball Spur, and five minutes later the Cubs arrive in a wagon, a piece of its canvas top flapping. The nine players and Frank Luther Mott sit stiff and shivering under the canvas.

The field is slightly elevated, the earth of the diamond reddish colored, sandy.

Chance and O'Reilly meet at home plate; water drips off their noses. Little Walter, the mean midget, a too large baseball cap covering his head, jumps up and down like a jester, splashing water with his tiny feet.

There is no disagreement; the game will go on. The players of the Confederacy take the field, stiffly toss the ball about. O'Reilly must have communicated with the other players, for all the reserves for the Confederacy have stayed home, except Bob Grady, the man Stan replaced in right field.

They play an inning. The infield is in close, the ball soft as a tomato. Johnny Baron hits what should be a grounder, but it dies when it is even with the pitcher's mound, and the third baseman, playing in, is able to throw him out easily.

In the bottom of the second inning of the day, a horse-drawn cab arrives from Iowa City. It is a hand-crafted affair like something out of a French novel, black-enameled wood, rocking like a baby buggy on huge, black springs. Except for being larger, it looks like one of the Amish carriages that still bounce along the highway right-of-ways west and south of Iowa City.

The door of the carriage opens and umpire Bill Klem emerges, wiry, red-complexioned, drill-eyed. Time is called. Chance comes over and shakes his hand, something I suspect

198

he does not do often. Klem is introduced to O'Reilly and Mott. He steps to one side and confers with Mott for a moment, the rain staining his blue suit. Then Klem moves in behind the catcher and, kicking the muddy soil, makes a place for his right foot. Mott ambles off to first base, where, it is agreed, he will act as base umpire.

"Play ball!" shouts Bill Klem, as the wind drenches us all with a new wall of water.

Klem is the feistiest, most diligent and honest, no-nonsense umpire ever to call a game. Klem *is* authority.

"How long will you let the game go on?" calls a dapper, white-haired reporter, the only representative of the press present today, during a break in the action.

"The game shall continue until one team wins, or until the captains agree to call it off."

"But you have the authority to terminate the game," cries the reporter. "You see what's happened; the Cubs have already lost a game because their first-string players are tied up here. You yourself were due to umpire in Chicago last night."

"The game shall continue until it is resolved," says Klem.

"But why?" asks the reporter.

"Sir," says Klem, drawing himself up until he is as tall as the reporter, who is not very tall. "I need not justify my decisions, any more than I need justify a call of ball or strike, safe or out. The game will continue because I believe that it should."

It always seems to take about two hours to play nine innings. Twenty-seven innings by noon. An hour break for lunch. Twenty-seven more innings by seven P.M., plus whatever can be squeezed in before darkness.

The rain does not seem either to speed up or to slow down the game. The ball is deader than usual. The infielders play in close, as if they were playing softball. The outfielders are barely recognizable as such. They play so shallow they could be mistaken for roving shortstops in the present-day major leagues.

There is no urgency to the game. Even in the pouring rain, there is the same easy lethargy of a sunstruck afternoon where bodies are bathed in sweat rather than rainwater.

"There is more than a contest of wills going on," I say to Stan as the Confederacy bats in the ninetieth inning. "No one can pitch for ninety innings, three consecutive days — there's something terribly wrong here. They're both pitching like it's the third inning; O'Reilly's curve is a joy, Brown's fast ball still rocks his catcher back on his heels."

"All I know is, it's great baseball," says Stan, shaking water off like a dog. "I've never played in this kind of competition. And I can keep up. I'm still hitting over .300. Lots of the Cubs aren't doing that."

Baseball is the only thing on the minds of these men. Those who marched to the Crusades had less dedication. But I seem to be the only one interested in what is really going on here. What, I wonder, are the real stakes of the game?

The headline on the *Iowa City Citizen* of July 6, 1908, is:

5000 ATTEND GAME

NO WINNER DECLARED

Baseball Challenge Continues

The truth at last. I remember what the July 6, 1908, newspaper at the university library in Iowa City says. Not a mention of the game. Not a word. Not a whisper. An ad for Hohenschuh Undertaking and, against all the odds of journalistic endeavor, a story about a man bitten by a dog:

Bitten by Angry Dog

George Dutcher Injured Yesterday While Parting Fighting Dogs

And in a column headed THE CITY:

> The stork visited at the Charles Dautremont
> home near St. Mary's schoolhouse, and left boy
> No. 3 in their care.

More reporting on the baseball game in today's paper, the
real paper:

> The game, scheduled as a double-header for
> Saturday only, was suspended at dusk on July 5,
> with the score still tied after eighty-five innings
> of play. A truly superhuman effort was extended
> by both teams. The starting pitchers, Three Fin-
> ger Brown for the Cubs and Arsenic O'Reilly for
> the Confederacy, were still flinging the ball
> when darkness forced suspension of the contest.
>
> We regret that no box score was kept after the
> seventeenth inning.

10

THE GAME SLOGS ON. The rain eases, the sky is close, thick as gray wool. A half-dozen fans sit under a dripping tarp. By midafternoon the teams pass the hundred-inning mark. The Cubs score a single run in the ninety-second and again in the ninety-ninth, but each time the Confederacy ties it.

Bill Klem insists on the lunch break after inning 111.

I wish I had my *Baseball Encyclopedia* with me. I believe the longest game in major-league history was a twenty-six-inning tie involving the Cubs, in — was it 1902?

By late afternoon the rain intensifies as black clouds sail in beneath the solid flannel sky and drench us all. Even Bill Klem is inclined to suspend the game temporarily. He calls the managers together for a conference. Rain strafes the field, hitting the earth and bouncing knee high. Chance appears unable to yell with his usual vehemence. Just when he and O'Reilly seem ready for a brief postponement, the rain eases as abruptly as it began. A moment later it is only misting, and the game resumes.

At supper everyone squishes off to the church hall, where a hot meal awaits.

The minister of the Twelve-Hour Church of Time Immemorial, Elder Womple, is a lanky, black-suited man with an equine face. Except when eating, he keeps his big, brown hands interlaced at waist level.

I am delighted to see that Sarah is there, a frilly calico apron making her look like exactly what she is, a beautiful girl in 1908.

"Oh, Gideon," she says as she plops a huge plate of meat and potatoes in front of me. "You look like a little boy who's been making mud pies and wiping his hands in his hair."

I suppose what she says is true. All morning the wet and mud-splattered players have touched my head for luck as their turn at bat approached. I can't see that I've brought them any luck, but I suppose it is luck that the Confederacy has not yet lost, that each time the Cubs score, the Confederacy comes back to tie the game.

Elder Womple begins what turns out to be an endless blessing of the food, congregation, and ballplayers, the town, district, county, and state, and the continent, world, and universe. Sarah stands behind my chair; her fingers, resting lightly on my right shoulder blade, slowly radiate heat.

"Uncle Tommy does go on," Sarah whispers when he finally allows us to begin eating. "No one ever burns his mouth on the food when Uncle Tommy's around to give the blessing."

After the meal, Elder Womple exchanges a few words, a very few words, with Frank Chance, then descends on me. My white hair seems to draw people to me. I must appear to Elder Womple to be the most susceptible to proselytizing among the bedraggled assembly.

"I understand you're a newspaperman?" he says to open the conversation.

"That's what people say."

"Kansas City's a fine God-fearing city, I'm told."

"Well, you know what they say, Jesse James was a regular churchgoer in Kansas City. I've always thought there was a clear message there."

"Indeed." Elder Womple cannot be certain that I am being facetious. "What church do you call home, Brother Gideon?"

"To tell the truth, I've never found the time to develop an affiliation."

"It's never too late to affiliate with the Lord, Brother Gideon. In fact, it would be very wise for you to consider the possibility, since I hear you've shown more than a passing interest in my niece. Our own ties to the church are very strong . . . if you know what I mean?"

"I know what you mean." And I try to smile with what I hope will be interpreted as naiveté.

"You are a believer, of course?"

"Of course; I have a strong reverence for the supernatural."

Elder Womple clears his throat uncomfortably. "That's not exactly how I —"

"Sarah has invited me to Wednesday Prayers," I say, loud enough for Sarah to hear, "your evening . . . you know what I mean. I'll be here."

"We'll look forward to seeing you again."

"Aren't we keeping you up? I mean, isn't noon really midnight, your time?"

"We never let sleep interfere with the Lord's work," says Elder Womple. "We manage. We sense that something of great significance is about to happen. The very air is charged with the Spirit."

Frank Chance shovels the last of the food into his mouth and slams his fork down on the wooden table.

"Let's get on with the game," he shouts, standing up.

"The Spirit," repeats Elder Womple.

☉

Day Three ends after the 145th inning with the game still tied. The Cubs retreat to Iowa City, the Confederacy players to their homes.

The next morning the Cubs arrive, not on the train, but in two large, gray-timbered wagons, each covered with a new tarpaulin.

Bill Klem has been housed at the home of Frank Luther Mott in Iowa City. This morning they arrive in Mr. Mott's Ford touring car.

All day, telegrams fly between Chicago and Big Inning. Rumors are going around that the game will be called at any moment because the Cubs have been ordered to return to Chicago.

Curiosity gets the best of O'Reilly and he sends me to the Big Inning telegraph office to inquire. I meet Little Walter toddling out, a sheaf of yellow telegrams clutched in his child-sized hand.

The telegrams to Frank Chance from the Cubs' owners say essentially the same thing but with increasing degrees of harshness: he is to return to Chicago immediately along with the other eight starting players. Some of the telegrams are so lengthy they take two sheets of paper.

Chance has sent only two wires, both less than ten words. The first read:

WILL STAY UNTIL GAME DECIDED STOP
CHANCE

The second was dispatched by Little Walter just before I arrived at the telegraph office, and was in reply to a threat by the Cub ownership to send police to return the truant ball-players:

WILL STAY UNTIL GAME DECIDED STOP DO YOUR WORST STOP
CHANCE

☺

Today the *Iowa City Citizen* displays, as it should, a banner headline: GAME CONTINUES IN RAIN. I remember the hundreds of issues my father and I perused at the University of Iowa Library with never a word about the game or the Confederacy.

ONLY 17 MARRIAGE LICENSES ISSUED IN JOHNSON COUNTY IN JUNE

THREE DROWN AT LAKE MUSCATINE

THE VICTIMS WERE: MAUDE GARNES,
ESTHER CROZEN,
CLYDE SLATER

Willner's was selling straw hats from 50¢ to $7.50, including "Merry Widows" and "Anti-Headache."

Classified ads cost one cent per word.

Deep in the night, after I have returned from again seeing Sarah, from almost making love with Sarah, the odors of her still clinging to me, the taste of her still on my lips, I am awakened from a hard sleep by a hand gripping my shoulder.

I pull my face from the pillow I have crushed to me. A scythe of moon bleeds across the floor and bedclothes. Above me, hunched like a monstrous spider, is Drifting Away.

"What? What do you want?"

"Stay away from the girl," he says in his booming monotone.

On the other bed Stan turns over, twisting the covers about him like a winding sheet.

"Shhh," I say. "You'll wake —" and I nod toward Stan.

"No one wakes unless I wish them to," he says at the same volume. Drifting Away's eyes glint like knives in the blue-black darkness.

"What do you care about Sarah? Why can't I see her?"

"Because I'll kill you if you don't stop," says Drifting Away, staring down at me, his huge hand burning my shoulder.

"But surely you had something to do with bringing me here," I whine, my voice much higher than I wish it to be.

"You slipped past Time," he booms. "I thought you might be a friend. But you are white. Sent to make me suffer." Across the room Stan spins in his bed, coughing, mumbling.

"At least tell me why you care."

"Stay away from her. I have killed before."

"Wait a minute," I say, sitting up, pushing his hand from my shoulder. "What would you have done if Onamata's father, Greasy Grass Man, had rejected you as a suitor, threatened you?"

"I'd have claimed her anyway. Killed if I had to," he says without hesitation.

"Then you have my answer. I feel about Sarah as you felt about Onamata."

I can't imagine why I display such bravado. It has nothing to do with courage, only compulsive honesty.

Drifting Away stands and glowers down at me.

"You are from outside Time," he says. "You and the girl together is unthinkable."

"But we haven't —"

"You will, if you go back to her. You have been warned."

He slips out the door without a sound. A few seconds later I imagine I hear the screen door close with a bump. I lie wide-eyed in the moonlight. Time passes. Stan continues to toss restlessly. I feel like a card in a deck that is being constantly shuffled. What is happening does not make sense. I get up and stare out at the silvered farm yard beyond the window. Everything is peaceful. Did it happen? Or did I dream it?

☻

They play sixty more innings on July 7. Sixty-four more on July 8. The rain continues, a steady, sincere, no-nonsense rainfall. The trees drip, the players drip, and the Iowa River rises an inch or two, its surface turning from turquoise to light brown, eddies swirling like tops beneath the large, mysterious tree. I do not stay away from Sarah.

On Day Six, the game is like a movie seen at fast-forward speed. The first batter hits the first pitch. Every batter hits the first pitch. The game speeds along like a fast freight.

They have played fifty innings by midmorning, a hundred and twelve by suppertime.

"Do you see what's happening?" I ask Stan, as play resumes after supper.

"Of course I see. Do you think I'm stupid?" he snaps. "One pitch to every batter. No foul balls. Every hit in play."

"Take a pitch the next time you're up," I say. "Break the cycle."

"I can't."

"Can't?"

"Won't. Damn it, Gid, the ball's there to be hit. I've got to hit it."

"Take a pitch."

"No." Stan breathes deeply. There is pain and incomprehension in his expression.

I make the same suggestion to other players. They ignore me. When Bill Klem calls the game for the night, a hundred and twenty-two innings have been played.

☙

The night before, or to Sarah the day before, I dutifully appeared at the Swans' farm. The rain had stopped almost as Bill Klem raised his arms to signal the end of play, so I'd had a dry walk there. Sarah was expecting me and came to the screen door when the old cinnamon-colored dog growled deep in his throat.

"I have to gather the eggs," she said. She produced a round wooden basket from the porch and carried it in the crook of her arm. She was wearing a long-sleeved, ankle-length dress with a paisley pattern of gold on indigo. I was dying for her touch. I pushed my face close to her neck as we walked. She giggled. She was carrying a small coal-oil lamp. Almost a toy.

The henhouse was a low, sod-roofed log building, windowless, claustrophobic. There was a double-decked row of nests inside the low chicken-wire door. I had to move carefully, stooped as if my back was broken. The smell was one of foulness tinged with ammonia.

Sarah had the basket on her left arm, the tiny lamp, which turned the oil the color of red vinegar, in her left hand. She reached under the sleeping hens and, as they clucked and scuffled, pulled out brown eggs and deposited them in the basket.

"I see your hens don't follow your religion."

"Don't blaspheme."

"I'm only making an observation. Didn't the donkeys kneel in prayer? Camels knelt down to pass through the eye of the needle. It seems to me your hens should be out filling their little craws with gravel, eating mosquitoes, working hard in the sight of the Lord, like their masters."

"You're making fun of us."

"No. Although I do have a facetious side, I need to be convinced. I know just enough about religion to be dangerous."

"Uncle Tommy has his eye on you," Sarah said. "He feels there may truly be something magical about you." She stopped, waiting for a reply, looking at me over her shoulder in the eerie red light as she plundered another nest.

"I get enough attention from the baseball players," I said. "If I had any magic about me, don't you think I'd have brought the Confederacy enough luck to end the game? Sitting in rotting clothes on a wet bench for twelve hours every

209

day, having my hair tousled by a bunch of superstitious farm boys, isn't my idea of fun."

"Reach up top there and get the eggs," said Sarah, pointing to the top row of nests. "I have to stretch too far." She was on tiptoes, her slender fingers just reaching into the mouth of the nest, beyond the whitewashed boards where a stubble of straw and the head of an orange-eyed hen protruded.

I moved my hand forward, then, feeling as if worms were wiggling from the palm of my hand toward my elbow, withdrew. I couldn't bring myself to put a hand into whatever might be under the complaining hen.

"I'm not a farm boy," I said lamely.

"Oh, honestly," said Sarah, exasperated. "Boost me, then. I usually bring along a bucket to stand on."

I gripped her hips and lifted her a few inches. Her hand swept under the hen and extracted a brown egg. Her lightness surprised me; it was like holding only her clothes.

"Either put me down or move me over. There are other nests."

"I like holding you," I said. I moved sideways down the row of nests, Sarah searching each one, until we were at the low door. We exited and, setting the basket and red-wine lamp on the ground, Sarah clasped her hands behind my neck and kissed me long and sweet. The little lamp glowed like something otherworldly. Later, we sat in the humid darkness on a many-pillowed porch swing, Sarah leaning back, her legs across my lap. Between kisses she kept bringing the conversation back to the Twelve-Hour Church.

"While Uncle Tommy doesn't necessarily trust you," Sarah whispered, "he feels you have a kinship with us. That there is something about you and time . . ."

"Very intuitive of him."

"Is there something about you and time?"

"Yes."

"Is that all you have to say?"

"I don't think I should say any more."

"Are you a prophet?"

I laughed aloud. "Hardly."

"This is serious. Uncle Tommy and some of the other elders think you may be a reincarnation of Gideon."

"I don't believe. I'm areligious . . . anti-religious."

"A nonbeliever can be called."

"For what?"

"We're not sure."

"Do you like to kiss and be kissed?" I ask.

"Very much."

"Does *that* need to be analyzed or explained?"

"No. That's inst—"

I kissed her and her lips parted, her tongue aflutter against mine. "Neither do I," I said between kisses. I cupped a breast and she kissed me harder.

"Follow me," Sarah whispered, pulling me toward the darkened interior. "We'll have to be very quiet. Orville's a sound sleeper, but —"

"I'll walk as if my life depends on it," I said.

☺

Day Eight. Cutting the grass. Frank Hall, in a yellow slicker, lurks like an expectant father, wary, hand-wringing, suffering with his field, as the rain softens it day by day and the players with Clydesdale-like intensity bruise the grass and desecrate the infield. There would be no game if it weren't for Frank Hall. Any other baseball field would be nothing but a quagmire by now. He has contoured the field. "Intuitive drainage" is how Frank Chance, in one of his rare good moods, described it. "A corps of engineers couldn't have done better."

Today, while the game goes on in a sifting mist that falls in layers like wet mosquito netting, Frank Hall appears at the right-field foul line, his two glistening black horses hitched to his mower. The sickle bar stands raised, the edges of each section honed silver, the blades blue, the bar so erect it might be holding a torch.

He hollers something to Wildfire Schulte, the Cub right fielder, then he releases a lever and the cutting arm is lowered in well-greased silence until it is within snipping distance of the earth. I can tell by the way he moves his head that he is clucking to the horses. They stride forward and the mower snicks along, shaving the earth; the horses' hoofs splash and the mower occasionally razors the water, sending up a fine, aquamarine spray.

The game goes on. The horses drift back and forth across the outfield, the fielders moving deferentially forward or back to accommodate the cutter.

Frank Hall waits until lunch to cut the infield grass. The team of horses turns in tight circles; the long tracks of the mower take many minutes to fade from sight. When he is finished, white-headed clovers lie like marbles in the rainwater.

Later in the day there is a cloudburst to celebrate the 500th inning of play.

▽

Day Nine. The *Des Moines Register* reports that it is raining in Johnson County only.

From the *Iowa City Citizen*, July 12, 1908:

BAD PLAY BY MATHEWSON

NEW YORK PITCHER DISAPPEARS TO GET IN
CHECKER GAME AT PITTSBURGH AROUSING IRE OF
MCGRAW

Pittsburgh, Pa., July 12 — Christy Mathewson, star twirler of the Giants' staff, was mysteriously missing many hours last night, and not until early this morning did he show up at his hotel.

McGraw was mad as a wet hen. Mathewson was scheduled to pitch one of the games in a double-header tomorrow, and McGraw wanted him to be in good condition.

No sooner was Mathewson in town than members of the checker club took him in charge and the star player spent most of last night at the game in the checker clubhouse in lower Allegheny. McGraw declares it is a scheme to make Mathewson ineffective against the Pirates, which the checker players indignantly deny. They think Mathewson is ruining his checker game by playing baseball.

Day Ten. Bewitched is the only word I can use to describe the players. They play on cheerfully under the cement skies, on an infield slippery as a greased cookie sheet, on an outfield spongy as a swamp.

"I expect a gator to reach up and lop off a leg one of these times," says Wildfire Schulte, but he says it not with trepidation or anger or even disgust, but with a grin a mile wide.

Stan is on first base when Johnny Baron lashes a ball toward the hole. It should be a single, but somehow Joe Tinker anticipates the play. I remember my dad saying, passing on secondhand information, "It was said Joe Tinker could read the angle of the bat as if it were a billboard with ten-foot-high letters." And that is exactly what he appears to be doing today. He knows, before Johnny Baron swings, where the ball will go if he beats it on the ground, and Tinker cheats several feet in that direction.

Tinker skids across the greasy infield; the ball pops like a pea into his glove, and moving like a ballet dancer he tosses the ball to an empty second base, knowing, trusting, Evers to be there. Evers is identical in height to Tinker but fifty pounds lighter. He is sometimes called The Crab, and though he's just short of his twenty-seventh birthday, he's gangly and skinny enough to pass for a teenager. In fact, he looks younger than Johnny Baron.

Stan, taking advantage of the slick base paths, begins his slide far short of second; his big body picks up speed on the lubricated earth, and from Evers's point of view Stan must look like a train as he bears down on the spindly second baseman.

But Evers's foot brushes the bag softly, like a bird landing on a bush without disturbing the foliage, and, launching himself in the air, Evers fires to first while hurtling over Stan's whooshing bulk.

"It's a pleasure to be done in by the best," says Stan, back on the bench. He looks as though he has spent the past several days digging ditches. "Did you ever dream we'd get to see Tinker-to-Evers-to-Chance in action? That I'd get to play against them? I'm playin' in the Bigs, Gid. I mean, it's the same thing, isn't it? I'm playin' against the Cubs. This is the Bigs, man!" He clasps me roughly on the shoulder with a muddy hand.

"I'm glad for you, Stan. I always knew you could do it."

"Gid, this is crazy, isn't it? Us playin' in this downpour?"

"Well . . ."

"But you know something, it doesn't seem any more unusual to me than playin' in a drizzle in some minor-league town."

"I understand."

"But what about you, buddy? Should you get mixed up with that girl? Don't get me wrong, it's just that when the game is over we're goin' back, aren't we?"

"I don't know, Stan. But it's sure something to think about, for both of us."

⊖

Day Eleven. It is during the 650th inning that the band arrives. My first thought is that they are from the Salvation Army, for they are wearing garish uniforms of a vaguely military cut. Johnny Baron mentioned a few days ago that the Salvation Army is in Iowa City, a Major Bushnell commanding a small mission in a failed bakery on South Capitol Street, near the railroad tracks.

For the past three days the game has slogged on with no spectators at all, the bleachers sitting empty and rain-washed under the close gray sky.

There are four members of the band, three men and a woman, playing a drum, fife, accordion, and tambourine. They congregate behind home plate, slightly to the right, near the corner of the first-base bleacher. At a signal from the leader, who is a corpulent, gray-haired man with a wine-red military cap that is held up by his large ears, they break into "The Battle Hymn of the Republic."

The resonance of the music is disconcerting, for there has been little sound the past several days, save the steady pelting of the rain, the crack of the bat, the occasional cawing of an outfielder shouting words of encouragement.

"I feel like I should be standing at attention," whispers Stan, who has been spelled in the outfield by Bob Grady.

The news from Chicago is that the Cubs have lost five games in a row and are fading toward the second division. There is a rumor that President Teddy Roosevelt has been asked to send troops to Big Inning to return the delinquent Cub players to Chicago.

The music soars. The four band members sing out in rous-

215

ing praise of their religion; their faces, turned skyward, are washed by the rain. They play music all afternoon and evening. When we go for supper, they break to eat sandwiches from a brown wicker basket, even though Elder Womple makes a special excursion to the baseball field to invite them to the church for supper.

"Who are they?" one of the ballplayers asks Elder Womple after the preacher has finished a long benediction.

"The Lord works in mysterious ways," replies Elder Womple, looking not at the questioner but at me.

When the game is called for the night, the quartet brings forward a creaking wagon, its box covered in pale canvas drooped by rain, and parks it near where the players for both teams now camp. The umpires are the only ones who commute anymore. Johnny, Stan, and I share a wagon donated by Johnny's family; it is crammed with homemade patchwork quilts and down comforters.

This night the rain has not stopped; it tattoos steadily on the canvas above us, increases in intensity, then lets loose a solid wash of water that forces the canvas down closer to us. Then it eases again to a rhythmic tapping.

Stan coughs wetly.

"How are you feeling?"

"Great. We're gonna win tomorrow. I can feel it."

He coughs again, harder.

"If you don't die of pneumonia first. How would you feel if a semipro team asked you to play under these conditions?"

"This is different. We've got a cause."

"We have?"

"Geez, Gideon, don't you see? If we — the Confederacy — beat the Cubs, we're all gonna be famous. The big-league teams will be courting us. This is my ticket to the Bigs."

"Stan, there's this matter of time . . ."

"Speaking of which, you must be doing all right for yourself — this is the first night you've been back before dawn. Don't *you* worry about time?"

"Yes, dammit, I worry about time. I'm so close to finding everything I never had — the real story of the Confederacy, and . . . someone to love who loves me back — that I don't think about much else. Can I stay here? Can I take Sarah back?"

"Well, I'm finding everything I never had, too. I want to play in the Bigs. You know how much I want that. Chance has been watching me. Little Walter says he's thinking about making me an offer to change teams. But . . ." He pauses for a long time as thunder rolls and lightning turns the air silver. "I've got Gloria back on the other side." Another long pause. "It's never the right time, is it, Gid?"

☉

Day Twelve. The rain continues. The ball diamond being on high ground is all that enables the game to carry on.

Behind the Cubs' bench, under the empty bleacher, Little Walter has built a small fire inside a tiny circle of stones, and over a makeshift grill he dries out baseballs. There are only about a dozen balls available, and after each one comes in contact with the mud of the infield or the water of the outfield, it is tossed to the midget, who sees it smoked and toasted until he considers it suitable to pass back to Bill Klem.

On nights when it clears off, the sky is a hard ocean-blue, sequined by stars. But by dawn it is raining again, sometimes little more than mist, sometimes a drilling, jackhammer rain, chilling us all to the bone.

The Iowa River is rising daily. Its surface ripples with tides, currents, undertows, as its speed increases. Its color has changed to the drab hue of a dusty road. There are reports of slight flooding on lowlands both north and south of Big Inning. Here, the water is lapping at the riverbank, teasing the roots of the holy tree near the Twelve-Hour Church of Time Immemorial.

The mysterious uniformed band continues to play — hymns, military music, and, strangely, "The Band Played On." The Cubs' third baseman Battleaxe Steinfeldt, who is a passable tenor, can be heard from his spot at third or from the Cub bench, singing, "And Casey would waltz with the strawberry blonde, and the band played on."

The twelfth day came to an end in the 753rd inning. It was also the day that a few spectators returned. A half-dozen raincoated and rubber-hatted fans appeared as though drawn by the music of the bizarre quartet.

July 15, 1908, from the *Iowa City Citizen:*

Iowa City Mayor Returns

MAYOR W. G. BALL RETURNED YESTERDAY FROM
SPIRIT LAKE WHERE HE SPENT THE PAST WEEK IN
THE KNIGHT TEMPLAR ENCAMPMENT

☺

When I am on the way to Sarah's, Drifting Away steps silently out of the roadside trees, blocking my path. My heart thrums in my throat, though I am not as afraid as perhaps I should be. My feeling is that if it is unthinkable for Sarah and me to make love, then it must be equally taboo to kill someone from outside Time. Yet Sarah and I *have* made love . . .

"You are a most ungrateful guest," says Drifting Away.

I've wanted to tell Sarah about Drifting Away but have been unable to find the words. I wonder if she'd believe me if I said, "There's a three-hundred-year-old Indian about fifteen feet high who threatens to kill me if I don't stop seeing you."

"Whose guest?" I fire back. "Why have I been brought here?"

"To fulfill your fondest wish. Why else?"

"My wish?"

"To see in person what happens to your baseball league. You and the girl should never have met."

"Sarah is important to me."

"Then you have learned one thing — that accomplishing your heart's desire is not all as wonderful as you expected."

I eye him balefully. "There is a saying where I come from: 'Anticipation is always nine tenths of the actual event.'"

He studies me like a teacher trying to decide how to discipline an unruly student. I don't like this feeling of being out of control, though when I stop to think about it I wonder how much I have ever been in control of my life.

"I want to know something," I say, hoping to distract him. "When the settlers threatened you, why didn't you leave? There was enough wilderness left to last you a lifetime. You must have known deep down that to resist was folly."

"The tree," says Drifting Away. "The tree by the river, the one the white people parade around. 'Its arms are the arms of Mother Earth,' said Grinning Bear, an old and wise medicine man, who was the first to realize its holiness. Grinning Bear spent a month without food, dreaming beneath its benevolent arms. I had built our tepee beside the tree; I would not be moved.

"Let me tell you about our holy trees. Usually we chose a sacred tree, cut it down and trimmed it, thanked it for giving up its life, worshiped it, performed our dances in front of it, made sacrifices to it, and finally burned it, returning its ashes to the earth near its stump. The cycle again, the roundness of life.

" 'This tree is too holy to cut,' Grinning Bear declared. 'It must be worshiped where it stands. Here we shall live, put down roots like this tree.'"

To a people who had never seen one like it, the tree must indeed have been impressive. It is a banyan-like tree, perhaps just a hearty weeping willow, but with a trunk that must be fifteen feet in diameter. I don't know enough mathematics to calculate the circumference. It is perhaps thirty feet tall, shaped like an umbrella with many long limbs lifted skyward, but heavy limbs, themselves as thick as ordinary tree trunks. And from each limb, at about five-foot intervals, a new trunk grows straight down until it reaches the earth, where it takes root. The tree has expanded until it is a small forest itself, a labyrinth.

I think of the roots, like pipelines, snaking out in all directions but especially toward the river; the longest roots must reach the water's edge, must wade in the tepid summer river.

"I can understand defending someplace holy to you."

"I made the mistake of thinking I was fighting honorable warriors. They murdered my wife."

"I know the story," I say. "I'm sorry."

We walk in silence for nearly a mile.

"Who's going to win the game?" I ask. "Or is it ever going to end? Is it part of your revenge to have twenty or so men play themselves to death in a rainstorm?"

"Too many questions," says Drifting Away. "But one more, from me: who do you want to win?"

"The Confederacy," I reply instantly.

"Are you sure?"

"Shouldn't I be? It's the odds. They should have lost in the first nine innings; they're amateurs holding professionals at bay. A few Indians holding off a well-equipped army. They're the underdogs, and . . . some of them are my friends."

"But consider the consequences. What if a few half-starved Indians defeated an army? Would it end there?"

"No, I suppose not. No matter how many soldiers you kill, there are always more over the next hill. They wouldn't give up. They'd take revenge."

"What if the other happened? What if the army eventually killed the Indians?"

"The whole thing dies out. Good has triumphed over evil. The world unfolds as it should."

"You are a quick learner."

"Then the Confederacy has to lose."

"Not necessarily."

"Meaning what?"

Drifting Away stops, sighs deeply, places a gigantic hand on my shoulder. "Do you know how long it has been, how many lifetimes have passed, since I have spoken to anyone? You believe in me. Otherwise you couldn't see me. How I've longed all these lifetimes to have an ally, to find someone, anyone, who believes I ever existed, that I will exist again."

I feel like Snow White being spared by the huntsman.

"I believe," I whisper.

"Whatever may happen I can't do the bidding of the grandfathers. I can't kill you. At least, not without reasoning with you. For I understand your passion. But please, give up the girl now. No good can come from your loving her."

"You know my answer to that."

"You must concentrate only on the game. However the game turns out, you'll discover what you came here to find out. Isn't that enough?"

"Before I met Sarah it would have been."

Drifting Away sighs heavily. "Don't add to my burdens. I will tell you about the game, the whys and wherefores of it. The grandfathers have determined that the time is right for me to earn the return of my murdered wife. Because my power vision was of baseball, the game is the thing. It is all the doing of the grandfathers. They have brought the greatest baseball team in the world here and pitted it against a group of farm boys. It can be likened to the cavalry fighting the Indians. My job, using whatever poor skills I have left after my endless exile, is to make the Indians win."

"Then at least we're on the same side."

"Unfortunately," says Drifting Away, "there is a problem."

"Maybe I'm here to help you, not to hinder you. Have you thought of that?"

"I have."

"And?"

"Stop for a moment and think. Think of the women in your life. The woman in mine. You know what no one else knows. You know of Coyote's visit to me, of the grandfathers' promise."

"Then it's the women. I've known there was something amiss. Tell me about it."

He frowns, turns away from me. I reach out for him, thinking he is about to leave.

"You don't have to tell me," I say to his back. "I know. I just don't want to admit I know. The spirit of Onamata was scattered to the four corners of the world, the four quadrants. For hundreds of years they've been inching closer together until now they're ready to reunite. Somehow all the women in my life are connected, aren't they? My mother, my sister, Sunny, and now Sarah. Onamata is in them, all of them."

"I knew you knew. So you see why it is impossible for you and the girl . . ."

"No! I can't give her up any more than you could have given up Onamata. My mother, my sister, my wife, were all dark spirits; Sarah is light. I won't give her up. I won't be moved."

"Then you had better change your allegiance. You had better hope the cavalry defeats the Indians, *this* Indian."

This does put everything in a different perspective. I've assumed I had some connection, however tenuous, with the Confederacy. Now I'm being told that if the Confederacy wins, I lose.

We walk on in silence. The moon reflects off the puddled

road and ditches, multiplying itself until it is like pale flowers underfoot.

"Then it's you who keeps the Confederacy in the game?"

"I help out where I can. I am not nearly as powerful as you would like to believe."

"The rain. Is that you, too?"

"The grandfathers. They don't always understand, I'm afraid. Or perhaps they do, for there is much Trickster in all of us. But these boys, and men, they play what the local people call 'good country hardball,' not skillful enough to compete with the Chicago Cubs. I stretch their tendons, put lightning under their feet, straighten errant throws, twist the three-fingered one's pitches until they hit the bat. That boy at short-stop makes plays only a major leaguer could accomplish. You must have been at least a little suspicious. Your friend, the lumbering one in the outfield — he has such desire. He has the heart of an eagle in the body of an ox. I try harder when he holds the bat."

"How long will the game last?"

"Until one of us wins. Me or the grandfathers. We both have great patience. It could last years."

Years. I visualize myself marrying Sarah, living in Big Inning.

"Wait a minute," I almost shout. "Are you sure there are grandfathers? What proof do you have? What you claim to believe makes you just as superstitious as the people from the Twelve-Hour Church, as all the religious hypocrites from this time and the time I come from. What makes you think anyone or anything is controlling your life? You may be responsible for your own destiny."

"Remember my power vision."

"Hallucinations brought on by fasting."

"The grandfathers sent Coyote with their message for me."

"Grief. Hysteria."

"I believe."

"There is no answer to that. At least consider what I believe. Everything is explainable. And events that aren't are just that — unexplainable. I don't believe there is any supernatural."

"As you wish," says Drifting Away, and vanishes with the tiniest of sounds, like a soft exhalation of breath.

I stand stunned, in the moist, silent darkness. I'll never view the game in the same light again. Everything I tried not to think of, the information I would sooner suppress than face, has been brought out in the open by Drifting Away. There is no reason to believe Drifting Away is lying. Still, there is the Trickster part of him. But if what he says is true, why are the grandfathers not his allies? Why is he fighting alone? Why are they testing him?

The game. It has come so close to ending so many times. The Cubs score; the Confederacy fights back to tie. I have to change my whole view of the game. Suddenly, instead of being just a very strange exhibition game, it is a matter of life and death for Sarah; if the Confederacy wins, I lose her. It may be life-threatening for me also, for I have no idea what my status is here in the past. I remember Drifting Away's words about the game going on for years. That I can live with. I hurry on toward Sarah.

11

DEEP IN THE NIGHT, wrapped in Sarah's arms in the hay-mow, a homemade quilt smuggled from the house separating us from the hay, from the overpowering odor of the drying clover, my dilemma, soothed by passion, does not seem frightening.

"What will we do?" I ask Sarah. "Where will we live?"

"I want a big house," she says, kissing down my cheek; her hair, damp and tangled, hangs over her face, making her look as if she's hiding from me. "Three stories high, like the biggest ones in Iowa City. Oh, there's one on South Clinton Street that I'll show you, if this game ever ends; it's right out of a wish book; it has a widow's walk, with all kinds of spindles and cornices; oh, it looks like lace and gingerbread; it's owned by a doctor —"

"Reporters don't make money like doctors."

"Gid, it doesn't matter. I was just dreaming, making believe . . ."

"You'll never have to worry about money," I hear myself saying, forgetting for a second where I am. "Actually money's not very important, unless you have someone you love very much who you can make happy by spending money."

I pull Sarah closer to me, tasting the salty dampness of her neck, trying to hold her so close that I won't be able to tell where her body stops and mine begins.

What *will* I do if I stay here in 1908? The possibilities boggle the mind. Sarah will be with me; Sarah will have that huge house with the widow's walk and whatever else she wants. I should be able to make a passable living by betting on baseball games, long-term wagers on pennant winners and World Series champions. If I only knew something about automobiles, or, better still, airplanes or television or cameras. Now I wish I had my *Baseball Encyclopedia* with me so I could bet on batting title winners and home-run leaders. But I think a lot of that information will come back to me as the situations take shape.

I'll invest my winnings in movies, in General Motors, Bell Telephone, Coca-Cola; what's good enough for Ty Cobb is good enough for me.

Maybe I can make money as a psychic, a prognosticator. I never paid much attention to history, but if I can predict the date of Archduke Ferdinand's assassination, the date of the end of World War I . . . When, I wonder, did it begin being referred to as World War I?

My adrenalin is flowing like electricity.

With my winnings, I could invest in publishing. In a few years I could arrange to meet a young fellow from Michigan named Hemingway.

But can I control the urge to change history? Can I stop myself from being in Chicago in 1919, from somehow keeping a Carolina farm boy named Joe Jackson away from the arms of scandal? Or this very fall, can I keep myself from traveling to New York and whispering in Fred Merkle's ear to touch second base always after a game-winning hit, no matter how large or hostile the crowd?

"Sarah, do you believe in magic?" I whisper.

"I don't think I'm supposed to. The church is pretty strict."

"Do you believe in me?"

"Of course; you're here."

"Well, I'm magic. If I told you I could take you to a magic place, more wonderful than the wildest things you've read about in magazines or books —"

"Oh, Gid, don't tease me."

"No. I'm not. I'd never do that. Remember you said there was something about me and time? Well, you're right, Sarah. Right north of Iowa City, about where the county road is, there is a highway — it runs from coast to coast, an interstate, divided highway. It's one of thousands of highways that cover America like concrete cobwebs; the whole nation is a network —"

"But why?" She is laughing at the idiocy of my suggestion. "What would travel on so many roads?"

"Automobiles. I've seen one or two here. Mr. Mott has one. Trucks, boxcars without tracks, the railways have become obsolete . . ."

"Oh, Gideon, there aren't ten cars in Johnson County —"

But I cut her off and lecture on about the wonders I know of, an evangelist myself, so sure, so absolutely positive of the truth I am speaking. Suddenly I know how a prophet must suffer, for all that I say sounds like no more than pie in the sky, delivered with fervor and sincerity.

I deliver a dissertation on electricity and how it will continue to change the face of America. "Moving pictures," I say. "Radio, television." I preach the doctrine of a talking magic box in the bosom of every family, of a man on the moon, of satellites like orbiting baseballs in the heavens, of pictures flashed instantaneously from Europe, Asia, Australia.

When I finish, I look down at Sarah with unrestrained pride, as if I've just discovered fire and demonstrated it for the first time to my mate.

"Gideon, that's silly," she says, laughing. But there is an edge to her laugh, a concern in her eyes. "I found a dime novel hidden under my brother's mattress one time. I read some of it; it was about robots and men flying in metal cylinders in space. You should be writing your stories down, you should —"

I am affronted. I cut her off again to rant about subways and skyscrapers, jet planes, oceanliners, atomic bombs. But eventually I run down and notice that Sarah is smiling tolerantly, like a mother who has listened to a child's dream.

As I stare at her face, still partially hidden by strands of hair, my dream of taking her back with me to the world of 1978 fades away. The culture shock would be too much. I would be taking her not to a world of marvels, but to a world of terrors.

"Sarah," I say, "I shouldn't tease you like that. I have an overactive imagination. There's only one cure for it. I have to make love with a beautiful, brown-eyed earthling named Sarah."

But even as Sarah pulls me to her heart, her mouth sweet inside mine, her love does not relieve my anxieties as it should.

☺

"What is it like being in the Bigs?" I ask Joe Tinker. We are walking in the twilight, along the banks of the ever-rising Iowa River.

"For baseball players it's as close to heaven as any of us will ever get," he says. "It's not an easy life. Lots of people still look down on us — we're suspect, like actors. Oh, the muckamucks make a big fuss over us when we win, say how we bring so much glory to the great city of Chicago, and all that hoopla. But try turning up at their house with plans to date their daughter, and see how far you get. Still, the Bigs are one of the only places where an uneducated farm boy can be a hero, win praise from tens of thousands of people.

"You have to want it bad," he goes on, looking at Johnny. "You have to have the heart for it. You've got to want to hear the fans roar like thunder, just for you. Being good isn't enough, you've got to want it so bad you'll walk through walls to get there; through walls, over mountains, over people, you set your eye on the top and never stop until you get there, and never let them move you after you do."

"How many of the Confederacy players are good enough to play in the Bigs?"

"That's hard to say."

"Why? You've seen them for over a thousand innings. They've played you to a stand-off."

"It all has to do with desire. With consistency. You have to be consistent in the Bigs. Guys who are heroes one day and bums the next don't last. There's a little bit of accountant or banker in a good baseball player. He's got to be able to do the same thing, and do it right, over and over, every day of his career."

As Tinker and I return to the muddy campground, Sarah steps from the shadow of a wagon wheel.

"I thought I'd surprise you," she says, smiling, crinkling her nose.

"Well . . ." I take her hands, which are small and soft in mine. "We could walk," I say.

"No," whispers Sarah, turning her face up to me.

"On the other hand, maybe *they* could go for a walk," I say, pointing to Stan and Johnny, who are discreetly leaning on the other end of the wagon.

"I'd thought of that, too," whispers Sarah.

"You wouldn't mind if I need a little privacy for a while," I say to Stan and Johnny.

"Oh, we have just hundreds of things we can do, don't we, John?" says Stan, his wide face cracking open in a smile.

"Sure," says Johnny Baron. "Last thing we want is our

sleep, after fifty-nine innings of baseball and being soaking wet for fifteen hours."

"I'm glad you understand," I say. "Come back about two P.M., Twelve-Hour Church time. That way it won't seem so late."

"You're all consideration," says Stan, but he and Johnny are already bulky shadows in the blue darkness, becoming more indistinct with every step.

"What about your brother?" I say to Sarah. "He's only one wagon over. Won't he be apt to kill me?"

"I won't tell him if you don't," says Sarah, pushing herself close to me.

"My mansion," I say, pulling back the canvas flap. I boost Sarah inside.

"I love you, Gideon," she whispers as we sink into the rainy-smelling quilts and comforters.

☉

The days grow shorter. The players are up by five A.M. Each team takes turns manning a chuck wagon, which dispenses coffee and flapjacks, as the first icicles of light touch the galvanized sky. As soon as the players, walking as if encased by fog, become recognizable, they adjourn to the diamond and Bill Klem, the umpire, can be heard hacking the phlegm from his throat, then demanding, "Play ball!"

☉

Day Seventeen. From the *Iowa City Citizen*:

> Ossining, N.Y. — Charles H. Rogers and Angelo Landiero were electrocuted for murder at the Sing Sing Prison this morning. The execution was successful.

GIRL WALKS ON ROOF ASLEEP

HAT CAUSES TRAGEDY

GIRL MARRIES A GHOST

———

Bessie Brown of Cameron, Oklahoma, is married
to a ghost.

☺

The band has as much stamina as the players. They play on,
and like pied pipers they seem to attract new fans each day.
The gathering of fans is pyramidal. Fifty fans one day becomes
two hundred the next, eight hundred the following day. The
next day is a madhouse as over three thousand fans fill the
stands and crowd around the outfield.

Trains several cars long run out from Iowa City every hour
on the Baseball Spur. The Twelve-Hour Church of Time Immemorial has set up concessions and the church hall is a
beehive of activity.

But there is something wrong with the fans; they are silent,
almost comatose.

"Zombies," says Stan, staring at the stands, concerned.

No matter what happens on the field, how spectacular the
fielding play, or how daring the base running, they remain
almost silent, except for a murmur of conversation that remains at the same level regardless of the action on the field.
They seem to be waiting for something. The only thing that
draws any response from them is the playing and singing of
the band. At one point a good percentage of the crowd hums
along with a rousing, Bible-thumping hymn, while not ten
people applaud a Tinker-to-Evers-to-Chance double play of
great skill and dexterity.

The fans are so silent they seem to have been sprayed with
ether. When the game ends for the day, the fans huddle in

the humid night. The rain, mercifully, has stopped. Under a pewter moon, the night scene is as eerie as desert.

The sounds tonight are of soft moans and disturbed dreams. The engine chugs back and forth on the Baseball Spur, delivering new converts. The band plays on. A not bad barbershop quartet joins them and in the wee hours sings softly:

> "Come on and join the army,
> I shall not be moved.
> Come on and join the army,
> I shall not be moved.
> Like a tree
> Planted by the water
> I shall not be moved."

Near dawn Sarah creeps into the wagon, cuddles into my arms, her cheek cool against mine after her long walk in the night air.

"I'm scared, Gid," she whispers.

Three feet away, Stan tosses restlessly. "Strike," he mutters and flops an arm against the canvas.

I hold Sarah tighter, as if our being close to each other can make her fears go away.

"There are thousands and thousands of people out there, Gid. The hill behind the field is black with them. They say there are ten thousand more in Iowa City waiting to travel out here on the Baseball Spur, thousands more walking. There's a five-hundred-car passenger train with the windows painted black, brought people from Chicago to Iowa City."

"Don't be afraid," I say lamely.

"We should go away," Sarah whispers, then kisses me, her mouth fierce, her teeth hard. "I'd go anywhere with you, Gid."

"I can't," I reply.

"Something terrible is going to happen to me if I stay here."

"I won't let anything happen to you. But I've got to stay here. I've got to know what happens."

> "I'm on my way to heaven
> I shall not be moved."

"Love me, Gid. Please. I'm afraid we'll never have the chance again." She twines her body around me. We sink deep in the feather comforters and scuffle out of our clothing.

> "Like a tree
> Planted by the river
> I shall not be moved."

Our heads are near the open flap of the wagon. The first silver tines of light prick the horizon. In the cold dawn I cannot believe I have reacted so negatively to Sarah's request to go away. I'm afraid I'm as bewitched as the rest of the players. We *should* leave. Once out of Johnson County we would be free of Drifting Away, the grandfathers, the Twelve-Hour Church.

But I can't leave. The last few days have been pure hell for me. I perch on the edge of the bench, dreading every Confederacy hit, knowing that if they win I lose Sarah. I'm scared of the Cubs winning, too, for that would toss me into a completely unknown situation. Could I stay here? What happens if Drifting Away loses? When I watch the Confederacy players come to bat with their backs to the wall for the umpteenth time, raindrops bouncing like tapioca on the infield mud, I know I don't want the game to end. I want to see more and more of this special magic. When the Confederacy ties the score, as it inevitably does, I switch my allegiance and pull frantically for the Cubs to get the last outs.

"Not yet, not yet," I whisper. The game must not end. I need more time to entrench myself here.

⊖

As the twenty-first day of the game begins, the crowd has swollen to what must be over ten thousand people; most wear yellow or brown slickers and stand like fenceposts in the driving rain.

The only statistics I've managed to keep are innings played. In twenty days they have played 1273 innings, an average of 63.7 per day.

Those who are statistically minded rebuke me for not keeping accurate records. My defense is, I never thought the game would go on so long, and if *they* wanted statistics, *they* should have kept them. Stan, as far as I know, is the only one who has kept his batting average.

"I'm hitting .301," he announces proudly, or "Down to .297, but wait till tomorrow."

There are times when the huge crowd becomes totally silent, so the only sounds are the band's soft playing, the quartet's harmonious humming; and the hoarse cries of the ballplayers.

The lightning began shortly after lunch. The sky became white on black, cloud over cloud, as the first flashes of chain lightning sawed across the sky. Then the dull afternoon was lit by fork lightning — snake tongues shooting out of the cold, white sky, followed by the reverberations of thunder.

The fork lightning is close and lethal. We can hear the crunch of it, the back-breaking snap of whatever it has struck, the cry of earth or tree, animal-like shrieks, death cries like rusty nails being pulled from a plank.

It strikes near the right-field line and kicks across the middle of the outfield, making the water appear to burn like gasoline as it passes.

"God's instrument!" an old woman on the first-base side screams. "Lightning is God's instrument!"

"Amen," intones a good portion of the crowd.

The game goes on.

"God's instrument!" she screams again as, from the direction of the Twelve-Hour Church, Elder Womple, black as a crow, solemnly plods toward us, a large, floppy Bible open in his hands.

"God's instrument, indeed," he intones.

O'Reilly delivers a high, inside fast ball to Harry Steinfeldt, moving him off the plate.

"God's instrument can shrivel the soul until it is tiny as a black pea."

"Amen," gabbles the crowd.

Steinfeldt strikes out on the next pitch, a wicked curve that breaks next to his knuckles.

"God's instrument can zipper open a chest, expand a heart, fill it with love for all mankind."

"Mmmmmm . . . mmm . . . mmmm . . ." replies the crowd.

"Praise God," roars Elder Womple, closing the Bible and raising both his arms above his head.

As Frank Chance stands in at the plate, the crowd, which is cramming the stands, ranging back up the hillside to infinity, stands too, hands raised in various attitudes of praise. Those used to such things stretch their hands toward the sky; those new to the idea raise their arms tentatively, self-consciously.

At the Cubs' bench, Little Walter stands on the wet board, his child-size arms extended upward.

From the throats of the throng rises a flutter of words, a mysterious melodious babbling, ebbing and swelling while chain lightning cuts across the sky like a band saw.

The game goes on. O'Reilly gives up a hit to Chance, a blow as sharp as the sound of a lightning strike.

Dual prongs of fork lightning send a puff of smoke floating into the air near the giant tree by the river. The second prong strikes the tree, which emits a terrible splitting sound.

The voices of the singers, the murmur of the band:

"Fighting sin and Satan
I shall not be moved."

Elder Womple: "We beseech Thee for guidance . . ."

But the crowd, the crowd — ten thousand people speaking in tongues, prattling, rattling, moaning, filling the whole space, volume rising, intensity increasing. In unfamiliar words, but strongly and strangely harmonious, like the beating of bird wings, is their mystical, musical babble.

The tree shrieks again, repelling the lightning, the force of it, the essence of it, gathering like a molten metal sun in the upper branches. Then, like Zeus pitching lightning bolts, the tree draws itself back like a giant catapult and fires the coiled lightning back at the sky.

Joe Tinker hits a single. Three Finger Brown strikes out.

The sky seems to accept the return of the lightning. It is like an orange tossed into a fog bank.

The gabble of the multitude winds down, a few voices trailing slowly off into silence.

In the western sky, beyond the ballfield, beyond the hill coated with spectators, the gray fog clouds begin to turn in a whirlpool-like gyration that quickly develops to a boil. The sky hisses and bubbles like a cauldron.

At the plate Jimmy Slagle takes a called strike, while the sky swirls, and the lightning, compressed, hovers like a fiery bird.

Suddenly the reprocessed lightning is pitched forth and, like a comet or a curve ball, hurtles toward the baseball field. The victim is Bob Grady, the Confederacy right fielder, who has been alternating every nine innings with Stan.

The lightning explodes, like a light bulb disintegrating. The single flash is blinding; dots dance before my eyes. The lightning is gone. Grady lies smoldering on the right-field grass.

"God's instrument!" screams the old woman.

"Guidance," Elder Womple is shouting.

From the mound, O'Reilly motions for Stan to take over right field.

He does.

Am I the only one not bewitched? Or am I, too? My inclination is to run to Bob Grady's body to see if anything can be done for him, to summon aid. Yet I do not move from the bench.

The game goes on.

Elder Womple preaches on. The band plays on.

As I watch, one of the white clouds, a cold, evil white that would ordinarily herald hail, drops low over the field. A lightning bolt like a spear flys earthward, pierces the ground beside Grady's body, quivers for a few seconds. Stan, who is standing not ten feet away, watching the angle of the bat, pounds his glove. A second lightning bolt arrives, then another and another, until they form rows on both sides of the body. The bolts are driven in at an angle until, if one could look into the earth, they must form a cage of molten energy beneath Grady.

The cloud drops even lower, swirling and frothing. Thunder rumbles ominously, calling the lightning bolts, calling them back to the cloud. The molten tines rise, bearing Bob Grady's body in the V of their embrace.

All that is left behind is a scorched silhouette on the right-field grass in the shape of a sprawled body.

I'm on my way to heaven,
I shall not be moved.
Like a tree
Planted by the river
I shall not be moved.

Water laps insidiously at the floating tree roots; the river-bank groans. The game goes on.

When play ends for the day, the huge crowd disperses as mysteriously as it arrived — some people walking, others crammed like cornstalks in wagonboxes, others by means of the Baseball Spur.

It is reported that the last train into Iowa City tipped silently into the swollen Iowa River as the tracks sagged and slackened. Several passenger cars were swept away in the direction of Missouri, horrified faces pressed fiercely against silted windows.

The rumor passing like pox through the milling crowd is that President Theodore Roosevelt is on his way to Iowa City by rail and is about to dispatch troops to Big Inning to return the defiant Cubs to Chicago.

After the game ends, in the deep purple twilight, eight Cub players form a small squad with Frank Chance as commander and quick-march about the baseball field, their cleats kicking up water in a fine, bluish spray, their bats smartly on their shoulders like rifles. Little Walter marches at the rear, running to keep up, yipping like a sheep dog.

Not to be outdone, O'Reilly, organizes all the Confederacy players in a marching formation and parades them about the field — all, that is, except Stan and me.

"I've been in a war, thank you," says Stan. "I'm a ballplayer, nothing else."

"What war?" says O'Reilly.

"A real war," says Stan simply, turning away.

"Don't look at me," I say.

"You do what I tell you," growls O'Reilly. "Get out there and march."

"Hey, I'm here as a volunteer, remember? I don't mind being mascot and bat boy, but there are some things I don't do. And marching is near the top of the list."

"You'll be sorry when we're attacked and you're unprepared to defend yourself."

"What kind of bullets do your bats use?"

"Don't be smart, boy. You strike me as one who is lacking in patriotism."

"You're the ones preparing to face United States soldiers," I point out logically.

O'Reilly stomps away, cursing. The two squads join together in a ragged column and continue, stepping on each other's heels. In place of Stan and me, they recruit the band. The puzzling red-uniformed quartet marches behind the ballplayers, fife singing like a teakettle, drum thumping.

⊝

Day Twenty-four, July 27, 1908:

> CUBS LOSE 14 OF 17 WITHOUT FIRST-STRING PLAYERS
>
> BARNEY OLDFIELD, THE FAMOUS DAREDEVIL AUTOMOBILE DRIVER, PASSED THROUGH IOWA CITY
>
> C. C. OAKES LOST TWO FINE HEIFERS BY LIGHTNING LAST WEEK

⊝

239

Theodore Roosevelt arrives at the Big Inning baseball grounds at about eight A.M., riding a flame-colored gelding with a brilliant white diamond on its forehead. He is accompanied by three aides, also on horseback; all four are coated in brown slickers the color of flypaper. Water drips from their hat brims. Water also drips from Roosevelt's rust-colored mustache. His aides look more like cavalry scouts or trail riders than presidential yes men.

"Mr. President. This is an honor," says Bill Klem, raising his hands to call time.

The president's horse sashays sideways, its hoofs splashing water. The stands are empty. The players, the umpires, Little Walter, the band, and I are the only ones present.

The players in the field move slowly forward, as if drawn by the president's presence. Those of us on the benches also step forward until we are congregated between the pitcher's mound and home plate.

The president, leaving his entourage along the third-base line, rides around behind home plate until he and his horse face the ragged and drenched ballplayers.

He clears his throat loudly. The rain has fogged his glasses. He stares at us avidly, a yellow neckerchief tied at his throat.

"Rumors of your magnificent achievement abound," he begins. "I wanted to see for myself. What inning are we in, Mr. Umpire?"

"The one thousand five hundred and fifty-fourth," replies Bill Klem.

"Then I hardly have to give my standard speech lambasting the doctrine of ignoble ease and praising the doctrine of the strenuous life. What I see before me *is* the strenuous life."

The president appears to be about five foot ten, with long legs on a thick body. He has a big nose, broad jaw, and large front teeth. As he becomes involved in his speech, he thrusts his head forward and works his jaw rapidly.

"It is far better to dare mighty things, to win glorious triumphs, even though checkered by failure, than to take rank with those poor spirits who neither enjoy much nor suffer much because they live in the gray twilight that knows not victory or defeat."

His voice is resonant. I think we are all standing straighter. I recall reading the memoirs of one of the soldiers who fought with him. "It was such fun being led by him," the man wrote.

"Though many must surely wonder why you are doing what you are doing, while many may criticize you, I want you to remember it is not the critic who counts, not the man who points out how the strong man stumbled or where the doers of deeds could have done better. The credit belongs to the man who is actually in the arena, in your case the baseball field: whose face is marred by dust and mud, sweat and blood; who strives valiantly; who errs and comes up short again and again; who knows the great enthusiasms, the great devotions; who spends himself in a worthy cause; who, at the best, knows in the end the triumph of high achievement; and who, at the worst, if he fails, at least fails while daring greatly."

A spontaneous cheer rises from our collective throats, is absorbed almost instantly by the rain-swollen air.

"Mr. President, we would be honored if you would take a turn behind the plate," says Bill Klem.

"I should be honored to do so, sir," says the president, dismounting in one fluid motion and at the same time making a signal for one of his aides to ride forward and lead the diamond-faced gelding off the field, "but, if you would not deem it inappropriate, I would rather take a turn in front of the plate."

"By all means, Mr. President," says Bill Klem. He nods toward Little Walter, who scuttles back to the Cubs' bench and drags a heavy black bat toward home plate as the Confederacy players retreat to their positions on the diamond.

President Roosevelt hefts the bat, takes off his hat and hands it to Bill Klem, shakes the water from his mustache, squares his shoulders, and tries to establish solid footing in the water-logged batter's box.

"I venture to say this gives new meaning to my credo, 'Speak softly, but carry a big stick,' " booms the president, then chuckles heartily.

All of us within hearing laugh politely.

Arsenic O'Reilly winds and tosses a looping, batting-practice pitch.

The president lets it go by.

"Don't patronize me, young man," he shouts at O'Reilly.

"Yes, sir," O'Reilly calls back, and I can see his face tighten as it does when he is facing one of the Cub power hitters with men on base.

O'Reilly takes his high leg kick and fires a fast ball over the outside corner, knee high. The president also lets that one go by.

"Strike one," calls Bill Klem.

"Much better," says Teddy Roosevelt.

"Does this count as part of the game?" someone asks. "If he hits will he be a base runner?"

As I watch, my mind is working on more than one level. I am recalling my father's book, *A Short History of the Iowa Baseball Confederacy.* On page 73, while describing the physical appearance of Drifting Away, my father inserted a footnote. At the bottom of the page it appeared thusly:

[1] *The only known likeness of Drifting Away appears on the American $5.00 "Indian Head" gold piece, personally commissioned by President Theodore Roosevelt.*

O'Reilly delivers another fast ball, and the president takes a mighty cut at the ball, missing by several inches, his knee-high boots squealing from the force of the swing.

"Bully for you, young man. Strike! Strike!"

O'Reilly closes his left eye as he goes into the wind-up, and sends another blur of horsehide straight down the middle of the plate. Teddy Roosevelt takes an equally vicious swing but does not connect. He turns and looks down and behind him to where Henry Pulvermacher clutches the ball in his warty hand.

"Excellent! Excellent! So much better than giving in to me. Never ease up. Always deliver your best ball."

Little Walter sidles up and takes the bat.

"Mr. President," says Bill Klem, "we'd like you to have the ball as a memento of your visit to Big Inning."

"I'd be delighted, sir. Delighted."

He accepts the ball from Henry Pulvermacher. An aide is advancing, leading the president's horse.

Suddenly I sprint from the Confederacy bench and meet the president face to face. "Mr. President, I must ask you something. The 'Indian Head' gold piece, what inspired its design?"

Teddy Roosevelt gazes critically at me for such a long time that I and the others present begin to feel embarrassed.

Roosevelt scratches his head, shakes his hat, reapplies it to his head before speaking.

"How could you know about that? Are you a mind reader?"

Now it is my turn to pause.

"No, sir," I finally venture. "It wouldn't make sense if I tried to explain."

"Well, young man, I didn't know anybody else knew about my change of heart. In fact, the five-dollar gold piece is not common knowledge. I've always wanted an American coin of definitive American design, something to rival the artistic beauty of ancient Greek coinage. Last year I wrote to Mr. Bela L. Pratt, an accomplished artist, and he took up the challenge. He, being aware that I champion the cause of the

American Indian . . ." He pauses, sees that the baseball players have no interest in our conversation, and takes the reins of the horse from his aide. We walk slowly in the direction of the Twelve-Hour Church.

"Mr. Pratt has shown me a number of designs, none of which have met with my approval, but last night, camped on the trail a few miles from here, I had a most extraordinary experience, and I now know what the design is to look like. In fact, I made a sketch or two." He digs a pudgy hand inside the crackling brown slicker, apparently searching for a shirt pocket; he produces a sheet of cream-colored stationery, folded over many times, and, shielding it from the rain, shows me several profiles of Drifting Away, some bareheaded, some in full eagle-feather headdress.

"*You* know Drifting Away?"

"The finest specimen I've ever seen. He dropped by our campfire last night; we visited until the wee hours. But how could you know I'm going to use him as a model for the new coin? I didn't know myself until a few hours ago."

"As someone wise once said, 'Things are out of kilter in Johnson County.' But I am acquainted with Drifting Away."

"But he doesn't know," says the president. "I made no mention —"

"He's very intuitive."

With a *harrumph*, the president clears his throat. "Well, we must be getting on. Good day, gentlemen." He salutes the scattered ballplayers, mounts his horse, and canters off in the direction of the river. The rain increases in intensity. O'Reilly curses and spits into the sodden air.

The fog is positively primeval. I feel as if a dinosaur might come slogging through the swamp of the field or appear head first out of the river at any moment, as if a pterodactyl might glide silently overhead.

The grainy water of the Iowa River, rising steadily, now a

bile-yellow color, laps menacingly at the roots of the giant tree by the church.

⊖

Walking in the last twilight on the edge of the trees in far center field, I stop and stand perfectly still. I concentrate on the essence of Drifting Away; as always, I alone have seen him lurking in the foliage, peering from the cornstalks along the right-field line, peeking around the corner of the Twelve-Hour Church. Suddenly he is standing beside me. I am shocked at how much he has aged in the past few days. He looks haggard. And I am sure he is shorter, much shorter.

"I'm surprised at you," I say. "Couldn't resist a shot at immortality."

Drifting Away smiles a little shamefacedly. "What do you mean?" he says, but it is clear he understands me.

"The coin and the president," I say. "I suppose you sat so he could see your profile in the firelight."

"We had a very pleasant meeting. The three of us have a good deal in common. We all practice what Mr. Roosevelt preaches. We are all somewhat larger than life."

"But what's happened to you?" I say. "You look positively —"

"I am tired. The game takes its toll on me. And it is not your imagination. I am smaller."

"How much longer can you keep the game going?"

"As long as they can." He stares up at the sky, which cleared as soon as play stopped and is now a peaceful robin's-egg blue tinged with pink. "Onamata is drawing nearer. I feel it. I will it."

"Can you tell me the *why* of this contest? Why are you being tested? Why aren't your grandfathers on your side?"

"You don't know?"

"No."

245

"You know of Onamata's murder but not of my great weakness. You see, I was on my way back to her. If I had been with her I would have saved her, or we would both have died with honor. But I let my weak body control my mind. A half-day's ride from Onamata I lay down and slept. The grandfathers saw, for they see everything."

"But how could you know she was in danger?"

"It was *in me* to know. My weakness caused her death."

"You shouldn't blame yourself. I've worried myself sick that my wife's comings and goings were my fault; my father had the same misgivings about my mother's disappearances. Could either of us have done anything to prevent being treated the way we were?"

"No. But I could have saved Onamata. She was my life. I have been doing what the people of the strange church over there would call penance. The grandfathers are giving me a final chance."

"What if I said I wanted to stay here, in 1908?"

He studies me for a long time. I know his answer before he speaks it. It is frightening that I can't discard my obsession with the Confederacy. I have never until now wanted to, but I always secretly thought I could. I guess I have been like an alcoholic who thinks he can quit drinking if he really wants to. I want Sarah more than the secret of the Confederacy — that in itself is a revelation.

"The girl spoke my answer to you," says Drifting Away. "'You can't live in the past.' I heard her say it."

"You heard?"

"I am always as close as your shadow," he whispers. And in among the lengthy shadows of poplars that stretch in the outfield I see my own. Sprawling in front of my shambling form is the chiseled profile from the five-dollar gold piece.

12

AS THE GAME sputters along, I can't help but be drawn into it in a manner far beyond the obvious. The sheer thrill of watching some of the greatest players in history is awesome. That they are struggling against forces they do not comprehend does not take away from the wonder of the game itself.

O'Reilly is always in the right place at the right time. He comes out of his delivery in an awkward fall, but there is cat in him and he is able to pounce on a bunt or a tapper to the mound so fast the eye is virtually unable to follow his movements. One second he is sprawling in the dirt; the next he has magically acquired the ball and is throwing to first. But what is a particular delight to watch is the way he backs up third or home on extra-base hits with runners aboard.

With Battleaxe Steinfeldt on first, the Peerless Leader, Frank Chance, slams the ball deep in the gap in left center. Steinfeldt is not exactly Man O' War on the bases; he would be happy to stop at third on the play, except that Chance has his head down, slicing around the bases, no doubt in his mind that he has a triple.

O'Reilly backs up third, but his head is up and **he is the first** player on the Confederacy team to realize that Chance is coming to third, making the play of import at the plate.

247

O'Reilly sprints down the line well ahead of Steinfeldt, who has to be frantically pointed toward home by the player coaching at third. O'Reilly is crouched like a shadow behind Henry Pulvermacher as Bad News Galloway's throw comes to the plate. Emanating from shallow right field, it should be a crisp one-bouncer into Pulvermacher's glove, but as the ball hits the slippery dirt between the pitcher's mound and home, it sizzles along the earth like a stone skimming water, and under the mitt of the surprised catcher.

But O'Reilly is there, the ball in his glove, all six feet four inches of him stretching out in a long dive as Steinfeldt slithers toward the plate. He tags Battleaxe on the forearm. Bill Klem signals the out. Chance, who had rounded third, scurries back to the bag. O'Reilly holds the ball high in the air, a trophy, a threat.

I remember my father saying to me, "Gideon, there's a lot more to watching a baseball game than keeping your eye on the ball." My father taught me the joys of watching a game when there were no base runners, when, to the untrained eye, nothing was happening. He taught me to follow that esoteric game of catch between pitcher and catcher, a game interrupted only by a lone and lonely batter attempting the seemingly impossible feat of striking a round ball with a cylindrical stick.

"You don't need base runners to enjoy the game," my father would say. "Notice how the infielders rise on their toes as the ball is delivered, ready to float in whatever direction the ball is hit. Keep an eye on the outfielders too, for if the signs have been flashed properly, they'll not only know what kind of pitch is coming, but whether it will be on the inside or outside part of the plate.

"But the real movement doesn't start until the ball is in play. *After* the ball is hit, *after* it has cleared the infield, especially if it is going for extra bases, you've got to train yourself to look back at the infield. While the outfielder is running down the ball, watch who is covering which base, watch to see who is backing up third and home. You'll be amazed at the amount of movement. Ah, Gideon, when everyone is in motion it's like watching those delicate, long-legged insects skim over calm water.

"The bunt is a ballet production all its own," he would go on. "As the batter squares around to drop the ball in front of the plate, watch the first and third basemen come huffing toward home, kicking up dust; watch the second baseman streaking toward first to take the throw while the shortstop covers second and the outfielders charge in to back up the bases in the event of an overthrow.

"You've got to watch the pitcher, Gideon. Watch the pitcher and you'll appreciate why baseball is a combination of chess and ballet. Watch him back up the bases, watch him get across to first on a grounder to the right side, see how the first baseman leads him, tossing to an empty sack, trusting him to be there.

"When it looks like nothing is going on, choose a player and watch him react to every pitch, rising like water, receding like water. Watch a different player every inning. It takes a lot of years of watching baseball to learn *not* to follow the ball every second. The true beauty of the game is the ebb and flow of the fielders, the kaleidoscopic arrangements and rearrangements of the players in response to a foul ball, an extra-base hit, or an attempted stolen base."

Someone ruffles my hair with a muddy hand and brings me back to reality. If only my father could be here. I miss him.

"I'm gonna stay," says Stan, grabbing my arm as we walk toward the church, pulling me to a halt.

"Stay?"

"Chance offered me a job. The Confederacy is every bit as good as the Bigs. Look at the way we're holding the Cubs to a standstill. And I'm hitting. As of today, I'm batting .308 against Three Finger Brown."

"Stan, this isn't real."

"Of course it is."

"Sorry. Bad choice of words."

"When this is over," Stan says, bright-eyed, standing in front of me holding my gaze, "I can play in the Bigs full-time, and even if I don't make it I can still come back to the Confederacy. Some of these guys are in their forties. I'll have years left."

"Stan, when this is over, there won't be a Confederacy. Something happens. The Confederacy never plays another game. The Cubs were never here."

"That *you* know of. This is real. *You* could be wrong, Gid."

"Stan!" I shout. "Where are your brains? You're like an accountant seduced by a five-dollar hooker, a man about to toss everything away because he's got hot pants thinking about glitter and sequins and damp sheets. You've pored over almost as many baseball records as I have. You know passages from *The Baseball Encyclopedia* like some people know scripture. Can *you* find any trace of the Confederacy? When we lived in 1978, were you listed in *The Baseball Encyclopedia*? Did you play for the Cubs, or any other major-league team, in 1908 or any other year? Quote me the record of that all-star big-league left-fielder, Stan Rogalski, born June 12, 1944, Onamata, Iowa. When were you born, Stan? If you played in the Bigs in 1908, or 1909, or 1910, when were you born?"

I look at Stan, at his face, which is as excited as if he just traded for a precious baseball card.

"What about Gloria?" I say with a sigh.

The minute the words are out, I'm sorry I spoke them. Stan tosses his head, frowns.

"Geez, Gid. I've chased a dream all my life. Ever since we were kids I've been gonna make it in the Bigs. I've got my chance now and I've got to take it."

He takes a deep breath and continues, "Now, 1908 was when baseball really meant something. It really *was* America. Saturday and Sunday afternoons, and weekday games starting at six P.M. in order to get through by dark. Feeling the dew starting to fall in the late evening, the grass getting frog-cool. The last batter like a ghost way up there at the plate —"

"Stan, do you know what I think about sometimes when Sunny is gone, while I prowl around that big, empty house, playing my horn and feeling sorry for myself? I think about Gloria, and how I'd give almost anything you can name if Sunny would follow my dream with me the way Gloria's followed your dream with you. Fourteen years of minor-league towns, crummy apartments, part-time jobs, batting slumps, injuries, never a pot to piss in or a window to throw it out of — only *your* dreams behind one more ballpark fence, in one more failing league, in one more stifling-hot town. And she's stayed with you every inch of the way."

I stop, both exhilarated and ashamed. The air is thick with guilt.

"Maybe there's a way I could bring her here. Do you think there is, Gid?"

"I don't know."

"If we're here forever, we have to make the best of it, right? It doesn't matter what's in future history. This is real enough for me. Think about the game you've been watching, Gideon. I've been a pro for years but I can't teach any of them a thing. They're playing the same game I was playing last month in Salt Lake, or that all the big-league teams were playing. That's what makes baseball the most wonderful game in the world. Move the Confederacy or the Cubs back to 1978, or bring one of those teams here, and they'd basically be equal. You can't say that about any other sport.

"Comparing football then and now is like comparing a jet-liner and a paper airplane. Knowing what I know, I could become a football coach here and be famous forever, or I could be a star at tennis or golf. But in baseball I'm a marginally good player here, just like I've always been a marginally good player. And look at me — I'm glad about it."

"Stan, look at me! Do I look like I'm having a good time? I'm living in terror that the game will end; that when it does, everything, including Sarah, will disappear. I watch the horizon. I wake with a lurch in the night, whether Sarah is with me or not. I stare out into the darkness as if we're surrounded by predatory animals. Sarah has begged me to take her away from here and I've refused because above everything else I've got to find out how the game comes out and why." I consider briefly telling him what I know, but decide there is no point in confusing him further. "We'll both do what we have to," I say. "Let's just hope our luck is good."

We stare at each other for a long time.

"Gid, I wouldn't trade these last couple of weeks for anything in the world." Stan smiles radiantly.

Just as there is no answer to Drifting Away's flat statement of belief, there is no suitable reply to Stan's state of rapture.

"I wouldn't either, Stan," I say. "I wouldn't either."

☻

Midway through Day Twenty-eight, a day when the clouds crowd close to the ground, sometimes making the outfielders unrecognizable from home plate, there is a sudden hissing from the sky that causes us all to look up.

The wicker gondola of a balloon is the first thing to become visible high over second base, as the sibilance increases. The players on the field all stare skyward as if trying to catch sight of a pop-up.

Then the balloon itself becomes visible, tall and tear-shaped, striped red, white, and green silk. The gondola settles, softly as a feather, on the grass behind second. The fog swirls about the balloon and about the players as if the vehicle has drawn the sky closer to earth.

There are two figures in the gondola, both clothed in cowled cloaks of heavy woven material. The balloon deflates softly, crumpling toward center field like a tower tipped over.

We all gather around the craft.

One man is apparently the pilot, the other the passenger. The passenger, an older man with regal bearing, climbs from the gondola, stretches luxuriously, and stares around with bright, all-seeing eyes. He is balding, with long white hair at the back and sides and a flowing white beard.

"May we be of service?" asks Bill Klem.

"I have traveled a considerable distance," says the old man. "This is one of my inventions," he adds, pointing to the balloon, "though I'm seldom given credit for it. I set down all the principles in 1505, but it took scientists nearly three hundred years to realize the potential of my ideas. Cautious types, afraid of their own beakers . . ."

"Oh, really," says Bill Klem, staring around. "As I said, can we be of service?"

"Don't be frightened, young men. If you help drag this craft to the sidelines, I'd like to watch your game for a while. That's why I'm here, and that's how you can be of service."

The players grab the lines of the balloon and drag it carefully over the left-field foul line.

It is Frank Luther Mott, who, mopping his brow, speaks the words, "Leonardo da Vinci?"

"It is good to be recognized," says the man, bowing slightly in Mott's direction. "This was a propitious time for a visit — more stirrings in this area than I've seen in a hundred years. Time is cracked and splintered, making passage here rather easy."

"Why?" asks Mott. "Why do you want to watch baseball?"

"I invented it, too," says Leonardo, "in 1506, to be exact. Unfortunately, I lived in a nation of bocce players. It took three hundred years for baseball to become popular. By that time, my name was no longer associated with it."

"You'll forgive us, sir, but we must get on with the game. You might care to sit behind home plate — that is the best vantage place."

"I know that," says Leonardo.

"It figures," says Stan. "Who else could come up with such perfect dimensions? Still, he's shorter than I would have guessed from his pictures."

"You've never seen the game played before?" Klem asks.

"One other time, but only from the air. It was 1870. But just as we arrived over a baseball field, there was an altercation of the elements, and we were sucked back."

"Back?" says Frank Luther Mott.

"The game. The game," says Leonardo.

And for an hour or more, as the fog rolls across the outfield in waves and a tingling rain pelts all present, the game carries on. Leonardo paces the third-base line, mumbling, making notes in a tall bound book he carries.

"Somehow I envisioned better weather," he says, as his assistant prepares the balloon for departure.

"We did too," says Bill Klem. "You've arrived at an unusual time in baseball history. But tell me, are you satisfied with what you have seen?"

Leonardo da Vinci smiles. "It took me years of calculations to get the distances just right. I'm pleased that it works in practical application as well as on paper. I think the game has some future."

"So do we, sir," says Bill Klem. "So do we."

$\ominus$

IMMORAL LETTERS CHARGED

COLFAX MAN IS ARRESTED WITH YOUNG GIRL

G. G. Gill, a real estate and insurance man living in Colfax, was arrested yesterday. The charge

against him is writing immoral letters to a young
girl. Gill is 40 years of age; the girl, barely 18.

THIRTEEN-FOOT CORNSTALK GROWN ON N.
VAN BUREN ST.

☻

On the thirtieth of July, during the early hours of darkness,
the massive statue of the Black Angel moved mysteriously
from Fairfield Cemetery to the lawn of the Old Capitol downtown, a mile or more. In the morning, the Angel was discovered with the dawn, standing like a monolithic crow on the
shiny grass, a glowing black in contrast to the building's brilliant white columns.

All day the citizens of Iowa City gathered in front of the
Angel, as if she were a visiting dignitary, a politician about to
make a critical speech. Occasionally someone knelt or made
an offering of food, wine, or clothing. A young priest read
from Ecclesiastes and crossed himself 101 times in rapid suc-
cession, imploring the statue to return to the cemetery, but
the Angel would not be moved.

☻

It is Missy Baron I am lonely for today. Missy, walking flat-
footed down the grassy road to the gate of her farm, swinging
her arms, skipping awkwardly every few strides, her sunbonnet, as always, slightly askew, on her way to meet me. I miss
kissing Missy's round, red cheek, taking her hand, skipping
with her on the way back to the farmhouse, or walking with
her the mile into Onamata, to my big, cool home.

Missy, I remember now, has no odor. She is like a fawn,
equipped by nature so predators cannot track it down. She
smells only of what she has touched — dandelions, marigolds,
her sleepy orange cat.

255

I remember one particular day, walking to town, holding Missy's soft, damp hand. I am talking of whatever comes to mind. Missy is there to listen; whether she does or not, I don't know. I never know how much Missy understands. She stops every once in a while to examine something, bends from the waist to eyeball a caraway plant, a Scotch thistle that is as large and purple as an upturned shaving brush, a piece of green glass peeking from the gravel like a bird's eye. Missy hums as if she is communing with the objects she views.

"We're going to a baseball game," I tell her. "Do you like baseball?"

Missy's face cracks wide in a grin that is so honest, so contagious, I can do nothing but hug her. Missy laughs — giggles, rather — and says something to me, a full, long sentence that I do not catch. Even knowing her all my life, I still can't always understand her. When Missy is excited, as she is now, her speech seems to emanate more from her nose than her mouth.

"There will be hot dogs," I say, jumping up and down, "and ice cream, and Sno-Cones, and peanuts."

Missy laughs, too loudly, on the verge of hysteria.

I remember Marylyle Baron admonishing me again and again, "Now don't you go getting Missy too excited. She doesn't know when to stop like you and me."

I stop my own motions; I hold Missy's shoulders and wait until she quiets down.

"Game," she says. "Baseball." And we resume our walk. Missy, head down, scuffs her shoes in the gravel at the side of the road, where small black-eyed Susans flutter like canaries in the grass.

It is a still, hot afternoon without a hint of breeze. The humidity is high and we sweat as we sit in the open bleachers in heavy sunshine. The sky is pale, the fans too hot to cheer.

Suddenly, the batter, a mile in front of a change-up, lashes it directly at us, or rather at Missy. I dive in front of her, not catching the ball but striking it down only inches from her face. The ball bounces in Missy's lap and rolls to her feet, where I retrieve it.

Missy's drink lies on its side in her lap. Even with a sealed top the orange drink seeps out around the straw and stains her skirt. A hot dog has left a mustard stain in the corner of her mouth.

"It's okay," I say. I'm not sure if Missy fully realizes what has happened.

"Oh, Gideon . . ." Then she sees the cup leaking in her lap. She sets it upright on the bench beside her. "My dress —"

"See what I've got?" I say, and hold up the shiny white ball. A combination usher-vendor-ballboy appears, not concerned over our welfare, but anxious to get the ball back. I wave him away. He stands for several seconds, giving me a dark stare. Their policy is to ask fans to return foul balls, but they can't *make* you return them.

"We were damn near killed," I say. "We get to keep the ball." And I place the round white orb in Missy's pudgy right hand.

"Is she hurt?" the boy says, in his capacity as usher.

"Only scared," I say, "and wet."

"I'll get her another drink," he says, in his capacity as vendor.

"Yeech," says Missy, setting down her half-eaten hot dog, which she has squeezed to pulp.

I take a paper napkin from my pocket and wipe her fingers. Then I wipe the mustard from the corner of her mouth. Suddenly I duck my head and kiss Missy's cheek, put my arm around her and squeeze her tightly. I realize I am shaking. Scared. I've always known I loved Missy, but until now I didn't fully realize how much.

"Did you see that catch I made, Gid? Did you see it?" Stan hollers as he charges in from the field.

"I saw it," I say. "You were great, buddy. You've still got a few miles left in those old legs. And the jump you got on the ball; that was experience showing."

Stan smiles wildly, pounds me on the shoulder. "It's all set," he says. "As soon as we beat the Cubs, I'm gonna switch teams. I'm goin' to Chicago. Utility outfielder and pinch hitter to start with, but I'll break into the regular line-up, see if I don't."

"I'm happy for you," I say. "I hate to bring up anything like reality, but Stan, you've seen the Iowa City newspaper. Where are the Cubs in the latest standings?"

"They've slipped to second last, but that's only because all their first stringers are down here."

"Stan, who wins the pennant in 1908?"

"The Cubs," he says automatically. Then the import of what I am saying begins to sink in.

"Stan, when and if this game ends, something happens; everything disappears or is wiped out of the memory of the world, including us, maybe. Stan, I feel as terrible about this as you do, but I don't think either of us can stay here. I'm gonna fight it. I may even die trying to stay here with Sarah."

I have to force myself to go on, for Stan's expression has gone from one of elation to the look he gets after going o for 8 in a double-header. "Stan, I'm not doing this to hurt you. I love you. You're the brother I've never had and the friend I've always been able to count on. If I've been impatient with you, it's because I tend to concentrate too much on my own troubles. Ah, Stan, I know what it is to have a dream on the tips of your fingers and not be able to gather it in. But you've got Gloria . . ."

"Why don't you run? Take Sarah and head for Chicago or Kansas City, or someplace where her weird family and that spooky church can't find you. Why don't you do it?"

"I can't," I say helplessly.

"Yeah, well, now you know how I feel about giving up the idea of playing for the Cubs."

⊖

Water has been flowing through the streets of Big Inning for days; houses on the lowest land have been evacuated.

As the water rises, everything that floats is washed into the current of the Iowa River and disappears forever in the direction of Missouri.

In Big Inning, the livery stable is the first building to collapse. With a groaning of timbers the long structure eases sideways and slowly folds itself flat like a cardboard cutout. There are strangled, gurgling sounds as the last air escapes between the shingles. One end is slightly higher than the other, for there are several carriages and a steel-wheeled corn wagon which have not been removed.

The water continues to rise. The storekeeper brings in two teams of dray horses pulling long, enclosed wagons. The stock is loaded up, and, with water lapping at the bottoms of the wagonboxes, the wagons lumber off toward higher ground.

As the residents of Big Inning begin to evacuate, as it becomes apparent that most of the buildings in town are in danger, Max Yocum, the house mover from Iowa City, anticipates that he will be the busiest man in Johnson County. He arrives in Big Inning with his crew of men and his team of sixteen Clydesdales, ready to jack up houses and commercial buildings and drag them to safety from the swirling streets of Big Inning to the hills behind the town.

But though he stays for twenty-four hours and the splashing of giant hoofs and the jingling of harnesses carry all the way to the ballfield in the deep of night, Max Yocum finds no takers. The citizens of Big Inning will not allow their buildings to be moved by man.

Water erodes the riverbank below the Twelve-Hour

Church. The building appears safe for the time being, but the yellow, curdled water continues to excavate the roots of the tree. Earth is swept away and the roots, long and hairy as seaweed, flail helplessly in the current.

A dozen more buildings follow the livery stable into the roiling current. The general store is turned sideways on its foundation. One of the insect-leg chairs from the ice cream parlor is tangled in the top of a lilac bush near where the store used to stand. The street looks like an old man's face, a tooth here, a tooth there, no two matching.

With most of the buildings gone, late in the night, section after section of the wooden sidewalks detach themselves from their mooring and float off like dead animals, eerie, bobbing and weaving in the stream.

By morning the water flowing down Main Street is eight feet deep. About noon, two houses near the south end of town let loose from their foundations with a scraping of brick and board and a screaming of nails. The small homes bob away in the current.

The churning waters continue to chew slowly at the riverbanks until the area fifty yards behind home plate looks like a green-tongued buffalo jump. Further upstream, the same water that floods Big Inning oozes over the plains until the grasses undulate as if blown by a strong wind. Water laps at the legs of the first-base stands and sprays the lowest two-by-fours that brace the bleachers behind home.

Late one evening, a half dozen of us sit under the stands, warming ourselves over the coals of Little Walter's fire, where he dries the baseballs one final time after play has been called for the day.

Someone wonders out loud if Cy Young will win 500 games in his career: he had 457 at the end of the 1907 season and appears headed for another good year.

"He'll win 511 all told, but this is the last year he'll ever win 20," I am tempted to say, but don't. Instead, I ask, "Is he the greatest pitcher ever?"

With that, the argument starts. Someone argues eloquently that the greatest player the game has ever known is a man named Brickyard Kennedy, a Brooklyn Dodger pitcher about whom I can recall nothing. Jack Chesbro's name comes up often; it is suggested that his winning 41 games in 1904 is baseball's greatest feat. Several of the Cubs argue that Three Finger Brown is the greatest pitcher alive.

As far as arguing about baseball goes, times have not changed a smidgen in seventy years. Back in Onamata, Stan and I sit on the porch of my house, watching fireflies spark in the darkness and argue compellingly, but not abusively, about baseball's greatest feat.

We never tire of doing it. We almost have a routine. It is like watching a rerun of a beloved movie. We discuss each worthy feat as if it were a preliminary to a main event. We remind ourselves of Hank Aaron's 755 home runs, Nolan Ryan's string of no-hitters, Cy Young's total wins, Al Gionfriddo's miracle catch off DiMaggio in the '47 World Series.

I tout Ruth's 60 home runs in 1927.

Stan recounts DiMaggio's 56-game hitting streak of 1941.

I extol Johnny Vander Meer's back-to-back no-hit games in 1938.

We talk of Rogers Hornsby's .424 season average, Hack Wilson's 190 RBI year, Gehrig's 2130 consecutive games.

Then we get down to business. Stan argues convincingly that Joe DiMaggio's 56-game hitting streak will never be equaled, that nothing can ever equal it for sheer magnificence of performance, for stamina, for going against the odds.

"Look," I counter, and I know my spiel by heart, "someone once described the pitching of a no-hit game as like catching lightning in a bottle. How about catching lightning in a bottle on two consecutive starts?" And I recount the details of

Johnny Vander Meer's back-to-back no-hitters on June 11 and 15, 1938, first against the Boston Braves, then the Brooklyn Dodgers. "Eighteen consecutive innings of no-hit ball; think of it. An accomplishment that will not only never be surpassed, it will never be equaled."

"Ewell Blackwell came within one out of doing it in 1947," counters Stan.

"Does that take away from it?" I demand, as I do every time we perform for each other. "Who's come close since? Nobody. Nobody ever will."

The conflict remains unresolved. Always will. We remain friends. In a few days we'll argue it all out again.

Here, under the grandstand, the person who favors Brickyard Kennedy remains unmoved, as do the supporters of Jack Chesbro and Cy Young.

The fireflies glitter in the humid night. The fire wastes away to embers.

Ꮎ

Late on the thirtieth day of the game, the Black Angel appears on the banks of the Iowa River, about halfway between Iowa City and Big Inning. The statue stands between the water and the Baseball Spur, squarely on railroad property, trespassing on the good will of Burlington Northern.

In the top of the 1898th inning, Noisy Kling connects with one of O'Reilly's fast balls and sends it not only deep to left, but above and beyond. Fleet-footed William Stiff gets a great jump on the ball and sprints up the slow incline of left field. The ball is over his head, but he appears to be gaining on it. We can actually see the trajectory of the ball, like a white planet being fired into orbit.

Stiff runs at a fierce speed, arms stretched in front of him. The incline grows steeper as both ball and ballplayer approach the horizon. Kling has rounded the bases and stands with one foot planted on home plate.

"I reckon it's a home run," he says, his voice full of uncertainty.

"Not if he catches it," says Henry Pulvermacher, and they both turn to Bill Klem.

"It will be a home run when I say it's a home run," he replies.

Stiff is now only a stick figure on the horizon, running upward toward the edge of the earth, the ball still just beyond his reach.

The ball, past its zenith, descends beyond the horizon an instant before the dark speck that is William Stiff appears to leap into infinity and disappear.

"Home run," says Bill Klem. "Next batter. Play ball!"

We never see William Stiff again. A few days later, though, the *Chicago Tribune* reports that a dazed man in a rotting baseball uniform, his shoes worn through to his bleeding feet, was found sprinting across the red sand of New Mexico, dodging the yucca and cactus, straining forward toward an imaginary fly ball. The sheriff's party that rode him down reported he had to be hog-tied before he could be taken to the hospital.

On the thirty-second day of play, as the Iowa Baseball Confederacy All-Stars take the field, in the top of the 2026th inning, the Black Angel of Death takes her place, defensively, in right field.

The Chicago batters are anxious to test the new right fielder. Finally, with two out, Noisy Kling hits a soft line drive down the right-field line. The Angel glides after the ball as if she is on ball bearings, cradles the ball in the cold feathers of her extended wing, leans back, and fires the ball to Bad News Galloway at second base.

At the plate, the Angel holds the bat with only her extended wing. She is a right-handed hitter. After taking a ball, she grounds on two hops to Tinker at short, who throws her out by a yard or more.

In the afternoon, Sarah, wrapped in a yellow slicker, the cowl thrown back, exposing her dark curls to the rain, stands alone and mournful along the right-field line. She stares in fascination at the Angel. I make my way to her but she seems unaware of me; I have to touch her arm to attract her attention.

"Isn't she beautiful, Gid? I've been close to her only once, up in Fairfield Cemetery. I'm scared of her and I'm attracted to her; I don't understand my feelings at all." I put my arm around Sarah, but it is as if I can feel her unconsciously straining toward the black monument in right field. At this moment I think I have some notion of what my mother and my wife have been through. Maybe even my sister, Enola Gay, has suffered the same fate. I understand that what they have done has not been done with malice. They have been pulled from the safety of their lives, drawn out into a hostile world by a mysterious force they do not understand.

I make my decision.

"Sarah," I whisper. I pull her around toward me, away from the Angel. "Do you still want to go away?"

"Oh, yes, Gid. Anywhere. I know something terrible is going to happen to me if I stay. Let's go now." She stares up at me, tears and raindrops mixing together on her cheeks.

"Not yet," I say. "Tomorrow. By tomorrow night I'll be able to leave. I promise."

"I hope I can hold on until then," says Sarah, clinging to me with fists clenched.

☉

On the afternoon of the thirty-third day, in the 2149th inning, with the rain pelting incessantly, the town of Big Inning completely obliterated by the flood, the holy tree clinging precariously to the riverbank, Bad News Galloway, our second baseman, cracks. With one out and Joe Tinker at the plate, Galloway throws his glove, with a resounding plop, into the mud of the infield, lets out a long, wild wail of despair, and charges off the field, crossing the foul line behind third base. He races in a splay-footed stagger, his arms flapping as if he were being attacked by bees, toward the church and the river. He passes the church, and when he reaches the tree and the riverbank he throws himself into the water, which is full of tree roots thrashing like snakes in a moat.

By the time any of us reach the bank, he is gone — swept away by the current, we suppose. But when we file sullenly to the church for supper, O'Reilly spots the body near shore, a long, whiplike root coiled around its neck.

We reel Galloway in and lay him out in the church hall. No one knows his first name. And Galloway, it turns out, is not a local resident.

"Showed up for ball practice one night in early May," says Henry Pulvermacher. "Said he was from the South."

Galloway boarded with a farm family out near Lone Tree, but when contacted, they are unable to supply any details. He received no mail. His belongings consisted of two changes of clothes, a few toiletries, and his baseball glove.

Elder Womple and the congregation of the Twelve-Hour Church are waiting to perform funeral rites. We walk in two loose lines, me at the rear of one, Little Walter, the other.

"Shame for a man to be buried without his family," says Chance, who appears to be mellowing as the days progress.

Little Walter steps forward, limping, his crew-cut hair protruding oddly at all angles.

"You be his father," he says to Chance.

"Well . . ." says Chance, clutching his cap in his hand like a schoolboy.

"And you," he calls in his shrill voice to a stout woman in a navy blue dress and matching wagon-wheel hat, "you be the mother."

"Wonder how big a family he was from?" says Henry Pulvermacher.

"He was the third of four," says Chance, taking the stout woman's arm. "Easy, Mama, we'll find us a seat at the front. Two brothers and a sister," he goes on.

Little Walter jumps about like a spoiled child. "You," he says to Johnny Baron, "are the younger brother."

He points to a tall, flat-chested girl of about twenty, with pale hair reaching to the middle of her back. "Sister!" he screeches.

He points me out as the older brother. I take the tall girl's arm and we stand beside the mother, immediately in front of the coffin, which is supported by two kitchen chairs. Johnny Baron stands next to Chance. The girl sniffles delicately. The big woman keens into Chance's shoulder as Elder Womple makes his way to the front of the hall. Chance has an arm gently around the woman's shoulders. "There, there," he says.

After the service, the congregation files past us, the family, and we accept their condolences.

"He was a fine young man," someone whispers, gripping Chance's hand in both of theirs.

"You take care of the family," a white-haired lady says to me. "You're the oldest."

I nod solemnly.

The ritual over, the pallbearers, three players from each team, prepare to remove the coffin. They heave, gently at first, then with some force, but the coffin remains suspended between the two kitchen chairs, stiff as if it were hypnotized by a side-show magician. Tug as they might, the coffin and chairs remain in place. With red faces and sheepish expressions the defeated pallbearers retreat. Bad News Galloway, it seems, will not be moved.

☻

From the *Iowa City Citizen:*

CUBA'S FIRST ELECTION

UNDER SUPERVISION OF THE USA WAS
MARKED BY GENERAL TRANQUILLITY AND
ABSENCE OF EXCITEMENT

WOMAN FEARS FRESH AIR

Enclosed in a nearly airtight wooden case which
has a glass front, Mrs. William Tryon arrived at
Salisbury, N.C., from her home in Fitchburg,
Mississippi.

☻

The Confederacy is batting. Bill Klem announces we will adjourn for supper at the end of the inning. Stan waggles his bat. Three Finger Brown goes into the wind-up. As he does, a light flashes across the sky like a laser beam or chain lightning. But it is neither: the aftermath of the flash is a flaming arrow spiked into the earth between the pitcher's mound and third base.

The arrow burns eerily, trailing black smoke like a candle. It came from right field, and all eyes turn in that direction. Far behind the outfield, on the green, rain-swollen hill, stands Drifting Away, large as a colossus. Except for his Indian headdress he might be Sagittarius the Archer, landed from the sky. He looks forty feet tall, bow poised, loaded with another flaming arrow. As the second arrow lands near second base, Drifting Away turns his back on the field, strides off into the rain-green poplars.

267

The players seem only partially aware of what has happened; they grumble like children wakened from a nap.

"Go after him," someone says, but without conviction.

Odors of food, bright as colors, waft from the Twelve-Hour Church.

"Let him go," says a voice.

"I smell frying onions," says another.

The arrows burn long into the warm twilight.

Sarah and I have agreed that we will slip away from the evening meal. We'll walk the Baseball Spur into Iowa City, take the train to a new life, to any place outside Johnson County.

We meet by the steps of the church. The water is ankle deep. I clutch my horn; Sarah carries a small black valise. Overhead clouds the color of wood smoke swirl like whirlpools, rush madly across the sky as if they are angry, as if they have a life of their own.

"Let's go," I say, taking Sarah's hand.

"Gid, I can't. I feel so strange. I feel like I'm rooted to the earth."

I glance at the sky. Amid the roiling clouds, forming, unforming, peering through the rush of darkness, I see the faces of the grandfathers. No matter how I deny their presence, they are still there. Faces, black, yellow, red, white; scowling, accusing, threatening. I feel a terrible weakness; I feel drawn toward the holy tree, which is now almost totally under water. I let go of Sarah's hand, venture toward the tree. The water is waist deep. I feel a touch of vertigo. Roots that formerly ran along the top edge of the earth, torn loose now, thrash around my legs, grasp at me.

A groan issues from the earth. The tree cries out and shifts a foot or more in the direction of the current. I think of Bad News Galloway, strangled blue by a tentacle of the tree, floating dead in the yellowish eddies.

I keep inching closer and closer to the tree, my horn held

high over my head. The water is chest high. I feel my footing slipping away. The water of the river actually feels warm. One more glance at the sky tells me I am doing what I must do. I do not cry out. I ease into the water slowly and quietly, like a spy setting out on a mission.

As I go down for the second time I feel cozy and languid, not at all panicked. I've never been able to swim; a boy named Melvin Boxmiller pulled my feet out from under me at the chlorined pool in Iowa City when I was a small boy. I fear water to the extent that I will never ride in canoes or rowboats. I hang on to my horn, fight for consciousness. I think I hear thunder roar. I picture lightning reflecting off the upturned horn. I rise to the surface again; even in my death throes I am keeping count. I catch a glimpse of the stern faces in the clouds. I remember how, as children, Stan and I would lie on our backs in the sweet-smelling grass, looking for pictures and shapes in the clouds. A root has wrapped itself around the small of my back, bracing me, making me comfortable in preparation for death. I sink. I clutch my trumpet. They'll find me this way on some sandy riverbank in Missouri: DEAD ALBINO FOUND ON DELTA, *Trumpet in Death Grip*.

To my surprise I rise again. What is supporting my back is the long arm of Drifting Away. As he swims through the eddying water, snakelike roots boil about us like eels, pulling us down with murderous intent. Drifting Away produces a knife and slashes us free, and we escape into the free-flowing current. Is it my imagination, or are the detached roots writhing in pain, bleeding dark fluid into the river?

A half mile downstream Drifting Away deposits me on the riverbank, coughing, mud-caked, my fingers still welded to the horn.

He shakes himself like a dog.

"In some societies you would be responsible for me for the rest of my life," I wheeze.

"What makes you think I am not already responsible for

you? If you were killed by the river, who knows what further mischief might occur?"

"Then what causes all this?" I wave a mud-encrusted hand to show I mean the flood and the endless game.

"Pride," says Drifting Away. "What else?"

"Is it so bad not to be moved? To stand by what you believe, no matter what? To have an obsession?"

"It is when obsession overrides love, takes precedence over brotherhood."

Suddenly Drifting Away grimaces in pain, grabs at his chest as if he is having a heart attack. The wind shrieks, thunder roars. The faces of the grandfathers, twisted by wrath, swirl above us at tree-top height. Drifting Away continues to suffer; he shrinks before my eyes until he is the size of an ordinary mortal.

"What happened?"

"I was supposed to kill you for trying to take the girl away. I could not. I've been punished. Whatever powers I had are gone. I can no longer keep the Confederacy in the game." He shudders.

I place an arm tentatively around the shoulders of this very ordinary-looking man.

"Thank you for my life," I say. "I'm sorry you had to sacrifice so much. Let's go back. Maybe together we can do something." Sodden and dejected, we start the long walk back to the baseball field.

⊖

But the Confederacy hangs in tenaciously. Like everyone else in and around Big Inning, they will not be moved.

Sarah stands in the exact spot where I left her, water swirling about her knees. Everyone, including me, carries on as if it is perfectly normal for a beautiful girl to stand for days in flood water, rooted to the earth.

13

DAY THIRTY-THREE. In the top of the third inning of the day, with two outs, a routine fly ball is lifted to center. As Ezra Dean camps under it, he suddenly twists violently, throwing his hands up as if fending off something. The ball lands in front of him and rolls by, Stan having to run it down and make a good throw to hold the runner at third.

While the play is being made at third, Dean, arms flailing, twists like cellophane on fire, runs full-out toward the river, passes the church, sidesteps the tree, and throws himself into the boiling yellowish water.

By the time any of us reach the riverbank, he has already been swept away.

The bloated corpse of a cow swirls by.

The Confederacy is down to seven players.

In the top of the 2204th inning, the Cubs load the bases. There is a conference at the Cub bench. A slow, choking sound emerges, a sound of suffering, but as the ragged players break up, I see by their expressions that what I have heard is laughter. It is the first time in days anyone has laughed, and the constricted throats treat it as an unfamiliar function.

What causes the laughter?

From the midst of the players emerges Little Walter, the

bad-tempered midget, dragging a thirty-two-inch bat, which is only an inch or two shorter than he.

O'Reilly runs from the mound, meets Bill Klem at the plate, and screams into his face. The old umpire bares his face to the storm for a few seconds, wipes the rain from his face with a tough-knuckled hand.

"There's no rule against it," he shouts over O'Reilly's protests.

O'Reilly is dancing like a giant leprechaun. The curses roll out of his mouth like ball bearings. His face is the color of boiled corned beef.

"I'll kill him, then!" shouts O'Reilly. He whirls away from Klem and rushes at Frank Chance, who has made his way to a spot between first and home. O'Reilly splashes past Little Walter, slopping water on him. "He's as good as dead," he yells. "If you send him to bat, he has to stand in the box, and if he does, I'll kill him. He can't get away from me. I can pick a crow off a fencepost at fifty yards."

Chance and O'Reilly are nose to nose, arms akimbo, the stubble on their chins almost touching.

"Get out there and play ball!" shouts Chance.

"He's your player," says O'Reilly, pointing a long, accusing finger at the midget. "He's your mascot — his death will be on your conscience."

"Pitch the ball," says Chance. "A quality crow-picker like yourself should have no trouble pitching strikes to a small person such as Walter."

"I heard you treated him like a son, that you loved him and he loved you. Are you willing to let him die so you can score the go-ahead run?" He whirls away from Chance without waiting for an answer.

He stops in front of the sopping midget.

"See how your *father* values your life. If you step in the batter's box, I'll drill the ball through you. You're nothing but a monkey. Frank Chance knows it. A monkey ain't human, ain't no loss. Same as sending a dog up to bat —"

The midget shrills two profane words at O'Reilly and splashes water with the end of the bat, as if he were operating a hand churn.

"He's as good as dead." O'Reilly hurls the words at Chance. "Do you care only for the game?"

"And you," says Chance coldly, "do you care so much you'd kill?"

Little Walter hefts the bat, changes shoulders at the last second, and steps into the left-handed batter's box. The water ripples over the tops of his little baseball cleats.

O'Reilly pumps and delivers a fast ball straight down the middle but head high.

"Ball," says Bill Klem.

The second pitch is even higher.

Little Walter pounds the plate with the bat, then has trouble getting it back on his shoulder.

The next pitch is high and inside, zippering an inch from the midget's nose.

"Ball," says Bill Klem, waving his left hand low to the ground.

"You were warned," O'Reilly shouts to the Chicago bench. "I'll not walk in the go-ahead run."

"Do your job," Chance roars back.

Little Walter edges an inch closer to the plate as he waggles the end of the black bat without taking it from his shoulder. O'Reilly pumps and fires. I close my eyes, gripping the edge of the bench. There is a split second of silence before the ugly, thwacking sound of ball on flesh. Another instant passes before the bat and the midget splash into the shallow water and lie as still as death.

There is complete silence as Chance picks up Little Walter. We have all gathered around to see the extent of the damage.

Walter's body is limp, his neck bent back. I suddenly realize that Walter is not a young man at all, but is possibly the oldest person present.

"Someone should call a doctor," I suggest.

Johnny Baron runs off in the direction of the Baseball Spur; the railroad grade is now the only safe way to reach Iowa City.

Chance lays Walter on a bed in Chance's wagon. It's impossible to tell whether or not he is breathing.

Eventually a doctor arrives, a white-haired man in a long black coat.

"Clear out of here and let me examine him," he says.

"We've got a game to play," says Chance gruffly, and we head back to the diamond.

The inning ends and the Confederacy comes to bat with their backs to the wall for perhaps the four hundredth time since this marathon began.

Swan and Pulvermacher are easy outs. The Cubs are one out from victory.

O'Reilly throws up his hands to call time.

"I'm putting *my* mascot up to bat," O'Reilly says to Klem. "You can bat in Galloway's spot," he says to me.

"Hey, wait a minute," I shout.

"Gideon Clarke, batting next," intones Klem.

"Shut up," O'Reilly says to me. Then to Chance he shouts, "It's only fair."

"What do you mean, fair?" I say, my voice rising.

"More than fair," says O'Reilly. "He's a bigger target."

Someone thrusts a bat into my hands.

"I want a batting helmet," I wail.

"What the hell's a batting helmet?" says O'Reilly.

I whirl and grab frantically on to O'Reilly's arm.

"What if he doesn't hit me?" I hiss. "I haven't held a bat in fifteen years. Ask Stan. I never could hit. He'll strike me out and the game will be over."

"He'll hit you; he's a gentleman, for all his faults," says O'Reilly, shoving me toward the batter's box.

"I thought I was part of the team," I say weakly. "I thought I meant something."

"You're a mascot," says O'Reilly contemptuously, pulling away from me, "a good-luck charm. What makes you think your life is worth anything? You're not a baseball player."

"Stan?" I look desperately to where he sits on the bench.

"Get a hit, Gid," he says. Or is it "Get hit"?

I look frantically back at the bench, then race back and take a lamp used by the Twelve-Hour Church people for night labor. It belongs to Orville Swan, who I'm sure would be happy to see me given a horsehide lobotomy. I fit the metal band of the lamp around my head. Anything for protection.

I edge warily into the batter's box. If I stretch out the bat, it reaches to the far side of the plate.

Bill Klem calls time, steps forward, and with his toe draws an outside line for the right-handed batter's box.

"Stand in," he commands.

"He won't hit me," I yell at O'Reilly. "You'll lose."

"Then he'll walk you trying," says O'Reilly confidently.

By the time the first pitch reaches the plate, I have bailed out of the batter's box and am huddled five feet away with my back to the plate. There are circumstances in which cowardice is a quite acceptable solution.

"Strike one," announces Klem.

"I told you," I shout at O'Reilly. "You can still pull me."

The second pitch curves toward me but finishes only inches inside. I am three feet outside the box this time.

I stare out at Three Finger Brown. His uniform is rotting off his body; the sole of his left shoe, flapping. He looks back from his blue-glazed face, weary, but his eyes burn so much I feel I can see the electric glow of them.

The third pitch is meant for me. There is no time to back

away. I sprawl face first in the mud. The ball passes where my chin had been seconds before and rolls to the backstop.

I barely get in the batter's box when he comes for me again, a fast ball straight at my ear. As I'm going down I know the ball is hitting the flying ends of my hair, but Klem simply shakes his head when I protest.

I stay outside the batter's box a long time, staring out at Brown, trying to guess what he is thinking. Chance walks across to the mound and places a hand on Brown's shoulder; they confer, their heads together.

I step in, but gingerly. Brown winds and the ball slams into Kling's mitt. I cringe, but the ball, true as a sixty-foot-six-inch piece of cut birch, is straight down the middle.

"Strike two," echoes Klem.

"Finish him off," yells Chance. A phrase of ambiguous meaning if I ever heard one. I think they have decided to settle for the strikeout and the win. Brown is taking too long, staring too intently at Noisy Kling, ignoring me. I haven't a hope of hitting his fast ball. But I'll give it all I have. I dig in and waggle the bat, staring over the top of my left elbow.

If he strikes me out, I survive unhurt, but we lose. *We. We* has come to mean Drifting Away and myself. Drifting Away will lose forever his chance to be reunited with his love. The foolish grandfathers will win. What will I have if the Cubs win? I can't take Sarah back with me. I probably can't stay here. I'm in love with a girl who has been standing for days in what is now waist-deep water, anchored to the earth because I tried to steal her away. I owe Drifting Away. I'll take a chance that my love for Sarah will be strong enough to . . . to survive.

In the batter's box, I straighten up, shake the rain from my hair.

"I thought you had good control," I suddenly scream at Brown.

He takes his eyes off the catcher and looks at me.

"You couldn't hit me if you wanted to. I'm too quick for an old man like you. You're pitched out."

His eyes glow like a Halloween pumpkin.

Chance calls something to him.

I jig like a madman in the batter's box. Out of the corner of my eye I see the Confederacy players, what's left of them, and the Black Angel, standing in front of our bench. O'Reilly's long, gaunt face is tense.

"Coward," I scream toward the pitcher's mound.

Brown goes into a quick wind-up, and a white speck streaks at my head. There's a grinding explosion like two cars colliding. *The game isn't lost yet*, I think as I fall toward the earth and unconsciousness.

⊖

When I wake, the Confederacy players are in the field. They have laid me out on our bench, like a corpse, my hands folded across my chest. I wonder if someone is summoning Father Rafferty to administer last rites.

I feel my head. There seem to be no dents. My head hasn't been mashed like a melon. In fact, the only damage I can find is a small bump on my forehead and what must be a tiny cut in the hair above my left ear. As I sit up, Johnny Evers lines out to shortstop and the Confederacy players are soon surrounding me.

"Nice going," says Stan. "He was set to strike you out until you jeered at him."

"What happened?" I ask, the universe turning slowly.

"Well, Klem let me run for you. And Johnny Baron tripled me home. We tied it up."

"No. I mean to me."

"Oh, Brown hit you on the miner's lamp, broke it to smithereens."

"I wonder if the church will expect me to pay for it?"

"Probably not," says Orville Swan.

"I was being facetious," I say.

☖

From the *Iowa City Citizen:*

> SENATOR WILLIAM BOYD ALLISON IS DEAD
>
> ----
>
> GOVERNOR A.B. CUMMINS ANNOUNCES
> AS CANDIDATE TO SUCCEED LATE SENATOR
>
> SEA LION ATTACKS KEEPER
>
> Mr. and Mrs. Charles C. Stevens have been
> blessed with a little daughter who came to live
> with them last Monday.
>
> BASEBALL GAME CONTINUES DESPITE FLOOD
> AT BIG INNING
>
> ----
>
> TOWN COMPLETELY SWEPT AWAY

☖

Day Thirty-five. The Cubs' hunchbacked mascot died during the night.

One of the players summoned Father Rafferty from St. Emmerence Church a mile outside Big Inning, after being unable to arouse Little Walter and noticing that his ragged breath was like someone feebly scratching a saw against tree bark.

The rain pelted down unmercifully.

Father Rafferty carried a lantern; his sodden cassock trailed glumly through the water.

"Over here," hissed Oilcan Flynn, holding open a canvas flap.

278

Father Rafferty climbed into the wagonbox. Little Walter lay on his back on a narrow board seat along one side of the box. Flynn and Frank Chance, unshaven, wet, and sinister, were crouched on their haunches.

Father Rafferty knelt, not so much as a religious gesture as to keep his head from hitting the low-hanging canvas. With two lanterns, the coffinlike space became unusually bright. The air stank with the fumes of burning coal oil.

Flynn was crossing himself furiously.

"Give him the last rites, Father," said Flynn.

"Did he ask for a priest?" said Father Rafferty.

"He's a dying man. Give him the last rites!" shouted Chance.

"Is he a Catholic?" said Father Rafferty.

"When they're dying, everyone's a Catholic," said Flynn.

"I don't think I like this," said Father Rafferty. He had moved, on his knees, across the damp straw until he was at Little Walter's feet. He unfolded his stole and hung it around his neck.

Father Rafferty stared at the wild-eyed Flynn, and at Chance, who himself may have been feverish, both crouched like animals at the end of the wagonbox.

"Have you had a doctor look at this man?" said Father Rafferty.

"Administer the last rites," cried Flynn, suddenly making a wild movement and producing a huge, rusty six-shooter that must have weighed ten pounds.

"Do you know for a fact that this man is Catholic?" said Father Rafferty.

"Unless you want to get to heaven before he does, administer the rites," said Oilcan Flynn.

"I have a considerable amount of work left to do in my lifetime; I don't think I want to die under these circumstances."

Flynn lowered the gun a little, his hand trembling. Little Walter shuddered and turned his head away.

"I suppose this certainly won't do him any harm," said Father Rafferty, crossing himself.

☺

I remember that at this time in 1908, the record of the *real* Chicago Cubs was 56–40. However, this day's *Iowa City Citizen* mentions that the Cubs have fallen into last place in the National League behind the hapless Brooklyn Dodgers.

The Cubs do everything but win. The Confederacy's seven players are virtually unable to score runs. Time and again the Cubs take themselves out of the game with amateur mistakes. Frank Chance passes another base runner to nullify what would have been a game-winning hit. On another occasion Harry Steinfeldt slips rounding third, flies into the air as if he had stepped on soap in a bathtub, lands like a sack of wet grain, and lies for perhaps thirty seconds while the Confederacy retrieves the ball and fires it in. Two runners are queued up behind Steinfeldt as if they are waiting to buy tickets to something. All three are eventually tagged out. The Confederacy survives another day. Drifting Away is visible to us all now, a bedraggled Indian lurking in the corn alongside right field. The Black Angel is growing smaller day by day, smaller but more beautiful.

Late in the night I am wakened by the end flap of the wagon suddenly being torn back. I expect to see Drifting Away. Instead I see Stan, his face stricken. He drops to his knees in the muck, folds his arms across the end of the wagon, lowers his head, and emits a deep, wracking sob.

"What is it?" I whisper. Our faces are only inches apart.

"I tried to go home, man," he says without raising his head. "And I can't. I waded down to the spur; I stood on the exact spot we arrived at."

"But I thought you —"

"I woke up," he says loudly, raising his head. "I woke up alone. An hour, two hours ago. Do I want to be alone for the rest of my life? I asked myself. You were right, Gid. None of this is worth anything without Gloria. So I went down to the spur and I said, 'Take me home.' I jigged around like an idiot. I raised my arms to the sky. But all that happened was that the clouds peeled off a big moon, the night got brighter, the river burbled, the church groaned and slid an inch or two closer to the river."

"I'm sorry," I say. "We can try again. I'll go with you."

"No. I know how much you want to stay here. I knew what I was doing when I dealt with Chance. It's my problem."

"You notice I'm alone, too," I say. No one seems to think it the least odd that Sarah stands rooted in the current near the church. I bring her food. Wrap a shawl around her shoulders. We chat as if nothing unusual is happening.

Stan puts his head down again.

"We'll figure something out," I say.

"I'll be all right in the morning," Stan says finally. "I'll be ready to play ball."

I drift back to sleep. My dream is punctuated with rifle fire. In the dream, the game goes on. Drifting Away fires at the players from the safety of the forest. A bullet hits the edge of the Confederacy bench, sending wood splinters dancing in the air. Another shot fells Harry Steinfeldt at third base; he is down in the mud, the uniform around his right knee already dark with blood.

Drifting Away, brandishing a long-barreled rifle, wades into the chest-deep water near the church and uproots Sarah, carrying her away, thrown over his shoulder like a sack of corn.

The players and the people of the Twelve-Hour Church mill about in confusion. Elder Womple, dark-suited, a black hat pulled low over his eyes, steps forward.

"Brother Gideon will lead us," he cries.

Everyone is like a hive of bees that has been disturbed, making outraged noises, drifting, leaderless. The band continues to make music behind the backstop, though a bullet has lodged in the accordion, making the bellows sound breathless and pathetic. The men from the Twelve-Hour Church have brought the lanterns they and their animals wear when cultivating the land in the dead of night.

I blow a blast on my trumpet to attract attention. I hand out baseball bats to the players and churchmen. Father Rafferty has turned up, a silver cross at his waist glinting menacingly in the firelight. Strapping a lamp to my forehead, I raise a baseball bat in my right hand like a sword, and raising my trumpet in my left, manage to blow "Charge!" As I do, I lead my unlikely and bedraggled followers toward the wilderness.

I wake with a lurch, one hand raised high over my head, my heart thudding like a drum.

☺

Chance magnanimously offers to allow the Confederacy to replace its dead and missing players. O'Reilly refuses, with disdain. He uses an expression I have heard Marylyle Baron use, "I'll go home with the one that brung me," meaning he'll stick it out with what he's got.

With Galloway gone, Oilcan Flynn and Johnny Baron cover the middle of the infield. Now, with Dean's loss, Stan and the Black Angel patrol the outfield, generally leaving right field untended except when a left-handed hitter is at the plate.

Today, O'Reilly, with southern courtliness, offers Chance the opportunity to replace the injured Battleaxe Steinfeldt. Steinfeldt's knee is swollen and swathed in a bloody bandage. No one knows how he was injured.

Chance, of course, refuses.

Harry Steinfeldt plays third base while lying on a cot, his injured leg straight out in front of him. Anything hitting his cot is declared a base hit. He does not bat. Chance, I believe, wanted to take him out of the game entirely, but Steinfeldt, like everyone else in Big Inning, will not be moved.

The riverbank behind the Twelve-Hour Church continues to be eaten away, as surely as if a serpent were raising its ruby-eyed head from the depths of the Iowa River and chomping it away bite by bite. There are a few gravestones sulking behind the church, ranging from small, upright white slabs to a twelve-foot obelisk of red-brindled granite.

The river is undermining the graveyard. As we watch helplessly, there is a massive splash and a yard of earth collapses into the churning water. The collapse has a domino effect, and a new piece of earth sinks perceptibly before our eyes, sighs, and is accepted into the river.

The men of the Twelve-Hour Church discuss trying to move the cemetery, decide time is against them. The river is altering its path. The holy tree, hopelessly undermined, clings precariously to the land.

The earth gives a sickening sigh and the two graves nearest the river sink down and away. The granite obelisk tips until it is pointed like a cannon about to fire over the river.

By evening the graveyard is gone. The people of the church are tense and pale. I'm glad I didn't see all the graves swallowed up. Reason tells me it is only matter, most of it long dead. Still, I have no stomach for it.

"Don't you think you should abandon the church?" I say to Elder Womple. "If the river shifts again, the building could go in a matter of minutes."

"We are not so easily moved," he says.

⊖

At dawn on Day Forty, in the bottom of the 2614th inning, O'Reilly approaches the umpire with the first line-up change in many days. Bill Klem casts a baleful glance toward the on-deck circle, where, ankle-deep in water, a huge Indian stands awkwardly, holding not a bat but a piece of root from the tree by the river, gripping it like a weapon, staring at the ground as though it is a river and he is looking for a fish to club for his breakfast.

If anyone had been keeping a scorecard, the entry would look like this:

D. AWAY   PH

"Away batting for Stiff," Bill Klem intones to the four members of the band, who are standing on the bleacher behind home. The band stops making music for the first time in weeks. Water sloshes malevolently against the bottom of the stands.

I wonder what sort of bargain has been struck. O'Reilly has a devious look about him. Yesterday he flopped down on the bench beside me and said, "I'm gonna tell you my story, kid." I made no reply, wondering what he expected of me; it occurred to me, as it had before, that I was older than the man calling me "kid."

"When you get back to that newspaper in Kansas City, you can write this up. I'm gonna name names —"

"I don't want to hear."

"You what?" O'Reilly glared at me as though I had just hit his best pitch for a stand-up triple.

"I don't want to hear. Those that can, do. Those that can't, talk about their failures. The world is full of men who would have been great major-league baseball players if something in their lives had been different. I don't want to hear your excuses."

O'Reilly spat into the dark water at our feet. He glowered at his knees until the inning ended.

Drifting Away is larger than life again. I don't think he has been forgiven by the grandfathers. What he is doing, he is doing on his own. As the huge Indian ambles up to the plate, he turns and, though he appears to be fighting the impulse, meets my eyes. He nods once, curtly. My heart sinks. The Confederacy is going to win. I am going to lose Sarah. I'm not ready for that. *I want the game to go on forever.*

I leap from the bench, my only thought to delay, to stop Drifting Away. I leap at him. His body is solid as the Black Angel's. I hang on his hip like a pestering child. I am peeled off by several of the Confederacy players.

"Don't let this happen," I yell to Chance. "He'll beat you."

"We're not afraid," Chance hollers back, "and since when are you on our side?"

The Confederacy players carry me back to the bench. On the mound, Chance laughs and pats Brown on the arm.

Bill Klem calls time in.

I notice that my captors have slackened their grips on my arms. With a sudden motion I push them over backward. They land on their backs in the grassy water behind the bench. Once again I tangle with Drifting Away, and the two of us roll in the muck near home plate. This time the players do not try to separate us.

Drifting Away clubs me on the shoulder. My whole left side feels paralyzed; sickness rises in my throat. As I struggle to get to my feet, my knee makes solid contact with Drifting Away's chin. I slip. He falls on top of me. But he is dead weight. I wrest the club from his grip, roll over until I am above him. I raise the club, the root of the holy tree.

I know I am free to bring the club down. I expect if I were to glance at the sky I would see wise faces of red, black, yellow, and white staring down at me. Then my eye catches a movement in the bleachers behind the plate: it is the grand-fathers, closer than the sky. The true nature of the band is revealed. The four blanket and buckskin-clad elders stand right behind the chicken-wire screen, their eyes fuming like smoke in their variously colored faces. Drifting Away's eyes are clouded but I still see my own pale reflection in them. I can't bring myself to defeat him. His quest has been so much longer than mine; he has suffered so much more.

My freedom, my opportunity for victory, lasts about two heartbeats, until Drifting Away recovers enough to toss me aside like a wearisome pet. He recovers the club and turns toward the plate, staggering slightly. He knows I won't attack him again. I had my chance to end his quest, and by doing so to fulfill mine. But I couldn't do it. Knowing he is vulnerable is enough. If I had defeated him, it would have been like batting out of turn. I'll manage. I'll bide my time.

Drifting Away takes a spot in the right-handed batter's box. He hefts the root, twitches his shoulders, stares around uncomfortably. Three Finger Brown rears back and the ball whizzes past Drifting Away; the big Indian swings after the ball is already in Noisy Kling's mitt.

"Way to go, Brownie," chirps the catcher.

The next ball is a rising curve that crosses the plate at cap level. Drifting Away swings late and lamely, like a girl.

The big Indian looks over at me, steps out of the batter's box. O'Reilly calls time. He and the Indian confer. O'Reilly shrugs his shoulders. I can read his lips saying, "Why not?" When he returns to the plate, Drifting Away moves to the left-handed batter's box.

Chance moves the outfielders around accordingly. Mordecai Peter Centennial "Three Finger" Brown winds up and sends another blue screamer toward the plate; it, too, is cap high but on the outside corner. Drifting Away begins his swing about the time the ball leaves Brown's hand.

The root makes full contact. The ball rises high and deep into the foggy right-field sky. Wildfire Schulte begins backing up almost before the crack of the bat. The ball soars as if it has a life of its own, as if it has grown feathers, and like a white dove it flies toward infinity.

I remember my father's words about there being no limit to

how far a ball can be hit or how far a good outfielder can go after it. Schulte sprints up the slope toward the highest point of land, his back toward the plate, his glove outstretched, his feet pumping. Drifting Away is on his way to second when the ball lands just beyond the tips of Schulte's fingers. It must be at least five hundred feet from home plate.

O'Reilly runs toward the third-base line, with me and most of the players behind or beside him.

"Touch the bases," O'Reilly roars, frantically waving Drifting Away on. The big Indian seems to glide over the water-covered infield, his moccasins barely touching earth. Johnny Evers runs to deep right field to receive Schulte's cut-off throw, which is right on target. Evers in turn fires to Noisy Kling, who is blocking home plate. The play is not even close. Drifting Away, in a blur of buckskin, appears to race right through Kling, across the plate, as the perfect throw from Evers whangs too late into Kling's glove.

The game is over.

☉

From the *Iowa City Citizen*, August 12, 1908:

> GOLLMAR BROTHERS GREATEST OF AMERICAN SHOWS
>
> Greatly enlarged and improved since last season as to now stand at the head of the circus business in America. More capital invested than in any other amusement enterprise on earth.
>
> To which is now added the fiercely thrilling, sensational, bewildering, gigantic new spectacle,
>
> *Fighting the Flames*
>
> Hundreds of characters and famous fire-fighters. Scenery showing a whole city. Larger than 100 theaters.

Six big circuses, given by 300 world-famous performers in three rings on three stages in the big hippodrome and the enormous aerial enclave.

More cages of wild and trained animals than any show on earth. The biggest herd of elephants ever collected. All nature of birds and wild beasts subdued and made to perform. A big collection containing the odd creatures of creation.

Presenting every morning at ten o'clock the most colossal, gorgeous Big Free Street Parade ever seen by human eyes. Inaugurating absolutely the biggest show on earth.

None should fail to witness the astounding sights, the hazardous rescues from toppling skyscrapers, terrific and terrible scenes of fire and ferocious ferocity. Cannonades of exploding combustibles. Superb and stupendous shows of spectacular splendors, monster outpourings of the flames' fierce furies. The lordship of all sensational features.

PART THREE

The
Post-game Show

The earth is all that lasts.
—Little Bear

14

THE PLAYERS of the Confederacy mill about congratulating each other. Drifting Away turned left when he crossed the plate and continued straight down the right-field line, where he met and embraced the Black Angel. The Angel's wings enfolded him and the two of them continued down the line, a statue and a myth halfway to being reunited.

The Angel was a good right fielder; she batted almost .300 and made only one error in the field.

I will know in the next few hours how much I have sacrificed and how much I have yet to sacrifice in order for Drifting Away to end his quest.

The rain is already lessening.

I have hope on my side. Perhaps there does not have to be any more death. Perhaps time can be defeated.

"What about the league?" someone asks.

"Too late to start the second half of the schedule," someone else says.

They look toward Frank Luther Mott.

"We'll discuss it," he says vaguely, his eyes glazed as if the Confederacy is already sinking like a pebble into the murk of history. "Maybe we'll start again in the spring if . . ." But the sentence remains unfinished. I suspect it will remain unfinished forever.

The black, metal-heavy clouds shrink away toward the horizon, turn ashen, dwindle. Dawn hangs on the rim of the clouds like quicksilver. The whole Iowa morning is bathed in a holy silver light.

The Cubs gather their gear. Both teams fade away.

Sarah has been released. She is surrounded by Twelve-Hour Church people. They are walking her to higher ground.

Stan, ragged as a hobo, stands in front of me.

"You can't stay here," he says to me.

"What about you? Have you changed your mind again?"

"No. No. I've been what I always wanted to be. I'd have sold my soul to be a major-league baseball player. I'd have done it, Gid. Chance offered me a contract. He says I could be a great hitter. Think about that — the terror of the league. A star." He pauses for a long time. "I'm not going to do it. Gloria should have thrown me back in the lake years ago."

"I've been telling you that all along," I say, and throw an arm over Stan's shoulder. "I still have every intention of staying. I have nothing to go back to."

Suddenly there is a rumble from the direction of the Twelve-Hour Church, and the building slowly settles toward the river, the timbers cracking and straining. A few people run from the church and climb to safety just before the water takes it.

"Sarah," I cry, but someone shakes his head, pointing down the puddled road toward the Swans' farm.

The church, and it seems the land beneath it, swirl into the current and the center of the church strikes against the giant tree. The water pushes ferociously against the collapsed building. I expect it to swing either right or left or perhaps the timbers will crack in the middle with half passing on either side.

But what finally happens is that the last roots of the giant tree pull slowly from the sodden earth; tree and building edge timidly into the current, foot by foot, until the tree is totally separated from the land. The long log church disintegrates in a cracking and splintering of wood. The whole conglomeration is drawn into the current. Tree and building are swept away.

"Elder Womple," someone cries. And I do believe I see his gaunt face amid the floating wreckage, which is soon out of view in the yellow froth of the river.

☻

The destruction is now complete. The town of Big Inning has been swept away. The backstop and bleachers are all that remain.

The sky is a blazing amethyst. Somewhere a meadowlark calls.

There is little to do but wait for night. Then I will walk with Stan to the end of the Baseball Spur and, if the sky is in tune, he'll be on his way home to Gloria. I'll stay behind as long as I can.

As we sit slumped on the Confederacy bench, I think I hear a click like the snapping of a picture with an old box camera.

As I raise my head the bleachers are no longer a bruised, sodden black, but owl-gray and *dry*. The earth at our feet is cracked in interlocking circular patterns. The field is mowed, manicured, immaculate. I know what I'm going to see as I turn toward the river, for the jingling of harnesses has already reached my ears, the heady odor of horses found my nose.

The church is there; the tree stands in the languid heat. Toward the river, I can see the top of Frank Hall's shack, which was swept away days ago. He will saunter into view at any second, gardening tools on his shoulder.

Soft music emanates from the church:

> "I'm on my way to heaven
> I shall not be moved."

"The town," I whisper, touching Stan's shoulder, my finger like a wand bringing him to life.

"What's happened?" he says softly, like a child waking from a pleasant dream.

We both look up and beyond the backstop. The town is there in the near distance.

"Was it a dream?" says Stan, his eyes looking as though they'll flood. "No," I say with conviction. "It happened."

"But what day do you think it is? Is it July Fourth, or forty days later?"

"It's August — look at the corn. Trust nature not to be fooled." The corn beyond the right-field line is tall, moist, smelling of life.

All I can think of is Sarah. I try not to let my panic show. I am afraid to search for her. Afraid not to.

Stan stands up, staggers slightly, as if getting his bearings, then, taking long, loping strides, heads for the center of town.

People nod to us as we walk on the hollow-sounding sidewalks. There are teams of horses tied to hitching rails in front of the stores; an Amish buggy is parked in the shade beside the livery stable. An automobile chugs down the street.

Henry Pulvermacher, in overalls, comes out of the general store, a box of groceries in his arms.

"Henry," I say. We both step in front of him, smiling as if he has rescued us from something.

"Beg pardon," he says, his wide-set blue eyes totally devoid of recognition.

'It's us," Stan says.

"Can I give you directions?" asks Henry.

"No. No, thanks," I say. "We just mistook you for someone we knew."

Henry nods curtly and continues on toward his wagon.

We walk along the street. The *Iowa City Citizen* is displayed in the window of the printer's office:

REDMEN ARE COMING

GREAT CHIEF DAY IN CITY

Wapieshiek Tribe to Hold 3-Day Convention in
Iowa City

NATIONAL LEAGUE STANDINGS

	W	L
Pittsburgh	64	39
New York	61	42
Chicago	58	45

Across the street Sarah is standing beside her father's
wagon. Orville is there, scowling over her.

"Sarah!" I cry, but she does not seem to hear me.

The very air around me is changing. The town is being
healed. It is like a cloud passing over the sun in such a way
that I can watch the shadows recede.

The sidewalk I stand on is still waterlogged, behind me a
jagged brick foundation. Another building sits cockeyed. We
are under the shadow. But across the street the sun glares,
the sidewalk is dry, the buildings stand square as soldiers. A
sign on the tallest false-fronted building on the far side of the
street reads ONAMATA GENERAL STORE. Behind me, the sign
says BIG INNING PRINTING COMPANY.

"Sarah," I cry again. Something holds me from stepping
into the red dust of the street, from running to Sarah, throwing my arms about her.

As I keep calling, waving frantically, Sarah looks up. She
stares across as if there is a great distance separating us. She
says something I cannot hear. Orville reaches out for her
shoulder, but she steps away from him. She moves forward
slowly as if picking her way through a passage rife with cobwebs.

When she has advanced three or four steps, she smiles

295

joyously as if seeing me clearly for the first time, and leaps into the street, her small feet sending up puffs of dust.

It is as if I have a glass barrier in front of me, a force field. I cannot run to meet her, nor, as I see what is about to happen, can I act as rescuer. An elegant, black-enameled car is chugging down the street and Sarah runs directly into its path.

All around are popping sounds, like hands clapped sharply together, once, like the sound a gun makes when fired outdoors. It takes me a few seconds to recognize what is happening. As I watch, the upstairs windows of buildings on both sides of the street bang shut. Later I will be told that, at Sarah's death on this humid August morning, every window in Johnson County slid shut.

The curious gather. Orville, with help, moves Sarah to the sidewalk, where she lies, pale as Snow White waiting to be wakened. I clutch on to Stan, rest my forehead against his upper arm. He is murmuring, a big hand clasped on my shoulder.

Sarah has no visible injuries; the only indication that she has been in an accident is a narrow tire track etched in red dust across the midsection of her white dress.

We are ignored, or more than ignored. It is as if the locals can sense our strangeness, can smell our alien qualities. Orville Swan glowers in my direction more than once but shows no sign of recognition, other than making it plain he considers me the instrument of Sarah's death.

Elder Womple arrives, and those who are members of the Twelve-Hour Church of Time Immemorial pray over Sarah's corpse. Father Rafferty appears like a black specter, the hem of his cassock dusty, his cross glinting like a sword in the blaze of sunlight. He stands a respectful distance away, fingering his beads, his lips moving silently. A doctor arrives from Iowa City, confirms what we already know. Mr. McKitteridge, the undertaker, is summoned.

The Baron brothers stand at the edge of the crowd, rubber-necking. They stare directly at us with memories blank as water.

I can endure no more. I raise my trumpet to my lips and break into a wild improvisation of "I Shall Not Be Moved." It is a wailing, caterwauling Dixieland-jazz-funeral-procession version. The sign behind me now reads ONAMATA PRINTING COMPANY.

"Tonight," I whisper to Stan, who is obviously embarrassed by my performance. I head off down the main street, strut-ting, high-stepping, my horn pointed at the sky, the notes, like flowers, burbling into the sun-rich day.

Some of my sorrow exorcised, I take refuge among the silent trees beyond the baseball field. I sit down, legs ex-tended. Purple asters, black-eyed Susans, and bluebells deco-rate and perfume the forest. A spear-shaped Indian paint-brush glows like a candle among the frilly wild grasses.

I cannot claim surprise at what has happened since the game ended. I knew what I was giving up when I spared Drifting Away. In a few hours I'll be back to my life in 1978. But what will I find there?

"I can be moved," I say to the forest. "I can move. I can change. I *will* change. I'll find Sunny. I'll save Sunny. I'll show her I can be moved. I'll destroy all my material on the Confederacy. I'll burn it while Sunny watches me. We'll get on with our lives."

⊖

Stan is silent and subdued as we make our way toward the Baseball Spur. A lamp throws a faint orange glow against the window of Frank Hall's shack. Frank sits on a chair in front of his cabin, which has a square washtub hanging, bottom out, on its wall. His cigarette glows in the warm darkness.

"Off to town, are you?"

We nod, self-conscious.

"Well, enjoy yourselves."

"We will," I say. "Take care."

He raises a hand languidly in a gesture of farewell.

We have barely mounted the grade to the railroad tracks when the ties disappear from beneath our feet and raspberry canes and tall weeds scratch at our wrists.

"We're home," I say.

"Have we been away?" Stan says. I glance at him quickly but he is grinning slyly.

"I'm heading out to look for Sunny," I say. "She's on her way home, I know."

"How do you know?"

"Something's going to happen to Sunny here in this time, just as it did to Sarah back there. Unless I stop it."

"Come on, Gid," he says, indicating by his tone that I don't mean what I say.

"No, it's true. I can stop it. I can defeat time. Where would she be? She's got to be close by."

Stan looks dubious.

"Think, man, where does she come from?"

"Highway," says Stan.

"We've got to get out to I-80, the Onamata exit." And I'm half a block along on the way to my house. "Come on, come on," I shout at Stan as he trudges in my wake.

"Gid, I'm goin' home. I want some reality for a change."

"Right." Like the Confederacy, this is my problem. "Go home, Stan. Kiss Gloria for me and don't take that goddamned job, no matter what."

"I'm gonna coach, Gid. That's what I'll do. See if I don't," he says over his shoulder. "Some little town like Onamata — farm boys; I'll teach them to hit. Send me a hitter or two to the Bigs . . ."

"You'll do it, Stan. I'm sure of it."

298

Grass is growing up around the wheels of my pickup truck, and the exterior of both truck and house are more sun-faded than I remember.

I pump the accelerator and eventually the truck roars to life.

When I get to I-80, I pull the truck onto the gravel at the side of the interstate. Pale dust is still rising into the moonlight as I leap out. Sunny is there, as I knew she would be, standing fifty yards down the highway. She looks tiny, waif-like; my heart wrenches in my chest. Her hand is raised hopefully as a car drones by in the direction of Chicago.

"Sunny! Get off the road," I shout as I run toward her.

"I changed my mind, Gid. I'm goin' straight on. Never comin' back."

"Sunny!" I race toward her. I'll sweep her up and carry her back to the truck and safety.

When I get within a few steps of her, she reaches down and grasps the small suitcase that has been in her company more than I have, and she races into the highway with me only a step behind. She crosses the eastbound lanes, runs into the ditch. The grass is cool and night-sweet. The clover tangles her ankles and she falls. I grasp on to her. She is light as a phantom.

"Leave me alone. I can't come back. I can't ever come back. You've never been able to see you're better off without me."

I hold tightly to her. She is straining, gasping for breath. With all her strength she swings the suitcase in an arc, the corner striking me on the side of the head. My knees are water; my vision blurs. I feel as if I'm going to vomit.

Sunny scrambles up out of the ditch into the westbound traffic. There is the terrible scream of air brakes, the sound of tires clutching in futility at the pavement. Silence. A door slamming. Muffled curses.

I pull myself painfully to my feet, stagger out onto the moonlit road, blood coursing down my face and staining my shirt.

A stocky trucker in dark green work clothes stands by the front fender of his truck.

"Oh, God," he says. "You're alive. What are you, drunk? I thought I hit a kid. I saw him, felt the bump."

"I'm sorry," I say. "I wasn't being careful."

I know we won't find anything if we look. I remember Sunny's words, "I'm like smoke." Maybe, like me, she has more lives than one.

"I thought it was a kid. You're sure you're alone?"

"There's no one with me," I say. "It's the moonlight shining through the corn. It plays tricks on the eyes."

"I'm glad to hear you say that." The trucker lets out his breath. "You gonna be all right?"

"I live nearby. My truck . . ." I point across the highway. I apologize. He grumbles about his load shifting.

"I thought it was a kid," he repeats. "Too many dexies and not enough sack time." He grinds the gears and the truck rumbles away.

⊖

It is nearly dawn when I reach my peaceful, white-painted home in Onamata. I am numb from lack of sleep, from grief, from my adventure. There is a sheet of white paper tacked to the door of the sun porch. More death, I think, and I am right.

The note is short and to the point: *John is dead.* The time of the funeral and the viewing hours at the Beckman-Jones Funeral Home are listed.

The note is signed *Mrs. John Baron.*

Not even addressed to me, and signed as if it were a grocery order. It is like having a mother write to her son beginning *Dear Sir* and ending *Yours Respectfully, Mrs. . . .* Then it strikes me that I have a mother who might well write a letter of that ilk. I excuse Marylyle. I may perpetrate strange acts in my own bereavement. For I have lost doubly. But there is more; for the fates, doubly is not enough. My life is being stripped clean.

Small-town people are so petty; it would be amusing if it weren't so sad. There are copies of a week-old newspaper, some of them yellowing on the front porch, some jammed between the screen and the front door. It's not a newspaper I subscribe to. There are copies of its front page and pages torn from national news magazines in the mailbox, among the junk mail and utility bills.

The FBI cornered my sister, Enola Gay, cornered her in my mother's mansion in Chicago, where she had apparently gone to pick up a large amount of money. Darlin' Maudie and Enola Gay would not come out. The place burned.

I'm afraid the next time I look in a mirror, my flesh will have been pared from my bones.

I know the neighbors are all behind their draperies, veined eyes peering out, wondering how I'll look when I read the news. They'll all be over tomorrow bearing casseroles and condolences, anxious to see how deep my wounds are. Anxious.

The biggest news in the *Iowa City Press-Citizen* is that the Black Angel vanished from Fairfield Cemetery about two weeks ago. The story has been in the *New York Times* and every TV network has done a feature on it. The FBI has been brought into the case because they think she may have been taken across state lines. There is even talk of the Mann Act being invoked, for a rampant rumor is that a particularly lascivious national magazine intends to publish explicit photos of the Angel engaged in many and various sexual acts with men and beasts.

The magazine's publisher is keeping mum, enjoying the notoriety, probably wondering what the hell is going on.

The magic appears to be gone. The hollyhocks are sun-faded, sternly silent as a church congregation; my dishes lie, scabby and evil, in the darkness of the sink. The house is oppressive. I am too exhausted to react to everything that has happened to me.

Overwhelmed, I flop on the porch swing, wake to bird chirps and sunlight. It is nine A.M. I drive to the Barons' farm.

As I stop the truck, Marylyle pushes open the screen door and steps out onto the verandah of her home. She walks carefully across the battleship-gray boards and sits down on her porch swing. The swing groans gently.

"Gideon," she says, "I'm so glad you're back. I didn't know how much I'd come to rely on you . . . And, oh, I'm sorry about your mama and sister. Wherever you've been, you must have seen the papers. They made a lot of it. There were TV crews in town, reporters milling around the yard . . ."

I have stopped at the bottom of the step. I can tell by the angle of her head that she's staring past me at the acres of corn that whisper in a feathery breeze.

"I'm sorry, too, Marylyle. I found your note. John's been a good friend to me all my life." There is a bed of snapdragons by my feet, some yellow as canaries, others the color of maroon velvet.

"I thought you'd want to know. John said you might be away for a long time. He even said you might not come back at all." She looks at me quizzically.

"I'm sorry about John, and I'm sorry I wasn't here when you needed me."

"It looks like we could have used each other to lean on, all right," Marylyle says. She hobbles down the steps and we embrace. Her body is sinewy but light, all tough angles, like caragana hedge. She is wearing beige running shoes, loosely laced, and her swollen feet make ominous bulges in the canvas.

"How's Missy taking it?" I ask. Marylyle gives no indication she has heard my question.

"Do you see this comb?" she says, turning her head so I can just make out the outline of a yellowish comb holding her ermine-white hair in place. "I haven't worn this in a coon's age. I found it down in the bottom of a dresser drawer. It's ivory; it's part of a set John gave me when we were courting, over sixty years ago."

"It's very nice," I say, not knowing what she may be expecting of me.

"These last days since John died, I've been longing for someone to talk to, Gideon. Oh, I talk to Missy, just as if she understands everything that's going on, poor dear." She pauses, stares around, distracted, as if she has forgotten something very important.

Am I going to share my total grief with her? Not yet, I decide. I can't heap any more sorrow on her just now. How can I tell her about Sunny? There isn't even a body. And how could I explain Sarah and the past forty days?

"I've got tea inside, Gideon. Would you like a cup with me?"

I follow her through the hall into the familiar kitchen, which smells of bread and cinnamon. Through the picture window we can watch the bees droning over her flower garden. It is full of golden marigolds, sweet peas, and cosmos.

"John helped himself along," she says, over steaming cups of tea doctored with lemon and honey.

"I'm not that surprised," I say. "He was a strong man, not one to put up with unwanted aggravation."

"The last time I saw John alive, he said to me, 'You go on to town, Mary Me Lyle,' using the special name he invented for me when we were courting. 'I've kissed Missy and given her a

303

dollar to spend in town,' he said. 'Now I'm gonna walk down
to the pasture.' And from behind the big green chair in the
parlor, he took out his shotgun. It had green-and-red flying
pheasants on the stock. 'Too many crows about. I'll try to do
in a few,' he said. I felt all hollowed out inside, as if his cancer
was eating at me, too. His eyes were sunk deep in his face and
I could see the pain there, bubbling up in his eyes no matter
how hard he tried to hide it.

"'If I'm not here when you get home, Marylyle, don't you
come lookin' for me. Phone the Pulvermachers down the way
— Gideon's gone off somewhere, you know. August Pulvermacher and his boys will come by.' He put one hand on my
arm and leaned in and kissed my cheek, the sharp white
stubble around his mouth prickling like nettles.

"I watched him walk off, swinging his left leg awkwardly as
he always did. It was all so — almost formal; we both knew
what was going on but we couldn't bring ourselves to come
right out with it.

"I give John credit. He was all tangled up in the barbed-
wire fence, back a quarter mile there. Young doctor from
Iowa City was very nice. 'A man as sick as he was should
never have been out hunting. The gun was too heavy for him;
he must have panicked when his sweater got caught in the
fence.'

"Accidental death all the way, was how it was ruled. No
one from the church said boo to me. I was so afraid they'd
want to plant John out in the wilderness."

"Where is Missy?" I ask, to take the conversation away
from John and to keep her talking.

"Missy was in her room playing with her dolls, but I think I
heard her go out. She'll be down in the pasture. She keeps
her room real neat," Marylyle says, as if I haven't been in
Missy's room a few hundred times. "Keeps her jigsaw puzzles
stacked up tidy as you please on those shelves you built for

her. She dresses and undresses her dolls. The doctors told us not to expect Missy to live beyond forty or forty-five, but she'll be sixty on her next birthday. Other than her heart condition, she's healthy as can be. Missy's been our sweet child for sixty years. I think she realizes that John is dead, but she's able to put it out of her mind."

How wonderful, I think, to be able to push grief far to the back of one's mind, like slipping cardboard boxes under the basement stairs.

"Marylyle," I say, interrupting, "I've got to ask you something."

"Of course, Gideon."

"Did you ever know a woman named Sarah Swan?" I try to keep my voice calm, casual. But my voice sounds to me as if it has broken, gone high and shrill. Marylyle looks up at me out of the corner of her eye, squinting. But if she suspects anything she doesn't let on.

"You been rummaging around the graveyard where the Twelve-Hour Church used to be? Or did you read about her in the old newspapers?" Marylyle recognizes my stricken look. "Is something the matter, Gid?"

"For someone who's lost almost everything, I guess I'm not doing too bad," I say bitterly. I still can't bring myself to mention Sunny or the real reason for my curiosity about Sarah.

"Oh, Gid, you know how I mean that. I all but raised you, boy; I know when something's bothering you, beyond what should be bothering you."

"Tell me what you know about Sarah Swan."

"She was older than me by three or four years. Sweet-looking girl; I didn't know her well. She belonged to that odd Twelve-Hour Church I mentioned. Tell you what, though, she was the first person killed by an automobile in Johnson County."

Suddenly, Marylyle begins humming, then breaks into song — the anthem of all of us who have in any way been involved in the mystery of the Iowa Baseball Confederacy:

> "Though my burden's heavy,
> I shall not be moved.
> Though my burden's heavy,
> I shall not be moved."

I want to laugh at the absurdity of it all. One of the properties of the thick, Iowa summer air must be stubbornness. We have not — any of us — allowed ourselves to be moved, whether by choice or by enchantment.

> "Like a tree
> Planted by the river
> I shall not be moved."

I stand very still.
Outside, thimble-sized bumblebees drone anxiously over the clover and bluebells.

> "If my friends forsake me,
> I shall not be moved . . .
> Like a tree
> Planted by the river
> I shall not be moved."

I shall not be moved. I wonder if Marylyle Baron realizes the irony of what she is singing. I don't suppose she even realizes she *is* singing, the look in her eyes is so distant.

Which ones of us have been moved from our goals, our obsessions, and what has it gotten us? Faces flash in front of my eyes: my father, Drifting Away, Frank Chance, Arsenic

O'Reilly, Stan, me, Sarah, Sunny, Missy, Marylyle — who of us has been moved?

Stan.

Which one of us is most likely to find happiness?

I shall not be moved. It sounds like a virtue. The words of the hymn certainly imply that it is. But my obsession with the Confederacy has cost me both Sunny and Sarah.

> "Don't let the world deceive you,
> I shall not be moved . . .
> Like a tree
> Planted by the river
> I shall not be moved."

"Marylyle?" I interrupt the song. "I'm going out to find Missy; I've been lonely for her." Marylyle stares at me for a second, as if she's not quite sure who I am. She has failed a lot in the weeks I've been gone. She doesn't speak but nods toward the pasture behind the house.

Two horses are grazing there. Barney and Babe are black and shiny as telephones, and they're at least as old as Mrs. Baron, if their age were in human years. They have white patches on their necks where collars have rubbed, and there are soft edges of white along their jaws and around their tired-looking eyes.

Missy is petting the velvet noses of the old horses, her sunbonnet askew; she is making sweet, birdlike sounds that they seem to understand.

I lean on the fence and watch Missy. She turns her attention to the flowers. There are tiger lilies, delicate as orange kittens scrabbling about her feet. Missy bends far forward, staring down into the face of a half-dollar-sized dandelion. She picks the dandelion and uses it like a tiny powder puff to dab at her nose and cheeks.

"Hello, Missy."

She is not startled by my voice. She looks up, her face breaking into a wide, trusting smile. Some of the pollen is on her fingers and her face.

"How'd you like to come home with me for a while?" I say. "I need some company, and there must be dishes that need washing." She holds out her hand to me; in mine, it is soft and damp as a child's.

As we come round the house, she looks over to where Marylyle sits on the steps, humming.

"I think your mom wants to be alone for a while," I say. "We'll phone her later, okay?" At my side, Missy skips once. "Let's walk," I say, steering her away from the truck. "I've got to open the house up. Let some light in. You can help me dust."

"Will you play your music?"

"My horn?"

"I hear you in the dark sometimes," she says, rubbing her cheek against my shoulder. I wonder if that is true?

As we walk we swing our arms. Our shadows in front of us are long as telephone poles.

I'm going to miss the magic. I will, I think, have to make my own magic from now on. I reach down for my horn, but I've left it at home, not even carried it to the truck with me.

I begin to hum, lively schottische music. Missy smiles up at me, her body absorbing my rhythm.

"Let's dance," I say. Missy giggles. Standing beside her, I place my right arm across her back to a point above her right shoulder. She raises her hand as if to ask a question, and our right hands join. We join our left hands at waist level. "One, two, three — *hop*," I sing.

> "One, two, three — *hop*,
> One, two, three — *hop*,
> And now we turn around."

I dance Missy in a tight circle in the warm dust of the road. We hop and turn again, on the road to Onamata. We stop, laughing. I hug Missy. As I release her, I run my fingers across the nape of her neck; it is wet under the ends of her graying, reddish hair.

I recall my father's words about there being a moment when each of us wants to be frozen forever in time.

We continue to laugh until I suddenly realize that we are not alone. Two people have appeared nearby. They are Indians. The woman has her back to us, is walking away. She wears a brown skirt; a white shawl covers her upper body. Two black braids bounce on her shoulders with each step.

We have danced almost onto the man's heels. He turns and looks curiously at us. We smile, both Missy and I, foolishly. The man is shorter than I am; he wears a red-and-black-checkered shirt and baggy trousers. He has a red bandanna tied around his head to keep his long hair in place.

"You look like you was enjoying yourselves," he says.

I take in everything about him, study him as if he were in an anthropological museum. His voice is soft, the accent local, from the nearby Sac-Fox Reservation. But he can't hide his eyes; they are the same. He can take whatever form he wants, but he cannot alter his eyes.

"You made it," I say. "Are you happy?"

"Sure we're happy. The old lady and me gonna meet her brother in Onamata."

He is only making conversation. Am I about to make a fool of myself again? The eyes. I'm *positive*.

"Haven't I seen you play baseball?" I ask.

"Baseball," echoes Missy, stamping a canvas shoe in the dust.

"Maybe in the stands. I haven't played in years and years. I only pinch-hit one time."

"I saw you," I say.

"Maybe I'll see you at the ballfield in Onamata," he says

and pauses a long time, as if puzzling over what he has just said. "After," he adds, staring straight at Missy.

"Yes, after . . ." I say. "Sarah." I breathe her name, just to hear the delicious sound of it. "I'm going to take one thing with me this time," I almost shout, my enthusiasm rising to the surface like cream. A copy of *The Baseball Encyclopedia*. A passport.

"Suit yourself," the man says as he turns away, already hurrying to catch up with his woman.

I take Missy's hand, so happy I think I might explode with joy. We look at our lengthy shadows on the road and realize that the magic has not deserted us after all. My shadow, lank, puppet-jointed, bears the headdress and profile of the classic Indian from the five-dollar gold piece.

"Look!" puffs Missy, pointing, striding forward.

About the Author

W.P. Kinsella was born in Edmonton, Alberta
in 1935, and still lives in Western Canada.
In 1982, his first baseball novel, SHOELESS
JOE, won the Houghton-Mifflin Award.
Kinsella is also the author of several
collections of short stories, including
THE THRILL OF THE GRASS, THE
FENCEPOST CHRONICLES (Totem Press
1986) and THE ALLIGATOR REPORT
(Totem 1987).

Also by W.P. Kinsella

THE FENCEPOST CHRONICLES

In the fascinating universe of W.P. Kinsella, there's no place quite like Hobbema, Alberta, where the Cree Indians of the Ermineskin Reserve live out their absurd, touching and hilarious adventures.

In **The Fencepost Chronicles**, Kinsella recounts 13 more wonderful stories featuring the delightfully crazy Frank Fencepost and his friend Silas Ermineskin—as they cause a riot on a nude beach in Vancouver, chit-chat with the Queen (in her bedroom!) and manage a bankrupt baseball team.

Throughout it all, Frank and Silas remain undaunted though not always unbloodied, as they and their fellow Cree pit themselves against travel agents, bureaucrats, used-car dealers, the RCMP and other denizens of the white-man's world.

ISBN: 0-00-223118-2 $9.95
A Totem Press Original

ORDER YOUR BOOKS TODAY!

FENCEPOST CHRONICLES is available at your local bookstore or order your copies today, direct from Collins Publishers.

To order, just indicate how many you want on the order form on the next page and enclose a cheque or money order for the full amount plus a postage and handling fee of $1.50 for the first copy and 50¢ for each subsequent copy.

Collins Publishers will enclose a free paperback catalogue with each order.

Collins Publishers reserve the right to show new retail prices on covers which may differ from those previously advertised in the text or elsewhere.

ORDER FORM

To order **FENCEPOST CHRONICLES** today, just
tick the titles you want and fill in the form below.

☐ FENCEPOST
  CHRONICLES   0-00-223118-2 $9.95

                        Plus Postage & Handling _____

                                    Total _____

Name_____

Address_____

_____ Postal Code_____

Send to:
Collins Publishers
100 Lesmill Road, Don Mills, Ontario
M3B 2T5